ALSO BY KIMBERLEY FREEMAN

Wildflower Hill

Lighthouse Bay

KIMBERLEY FREEMAN

A TOUCHSTONE BOOK
Published by Simon & Schuster
New York London Toronto Sydney New Delhi

For Mary-Rose:
what's said on the mountain, stays on the mountain.

Touchstone Books
A Division of Simon & Schuster, Inc.
1230 Avenue of the Americas
New York, NY 10020

Originally published in 2012 by Hachette Australia Pty. Ltd.

First Touchstone trade paperback edition April 2013

TOUCHSTONE and colophon are registered trademarks of Simon & Schuster, Inc.

For information about special discounts for bulk purchases, please contact Simon & Schuster Special Sales at 1-866-506-1949 or business@simonandschuster.com.

The Simon & Schuster Speakers Bureau can bring authors to your live event. For more information or to book an event, contact the Simon & Schuster Speakers Bureau at 1-866-248-3049 or visit our website at www.simonspeakers.com.

Designed by Akasha Archer

Manufactured in the United States of America

10 9 8 7 6 5 4 3 2 1

Library of Congress Cataloging-in-Publication Data is available.

ISBN 978-1-4516-7279-4
ISBN 978-1-4516-7280-0 (ebook)

The Times
Brisbane, May 1901

It is believed that all twenty-two souls aboard the barque *Aurora* have been lost in a hurricane off the eastern coast of Australia. Aboard the ship was Mr. Arthur Winterbourne, first son of the late Lord Winterbourne, the London jeweler. Mr. Winterbourne and his wife were accompanying a gift to the new Australian parliament from HRH Queen Victoria. It is understood the gift is a mace, a ceremonial club made of gold and precious gems, and it is priceless. Mr. Percy Winterbourne, the second son, is expected to travel to Australia to conduct a search for the object.

Prologue

The woman's white skin dazzles in the harsh sun. Her pale blue dress clings wetly to her ankles. The sky makes her eyes ache: it is as though she can see behind the blue to the great arch of the cosmos. The sand squeaks beneath her bare feet. Her shoes were swallowed by the sea. All of her belongings, her husband. All lost, spinning down in cold, dark salt water. All except the chest she drags behind her in the sand.

One footstep after another. She has not seen another human face since that of her husband, as his grip slipped and he vanished between the ship and the lifeboat. He looked almost surprised.

Her arms ache from dragging the chest, but she will never let it go, not while there is breath in her lungs. Inside is something so precious that it makes her heart squeeze against her ribs to think of losing it. The sea roars and retreats, roars and retreats, as it has done since she started to walk. At first she found the sound soothing, but now it irritates her. She wants quiet in her head. She wants silence to think about what has happened, what she has lost, and what on earth she should do next.

One

2011

Libby sat at the back of the small parish church mourning the man she had loved for twelve years. In a congregation of nearly eighty people, not one offered her a warm touch or a sad smile. They didn't even know who she was. Or if they did, they didn't show it.

It was a relief in some ways: at least there were no sidelong glances, no murmurs passed from lips to ears behind hands, no cool shoulders on either side of her in the pew. But in other ways it was a sad acknowledgment of the grubby truth. Nobody knew that the man they had come here today to bid farewell forever—the man whose strong body and brilliant life force somehow fit in that narrow box at the front of the church—was the most important man in her world. Mark Winterbourne, dead at fifty-eight from a ruptured aneurysm. He was mourned by family: his wife Emily and their two adult daughters.

Libby wasn't sure about the rule for secret lovers of the deceased, but she assumed it involved sitting in the back pew with one's heart aching as though it might crack into pieces while reining in the impulse to stand up and shout, "But none of you loved him as much as I did!"

On her birthday. Her fortieth birthday.

Libby discreetly touched her handkerchief to her leaking eyes again. The church was chill. February snow still lay on the ground outside. She shivered in her long-sleeved jacket. Mark wouldn't have approved of what she was wearing. He had never liked her in tailored clothes: he said he spent enough time with people in suits. He liked her in jeans, loose dresses, or nothing. When she had pulled on the jacket this morning, an attempt not to stand out in a crowd that she knew would be immaculately dressed, she had remembered the last time she'd worn it. Mark had said, "Where's that lacy shirt I like? Wear that instead." The thought that Mark would never again complain about the jacket had hit her hard. Never again in the whole, long future of the universe would Mark say anything to her. Never again would his eyes crinkle with his quiet laughter. Never again would his hands clasp hers, would his lips claim hers, would his body press against hers . . .

Libby's scalp pinched from trying to hold the sobs inside. It wouldn't do for this unknown woman in the back pew to break down and let loose a secret held tightly for so long. Mark had always been adamant: his wife and children must never be hurt. They were innocent, they deserved no pain. Mark and Libby had to carry the entire burden. And what a terrible burden it had been, what an exhausting dance of soaring hope and blinding guilt the last twelve years had been.

The first of the tributes started, and Libby listened for a while, then decided these descriptions of Mark were not *her* Mark. So she closed her eyes and thought about what she would say, if she were free to say it.

Mark Winterbourne died at fifty-eight, but don't make the mistake of thinking him a typical middle-aged man. He was tall and well kept, with a full head of hair and a flat stomach and hard thighs that were a testament to his healthy lifestyle and love of long-distance running. He was smart and funny and determined. He let nothing slow him down. He overcame childhood illnesses, dyslexia, the death of his father when he was only fifteen. We had so many good times, hidden and stolen though they were. Even after twelve years together, he took my breath away. He was generous, sweet and kind. So kind. The kindest man I have ever known. Hot tears squeezed from under Libby's eyelids and ran down her cheeks. She opened her eyes, and saw that Mark's wife had bent her head and was sobbing into her hands in the front pew. The vicar had come down the stairs to put his arm around her. Libby's ribs squeezed tight with guilt. She should never have come.

The train back down through the Channel tunnel to Paris was largely empty, and Libby put her bag on the seat next to her and laid her head on it. Now the great hollowness could start in earnest. Mark was buried; the line between her old life and her new one had been marked in six feet of soil. She tried not to think of the things that she and Mark had never done, the things he had wanted to do but she had refused. Things that she needed to do herself, now that she was alone. Now that she was so keenly aware of how tenuously life was held. The train bumped and swayed and Libby breathed deeply. In, out, aware of her breath, so temporarily housed in her warm body.

"Claudette wants to see you."

Libby looked up. She was just unwinding her scarf and hanging her bag on the back of her chair. Here at Pierre-Louis Design the cubicles were as bland as the reception area was bright. Libby worked all day on her large-screen Mac designing glossy brochures for jewelry and fashion houses while surrounded by gray furniture and beige room dividers. Gradually the entire building was being refurbished, but somehow the refurbishers never made it to her quarter of the workplace.

"Why does Claudette want to see me?"

Monique, Claudette's secretary, blinked back as though surprised. "I don't know. But she said to seize you the moment you came in."

Libby sighed. It had been hard enough to get up in her little flat in Levallois. The weight of her limbs had astonished her. She had managed to take off the last five days, since Mark died, by claiming illness, and it *was* a kind of illness. An ache from toes to scalp. But it would never go away. She would never be fit for work. "All right," she said. "I'm coming."

Libby's French had been of the awkward, high-school variety when she'd first arrived in Paris twenty years ago. Now she was fluent, could think in French, but she missed speaking English. She missed the nuance available in so many synonyms, she missed being able to string adjectives one after the other like pearls, and she still had to hesitate if she was trying to express herself in French while upset. Claudette, her boss, had a reputation for upsetting her staff, so Libby was on her guard.

Claudette's office featured floor-to-ceiling windows through which, if she desired, she could watch the Seine all day. But Claudette had purposely placed her desk so her back was turned away from the view. It had been the only change she'd made on her arrival eight months ago, but it had been a telling one. In Claudette's opinion, there was no time for looking out windows, and the relaxed atmosphere that Libby had once treasured about her work had gradually withered and died.

"Ah, Libby," Claudette said, indicating the chair at the side of the desk. "Do sit down. We need a little chat."

Libby sat down, realized her heart was speeding and tried to take a deep breath without Claudette noticing. She crossed her legs and waited while Claudette fixed her with icy blue eyes. The window was open, and she could hear the traffic on the two bridges that bracketed the tip of the Ile Saint-Louis.

"Happy birthday," Claudette said at last.

Libby was taken aback. "Thank you," she said.

A pause. Claudette still hadn't smiled.

"Is that all?" Libby asked.

"I am suspicious," Claudette said. "You took five days off over your fortieth birthday."

"I was unwell."

"And yet you look well this morning."

She did? "Because I've had five days off."

Claudette narrowed her eyes, then leaned back in her chair, turning a lead pencil over and over in her fingers. "I must believe you, I suppose. I simply do not like being made a fool of, Libby. Five days' leave costs me a lot of money. I would hate to think you were taking advantage of your employer, simply because you had a milestone birthday to celebrate."

Claudette was famed for these little offenses, so Libby didn't bite. "I assure you I was incapable of coming to work."

"And yet Henri saw you on the platform at Gare du Nord yesterday afternoon."

"I was coming back from London, from seeing my specialist."

"Specialist?"

Libby held her ground. "It's private."

Claudette frowned. Libby fought back guilt. It wasn't in her nature to lie, even after twelve years with Mark.

"I can do nothing but accept you are telling the truth," Claudette said with a little shrug.

"It is the truth," Libby lied.

Claudette glanced at her notebook. "While I have you here . . . I heard this morning that Mark Winterbourne died. You handled his account, yes?"

Libby's heart screeched, but she tried not to give any outward sign. "Yes."

"Can you call his office today and see who is taking his position? We've had his account for twelve years and I don't want to lose it. The Winterbourne catalog is one of our signature productions."

"Call them today? We don't normally sign the contract until mid-year."

"They'll be distracted. Everything still up in the air. We can't risk another studio getting the contract." Claudette shook her head. "He died of an aneurysm, you know," she said. "I heard it was genetic. He's not the first Winterbourne to go that way, apparently."

Libby winced. She hadn't known that. Of all the intimacies they'd shared, he'd never mentioned a predisposition to drop dead suddenly. Had he not told her because he wanted to protect her from worry? Or had he not told her because she was only his lover?

Claudette shrugged. "Life is short. Let's get the contract. Call them today."

Libby returned to her desk with her stomach churning. How could she dial that familiar number now, knowing that he wouldn't be there to take her call? How could she go on working on the catalog without Mark to plan it with her? Her job, once the sweet refuge where contact with Mark was sanctioned, had emptied out. There was nothing except the beige room dividers and cranky boss. She stared for a long time at her blank computer screen—she hadn't even switched it on—wondering if anyone ever recovered from such a loss. Then she stood and picked up her handbag, scarf and coat and, without a word, left the office.

She wasn't going to call Winterbourne Jewelers. She was going to call her sister.

*L*ibby perched on the edge of her rented couch in her rented flat on Villa Rémond and tapped out her childhood phone number; familiar yet half-forgotten, stretched out of shape by international dialing codes. As it rang, she noticed she was holding her breath. She forced her shoulders to relax.

"Hello?" a voice croaked, and Libby realized she had made the error of not checking international time zones properly. She had woken Juliet.

Voiceless with embarrassment and self-blame, she allowed the silence to go on a little too long.

"Hello?" Juliet said again, this time with a tinge of fear.

Libby hung up. She didn't know what else to do. Who was she kidding? Juliet wouldn't welcome her coming home. If she knew that was what Libby planned, she might actively discourage her. *Don't come back. Ever.* That's what Juliet had said to her. And Libby had replied, *I never will. Ever.* For twenty years, Libby had made good on that promise.

But things teenagers say to each other shouldn't be plans for life, and there were good reasons for going home. Mark's voice started up in her imagination. *You'll paint. We'll look at the sea together. Maybe get to the bottom of the Winterbourne family mystery. How could I* not *buy the cottage? Our annual retreat.* Then he'd handed her keys that she'd swore she'd never use, and a title deed that she swore she'd never read. Once in a while he'd mention it, always before an opal-buying trip to Australia. Checking if she was sure she didn't want to go. But she'd held firm. If Juliet had seen her with Mark . . . God, if Juliet had *told* Mark . . .

Libby glanced around her flat. It had always been too expensive, but she'd stayed because Mark wanted her to live somewhere central. She focused on the door to the bedroom, holding her breath, certain that at any second Mark would walk out, tall and strong, dressed only in his boxer shorts and his blue silk robe, his dark hair curling over his ears. And he would smile at her and touch her hair and he would be flesh and blood and breath. But he didn't walk out. He never would again.

And one of the only other people who knew what that loss felt like was Juliet.

*L*ibby and Mark's favorite café had been on Boulevard Saint-Germain, a café whose art-deco interior had barely been touched since the 1930s. They always sat just outside the entrance, at the table to the left of the door. Mark became irrationally irritated if they arrrived and somebody else was at their table. He always had a copy of *The Guardian* with him, usually bought from the international newsagent, but sometimes it was the copy he'd brought with him from London.

Today Libby arrived at the café alone, placed the folded copy of *The Guardian* where Mark would have sat and ordered their usual: a café au lait for her, an espresso for him. Then she waited for the drinks to arrive, taking in the familiar view of the pale cream and white neoclassical buildings on Rue Saint-Benoît, the traffic, the pedestrians in their dark coats, the unfurling leaves on the elms overhead. She breathed in the scents of Paris—exhaust fumes, cut lilies, rain on pavement—and wondered how it would be possible to leave. The farewell party at work had seemed as though it were happening to someone else; some happy, unconflicted woman with no dark past and a bright future.

"You are expecting your friend?" the waiter said to her as he placed Mark's espresso next to the newspaper.

Libby forced a smile, but her heart pinched. *No, he's never coming again.* She sipped her coffee while Mark's cooled in the morning air. She closed her eyes and imagined a conversation with him, drawn from so many of their conversations.

"How was the journey down?" she asked.

"Good," he replied. "I got a lot of work done on the train."

"Have you been busy?"

"Always." A slight smile, a tap of his knuckles on his newspaper that said, *Let me read.*

Libby opened her eyes. Gray clouds had gathered overhead and a damp chill was in the air. Her flight was leaving in three hours. Behind her ribs, her stinging heart pulsed coldly. Everything ached. Slowly, she drank her coffee. The last time. She gathered her bag and keys and stood. The last time. A light shower started as she walked away. She turned to look behind her. Mark's coffee sat untouched on the table, his newspaper flapping in the breeze.

"Good-bye," she said, leaving Paris and Mark behind her.

The last time.

Two

The ocean.

Libby's breath caught in her throat as she peeled off the high-way and down onto the oceanfront road for her first glimpse of the wide Pacific. It was a perfect February day. The blue sky was cloudless, and the sun shone white-yellow above the water. The ocean sparkled in shades of blue and green, underlit with gold. The afternoon sea breeze was picking up, ruffling the water into whitecaps and buffeting under the wings of seagulls. At the top of a cliff, Libby pulled the car over. She crossed the road to the grass verge and took a moment to breathe it in.

That smell. So familiar, waking in her long-buried feelings. Seaweed. Salt. A smell both invigorating and overpowering. She inhaled great lungfuls of it. From here she could look to the north and see the promontory that curved around the northern tip of Lighthouse Bay—her childhood home—with the old lighthouse catching the sun on its limewashed bricks. Her heart stammered.

Libby turned and crossed the road back to her car. She'd bought it two days ago, still jetlagged from her arrival in Brisbane. She hadn't driven a car in years. There was no need in Paris, and during any holidays she spent with Mark, he would drive. He was precious about his Mercedes and any suggestion that she could take a turn at the wheel was met with a quick but gentle refusal. Driving this little Subaru off the lot had been an interesting experience. She dropped the clutch, kangaroo-hopped it to the driveway, then had to remember how to hill-start before she could make it out onto the incline into traffic. But it had come back to her quickly, and she took heart in that.

Libby started the car and pulled back onto the road that wound along the cliff's edge and to the north. The cliff slowly tapered down, and the white-golden beach came into view. It was empty but for a few fishermen and the occasional mad sunbather braving the midday heat. Lighthouse Bay was too far north to be convenient, like the famous beaches of Noosa and Peregian. When Libby had left town in the late 1980s, it had been a backwater, a place young people escaped from to the bigger smokes of Brisbane or Sydney. But as the road guided her up into the town, she could see that things had changed. The main street was now a shopping strip. Beach-clothing stores, al fresco restaurants, a gourmet ice creamery, shiny takeaways, a large bottle shop. The slow but determined creep of progress was visible in a small shopping complex, with white painted plaster and lots of glass windows and a smoothie chain store with street frontage.

Then there it was, almost exactly the same as the last time Libby had seen it, perhaps with fresher paint: her father's B&B. When Libby was a child, the summer would see all four rooms full, and the winter would see Juliet and Libby playing in them empty, pretending to own a castle. But no, it was her sister's business now, with JULIET's painted on the front window where once it had said REGGIE's. Libby slowed but didn't stop. There would be time to see Juliet soon, but not now. Not while Libby was grappling with the strangeness of being back here. In the place she said she'd never return to. Ever.

The road branched off in two directions now. One would take her back to the beachfront and then to the cottage. The other would take her a little farther inland, through the suburb she had grown up in, and past the cemetery where her father was buried.

Libby indicated and headed towards the cemetery.

Lighthouse Bay Lawn Cemetery was small and shady. She parked her car on the street and walked along parallel to the low iron face until she reached the gate. It squeaked open, then clanged closed behind her. For a moment she was bewildered. He was in here somewhere, but where? She walked along between the headstones, glancing at them for familiar letters. Around the fish pond and down the narrow path towards the back fence. Finally she found it.

Reginald Robert Slater. b. 1938, d. 1996. At rest.

Libby read the simple inscription over and over again. He'd only been fifty-eight when he'd died; the same age as Mark. But at the time she'd thought him old. She'd thought his sudden death from a heart attack par for the course for the elderly. No lingering death from sickness that would have tempted her to come home and say good-bye. She hadn't even come to the funeral: it was simply too far from Paris.

A butcher bird on a nearby tree started to sing, breaking into the thoughts that had made her squirm with guilt. She wished she'd brought some flowers to put on his grave, but she realized that it would have been an empty gesture. Libby raised her eyes and took in the rest of the cemetery. Her mother was in here somewhere too, but she had died before Libby's second birthday, just three days after Juliet was born. Libby had no recollection of her and had never missed her. Not the way she was suddenly and unexpectedly missing her father.

She could hear the sea drawing and shushing in the distance. She was struck by a raft of sensations so fierce and overwhelming that she thought it might knock her to her knees: grief, regret, aching love, cold guilt. Sometimes, in the days since Mark's death, Libby had wondered why on earth she was still alive. Why hadn't the pain killed her yet? It seemed impossible she could feel this bad and not die of it.

But she went on. Broken inside, but still moving her body, still breathing in and out. She walked down the row of graves back to the car, idly reading headstones. Most names were unfamiliar. But one, under the spreading branches of a tree, she knew very well. *Andrew Nicholson*. Andy. She wondered if Juliet still visited his grave.

Libby slid back into the car. Today, she couldn't face seeing Juliet. Today, she would deal with the simple yet overwhelming task of seeing the cottage Mark had bought for her—for them.

She recognized the cottage as soon as she saw it, standing there alone on the bottom of the gravel path to the lighthouse. Not just from the photographs Mark had shown her, but from her own youth. She stretched her memory backwards for local history. The cottage had been built in the 1940s as the new lighthouse keeper's residence. When she had lived in Lighthouse Bay, the cottage had been empty. Pirate Pete had chosen to live in the lighthouse, which was a relic of the nineteenth century. And now thinking of Pirate Pete brought more recollections. She and a group of her teenage friends, daring each other to go up the path towards the lighthouse and knock on the door. Giggling like fools. Pirate Pete swinging open the door, his long gray beard and his icy eyes. "You kids leave me the hell alone!" Pirate Pete had featured heavily in their late-night slumber-party scary stories. Except he wasn't a pirate, of course. He was just a lighthouse keeper and, perhaps, a lonely old man.

She pulled the car into the overgrown driveway and turned off the engine, then sat there for a few minutes, hands locked on the steering wheel, letting the thoughts and memories wash over her. In her handbag were the keys—keys she thought she'd never use. Libby sighed. This wasn't what she'd expected to do with her life this week. She hadn't expected to return home, in mourning, with no job, to a cottage that she owned but had never seen the inside of.

Mark had traveled to Queensland once a year to buy opals. Six years ago, he had taken a side trip to nearby Winterbourne Beach, a place named after his family and a popular diving location because of a legendary treasure his family lost in a shipwreck at the turn of the twentieth century. "While I was there, how could I not go to see the place where my baby girl was born and bred?" he'd said. "The cottage was for sale and I wanted a way to show you how much I love you."

Blinking back tears, she scooped up her handbag and climbed out of the car. The first key she tried fitted the front door lock, and then she was inside.

Musty. Old things. Itching dust. The windows were covered in a fine crust of salt, fogging the view of the outside world. First mental note: get windows cleaned. She crossed the living-room floor—brown tiles, thin brown rug, old square wooden table, no chairs—and unlatched the aluminum sliders. With a heft, she pulled each one open, letting in the sea breeze. It may have been originally built in the 1940s, but the decor was wholly 1970s. The kitchen bench was bright green laminate, the splashbacks were made of tiny tiles the color of pond scum. The gas stove was laced with cobwebs and dotted with cockroach droppings. Second mental note: scrub everything with industrial-strength cleaner.

A short hallway led to a miserable bathroom, a laundry with a back door, and two bedrooms. The first, the main bedroom, was painted pale pink. The bed was wrought iron, king-sized, with a mattress on it still in plastic wrapping. A quick check of the cupboards unearthed pale green linen, also still in wrapping. She stopped and took a breath.

Once, they had almost come. Mark had organized the time off work, Libby had chosen colors for the bedroom. These colors. But a week before their flight, her feet had grown cold. "Just give me another six months," she'd said. "I'll write to Juliet and see how she feels about it all. There's a lot of bad blood."

"What kind of bad blood?"

But she'd never been able to tell him. Her hold on him was already so tenuous: if she'd articulated her shame, her guilt, would his feelings have cooled? Six months became a year. A year became two. She hadn't written to Juliet, and he'd stopped asking: maybe he thought he could work on her slowly over time. But time had run out.

The second bedroom was not really big enough to be a bedroom; it was more of a studio, with a whole wall of sliding aluminum windows. It was set up as an art room; two blank canvases stood on easels, cobwebbed. It made her sit down on the floor and cry.

When Mark bought the cottage, she had wondered why he would pressure her into going back to a place she'd sworn she'd never return to. But all he'd wanted was for her to give up the job with Pierre-Louis and take life easier, relax and paint, her dream since she was a child. And here it all was: a little cottage, a view of the sea, a way to get started. And Mark wasn't here to see how grateful she was, how much she appreciated this gesture of love.

Libby cried for what seemed like an age, then pulled herself to her feet and palmed tears off her face. She flicked the light switch: nothing. No electricity. She returned to the kitchen. The fridge was standing open, empty. Nothing in the pantry. No cleaning products or dishcloths under the sink. She needed the basics. That meant a trip to the general store. The longer she was in town, the greater the risk she'd run into her sister accidentally. But she couldn't bring herself to go to the B&B just yet. One more good night's sleep and then she'd do it. Definitely.

The sticky heat made her tired. Libby just wanted to curl up and sleep. But she had to spend the afternoon getting the cottage in order. She dressed in a sleeveless cotton top and shorts, tied back her long, dark hair and summoned as much energy as she could. By sunset, she had a light scum of perspiration and cobwebs all over her. She considered a shower, but then remembered she was on the sea. So, instead, she found her bathing costume and headed to the beach.

Years of city living a long way from the sea had made her wary. What if there were jellyfish? Sharks? But the water was blue-green and clear and warm, rolling all around her. She waded in to her waist, then dived into a wave. The constant pull of the waves was replaced by the sound of water bubbling against her ears, then she was up again, gulping air and laughing. The idea that she could be out this late in nothing but a bathing costume, swimming in the sea, was ridiculous. In Paris at this time, she'd be layering on gloves and a scarf for the walk back to the Metro, grinding for space with other commuters. Here on the beach, the only other person was a fisherman up to his ankles in the tide, half a kilometer away.

She floated on her back for a while, letting the waves carry her. Salt water on her lips, hair streaming behind her. Then she waded back out onto the beach and sat on the sand to dry by air. The sweet bruise of dusk in the sky; brazen pinks and golds gave way to subtle purple and pewter. She was wrapped in velvet: the soft sand, the sea mist over the headland, the temperate breeze, and her own human softness, her flesh and muscle and aching heart. Libby closed her eyes.

When she opened them again, the fisherman was gone and dusk was falling away to night. She rose and dusted off the sand, and trudged back up towards the cottage. The beach was separated from civilization by a strip of vegetation: banksias, pandanuses, mangroves. Ghost crabs scuttled away from her as she made her way up the sandy path to the street. She let herself into the cottage and was pleased that the musty smell was gone. The sea breeze was rushing in at the windows, making the light lacy curtains flutter. She made a peanut-butter sandwich, showered off the salt quickly under unheated water, and thought about making a start on setting up a canvas and opening some of the boxes of paints. But weariness had other ideas for her, and she climbed into bed instead.

Around 11 pm, she woke wondering what had prickled her from sleep. A car engine. She lay in the dark awhile, listening. The car wasn't moving away or moving closer, just sitting in the same place.

She rose and pulled back the corner of the curtain. Yes, a car sat on the road right outside her house. Headlights on. Motor running. Not moving. Libby watched it, curious. Then, with a slight thrill of apprehension. It was too dark to see what kind of car it was, let alone the number plate. Five minutes passed. Ten. Finally, it pulled into the street, did a U-turn, its tires crunching on the gravel shoulder, and roared off.

Three

It wasn't a good day for an entire mothers' group to come in. Cheryl had called in sick at seven, and Juliet hadn't been able to track down Melody to start early. Juliet reasoned that if she left the dirty linen in room number two, she could manage the tea room by herself until lunchtime when Melody was due. Then after lunch she could slip upstairs and strip the linen, make beds, give the only occupied room a quick vacuum, and be down in time for the after-school trade. But this plan relied on a normal morning.

"I hope you don't mind," said the round-faced young woman with the equally round-faced baby on her hip, "but we had intended to meet at my place and I forgot the renovators were coming to build my new linen cupboard. Just too much noise."

"Of course I don't mind," Juliet said, smiling, frantically doing calculations in her head. There were twelve of them. Even if every single one of them ordered scones with jam and cream, there would still be fourteen scones left over for her regular customers. Should she get started on a scone mix now just in case? Before they all started asking for bottles to be heated and coffees made a dozen different ways?

Juliet didn't have time to resolve this question. The orders started coming and she started running—carefully and gracefully—between tables and kitchen, ruefully eyeing the four unopened loaves of bread set out to prepare ready-made sandwiches for lunch. Today would be a nightmare and that was that. She simply had to put her head down and work hard. Luckily, working hard was something Juliet was well used to. She tied back her long, brown hair and got on with it.

Juliet's B&B and Tea Room, or as her business was popularly known, Juliet's, owed a little of its success to location: it was right on the beach, with a wide wooden deck undercover for toddlers to feed seagulls and harried mothers to soothe their sleep-deprived eyes on the sea. But the business owed most of its success to Juliet. "She's a marvel, that Juliet," she heard people say frequently. Once or twice she'd heard, "Married to her job too," but only after she'd turned away the affections of Sergeant Scott Lacey, former career ratbag at Bay High who now enforced the law at the local police station. But Juliet was neither a marvel nor married to her job. When her father had died fifteen years ago, he left the business behind and somebody had to pick up the reins. She'd only been twenty-three, but she knew she couldn't let all her father's work go to waste. She'd added the tea room, renamed it Juliet's, and hadn't had a day off since. Even away for three weeks on a meditation retreat in New Zealand, she had phoned Cheryl every day to check in, solve problems, and add to the enormous to-do list for her return.

At eleven-thirty, while Melody cleared the tables on the deck, and Juliet frantically made sandwiches, and the phone rang unanswered in the background, the bell over the door went and Juliet thought, *Please, no more customers. Just give me ten minutes to make these sandwiches.*

But then Melody came to the kitchen door and said, "Juliet, somebody here to see you."

Juliet looked up, wiping sweat off her forehead with the back of her hand and blowing a strand of loose hair out of her eyes. "Who?"

"She says her name is Libby."

Despite the sticky warmth in the kitchen, Juliet's entire body went cold. "No. Are you sure?"

Melody spoke warily. "That's what she said. Is everything okay?"

Juliet never swore. It wasn't that she was prudish, it was simply that the words were often spoken with such anger or coarseness that they made her flinch. But on this occasion, as she put down the butter knife and pressed her palms into the stainless-steel work bench, she shouted, "Fuuuuuck."

Melody, only nineteen and now more frightened than puzzled, backed away. "It's okay, I'll tell her you're too busy to see her now."

Juliet untied her apron. "No, no. I'll see her. She's my sister. The one I haven't seen in twenty years." Her heart looped a fast rhythm. Twenty years. Not since . . . Juliet shook her head. "Here," she said, handing Melody the apron. "Make four ham and salad, four turkey Swiss and cranberry and four . . . oh, use your imagination. Where is she?"

"Out on the deck. I haven't finished cleaning up after the mothers' group yet."

Juliet swallowed hard. Her mouth was dry. She went out through the swinging doors, across the carpeted tea-room floor and out to the deck. Libby sat with her back to Juliet, wearing a crisp cotton shirt and expensive-looking jeans, her black hair gleaming in the sun. Juliet's hand went self-consciously to her own sweaty hair, knotted at her nape. All around were tables full of empty cups and plates and spoons. Seagulls were feasting on the half-chewed remnants that toddlers had dropped. Juliet flapped them away.

Libby turned. "Juliet," she said, jumping to her feet.

"I hadn't expected to see you." Did that sound too cold? Should she have said, "I'm glad to see you"? *Was* she glad to see her sister after twenty years and approximately eight Christmas cards that always arrived in February? No, what she wanted to say was, "Why are you here?" because she was afraid—suddenly, seriously afraid—that Libby was here to claim her half of the business that their father had left to both of them.

"I'm sorry," Libby said with that winning smile that had turned every boy's heart at Bay High. Every boy except Andy. She spread her hands. "Jet lag. I'm not thinking straight. I should have called."

"I have spare rooms, but they're not ready yet. It's been a really busy morning and–"

"I don't need a room. It's fine."

"Then where are you staying?" Surely if her sister had booked an apartment with one of the holiday letting agencies, somebody would have told her.

"The lighthouse cottage on the hill. Hey, let's sit down and talk."

Libby's failure to see that Juliet was busy rankled. "I can't. It's nearly lunch and I've loads to do. That cottage isn't for rent. Some English businessman bought it."

"He was a friend of mine."

"Excuse me, Juliet?"

Juliet turned. Melody stood at the door.

"I've just taken a call from the Lighthouse Ladies Book Club. They want to come down for high tea at one-thirty. There are eighteen of them."

Juliet's shoulders sagged. She returned her attention to Libby. "I'm sorry, but I can't stop and talk."

Libby's pupils contracted. She was offended. Juliet hardened against her. If she couldn't see that turning up at rush hour after twenty years was a bad idea, then that wasn't Juliet's problem. "How long are you staying? Can we talk some time when I'm not so busy?"

"Sure," Libby said, shouldering her handbag.

Juliet watched her go. Years of bitterness and regret and sorrow and fear churned in her gut. But then she was far too busy to think about it.

The Breakers Room of the Lighthouse Bay Surf Club was where all the wedding receptions, Melbourne Cup lunches, and community meetings were held. Juliet's first job in her teens had been waitressing in the Breakers Room: handing out canapés and glasses of the second-cheapest champagne. This afternoon, though, she was sitting on a hard plastic chair among two dozen other community-minded people, listening to a handsome, slippery eel named Tristan Catherwood talk. He represented a company called Ashley-Harris Holdings, who had been circling Lighthouse Bay like wolves for years. Every proposal the company had put forward had been knocked on the head by the shire council: the eight-story tourist resort, the five-story tourist resort and, lately, the three-story tourist resort. It seemed, though, that Catherwood and his mob just didn't get the message: nobody wanted a tourist resort in Lighthouse Bay.

But that wasn't strictly true. Some folk believed that a bona fide tourist resort—the kind with a gym and a fancy pool with thatched-roof pergolas and slot machines in the bar—would put Lighthouse Bay on the map. No more sleepy town with just enough holiday apartments and B&B rooms for the small family-orientated tourist trade. Big trade, big money.

But Juliet didn't want big trade in the Bay. Big trade meant chain stores, and she feared she was only one chain coffee shop away from losing her business. The thought made her feet tingle, as though she were falling. Everybody knew Juliet's made the best coffee in town. Her breakfasts were famous. But in the dark part of her imagination she could see her customers deserting her to sit at veneer-and-chrome tables and sip lattes from logo-stamped cups, while she maintained four empty B&B rooms and baked scones for nobody.

She shivered. The air conditioning must be up too high.

Sustainable. That was the word Tristan Catherwood kept using, as though he knew what it meant. As though he had a clue what a delicately balanced ecosystem a small seaside town was, and how easily it could be tilted into wreckage.

"At Ashley-Harris Holdings, we have *listened* to your concerns, and we are working *very hard* to come up with a *sustainable vision* for Lighthouse Bay's future, while *maximizing* the benefits for your *community* and our investors." The dramatic emphasis was insulting: as though he were talking to a roomful of deaf pensioners.

Juliet glanced around. Well, there were a few deaf pensioners, but still . . .

Ashley-Harris always served tea and biscuits after these community consultations, but Juliet could never bear to stay and chat afterwards. Tea bags and store-bought biscuits were an insult to her. Would it have killed them to buy some locally made produce? She passed through the bar, cautioned herself against stopping to down a swift Scotch, and headed across the park and onto the beach to clear her head before returning to work. Why did she torture herself by going to the community consultations? They always left her with a raw feeling in her gullet that wouldn't fade for days. Eventually Ashley-Harris Holdings would find a way to build their tourist resort. They would find a piece of land and a way to appease the council and the future would come rushing in to Lighthouse Bay, the way high tide rushes in to the beach at night: swirling and inescapable and pulling her in directions she didn't want to go.

Up ahead, she could see a large dark shape on the beach. At first she thought somebody had left their clothes on the sand while they went swimming but, as she approached, she recognized a big sea turtle.

Juliet held her breath and jogged towards it. In many ways, it would be worse if it was still alive. A turtle that size would weigh too much for her to lift and if it was sick enough to be stranded it probably wouldn't live anyway. But this turtle was already dead, with sightless black eyes and the corner of a blue plastic shopping bag protruding from its mouth. It had mistaken the bag for a jellyfish, then choked on it. Rubbish, especially plastic rubbish, was now the leading killer of sea turtles in these parts.

Juliet wished that Tristan Catherwood were standing beside her right now. "Sustainable, Tristan?" she would ask. "How are you going to stop all those tourists from unwittingly killing our native marine life?"

Juliet sighed, turning her eyes out to sea. The breeze lifted her long brown hair and tugged at her loose cotton dress. She didn't understand why the whole world was so seduced by the idea of bigger, better, more. What was wrong with things staying the way they were? She cast a glance towards the old lighthouse, thinking of Libby. Lighthouse Bay had always been too small for her, and Juliet had been so glad when she'd left. She'd never expected her sister to come back. She still didn't fit, with her glossy dark hair and her unlined white skin, looking as though she'd never worried about anything. Twenty years in Paris, doing . . . Well, Juliet didn't really know what Libby had been doing in Paris. But if she thought she could come back and take half the business she was mistaken. Juliet had done all the work. Perhaps she could remortgage and pay Libby out. Juliet felt her mind whirl with the particular brand of crazy that thinking about money induced. She stopped herself, told herself to focus on the moment at hand.

Late-afternoon shadows were making their way across the sand. Juliet trudged back up towards home to call Coastcare. They would want to come and take the turtle, cut it up and examine it to see what had killed it. But what had killed it was obvious: progress for the sake of progress, without care or conscience. The stock in Tristan Catherwood's trade.

By ten o'clock each night, everything was usually perfectly quiet. All the jobs had been done, the kitchen and tea room were clean, the guests were asleep, the paperwork was filled in and filed. That's when Juliet finally relaxed with a pot of tea for an hour before bed. Tonight, she had an overnight guest in her apartment: her friend and co-worker Cheryl's seven-year-old daughter. Cheryl worked one night shift a week at the surf club to help pay for private school fees. As a single mother, she had few late-night childcare options, so Juliet helped out. Katie had been fast asleep by eight on the roll-out bed in Juliet's bedroom.

Juliet closed the spreadsheet on her computer and opened the Internet browser, and started poking around the same old sites. It was a warm evening, and she leaned over to slide open a window. She could hear the sea but, maddeningly, couldn't see it. Ten years ago she had moved out of the apartment that faced the water and turned it into two B&B rooms. She'd moved here into the back apartment, hoping at the time it would be temporary: that marriage and children would mean a move to somewhere bigger. But here she still was. Juliet didn't mind the size of the apartment so much. She had an industrial kitchen downstairs if she wanted to spread out and cook something ambitious, and it was easier to keep a small place clean considering her busy hours. What she minded was that there had been no marriage, there had been no children. Now, at thirty-eight, she felt herself being dragged through an ever-narrowing window. If she wanted to be married and have babies before the window closed, she had to meet Mr. Right four years ago.

The door to her bedroom opened and Katie stood there in her pajamas, blinking against the light.

"What's wrong, sweetie?" Juliet said.

"I had a bad dream." The little girl padded over and climbed onto Juliet's lap, snuggling against her. "Where's Mummy?"

"She's still working. She'll be here to get you in the morning." Juliet stroked Katie's fair hair. "Are you going to help me with the breakfasts in the morning?"

Katie shrugged. She was dazed with sleep.

"Don't worry about bad dreams. They go away when you open your eyes."

Katie remained silent, pressed up against Juliet's body. Juliet could feel the little girl's heartbeat. *Tick-tick, tick-tick, tick-tick.*

Finally Katie said, "Who are all those pictures of?"

Juliet glanced at the screen. "Men."

"Are they all your friends?"

"No. I don't know any of them." Juliet fought with embarrassment. She hoped Katie wouldn't mention Datemate to her mother, who still had hopes that Juliet would finally give in to the pleadings of Scott Lacey. "It's just a website you can go to if you want to meet new friends."

Already Katie had lost interest. She was yawning widely.

"Here," Juliet said. "Let's put you back to bed."

She lifted Katie and took her back to the roll-out bed, tucked her in and sang her another lullaby, then she closed the door quietly and returned to the living room. The array of male faces was still there. She had never contacted any of these men. Not once. But she spent a lot of time scrolling through them, reading about their interests, their political and religious beliefs. Some of them sounded lovely and genuine, some of them were raging egomaniacs. Some were handsome, some plain but sweet. But none of them, not one, had yet persuaded her to sign up, make contact, meet for coffee and a chat. She glanced at the framed picture of Andy she still kept on the bookshelf: forever preserved at nineteen.

"Juliet?"

Juliet turned. Katie was at the door again.

"Will you lie down with me? I'm frightened."

Juliet shut down the computer and stood. "Come on, then." Lying in the dark singing to a seven-year-old wasn't her idea of the ideal Friday night, but things were as they were. Cheryl was seven years older than Juliet, had been Juliet's age when she'd decided that single motherhood would be better than no motherhood at all. "The problem is," she'd said at the time, "men in their forties want women in their twenties."

Juliet didn't know how many of Cheryl's common wisdoms about men and what they wanted were true, so Juliet tried to remain positive. *When it's meant to happen*, she always said.

But sometimes, in the darker hours of the night, she suspected it was never meant to happen, at least not for her. She'd had her one chance. She'd had her true, mad, deep love. Perhaps it was greedy to expect it to happen again.

Katie wrapped a strand of Juliet's long brown hair around her index finger. In the distance, thunder rumbled. "Don't leave," she said.

"I won't," Juliet said softly. "Close your eyes."

She watched as the child fell asleep, then stayed a little longer as the storm rolled in, happy to have some company in the dark.

The jet lag took days to lift. Libby was still having trouble sleeping. Her mind was a whirl of questions: some practical, like when her belongings would arrive from Paris; some less straightforward, like how she could get used to this new life and make it up to her sister. She closed her eyes. She tried her left side, then her right, then gave in and got up. She could hear the distant grumble of an approaching storm. She switched on her torch and went to the back room—the art room, as she already thought of it—and slid open the window. Cool sea air and the rushing sound of waves flowed in. Lightning reflected in the clouds in the distance. She stood her torch up in an empty cup so that it shone on the ceiling, giving her enough light to start unpacking the supplies. Maybe this way she could tire herself enough to sleep. Mark had thought of everything, of course. Not just the view and all the light she would get from those windows. The easels, the canvases on cedar stretchers, a rolling chest of drawers full of paints, brushes, palettes, palette knives, bottles of linseed oil and gum and turpentine and varnish, a roll of rags tied with a blue ribbon, even jars of shellac, beeswax and pumice sand. The smells—oils, solvents, wood, earth—filled her head. A shelf was lined up with inks, nibs and watercolor paper, books of art by Cézanne, Monet and Turner: all her favorites. So Mark *had* been listening. As the wind grew gustier and the thunder closer, she removed things from wrappers, lined them up tidily in drawers, going through the process robotically; both because she was tired and because she was barely able to enjoy the fantasy scenario without Mark by her side. He had purchased these things and put them here assuming one day they would open them together, that he would be able to see her face and hear her squeals of delight, have a glass of champagne with her and toast her new art room at her beach cottage. But in her stubbornness and her fear she had refused to come here with him. Now he was gone. Now it was too late to tell him how grateful she was for his generosity, and especially for taking seriously her dream of painting.

When the rain started in earnest, she remembered all the windows were open, so she grabbed her torch and hurried to the lounge room and kitchen. The wind was gusting madly by now, tying the curtains in knots, laden with the sweet, damp smell of rain. Libby slid the windows closed and was left with sticky humidity. She was tempted to reopen the windows but knew it would mean rainwater to clean up in the morning. She went to the other side of the house and opened the front door. From here she could see the stormy sky without getting wet, so she watched for a while as the lightning flashed and the trees were torn this way and that in the wind. Then she glanced up towards the lighthouse.

There was a dim flickering light in one of the windows. Libby squinted, sure she was seeing things. Surely the lighthouse was empty. But there was unmistakably a light, like candlelight. Who was in the lighthouse, with a candle, at this time of night? The nerves in her belly tingled a little with fear, as she remembered how spooky the lighthouse had seemed to her all those years ago. Pirate Pete had cast a long shadow.

No, tiredness and the storm had made her jumpy. She went back to bed, pushed off the sheets and slept naked and uncovered in the sticky warmth. She didn't sleep well, dreaming of flickering lights in windows, and a cold ocean roaring like a great beast.

Four

1901

*I*sabella can do nothing but trust the sea. There is no ground beneath her feet, so she curls her toes lightly on the planks of the anchor deck as she watches the great waves roll beneath her. The sun is bright and wind flaps the sails and rattles the cleats. She pleads quietly with the ocean: "Keep us safe, for we are not fish; we are men and women, and we are far from land." Every morning she comes out here and says her little prayer, in fair weather and in foul. So far, they have been safe. And while she knows rationally that her prayer can't be the reason they are safe, somehow she still suspects it in a superstitious corner of her heart.

"Making a spectacle of yourself again, Isabella?"

Isabella turns. Her husband, Arthur, stands down a few steps, in front of the deck house. His arms are folded and, under his thin pale hair, he wears a frown. Or perhaps that is his permanent expression, at least for her.

"Don't fret," she says, a little too boldly for his liking, no doubt, "nobody can hear me."

"They all know you're standing up there, lips moving, talking to the sky."

"Talking to the sea, actually," she says, moving to the stairs.

"Shoes, Isabella. Where are your shoes?"

Shoes. Today it is shoes. Yesterday it was unbound hair. The day before, gloves. Gloves! Why insist that she dress as though she were going to high tea when she simply wanted to get above deck for fresh air and sunshine? Nobody on this wretched ship cares what she wears, surely. "My shoes are in our cabin, Arthur," she replies.

"Fetch them. Wear them. I can endure you going without hat and gloves, but shoes are a necessity." His eyes drop, as they often do, to the black ribbon around her wrist. His complexion, usually florid, deepens to red.

She pulls her sleeve over it. She doesn't want to have that argument today. *Why do you insist on wearing that old piece of tat? Winterbourne Jewelers are world renowned and you wear a ribbon? You won't even wear your wedding ring.* She doesn't want to tell him again that her wedding ring doesn't fit, because she suspects he made it that small on purpose, hoping it would become trapped on her hand.

He shakes his head slightly. "Have a care for your appearance, Isabella. Remember the Winterbourne name."

"Very well, Arthur." She cares nothing for the Winterbourne name and only a little more than nothing for her husband. Once she was the same as other women; once she had a soft heart. But time and sorrow have worn down her goodwill, thinned it until it is barely there. She goes below deck only half-intending to find her shoes, hesitates outside the saloon. From here she can see down into the dark end of the ship, a place so full of trapped gloom and the smell of unwashed men that she can barely breathe. Seventeen man the ship, and even now after eight weeks at sea she cannot name a single one beyond the Captain and First Mate. She is both frightened and compelled by their rough maleness. Meggy, who is sitting in the saloon knitting, calls out to her.

"Isabella?"

Isabella turns and smiles at her friend. A ship is no place for a woman, but for two women it is bearable. "Shoes," she says.

Meggy grimaces, scrunching up her pretty face. "Yes, one must wear shoes. Sharp things and rough things everywhere."

"But it's so much easier to climb the stairs without them." The staircase between the main deck and 'tween deck more closely resembles a ladder. Here in the saloon there is light from the small round windows. There is even a semblance of civilized comfort in the mahogany dining table, the embroidered cushions, the hanging lampshade. The Captain's desk is laid out tidily under a porthole. Books and maps, though Isabella would be surprised if he read and even more surprised if he could follow a map given the frightening amounts of whiskey he consumes daily. Isabella, still shoeless, sits next to Meggy and picks up her embroidery ring.

"Still," Meggy says, "you don't want to stand on a nail. Much more blood than falling down stairs." She speaks with the weary authority of one who has been on many voyages, seen many shipboard injuries. And indeed she has. Meggy Whiteaway is one of the reasons Isabella is here. Meggy travels a great deal with her husband, the Captain, and longs for female company. Life aboard a cargo ship is not a natural environment for a woman, and Meggy has been pressing Isabella for years to join them on a journey. Arthur and the Captain are old school chums. Isabella met Meggy the day she married Arthur and has always liked her, or felt sorry for her, or perhaps both.

Another reason Isabella is here, of course, is the parliamentary mace. Commissioned by the Queen, designed by Arthur Winterbourne, made lovingly on British soil and destined for Sydney, where it will be handed to the new Australian government to celebrate federation. Arthur wanted to accompany it, and so Isabella came too. Better than staying in Somerset, prey to his viperous family.

But Isabella knows the most pressing reason she is aboard the barque *Aurora*. She is here because it solves, temporarily, the problem of What To Do About Isabella, a question she hears whispered behind hands in the parlor at her mother-in-law's house, as much as she sees it in the eyes of her husband. There was a time when she might have felt ashamed that she had brought them all so much worry and embarrassment. But social shame became beyond insignificant when she lost Daniel.

"Are you well, Isabella?" Meggy is saying, her round blue eyes soft with concern. "You look quite pale."

Isabella fights tears. Isabella is always fighting tears. She shoots out of the seat. "My shoes," she says, half an explanation, and takes herself off alone to her quiet cabin.

*I*sabella is awake early, lying in her narrow bed considering that cold nausea known only by mothers who have lost a child. Each day when she wakes, there is perhaps two or three seconds of reprieve, and then the sadness floods back in and she is reminded that her life is ruined. The fall, from unknowing to knowing, is agony. She would prefer to simply wake into sadness. But those few seconds of reprieve mock her every morning: they are a false time, a cruel promise of happiness that cannot be kept, just like the fifteen and a half days that Daniel lived.

But life ticks on, and Isabella knows she must get up and go to the anchor deck to say her prayer to the ocean. She slips through the fore hatch and immediately sees Meggy sitting up on the anchor deck with a forlorn expression, her red-gold hair catching the morning light. Curious, Isabella approaches, sits down next to her. Arthur often complains about the way both she and Meggy "pose like children" around the ship. Ladies, he thinks, should never sit anywhere but in a chair. But just in front of the ship's wheel is a wonderful place to sit with her knees under her chin and feel as though she were skimming fast along the edge of the known world with the sunshine in her hair.

Isabella had kept her decorum for the first little while on the ship, but the farther she got from home, the quicker she shed her manners. As they sailed from Bristol, down the river Avon, past St. Vincents Rocks, she still wore a hat and gloves. When they hit contrary winds just two days later, and she couldn't stand up without vomiting, she soon removed everything that was likely to intervene between her and getting to the side of the ship quickly. Within three weeks they had moved into the trade winds, and the speed of the ship and the pressing warmth made her feel reckless enough to abandon her corset. She breathed for the first time since she was a child.

"Up early, Meggy?" Isabella says.

Meggy faces the quarter deck, not the bow. "Couldn't sleep." Her eyes follow someone on the main deck, on the other side of the wheel. Isabella studies her a few moments, then realizes she is watching the First Mate.

"Mr. Harrow interests you this morning?" she says softly, leaning against Meggy briefly.

Meggy's eyes flicker and return to Isabella. "Do you not think he is splendid?"

"*Splendid* is perhaps not the word I would use." Isabella turns to assess him. He speaks with two crew members down on the quarter deck. He is a little man, shorter than Isabella, but perhaps that doesn't matter so much to Meggy, who is a tiny woman with a body shaped like a bell. Isabella wars inside herself. She wants to protect Meggy, but she is also exasperated by her friend's foolishness. Women with the twin curses of beauty and breeding do not choose where they love. "Meggy, you know how unsafe it is to harbor a secret love for him."

"I don't love him, Isabella. I just admire him so terribly much. His wife, Mary, died last year. He nursed her until the end; he was there to hear her last breath."

"How do you know?"

"I overheard him telling Francis, on our last voyage. Do you not think it a wonderful thing when a man loves so deeply? They are meant to be so strong and hard, yet in their hearts they can be so soft."

Isabella doesn't answer. She is imagining if she were sick, dying. Arthur would simply stay away until it was over. Just as he did when Daniel died. Isabella didn't see him until after the funeral, an event that took place without her knowledge. Arthur had been afraid she would make a scene.

"How terribly sad, for him to be a widower so young," Meggy breathes. "What misery he has endured."

Isabella glances at Meggy's face. Her friend's eyes are shiny with tears. A knotted, angry feeling hardens within her. Meggy has never once cried with Isabella about Daniel, and losing a child is far worse than losing a wife. Meggy, who has never had a child of her own, had merely said, "You'll have another, and this sadness will turn to sunshine," as though children were like tea sets and the loss of one could be compensated easily with the purchase of another.

Isabella gets the devil in her.

She stands, calls out, "Mr. Harrow!"

Meggy shrinks up, knees against chest, putting Isabella in mind of a spider when one raises the broom at it. "Isabella, don't!" she hisses.

But it is too late. Mr. Harrow turns towards them and raises his hand in a wave. Meggy climbs to her feet, in the hope of escape. Isabella beckons Mr. Harrow with one hand, while capturing Meggy by the upper arm. Isabella is strong, tall and queenly; Meggy cannot get away. Mr. Harrow's shiny pink face is curious as he approaches.

"Yes, Mrs. Winterbourne?"

Meggy has turned her face away, deep red with embarrassment. The first tendril of regret touches Isabella, but it is too late. Her mouth has already started to form the words. "Mrs. Whiteaway and I were just having a little chat, and it seems that Mrs. Whiteaway admires you greatly."

Now it is Mr. Harrow's turn to glow with embarrassment, and Isabella can't for the life of her recover the evil spark that has made her start this nonsense, and shame creeps across her skin. She releases Meggy, who runs past them and down the fore hatch with a sob. Mr. Harrow watches her, then turns back to Isabella. She cannot read his expression. Is he angry? Puzzled? Perhaps he is sweet on Meggy too?

Ah, of course he is. They travel all over the world together, and it's "Mrs. Whiteaway" this and "Mr. Harrow" that and dropped eyelids as they pass each other in the narrow wood-paneled corridors of the saloon.

"I'm sorry," Isabella manages. "I don't quite know . . ." She trails off, nods once, then goes to the anchor deck to recite her morning plea to the ocean.

She realizes it is unlikely Meggy will speak to her for the rest of the journey and for a few hot moments she doesn't care. But then she cools again, and despairs because she is a woman who is too broken to reassemble herself nicely when the situation requires. Too broken, surely, to move among other people, whose hearts are whole.

The ship is large, but the rooms are very close together. Isabella and Arthur have two cramped bunks in what is otherwise the bosun's cabin. The bosun, for this journey, sleeps with the crew at the dark end of the ship. At night the ship creaks. The sound of wind gusting outside. The sea slapping the boards. But Isabella has never slept so well in her life, rocked in the arms of the ocean.

At night, when she lies in her bunk, she can hear Arthur and the Captain talking in the saloon. They don't know she can hear them, because they talk about her readily and clearly. Her body tenses as she hears her name.

"My wife is inconsolable this evening, Winterbourne. Isabella's gone and done something silly."

Arthur harrumphs. There is the sound of a drink being poured. "Did Meggy tell you what she'd done?"

"Wouldn't divulge. Simply said that she'd embarrassed her greatly, and that she is as wild as a spitting cat."

Isabella's heart wilts in her chest. Meggy has turned on her. She knows why, but she still feels betrayed. Why can nobody be kind to her? As kind as she needs them to be? Is there something in her face or bearing that invites people to unkindness?

"Ah, yes. That's Isabella," Arthur grumbles. "She wasn't always this way, Francis. When I married her she was much more amenable. The infant's death . . ."

"I have to speak plainly to you, Winterbourne. She can't keep using that as an excuse."

"Some women never recover from it."

"Because they don't want to. They're in love with their own grief. You say Isabella was more amenable at the start, but I remember she had a will of her own even then. When the child died, nobody stopped her from raging and rambling. Everyone made excuses for her, so she learned quickly that she could do as she pleased, even if it upset others."

Isabella doesn't know where to take greater offense: the idea that she has learned to behave badly, like a mistreated dog, or the fact that they are talking about her perceived failings so openly. But no, the thing that stings the most is the way they use the words *the child* and *the infant*. He had a name. Daniel.

"I don't know what more I can do, Francis. I sent her out with a friend's wife one day and removed every trace of the child. The cradle, the clothes, the little rabbit my mother had knitted. She flew into a rage, of course. I had to grasp both her hands quite firmly to stop her from clawing my eyes out."

Quite firmly. He'd left two black bruises that hadn't faded for a week.

And then the Captain says what Isabella feared he would. "Meggy tells me the ribbon around her wrist is significant."

"Really?"

She can hear the penny drop even from her bed.

"We were having this very conversation today. Isabella, the baby, the way she refuses to get over it. And Meggy revealed that inside the ribbon, pressed against her wrist, Isabella has sewn a baby bracelet that you missed. A coral one, made by Isabella and her sister when they were children."

Even as he says these words, Isabella is running her fingers over the familiar lumps under the ribbon. Yes, he had thrown it all away. She had come home from an interminable day in Bath with Mrs. Evans to find the nursery stripped bare. Only this bracelet, in the back of a drawer, had been missed. As children, she and her sister Victoria loved to make jewelry. Their father had been a jeweler, though not on the scale of the Winterbournes, of course. He had a small workshop in Port Isaac, the seaside town where Isabella grew up. He had handmade unique pieces for his rich bohemian clientele, often European nobility; and he'd taught his daughters all the techniques for wrapping stones in wire without soldering. She and her sister were eleven and twelve when they made the coral bracelet, each link held tightly in a coil of silver wire, with only enough beads to make a tiny thing. Victoria had kept it in her jewelry box for years, for they had always agreed that whoever had a child first could have it. It had arrived at Isabella's house the day before Daniel was born, in a special package from New York, where Victoria now lived, married but so far childless.

"You'll have to take it off her, Winterbourne. Throw it in the sea. She'll never get better till it's gone."

Isabella's heart is hot with fear. She knew he would suggest it, she knows Arthur will agree with it. But it is the only thing that remains of Daniel, the only thing that is keeping her in one piece. Quite simply, if she loses this string of coral, she loses herself. So she unties it immediately and slides it under her pillow. But it is not safe there, not for long. It will be the second or third place he looks, if he is determined to take it from her.

There is one place the bracelet will be safe, if she dares to put it there.

Five

Supper is always served in the saloon, and that is where tonight's plan starts. For everything to work, Isabella must go ahead of her husband to bed, so when the steward brings them a slab of undercooked, oversalted pork with a few sunken potatoes swimming in its gravy, she feigns a sudden fit of illness. Though in truth she scarcely needs to feign illness, looking at that food. How she longs for fresh meat and newly dug potatoes.

"Oh," she says, her hand flying to her lips.

"Isabella?" Arthur says, with his usual wary tone.

"I feel suddenly unwell," she says.

Meggy, who sits silent and stony across from her, won't meet her eye. The Captain is busy sloshing claret into his crystal glass. This leaves Arthur in charge of the problem.

"Will you eat with us?"

"I think not," she says. "I will go directly to bed."

Arthur opens his mouth to encourage her to stay. He is a man who worries constantly what others will think of him, and any perceived lack of manners on her part makes him huff and puff like a steam train. But she suspects he has reckoned that illness will only make her manners worse, so he holds his thoughts, and waves her away with one doughy white hand.

Once the cabin door is closed behind her, she unbuttons her bodice and unhooks her stays, slips off her skirt and hangs them all in the narrow wardrobe built into the nook behind the bunks. She throws on her nightgown and stands still a moment, heart beating hard, straining her hearing for the sound of footsteps. Nothing. Hung on the door is her husband's waistcoat. Isabella reaches into the pocket. When she has what she is after, she lies down on her bed. But she doesn't sleep. She lies still and listens to them. The clink of silver on china. Their conversation: always the weather, though she understands such an obsession out here at sea. Just the previous week, when they were sailing out of the East Indies, a storm had come upon them so fast and unexpectedly that she had been sure they would all perish. They live or die by the weather.

Isabella hears Meggy's soft tones retreating. Isabella relaxes a little: she needs Meggy—who has uncannily sharp hearing—out of the saloon. Then, Arthur and the Captain resume their conversation. The constant unstopping of the bottle of claret, the clunk of their glasses on the polished wood. Every night after dinner, Arthur drinks with the Captain. And the Captain drinks a lot. The drunker they are, the louder their voices become.

She listens to them a long time. They talk about the weather, old friends, about Isabella. Arthur tells the Captain about the new house he intends to build on their return to England, and for a little while he sounds excited and happy. Isabella does not feel sorry for him. She does not want the new house, because Arthur's mother will then move in with them. And if she is there, it is likely Percy will be there often, and Isabella never wants to see Percy again.

Eventually Arthur resumes his usual sour tone. "How well do you trust your crew?" he asks the Captain.

"Well enough. Why?"

"There are seventeen of them and they are a low sort of men. Can you be sure nobody is stealing anything from you?"

"They'd have nowhere to hide it, Winterbourne," the Captain slurs, managing to find a sibilant consonant in every word.

One of Arthur's chief concerns in life is that he will have something stolen from him. Several servants back in Somerset have been sacrificed to this fear. In fact, his whole family appears to share this unfounded fear: unfounded, for it has never happened to any of them, to her knowledge. Perhaps it is working with gems that does it to them: small, precious things that are easy to hide and transport. But Isabella has always thought it ghastly that people who have so much should be so fearful of losing a little of it.

"If one of them should think to touch the mace," Arthur continues, and now Isabella realizes just how drunk he is. With his drunkenness, all his morbid thoughts come to light like frightened bats flying from a cave.

"Nobody's going to touch your mace."

"I'm wary," he says. "I have the key on me, day and night."

Isabella smiles, as she has the key in her hand at that very second. He pins it inside his waistcoat pocket, and his waistcoat is hung on the inside of their door just before supper every night. He hangs it, rolls up his shirt sleeves, washes his face and hands in the china dish by their beds, and thus the day is over and the night has commenced. Arthur is a man who revels in routines.

The Captain mutters something else to Arthur, and then they are off on another topic of conversation. She waits a few more moments, then decides if she waits too long Arthur will be beyond drunk and want to fall into bed, so she quietly peels back the covers and climbs down the ladder.

A thing she has had to get used to on the ship is the constant lurching movement of the sea beneath her feet. So she stands, waits until she is sure of her footing, then goes to the door. There is no latch, so it tends not to stay properly closed. It is ajar an inch: enough to hear somebody approaching and to let in a little reflected lamplight from the saloon. Her pulse thuds dully in her ears. When she is certain they aren't moving from the velvet seats to which their drunken backsides are glued, she moves back and crouches beside her husband's bunk and feels underneath it for the walnut chest.

Her fingers find the brass handle on each end, and slowly, slowly, she begins to pull.

A sudden lurch as the ship pitches down a wave; the chest scrapes against the wooden floor and she overcompensates, falls backwards, fingers flying off the box. She falls inelegantly, and certainly not quietly.

"What is that?" Arthur says.

Isabella quickly clambers to her feet, shoving the walnut chest back under the bunk with her foot, securing it in place with her trunk, and then the door to the cabin is open and Arthur is eyeing her in the dark.

"Isabella?"

"I came down to get a drink of water, and fell from the lowest rung," she says, gesturing to the ladder.

His eyes catch on her bare wrist, where the black ribbon has been. "Are you still unwell?" he says at last.

She nods. The key to the box burns a guilty hole in her palm.

"Go back to your bed. I'll bring you water."

And she can do nothing but go back to her bed. He returns

a few seconds later with a cup of water, which she drinks while
he waits. The Captain appears at the door and says, "I'm off to
bed now, Winterbourne."

"Good night, Francis. I'll do the same."

No! Here is her plan foiled, and here is the wretched key still
in her hand. How is she to return it to his waistcoat before he
notices it missing, if he is here in the cabin with her?

Arthur undresses and bids her good night. With a grunt and a
struggle, he climbs onto his bunk below her. She lies above him on
her side, and waits for him to sleep so she can decide what to do.

Finally, the familiar trumpet of his snoring alerts her to his
deep drunken sleep. She decides the only safe course of action is
to climb down, slip the key back in his waistcoat pocket, then go
back to bed and do it all another time.

Once more she peels back the sheets. Once more she climbs
down the ladder. As her bare ankles pass his sleeping body, she
shudders deeply, as one might when one walks past a snake.

And once her feet are on the floor, she no longer wants to put
his wretched key back. Not yet. She stands next to him in the
dark, and he doesn't hear her. He doesn't wake. A mad courage
seizes her. She crouches and reaches under his bunk.

If he wakes, she will be discovered. She knows this, and still
she does it.

Gently, she pulls the chest out until it touches her knees. The
chest is narrow but three feet long, and she has to feel along its
length for the five locks. In the dark, she fumbles with the key.
An eternity stretches out between her finding each one, guiding
the key into the lock, turning it with a soft snick. She barely
breathes the whole time. There is no light in the gray room. She
finds her way by touch.

Finally, she cracks the chest open. Two fine gold chains stop the lid from falling all the way back and smacking into the floor. She lifts the layers of black velvet and sees the dull glint of the mace: gold, studded with precious gems. She carefully feels around in the chest for the edge of the velvet cushion on which the mace rests, eases up the corner, slips her precious black ribbon out of the front of her nightgown and tucks it under, then releases the cushion and closes the box.

Snap.

Too confident, she drops it the last half-inch. The noise seems impossibly loud in the dark. Her body ices over and she can't move. Her heart thumps out of her chest; even her eyeballs seems to pulse. Arthur stops snoring, makes a grunting noise.

Then, slowly, rhythmically, he starts again. She has never been so glad to hear him snore. She almost laughs.

She feels around the box again for the locks. One by one, she fastens them. A kind of reckless certainty has gripped her. All will be well, so she takes her time, quietly pushes the mace under the bed, then slips the key into Arthur's waistcoat.

Up the ladder. Into bed. She doesn't sleep for hours and hours because the excitement takes forever to cool from her blood.

For now, Daniel's bracelet is safe. It will at least get to the other side, Sydney, where Arthur is to hand the mace over to Mr. Barton on behalf of the Queen. Isabella anticipates more key-stealing and tiptoeing about before the ceremony, of course, but for the present she is simply glad that the black ribbon is not in danger of going overboard. The rest she can work out when she is finally off this stinking vessel.

The next few days are bleak. A black cloud descends on her. At first she thinks the darkness is caused by her not having the bracelet around her wrist, and perhaps that is a little of the reason. But more likely it's the weather, which has turned leaden and windy and rough.

The place to be, on a ship in stormy seas, is above deck. Below deck, without her eyes to find a horizon, the roiling seasickness can set in. So she spends hours every day up on the anchor deck, the voices of men shouting and swearing behind her, watching the gray sea and the gray sky and trying to stay clear of the rain under the canvas cover. Ordinarily, Meggy would have joined her, but Meggy avoids her now, preferring to mark the time embroidering in the saloon. Life goes on below deck, all the little mundane details of lived experience tick along, pushing time into lines. Above deck, with nothing in sight but endless sea, time stops and she is pitching and yawing through an eternal gray moment. It is like her sadness, this interminable journey. She sees no land, she can predict no end, all is storm-beaten.

And sometimes when the rain comes hammering hard, but never cold, and she has to shrink under the last dry space behind the ship's wheel, she hears Mr. Harrow barking orders and she thinks about what Meggy told her. He lost his wife. And here he functions perfectly well. She would not be able to sail a ship. She would run it aground in her grief, surely. But, while the Captain fumbles through tasks, Mr. Harrow is calm and capable. Sometimes she steals glances at him, looking for the pain on his face, but she doesn't see it. Then she realizes she is being as bad as Meggy, and she puts her face on her knees again and waits and waits, through time and distance and stormy seas.

Then the first gray light glimmers at the hem of the darkness. Isabella sees Mr. Harrow in the galley. He, like her, is searching for something to stop up the hunger until lunch. He crouches with his head in the cupboard.

When she says, "Good morning," he startles and hits his head.

"I'm so sorry," she says.

"It's fine," he replies, standing, rubbing his head. "Are you looking for food too?"

She nods. "I hid some dried apple in a tin at the back, behind the flour."

He returns his attention to the cupboard, smiling. "Ah, very clever." He pulls out the tin and attempts to prize off the lid. "Did you put this lid on yourself?" he says, with effort.

She laughs, spreading her palms apart. "My mother used to say I should have been born a boy. 'Strong as a goat, wild as a blackbird.'" Remembering Mother's old saying makes her instantly sad. She doesn't feel strong and wild anymore.

He has the lid off now and is offering her the tin. She selects a handful of sliced apple. Mr. Harrow is about to slip past her on his way out when she stops him.

"Mr. Harrow, wait," she says. She watches her hand on his forearm as though it isn't her own. She didn't realize she was going to speak to him, but a compulsion has seized her.

He waits, and a small stretch of time binds them together in expectation.

Then she says, "Meggy told me about your wife."

And there it was: the raw pain that she has been so longing to see on his face. Finally, she has found somebody *who knows*. To her horror, the corners of her mouth curl up as though to smile. She pushes them down again.

But then the vulnerability in Mr. Harrow's face is gone, hidden under a constructed expression of acceptance. "Yes, I did lose Mary. It was very difficult," he says. "But life must go on."

"Must it?"

Her question flummoxes him. He opens his mouth to speak, then doesn't. Rather, he remains still with his lips slightly parted.

"My son, Daniel, died nearly three years ago," she says in a rush. "He was fifteen days old. Born perfectly healthy, growing well. Then one morning my eyes opened late—too late in the morning, too bright—wondering why he hadn't woken me. He hadn't woken me because he was dead, Mr. Harrow. Dead and cold." Here her voice breaks and she puts her hands to her mouth to stop up the tears. "Because I was out of my mind with my grief, my husband's family saw to it that the child was buried without me in attendance. I didn't even have a chance to say good-bye to him."

"Oh, my dear Mrs. Winterbourne," he says, and gently pulls her hands away from her face and holds them in his rough fingers. "It is terrible to lose a loved one, but the sun *will* shine again."

"It cannot." Now she doubts him. He has only lost a wife, not a child. What can he know about her pain?

Mr. Harrow searches for words. The ship rides over a bump and swell, setting the hanging spoons clanging against each other. Finally he says, "Such sadness doesn't just bruise, then fade away. It devastates. The only way back is to rebuild, stone by stone. And sometimes one hasn't the energy, or the inclination, and one sits among the ruins and waits for something to change. But nothing changes unless we stand up again, and keep picking up the stones."

Her heart lightens and darkens over and over as he speaks: hope, despair, hope, despair, fast-moving clouds over the sun. He does understand, but he is telling her she has to try to get better. Does he not know that if she recovers from Daniel's death, then she loses Daniel a second time? Recovering is a kind of forgetting.

But she has longed for the comfort of words such as Mr. Harrow's and perhaps Mr. Harrow has longed for a fellow soul to share his sorrow too, so they stand there for a moment together, hands clasped, tears brimming. And that's when Meggy comes in.

"Oh," she says, her pale eyes taking in their stance, their clasped hands, their searching eyes. At first Isabella does not understand the import: there is nothing romantic about the moment Mr. Harrow and she are sharing. But, by God, it looks like it.

Mr. Harrow, alarmed—for Isabella suspects he is sweet on Meggy—drops her hands and takes a step back, knocking his head on a hanging copper pan.

Isabella says, "Meggy, wait." But Meggy has already turned and hurried off.

Mr. Harrow rubs his head. "I should go," he says.

Isabella nods, and is left alone in the galley a few moments later, wondering when she will harvest the inevitable consequences.

Dinner is cooking in the galley, and the smell of stewing meat is trapped in the saloon where Isabella sits alone, working on her embroidery ring. She has made many mistakes this evening, and has spent so much time unpicking misplaced stitches that she may as well not have started work at all. Meggy is nowhere in sight. Isabella begins to hope, faintly, that Meggy has decided to keep to herself about the scene with Mr. Harrow. But the hope does not last, for at dusk Arthur thunders down the stairs and a moment later is standing in front of her, his brows drawn down so hard that they create grim shadows on his face. Isabella puts aside her embroidery ring and tries not to blink, or flinch, or indicate in any way that she knows what is coming.

"Whatever is wrong, Arthur?" she says. Forcing her hands to be still, she takes a match and lights the oil lantern above her head, closing the latch softly.

For a few moments, he can't form words. He splutters and spits, then finally says, "I will not tolerate you showing such attentions to another man."

She maintains her feigned puzzlement, but feels the sting of Meggy's betrayal. "And nor should you tolerate it, and nor should you ever need to tolerate it," she says evenly.

"Don't play the innocent with me!" he shouts, and she imagines that everyone below deck, all the way down the corridor to the crew's quarters, hears it. The ship may be one hundred and sixty feet long, but everything is close to everything else below deck. Arthur, sensing he is embarrassing himself, drops his voice. "Meggy saw you with Harrow."

"Mr. Harrow was comforting me," she says. "There was nothing in his touch beyond ordinary human compassion."

"Comforting you over what?" He says this with bafflement, truly believing she has no need for comfort.

What boiling hatred she feels for him then, for his blindness and his complete absence of compassion. "Mr. Harrow's wife died. I thought he might understand how I feel about Daniel's death."

"How you feel, Isabella, is not something to broadcast about to strange men on a—"

"To a fellow human, who has also suffered a great loss," she says, her words riding over his even though she knows it is the habit of hers he despises the most. *Isabella, you ought to listen more and speak far less.*

Arthur splutters a little more, pacing in the small space, his shoes clacking on the wood. The smells of rain and rime are strong, and she thinks about the sea out there restlessly churning; and the restless churning is in her guts too.

Finally, he says, "The child's death hasn't made you special, Isabella. You are still merely the woman you always were. You deserve no special treatment, you are not above the rules of proper society." His eyes flick to her wrist. "At least you have taken off that tatty ribbon."

She bristles, but doesn't bite.

He squares his shoulders, twitches his nostrils. "You are to stay below deck until we reach Sydney."

"What? No!"

"Stay here in the saloon or in our bedroom. Keep Meggy company. I don't care what you do. But stay away from the crew. Guard your modesty. And don't go about seeking comfort for old wounds that have long healed, just to draw attention to yourself."

"I haven't healed!" she cries. But he has already turned and disappeared up the fore hatch. She wants to carve her embroidery scissors into his forehead; perhaps write Daniel's name there, to put back into his mind the baby that he lost, that *they* lost. Isabella feels she shall go mad. Every nerve in every tooth is tingling with frustration. The rage builds inside her, under her ribs, around her heart. She wants to break something or someone. Right now, it's Arthur, but if Meggy came down the hatch she would enjoy tearing her face off too. Where does this violence come from? She was once a gentle woman. How gentle her hands were, when she held the light, sweet limbs of her son.

Confined below deck. The trapped air and the smells from the cargo hold, not to mention the crew's quarters. She'll be sick. But Arthur won't care if she grows sick. Why does he want her at all, if she is such a disappointment and an irritation? How can he bear to be married to her any more than she can bear to be married to him?

Isabella realizes she is crushing her embroidery ring hard between her hands, and the needle has pierced her palm. She gently removes it, and a perfectly round drop of blood forms. She finds herself transfixed by it, by the delicate patterns of lines on her palm. She presses just beside the tiny puncture and the ball turns to a drop, and runs down her wrist.

Escapes.

She is a long way from home. If she were to disappear while in Australia, how would he ever find her? She could find a passage to America, where Victoria lives. And now the plan crystallizes even more clearly. Her sister's last letter told her she is expecting a baby. Isabella could take Daniel's bracelet to her and, loath to give it up though she would be, his spirit could live again in her sister's child. In that moment, seized by the sudden searing rightness of her idea, she wants nothing more than this.

Isabella feels light for the first time in years.

Six

Isabella sits on her bed. The door to the cabin is shut and held fast by a trunk full of clothes. She has a fountain pen and a scrap of paper, and on it she makes a list of the jewelry laid out in front of her.

1 ruby and diamond bracelet
1 gold pendant with sapphires
1 gold pendant with pearls
1 platinum pendant with pearls and amethysts
1 pair diamond and peridot earrings
1 pair French opal and gold earrings
1 Hungarian emerald brooch
1 enamel pansy brooch with diamond
1 ruby and pearl platinum brooch
1 moonstone and diamond ring
1 sapphire ring

This is everything valuable she owns. Shoes and dresses cannot be sold so easily, but this jewelry can. Each of these items was a present from her husband or his family, but she wears none of this jewelry. When pressed, on a special occasion, she allows herself to be guided by Arthur on what will glitter most beautifully under candlelight, but for the most part the jewelry stays in its silk box, a hidden reminder that she is owned by the Winterbourne family, for every one of these pieces is a Winterbourne original. She has been owned by the Winterbournes since they bought out her father's business at what Arthur's mother always called "a vastly inflated cost."

Every one of these pieces belongs to her too. There can be no accusation of theft. She is almost certain.

Once she has finished the list, Isabella packs the jewelry away in the bottom of her trunk, then folds the list and slides it under her pillow. She lies down with her hands behind her head and closes her eyes. There is no window in the cabin, so even though it is daylight outside the room is gray. The ship rolls on.

Over and over in her mind she turns the delicious thought that if she sells her jewelry in Sydney, she will easily have enough for a passage to New York to meet her sister. And not on a wretched sailing vessel like this one; on a nice, big, stable steamer. Her fantasy grows more detailed by the moment, and the more detailed it grows the more she convinces herself that it is meant to be, pre-ordained somehow. She is merely fulfilling her destiny. The Winterbournes think her unstable and mad, and perhaps she is. If so, then why shouldn't she run away? Both her father and Arthur's are dead, and they had arranged the union. Foolishly. What remains of her husband's family doesn't want her: she would be freeing him to marry another woman, perhaps one who can give him another child. Her womb refuses to quicken again. She believes it still longs for Daniel, as she does. Perhaps his new wife might even enjoy his weekly visits to her body. Though she can't imagine that. She remembers being fifteen or sixteen and wondering about the secrets of lovemaking, and thinking it all sounded very thrilling. Either she was mistaken or Arthur is very bad at it.

The weather has been growing worse. Perhaps she is feeling it is worse because she has been shut in her cabin for two days now. She could sit in the saloon where there are salt-splashed windows, but that would mean sitting with Meggy and Arthur. The seas are very stormy and the rain is unrelenting. She has glimpsed Mr. Harrow and the Captain in the corridor, both soaked to the bone even with the protection of their moleskins, their shoes squelching, and she fights the superstitious fear that the bad weather has come because she has stopped making her daily pact with the sea.

The Captain in particular looks haunted. She can't imagine why; he has surely been through bad weather before. She wishes she could ask Mr. Harrow what is going on, but she dare not in case Arthur sees. She could ask Arthur, but that would mean talking to him.

Isabella sometimes tries to remember a time when she didn't hate Arthur, and perhaps there was a brief moment, when she was expecting Daniel. For a few months, he softened. He was pleased that she had a child on the way so soon. Pleased in the way that somebody might be pleased with a dog who has fetched his slippers, perhaps, but pleased nonetheless. He'd brought the enamel pansy brooch home from work one day, on a whim, to give her. She'd even worn it for a while, so relieved was she that his sternness seemed to be dissipating. Hopeful, even, that being wedded to him for life might not be the misery she anticipated.

Yes, she liked him for a little while. He still seemed remote and terse, but she thought she saw in him the makings of a good father: one who might dote upon the baby with her. When Daniel was born, he didn't live up to that fond dream.

The first time Arthur saw Daniel, Isabella was in bed, dozing.

It was late afternoon and Daniel was sleeping peacefully, three days old, his tiny fists lying soft around his ears, his little mouth puckered up and sucking on an imaginary breast. Arthur came in with a thump and a clatter at the door, and said to her, "Why are you in bed at four o'clock?"

She startled awake, but Daniel slept on. "I'm sorry, Arthur," she said. "I am so very tired. The little one wakes all through the night."

"Then you should have a wet nurse as I suggested. You can't lie around in bed all day like a slattern."

The idea of somebody else feeding her child was abhorrent to her. She sat up, trying to gather herself: a difficult task as she'd given birth only a few days before and she was sore and seemed to leak from everywhere at once. "Please, Arthur. Just let me mother him the way I choose."

"Well, if you are determined, and I see you are, ensure that you speak to my mother. She raised two sons and I wager she never once slept in the daytime."

Isabella would sooner eat poison than ask his mother for advice. The first Mrs. Winterbourne has all the outward appearance of an angel: soft curves, fair curling hair, wide blue eyes and a bovine smile, but beneath that surface she is made of wire and stones. Isabella has never told Arthur how, on the evening of their wedding dinner, Mrs. Winterbourne took her aside and told her she thought Arthur had married beneath him, and she'd best paddle as hard as she could to catch up with the manners and comportment that her sons were born to. She has never told him because she suspects he would probably agree. Every one of his family would agree, especially unctuous Percy and the trembling mouse he calls his wife.

Arthur paced over to the cradle. A late-afternoon sunbeam fell through the shutter and lit the creamy lace sheets, and illuminated her son's impossibly soft cheek. "I don't want him to be soppy," he said.

"He is only new in the world," she murmured. "Let him be soft awhile."

Arthur folded his hands behind his back, as though fearful he would be tempted to pick the child up otherwise. He pushed his lips into a pout as he surveyed his son, much the way she'd seen him consider the cut of a diamond. "He is smaller than I thought he would be."

"Just under seven pounds," she said.

And that was it. He turned, hands still folded behind his back, and left the room. She rose and leaned over Daniel's cradle, stroked the fluff on his warm head, breathed his milky sweetness and vowed that she would love him enough for both his parents.

Isabella opens her eyes. It is too much: the memory of Daniel—warm and breathing, not cold and still—has turned a knife in her heart. How she wishes she could open up the walnut chest and retrieve her black ribbon, and spend the afternoon rolling each link on the coral bracelet between her thumb and forefinger, milking it of the last impression of her baby's living warmth. But she daren't. It must stay hidden until Sydney. In Sydney she will get it back and she will somehow get out of this miserable marriage and away from Arthur and his poisonous family. Then this wretched storm would stop, and calm seas and sunshine might be hers once more.

Two mornings later, Mr. Harrow seeks her out, clever enough to do it while Arthur is otherwise occupied up in the cargo hold with the Captain and Meggy, sorting out a dispute about marble tiles. As well as bringing the mace to Australia, Arthur is exporting expensive tiles and carpets. The less Isabella knows about business, the happier she is. But Arthur is quite tense about the deal, and tense too that the crew will steal or damage the goods.

When Mr. Harrow knocks on her cabin door, her heart startles a little. She doesn't want to endure another of Arthur's lectures.

"Mr. Harrow?" she says, warily.

"I'm sorry, Mrs. Winterbourne. I shall be very quick. Is it the case that you have been confined below deck because of our . . . interaction in the galley the other day?"

Isabella knows a woman of her standing should dismiss him lightly, never drawing attention to the private matters of her husband. But she sees little point in such manners. "Yes. I did explain, but he's an angry fool."

"I feel terrible," he says. "Do you want me to speak to him?"

"No, it will only make matters worse."

He glances around. "If there's anything I can do . . . I was touched deeply by your loss."

"And I yours," she says, and she means it. A little glimmer starts in her heart, and hope rises. Perhaps the ice is not permanent after all.

"I'm sorry it took me so long to realize what has happened. We've been rather run off our feet by the weather."

Mention of the weather picks at a little thread of unease in her gut. She realizes that last night she dreamed of the gray sea rising up and up, through the boards, through the cabin, engulfing Arthur's bunk and then sloshing around her blankets, carrying the black ribbon away while she tried to reach for it with hands as slippery as fish fins. Yes, the weather has been on her mind. If only she could get above deck and talk to the sea.

"The weather is normal, though? For this part of the world and this time of year?"

Mr. Harrow shakes his head. "I must say, Mrs. Winterbourne, that the Captain and I are in dispute. It seems to me there must be a hurricane nearby. He argues that it's too late in the year for a hurricane but . . ." He drops his voice low. "Captain Whiteaway does not like bad weather."

Tingles of hot ice lace her skin. "So then why does he persist in the journey? Should we not come to port until we are certain it isn't a hurricane?"

"He deals with his dislike of bad weather by insisting it isn't happening." Mr. Harrow snaps his mouth shut at the end of this sentence, an outward sign that he believes he has spoken too much, and too contrary to the Captain. "Don't concern yourself. We are all good men, and we will be safe."

"The Captain drinks too much," she says plainly.

He replies in a near-perfect impersonation of the Captain's voice. "'It's how I unravel the knots in my stomach.'"

"The amount I've seen him consume at dinner would indicate a large volume of knots."

Mr. Harrow tries a smile. "As I said, don't worry. Let the men aboard mind the weather, and you mind your own affairs below deck." Then voices from the other end of the corridor have him backing out quickly, with no word of farewell.

Isabella ventures into the saloon and stops to look at the map spread out on the Captain's desk. Captain Francis Whiteaway has traversed the globe, from north to south and east to west, for twenty years. So far as she knows, he has always drunk heavily, he has negotiated much bad weather, and he has always returned to England safe and whole. If he says it is too late in the year for a hurricane, then perhaps he is right. Mr. Harrow is, after all, a scant few years older than Isabella herself. She eyes the half-empty whiskey decanter. How many times has she seen it filled, then emptied again? Her fingers trace the east coast of Australia, pale pink against a turquoise sea. They are here, somewhere. But there are no storm clouds on this map, and the sea is as flat and still as the lid of a tomb.

*I*sabella thinks herself alone. It is after breakfast, and the weather is making her sick. The sea lifts them and dumps them, over and over. She is confined below deck but can't bear another long day in her cabin, and needs to avoid Meggy and Arthur, so she takes the walk down to the dark end of the ship. She carries her fountain pen and her list. She hopes to find somewhere quiet and away from the eyes of others to add up the worth of her jewelry, and budget how much she will need for her voyage to New York, food, coaches . . . There seems so much to organize and at night the swirl of thoughts keeps her awake. Pinning them to the page will help. It will also give her something to take her mind off the weather.

All the crew are on deck, managing the sails. She goes down to the cargo hold and sits on a stack of tiles covered with a rope net. The light is dim, but she smooths out her list on her lap and starts to jot down notes.

The ship shudders and shakes. She takes a deep breath and keeps going.

Her senses prickle. She is suddenly aware that she's not alone. She looks up, her hand instinctively covering the page on which she writes.

"Writing a love letter, Mrs. Winterbourne?" says Captain Whiteaway.

Isabella quickly folds the list. "No, I'm not. I'm making a list."

"Of what?"

"Private thoughts," she replies. "Nothing to concern yourself with." She peers at him in the gloom. He is drunk already. "Why are you not on deck with the others?"

"I came to see if the cargo had moved. We hit quite a bump back there."

"I felt it." She wants to ask why he came himself, rather than sending a crewman, but the answer would be that he was drunk, or lazy, or afraid of the bad weather and pretending it wasn't happening. He is here because he is incompetent, and no man will ever admit that about himself.

His eyes haven't left the piece of paper in her hand. "What secrets are you hiding in there, Isabella?" he says.

"No secrets."

He holds out his hand and makes a "give it to me" gesture.

"It's private."

He looms over her, a six-foot slab of meaty man with hot brandied breath, and now the horrible memories are awakening again in her mind. Her mouth moves to protest, but only a little popping noise comes out.

The flash of remembrance: the conservatory at her mother-in-law's house. Early in the morning before anyone was awake. Her heart still shredded with grief, her breasts still swollen with milk. And Percy Winterbourne, Arthur's younger brother, forcing himself on her.

Frost on the grass outside, the sour smell of ashes in the fireplace. His hand clamped over her mouth, the taste of his skin, her frantic breath searing her nostrils. "A little of this?" he had said, roughly squeezing her tender nipples through her gown. Pain and shame in equal measure. Her struggles had made him angry, rougher. Then the maid had come in and he'd leaped away from her, smoothed over his waistcoat and pretended nothing had happened.

And when she told Arthur later, he had called her a liar.

"Leave me be!" Isabella shrieks, frightened and, bafflingly, ashamed.

Captain Whiteaway stands back. His conscience has been pricked awake; Isabella is pale and trembling. He drops his hand. Saves face by saying, "I'm not interested in your women's nonsense anyway. But if I find out you and Harrow are writing love letters to each other, I'll fire him and put you out at the next port. Arthur is my good friend."

"It's not a love letter," she manages. "It is a list. Just a list." But her words may as well have not been spoken. He is stroking his hand over his beard, turning away.

And after all it isn't "just a list." It is a plan, it is a ticket out of misery, it is a first step in escaping her husband.

It is three in the morning, the deepest hour of sleep. Isabella hears knocking and shouting, but it takes a few moments for her to realize this knocking and this shouting is meant for her. Arthur's voice. "Isabella, wake up!"

She opens her eyes. Everything is moving. She sits up, trying to steady herself. The ship is moaning. It pitches, then it yaws. Howling wind outside. Fear kicks her heart. "What is happening?"

"Get dressed. Francis is taking us into sheltered water. He's going to try to beach us."

"Beach—"

"Just get dressed, woman!" he roars. "I'll be back for you in two minutes." Then he is gone, slamming out of the cabin. She hears his voice outside in the saloon, Meggy's voice. She hears them go up the ladder while she is still lacing up her dress with shaking hands.

The sea has teeth. Isabella always knew it: she never became too enamored of the sea's beauty to see its cruelty. The sea has teeth and they are snapping at the ship. Arthur should never have confined her below deck. She was keeping them safe with her morning prayer, showing her respect, reminding the sea that she never once took her safety for granted. Isabella is cold at the center. This can't be happening. This ship has been at sea for decades: why would this happen now, while she is on board? It is too unfair. Isabella bends to fasten her shoes. The ship lurches, stands for a moment as if on its beam ends, then slams back onto the water. Everything around her falls down; she falls down. The hatch above the saloon bangs closed. She picks herself up and runs out of her cabin and up the ladder, pushes on the hatch and finds the way blocked. She thunders with her fists on the wood. Around her feet are shards of broken crockery.

"Help!" she shouts. "Help! There is something blocking the fore hatch."

But how could they hear her over the thundering sea?

"Arthur!" she screams. "Arthur!"

"Isabella!" His voice is muffled through the wood. "Bring the mace. A beam has snapped and is blocking the hatch. We are removing it now. Be ready and bring the mace."

She returns to the cabin and yanks the chest from its hiding position. She hefts it unsteadily. The key to the chest is in Arthur's pocket, so she can't open it and remove her precious prize. But she hauls it to the bottom of the ladder and waits. She tells herself not to panic. They are beaching the ship. They will stand on land. The wind and the rain will not be so frightening on the land. Again, the ship pitches violently. All the windows on the leeward side suddenly shatter, and the sea pours in. Isabella yelps. The lantern light has extinguished. Dark cold water swirls around her feet, pulling off her shoes, and her heart slams in her chest.

"Help me! Help me!" she screams. The sounds above her are terrifying. The snap of wood and the twang of ropes stretched past breaking point. Every time the ship pitches, more water foams in, but they are not sinking.

Not yet.

"Push on the hatch, Isabella!" Arthur calls.

Isabella pushes, the sinews in her arms straining. On the other side, the grind of wood on wood, then the hatch shoots up.

Arthur's hands are there. "The mace!" he says. Isabella understands that, for the first time in their relationship, they are fixed on a common goal: save this wooden chest from being swallowed by the sea.

She hefts it up the ladder, bumping the walnut chest on every step. Pushes it towards Arthur, who pulls it through the hatch, then offers her his left hand. She is on deck now, and it is chaos. Foaming sea, sails in ribbons, ropes knotted chaotically by the wind, the sky screaming in the rigging.

"What's happening?" she asks.

"Francis is bringing us to the beach. But he needs to get the ship before the wind."

Isabella looks around. Rain fills her eyes. The sea surrounds them. "I see no land."

"Over there." Arthur gestures widely. "Somewhere." He stands with an ankle on either side of the walnut chest.

Then a man screams. "Breakers! Breakers!"

Isabella has only a moment to turn her head and see the white foaming breakers before the sickening grind of the ship on the rocks vibrates up through her ribs and heart.

"Abandon ship! Abandon ship!" This is the Captain, standing at the wheel, surrounded by shredded sails and wooden debris. "Every man for himself!"

All Isabella's joints turn to water. Arthur is already hefting the chest towards a lifeboat. She scrambles after him amid chaos and noise and salt water and rain. He fumbles with ropes and she helps. People are crawling into lifeboats on the starboard side. She searches faces, looking for Meggy or Mr. Harrow, when a huge wave turns the ship suddenly forty-five degrees and it slams onto the reef again. With a huge plume of foam, the wood disintegrates. Where there were men and movement, now there is only gushing sea. Her heart is too big for her body.

"Quickly, Arthur!" she shouts. She looks around for the Captain, for Meggy, for anyone. Perhaps there are people still taking the last lifeboat off the prow.

Arthur lowers their lifeboat and by some miracle they are now both in it and bobbing on the shallow water over the reef. Arthur takes one oar and Isabella the other and they push themselves into deep water, the walnut chest between them. The waves want to keep carrying them back towards the ship, which Isabella can now see has broken in half. She thinks about her jewelry back on board, but cannot feel sorry for its loss. If she lives, she will think herself lucky. If Daniel's coral bracelet survives too, she will think herself rich beyond measure.

Then Arthur half-stands to get his oar against a rock and push away. A wave catches their little boat and he tips into the water.

"Arthur!" Isabella screams. His oar is still sticking out of the water, so she grasps it. He holds the other end tightly, swallowing water and struggling.

"Pull, you useless woman, pull!" he screams.

"I *am* pulling!"

But then the water is over his face and, pull as she might, she cannot bring him closer. Suddenly, the force is reversed, and she realizes he is pulling her. If he is going to drown, he will take her with him. But before she can register this properly and drop the oar, it flips up. Light. Arthur is gone.

Isabella feels her own lightness, her own lack of substance. Her death is just over there, an arm's-length away. A swelling wave beneath her lifts the lifeboat, and pushes it away from the ship. She surfs down it, shouting with fear, unable to hear herself over the storm.

But now she can see land, and she starts to row.

In spite of the mad currents.

In spite of the rocks.

Because in the chest is the last memory of her son.

She rows. Through the black water. Through the storm. Through the pelting icy needles of rain. For Daniel.

Seven

*I*sabella focuses on one task at a time, because to think of anything beyond the immediate present is to feel searing terror. She must seek shelter, but beyond the vast empty beach is a dark tangle of spiny trees that are black and nightmarish in the dark. The sight of them makes her stomach turn to water. Instead, she drags the lifeboat up the beach to a rocky shelf protruding from the white sand. Once, twice, she heaves. On the third attempt, her arms burning, she manages to flip the boat over. One side becomes wedged against the rock and she crawls underneath it for shelter, tucking the walnut box with the mace in it against her body.

The rain hammers on the bottom of the boat. She curls into a ball. A gap between boat, rock and sand, only a foot at its highest point, keeps her from being in perfect airless dark. The sea roars and crashes. She waits for the others to come. Her body shivers uncontrollably: cold from the rain and sea, colder from the fear and shock. Nobody comes. Her eyes are fixed on the water. No other boats. No brave swimmers. Nobody.

Arthur doesn't come. Nor Meggy. Nor Captain Whiteaway. Nor Mr. Harrow.

The black night lightens to gray after an hour or so. Dawn is not far away. Where are they? They are taking a long time to get from the wreck to the shore.

Under the boat, she waits.

The rain and wind ease a little, but it is still too stormy to leave her shelter. She remains on her side in the sand, eyes fixed on the sea, while weak daylight struggles through the clouds. And still nobody comes.

*A*round the middle of the day, the rain stops. Isabella crawls out from under the boat to stretch her legs, and finds they can barely support her weight. She sits on the sand. She cries. The tears blur her vision as she surveys the world around her. Will anyone know she is here? Will there be a rescue ship? Isabella doesn't know how such things work. But she fears that there will be no rescue ship. She sits on a vast beach, looking out at a bay shaped like a cauldron. Out there somewhere, in the storm-tossed water, is her husband. He is dead. They are all dead. A chill spreads through her veins. She struggles to her feet and forces her legs to work. She paces the sand, muttering, "They are all dead," over and over, to see if the thought will sink in and become more ordinary.

They are all dead.

She walks to the edge of the water, lifts her skirts and wades in up to her waist. The water is warmer than the air. She relieves herself, a flush of shame on her cheeks even though there is not a soul around to witness it. Then she returns to the beach, to the shelter of her upturned boat. That is enough for today. Her stomach grumbles: she is hungry but has no appetite. She will worry about food tomorrow. For the rest of the day she lies in the sand under the boat. More rain moves in. Exhaustion finally catches her. At dusk, she sleeps.

*   *   *

*I*sabella wakes to see the rain has cleared. The dawn sky is smudged by only a few purple-edged clouds. There will be sun. The thought lightens her mood, but only temporarily, for the night has brought something else to the beach.

Bodies.

At first her heart leaps, and she thinks they are sleeping. But as she walks towards them, it becomes apparent that the angle at which the two men are heaped upon each other is unnatural. Their legs are tossed by the waves running onto the shore.

Isabella turns sharply and walks back in the other direction. She doesn't want to know if they are her friends or simply crewmen. She feels the great emptiness inside her. She crawls under her boat and sobs for hours.

But now she knows it is time to leave.

As well as the bodies, pieces of wreckage have washed up along the beach. She picks through it, looking for anything that might be of use. There is nothing. Splintered wood. No bottles or barrels of food, no clothes or shoes. She glances over at the bodies again, but quickly looks away. She won't steal clothes off corpses. Isabella's eyes go to the mouth of the cove. If she walks up to the tip of the headland, she will be able to see better where she is. There may be a town. The thought cheers her. She may see houses.

She may see endless beach hemmed by spiny forest.

Isabella breathes deeply. First she must get Daniel's bracelet out of the chest.

Around her upturned boat, rocks of varying sizes lie in random patterns. Isabella chooses one and pulls the chest out from under the boat. She takes aim and smacks the rock against the lock, and the impact shudders up her arms and into her shoulders.

The imprinted brass decorative clasp pops off, but the lock doesn't break. Her husband's fear of thieves has made him use sturdy locks, firmly screwed from inside and out.

Isabella wonders if she is a thief, as she rips off the bottom of her petticoat and twists it into a rope. She threads the rope through the brass handle and stands, pulling the box behind her.

She trudges through the sand. The sun is high and hot. She stops, takes off her remaining petticoat and wraps it around her head like a long scarf, pulling a few inches of the white cotton forward to shelter her face. Then she picks up her rope and walks again. The sand squeaks against her feet. The rhythm of the sea times her footfalls: five steps as it draws, five steps as it surges. She comes to the base of the long arm that shelters the bay and scrambles up, yanking the walnut box up behind her. Long, tough grass covers the ground and prickles her feet. The trees she can see hemming the beach are shades of gray and olive. She is sideswiped by a sudden longing to be back in England, where the sunshine is gentle and the trees are dark green, where she had shoes and knew what would happen next.

She marches on, up the headland. The sun peaks, then goes over, changing the shadows of the grass on the sand. Then, finally, she is at the tip of the headland. She dares not look yet. There is a rock with a shallow pool. It is too high to be full of sea water, so she knows it is rainwater. She drinks it, even though it is gritty. She wishes she had collected water yesterday when it rained, then acknowledges she had nothing to collect it in.

She lays down the box, stands tall and bravely looks. Back to the north first. Nothing. Countless miles of sand, a headland in the distance, obscured by sea mist. Now she looks south. More nothing. More sea mist. More green-blue ocean, roaring and wild beyond the shelter of the bay.

Endless. Endless.

She feels her smallness. She feels the immensity of the world. She feels the silent indifference of God. She feels the power of the ocean and her own limp weakness. Isabella's knees buckle beneath her. She lowers herself to the spiky grass, and it pokes her through her dress. She puts her forehead on her knees and wishes, fervently, that she had died like all the others.

She sits like that for a long time, heart thudding in her ears, the ocean crashing all around her, longing for small, quiet places and shelter and food. Then she lifts her head. She cannot sit here forever, for she will surely die. To the north there are clouds. They may turn into storm clouds. The ship was heading south, so there must be something to the south. Achingly distant, perhaps hundreds of miles. But there is *something* there, and so that is where she must go. She cannot stay where there is nothing. Her stomach already gurgles with hunger and the sun is drying all the rainwater. She is too frightened to go through the trees: just looking at them makes her flinch. So she will head south along the beach.

She wants to cry, but crying will avail her nothing. Crying didn't bring Daniel back. Crying won't save his bracelet or give her a way to New York to find her sister. She stands, grabs the petticoat rope and clambers down the other side of the grassy verge and back onto smooth, bare sand. And she walks, dragging the walnut box behind her. Better to walk in the cool of evening and rest during the hottest part of the day. She walks until the stars come out, thousands of them glittering in foreign patterns in the black sky. She walks until midnight chases the last of the heat off the land. She walks until her feet and legs feel like liquid, and then she heads up to the edge of the spiny forest and lies down in the sand to sleep.

*   *   *

*I*sabella realizes she has never felt hunger before. She has felt the faint gnawing of an empty stomach before breakfast, perhaps. But hunger is more encompassing than that. It makes her innards feel raw. The sun is hot when she wakes and she knows it is suicide to move while it is up. She is less fearful of the forest now, and goes in a little way for the meager shade. Here, there is still rainwater caught in puddles, so she can at least wet her mouth so it doesn't feel like cloth. Even with the shade over her face, her skin is growing cracked and dry from the salt and the wind and the reflection off the sea. Her hands are pink with sunburn and raw from dragging the heavy chest. She turns them over in front of her face, wondering where her wedding ring is now.

With all her other jewelry, in the silk box, at the bottom of the ocean. Only a few short days ago, she was counting it out, planning her escape, writing her list. All of it has washed away.

She sits, grasps her knees and leans forward, trying to get comfortable on the sand and leaf fall. But her stomach is aching and she needs to eat. Anything. She looks behind her. The trees are dense. If this were England she'd know where to go looking for wild blueberries or a peach tree. The thought of fruit makes her mouth water. She rises, leaving the chest for now. There is nobody nearby to steal it. She makes her way a little into the trees, twigs scratching her arms. She is overwhelmed by an intense, foreign smell, sour and pungent. These trees and bushes look as though they could never bear fruit. Everything seems barren, dried out, starving itself.

She freezes at a slithering sound in the bushes, and backs away. A snake? Or something worse? She heads back to the chest, sits with it and tries not to think about food or water.

*   *   *

Isabella knows, of course, that the Winterbournes will come to look for the mace. She wants to be rid of it, so she can be free of them. Especially free of Percy. She is already plunged too deep in horror to imagine what he would do if he found that she had it. She spends the hottest part of the day trying again and again to prize open the chest. She uses rocks and sticks and sharp-edged shells. She crushes one of her fingertips. It goes blue, but the chest is still closed. The key is in her husband's pocket. Perhaps he is washed up on the shore by now, or perhaps he is deep in the ocean. Once she reaches civilization, she can open it. The box is only wood, after all. She must borrow tools and open the chest and get Daniel's bracelet out. Then somehow she must get to a port that sails to New York. The Winterbournes will think her dead, and not come after her. She is free, as long as she can survive and as long as she can rid herself of the wretched mace.

The shadows grow long and she stands and begins to walk again. She is slower today: four footfalls for every draw and every wash of the waves. Hunger makes her weak, but just before dark she sees ahead that brown creek water has carved a furrow in the sand. She trudges up the beach and into the woods, bends at the side of the stream and scoops handfuls into her mouth. The heavy rain has made the creek run fast and full. The water has a strange mineral taste, but she doesn't care. She drinks until her stomach aches. She decides to spend the night and next morning here, where she can hear the running water and know she will not die of thirst. The ground cover is soft. She lies for a long time without sleeping, blinking up at the foreign stars through the spiny leaves.

*   *   *

*H*unger prompts Isabella awake the next dawn. Her feet are raw, her hands are blistering, but all she can feel is hunger. She is not a woman anymore, just a vast ache. She must find food. She knows she must be brave and go deeper into the woods.

With weak and shaking fingers, she winds the chest in the petticoat rope and straps it to her back, tying knots and adjusting it over her shoulders. She has seen drawings of native women carrying children like this. She moves slowly, following the creek, picking her way over rocks and twigs and marshy leaf fall. The foliage is thick, but she manages to find a narrow, sandy path. She hears strange birds and longs for blackbirds.

Then, movement from the corner of her eye. She flinches, turning her head to see a large gray-brown lizard with its legs wrapped around a narrow tree trunk. It looks at her; she looks at it.

Along with her fear and revulsion is the realization that if she can catch it and cook it, she can eat it.

But its big claws look sharp and she hesitates long enough for it to scamper farther up the tree and onto a branch. Now Isabella can only see its tail, and she wishes she had been more decisive because her stomach is roaring with hunger and she feels weak and dizzy.

She looks behind her. The trees have closed out the view of the beach, but she can still hear the ocean and knows she can find her way back.

Farther into the forest? But why? What does she hope to find? Despair seizes her, but she doesn't fall to her knees, she doesn't pound her head against a tree. She keeps trudging, bruising the soles of her feet on rocks and fallen twigs. Her eyes are searching all the time. She doesn't know what is edible and what isn't.

Now she sees a shrub with curling yellow flowers and egg-shaped berries. Several of the berries have fallen on the ground. Isabella bends to pick one up, and turns it over in her fingers. What if it's poison?

If it's poison, she dies quickly, rather than slowly.

Isabella eats the sweet, green berry. Her teeth grind against a seed, which she spits out. She eats all the fallen fruit, then picks more off the shrub. The ones she picks are hard and sour. She goes farther into the forest, looking for more fallen fruit. Her stomach howls. There is no way a handful of berries can satisfy her, but at least she is eating something.

The sun is growing warm in the sky now, and she can't bear the trickling sweat under her breasts. Her back is aching, so she unties the chest and rests it between dark tree roots. She sits on it, trying to keep her sunburned hands in the patchy shade.

Movement in the undergrowth, something white flashing. Isabella peers warily, then stands and moves to it. It is a seagull: injured or old, flapping one of its wings, unable to fly or move away from her.

Instinct overrides everything. She hasn't eaten anything but berries in four days. She looks for a rock, finds one and, screwing her eyes half-shut, brings it down on the bird's light skull. It stops struggling.

Isabella's stomach flips over at the thought of what she has done. She has never killed anything, and in her weak, vulnerable state, her heart wrings for the gull, for its struggle for life, for its ghastly death. She crouches next to its mangled corpse, her hands in her hair, and sobs. The sobs crack the fresh sea air, they thunder through the spiny woods, they sink into the ground and make it shake.

Hunger reminds her she must stop crying. She must get on.

She picks up the bird by its feet and rests it gently on the chest, refusing to look directly at it. She has seen Cook pluck and gut a bird, so she knows roughly what to do. But she has never started a fire. She concentrates on one task at a time. She finds stones to make a pit, finds kindling, finds a couple of good dry sticks to rub together. There is blood on her hands and she tells herself not to be squeamish, that blood is always part of eating. It is spilled regularly in kitchens across the world. She rubs the sticks, she rubs the sticks, she rubs the sticks. Nothing happens. She tries again. She sits back on her haunches and lets out a shout of frustration that tears her throat. She rubs the sticks. Where is the fire? *Where is the damned fire?*

A noise. She startles, whirls around.

A dog. No, a wolf. Something between a dog and a wolf stands on the other side of the chest. She sees it, sees her dead seagull and lurches forward.

The wild dog also lurches. Its jaws open wide to pick up the seagull just as Isabella's hands touch its soft feathers. The wild dog doesn't hesitate. It drops the bird and fastens its strong, sharp jaws on her hand. Isabella screams. Hot, pulling pain. She tries to pull back, but the wild dog has her hand. She brings around her other hand, forms a fist and punches the wild dog's head. It drops her, she leaps backwards, and the dog is gone—with the dead gull in its mouth.

"No!" she shrieks. "No, no, no!" Blood trickles from her wounded hand; the shape of the beast's mouth is perfectly re-produced on her sunburned skin. She pulls the petticoat off her head and wraps her hand in it to stop the blood flowing. The emptiness inside, the emptiness outside. Everything is empty. She slumps heavily over the chest and cannot move.

*　　*　　*

By the early evening her mind is playing tricks on her, because she thinks she can smell roasting meat. She stands and sniffs the air. Her mouth waters. But she knows that she must be imagining it, like a mirage in the desert—only it is not water she craves, it is food. She is up now, and she straps the chest to her back once more and determines to eat something, even if it makes her sick. She can't go any farther without sustenance. Recklessly, she picks the pink berries as high as she can reach off one of the spindly trees and sucks on them. She fights her way through tree branches and tangled undergrowth, ignores the crisscross of scratches through her shredded sleeves, stops frequently to drink from the creek. Her head pounds, and her thoughts are dark and tangled. "Sh," she says to herself. "Sh, sh." *Smooth out those thoughts. If you can eat, then everything will be fine. Everything will be fine.* Once her stomach is full she can head directly south again. She will find a town and there will be food: roast beef and new potatoes, Yorkshire pudding and jam gravy.

Isabella is too busy talking to herself to hear the footfalls. A dark shadow has her looking up, has her heart leaping into her mouth. Two black men stand before her, wearing nothing but armbands made of shells. Each of them holds upright a long spear.

She shrieks. She takes a step backwards to prepare to run, but her bare foot strikes a dropped branch and now she is falling instead. The chest is on her back, and it hits the ground hard, and she hits it even harder. Pain crushes into her neck and she cries out, her hand flailing into the air. The darkness is instant and inescapable.

Eight

The field of her vision is a narrow slit; jolting movement; bright and dark. She closes her eyes again, wants to sink back into the dark, soft place. But something doesn't feel right. She forces them open again, pain screaming into her head. She tries to move her arms and legs, but they are slack and weak. She blinks rapidly, realizes she is being carried—cradled like a child—by one of the natives. She struggles and he presses her more firmly against his naked chest. She raises her hands to scratch his eyes, but he captures them easily and holds them down against her stomach. He says something to his companion, and Isabella realizes she no longer has the walnut chest. Thieves! Kidnappers! What will they do to her? She shouts and curses and struggles, but she is weak and injured.

The man who carries her says something to her tersely.

Tearily, she shakes her head. "I don't understand."

He reaches for her throat and she flinches, but then she feels his fingers on the back of her neck and they come away bloody. Isabella reaches for the same place, and feels a stinging gash, oozing blood. Pain sings through her spine.

The two naked black men take her farther into the forest, across uneven ground. Their feet must be like leather, because they are swift and light. She feels like the gull: too wounded to fight. Her own ghastly end is coming.

But then she smells the smoky roasting meat. The natives bring her down into a grove that the creek runs through, overgrown with green foliage. On the other side a dozen more black people collect around a fire. Five small huts stand off to one side. Women tend to fat babies, or hold roasting meat on spears over the fire; men talk or sit on rocks sharpening spears or fixing weapons. Not one of them is wearing clothes. Isabella has never seen a naked man, only Arthur in the dark bedroom. She doesn't know where to direct her gaze.

"What are you going to do with me?" she says. Do these natives eat humans?

But then her captor places her carefully on the ground and calls out. Within seconds a large woman with soft eyes and pendulous breasts approaches, and her companions explain the situation in their native tongue. The woman helps Isabella to sit, and mimes putting her hand to her mouth. They are asking her to eat.

"Yes!" Isabella says. "Yes. Food. Yes."

More calling to each other in their native tongue, then she is offered the spear with the roasting lizard on it. She pulls off a chunk of white flesh and puts it to her lips without a second thought. The flesh is soft, a little chewy, and tastes smoky. As hungry as she is, she thinks it the best meal she has ever eaten.

As she eats, the woman talks softly, cleaning the wound and dressing it with sharp-smelling ointment. She turns her attention to the bite on Isabella's hand, tuts and makes a few more comments. Isabella tells her that she can't understand, but the woman talks anyway. A child, just learning to walk, toddles up to them and grasps Isabella's free hand. Isabella smiles, charmed by the child's round cheeks and dark eyes. The child pushes up the sleeve of her dress and admires her white skin with awe. Something about the child's touch encourages her to relax. The child is happy and well. That must mean the people who raise him are good people.

She turns to the woman and says, "Thank you," warmly, with a smile. The woman may not know the words, but she understands the sentiment.

The woman gestures towards the huts and then points at the sky. Dusk is closing in. The woman is offering her shelter for the night.

Isabella looks at the hut, with its open front. Clouds have been gathering over the afternoon, and it might rain. The chest is still where she fell. But who is there to steal it? It could do no harm, surely, to stay here overnight. Sleep somewhere soft and sheltered, perhaps even have more to eat in the morning.

Isabella nods. "Yes, thank you."

Isabella lies among the soft leaves and animal skins and sleeps like the dead. When she wakes, the soft-fingered woman is there again offering her food, re-dressing her wound. When Isabella makes to stand, she is pushed back down. The woman clicks her tongue. The message is clear. *You are not well. You must stay a little longer.* Isabella gratefully accepts. She spends the day watching them come and go, with fish and lizards and wild dogs to eat, with baskets full of berries and fruit that Isabella recognizes from her long walk. They feed her well. Rain moves in. She wonders if these are the only people for hundreds of miles, if she should just throw her lot in with them and become part of their tribe. She would, at least, never go hungry again. But the desire to return to the chest, to Daniel's bracelet, is strong. She needs to be with her own family, her sister. She vows to keep moving as soon as morning comes.

She is dreamless until just before dawn, when a confused tangle of images chase themselves across her mind's eye. She is pregnant with Daniel again, blood is pouring out between her legs, but when she looks down at the sand there is no baby, just the cold corpses of her shipmates. She gives birth to death. Isabella snaps awake, tries to take comfort in the fact that she is alive and safe. But there is no comfort. There is only misery, gray as the gloom before dawn.

Isabella rises. Nobody is awake. She must get away: that dream is surely caught in the trees around her now, seeped into the sandy ground, will hang around all day, all week. Her head has stopped aching and she is strong enough now to keep moving. She needs to get back to collect the chest and head south, where surely there are buildings and cooked meals on plates. Quietly, on soft feet, she tiptoes past the natives through the dark trees in the dim light. The chest lies, unmolested, where she fell. She re-ties the rope through the brass handle, and drags it behind her once again, down the empty beach.

Clouds cling to the sky, dark and churning. There will be more rain, but at least it will be a reprieve from the searing sun.

Isabella's heart catches on a hook. Is that a flash? She looks to the clouds to the south. Was it lightning? Or was it—

There. Again. A light, barely noticeable in the pre-dawn gray, sweeps across the clouds and is gone.

A lighthouse. Meaning returns. Focus intensifies. Hope is reborn.

For where there is a lighthouse, there is a lighthouse keeper.

The beach goes on forever. The sea is almost emerald today, with caps whiter than newly fallen snow. On and on it rushes and roars, and Isabella places one foot in front of the other, dragging her load behind her in the sand. The rhythm of walking and stopping begins to change. Creeks are regular enough that she doesn't go thirsty; and she now knows which berries and fruits are edible, even if they taste hard and dry. But she is human. She is wearing out. The stops become longer. The walks slower, shorter. Walking becomes trudging, lumbering, falling with only her knees to catch her. She tries to move forward a little every day: between late afternoon and nightfall, slowly, preserving her energy. A vast, aching emptiness surrounds her, pervades her, inhabits her. *Alone, alone*, the ocean seems to say. *Alone, alone.* Slowly, ponderously, endlessly. If she walks, she is quiet; but when she stops, she speaks without knowing she will speak. She hears her own voice and is alarmed. Why is she speaking? What is she saying? She tells herself to stop, but hears her voice again a few minutes later. Isabella lets the talking continue. She is too tired to control her thoughts. Focus slips away from her, and her mind opens and she can see behind the world now, the great gears turning and the bright hot reality of its meaninglessness. Now she has seen it, she knows she will always feel it inside herself. Safety, food, even happiness may come to her one day, but it is too late. She already knows the truth about life.

Her arms ache. She keeps going.

She keeps going.

*I*sabella doesn't count the days. She refuses to go back over them in her mind, because to do so makes her feel the throbbing exhaustion, the desperate fear that there really is nothing to the south. Nothing at all. The nights have been clear with no clouds for the light to reflect off, so she doesn't see it again. She has always been prone to excessive imagining: perhaps the lighthouse was a fantasy. Each day, before she starts to walk, she wades into the warm sea water to clear her head and clean her wounds and gather her courage, and lets it carry her a little while. Her gown, once a good going-to-town dress, is shredded and misshapen, encrusted with blood and dirt. It floats around her like a giant jellyfish. She closes her eyes, feels the motion of the sea. Then opens them and looks south.

And on this day, she sees it. She sees it clear and bright with her own eyes, not half-imagined against clouds.

A light. The lighthouse, sparking into life in the misty distance.

She lurches out of the water, its weight making her cumbersome and slow. She is not hungry now, not tired, nor sore. She is focused solely on getting to the lighthouse. It is perhaps fifteen miles now. Perhaps she can be there tomorrow, before it sparks into life again.

And then, whatever comes next.

*I*sabella hardly sleeps for excitement. She fights the urge to walk all night; she knows she won't make it without collapsing. Finally, she drops off. When she wakes, she can see it. The headland beckons, under a light sea mist. She can see the lighthouse now, red and white. Not far, not far. She gathers fruit and drinks from a stream, but she is restless to keep moving, even in the sun and the heat, beyond endurance. The end is finally in sight.

Little by little, walking slowly, resting often, she makes her way down the beach.

But she cannot make it. Not in one day. If she were well and unburdened and walking in the shade of tall oaks, perhaps. But she fears killing herself by pushing too hard. Midmorning she shelters again in the woods. Late afternoon she walks. She sees the light come on and wants to sob. She had wanted to be there by now. She doesn't want to die this close to refuge.

She sleeps long and hard. Her body has reached its limit. She cannot risk walking in the heat, so she waits through the day, then climbs to her feet only when the sun has moved into the west. Her legs are like jelly, her feet sting. She draws herself up, pulls on the loathsome petticoat rope. Nearly there, nearly there.

One foot. The next foot. The beach grows increasingly rocky as she nears the lighthouse. One foot. The next foot. Each step takes an age. *Live, Isabella,* she directs herself sternly. *Don't collapse now.*

The lighthouse can only be reached by a rocky climb of about ten feet. She considers going around through the bushes, but fears losing her way without the direct line of the ocean beside her. She ties the wooden chest to her back again and begins to climb.

Dusk is settling around her. Seagulls wheel above and the breeze grows fresh. She is bent over, picking a path over the rocks with bare hands and bare feet, groaning, gasping. She slips, pitches forward and gashes open her injured hand on a sharp rock edge. But nothing will stop her now, not even fresh blood. Forward, forward. Up and up. Until at last she is at the top and the lighthouse bursts into life just as she looks up at it. Her beacon in the dark. Now she is here. Now everything must be all right.

It must.

Her head swims. Her ears ring.

She rounds the lighthouse on feet made of lead and finds a tiny cottage attached, no more than a wooden box built out of the side of the lighthouse. It takes the last of her energy to lift her hand and knock weakly at the door. She fears there will be no answer, so she waits only a few seconds before knocking again. This time she calls out too. "Help!" Her voice is so thin it frightens her. "I need help." She realizes that she has left a smear of blood on the door from her hand. She turns it over in front of her. The blood is dark in the half-light.

The door swings open. Isabella looks up into the black eyes of a tall, lean man of about forty years. His eyes widen when he sees her.

"Please, please," she says. It is all she can say. Other words have fled, and now she is falling forward, crashing to her knees. He catches her in strong arms, takes her weight and draws her inside. She has an impression of dim spaces, flickering light, then everything goes gray.

When she opens her eyes, it is nighttime. There is candlelight and she is lying on top of rough blankets on a small bed.

She blinks, reorientating herself. Sitting on a stool next to the bed is a bearded man with a serious expression. The lighthouse keeper. She is at the lighthouse at last. She groans with relief.

"What is your name?" he asks, gently.

She opens her mouth to give him her name, but then stops herself. What if the Winterbournes come looking for her?

"Mary Harrow," she says.

"Do you think you can stand, Mary Harrow? I have soup and bread, and clean water. You ought to eat, get your strength back."

"How long have I been asleep?"

"Six hours. It's nearly midnight."

Isabella sits and gingerly lowers her feet to the floor.

"Here, let me help you," he says. With his arm around her waist, he leads her from the bed, past a spiraling staircase to a small, low-ceilinged room. There is a sink, a round table with a single chair, a cast-iron cooker. A smell of cooked fish and tobacco lingers in the air. He slides her onto the chair. She sees the wooden chest, still tied in the petticoat rope, sitting by the door on the bare floorboards.

Isabella sits quietly. The lighthouse keeper is in charge now; she can stop. He goes to a chest under his sink for a box of first-aid supplies, then lights a lantern and positions it on the table close to her outstretched palm. While he cleans and dresses the wound, he doesn't meet her eye. His head is bent in concentration, so Isabella has ample opportunity to study him: his dark curling hair and neat beard flecked with gray, his serious eyebrows, his agile fingers.

"Where are you from?" he asks her, at last.

"I can't say."

"What was that box on your back?"

"A burden I soon hope to rid myself of."

He bends to look at the chest, and she flies from her seat and throws herself in front of him. "You mustn't touch it."

Startled, the lighthouse keeper recoils. He speaks to her as he might speak to an injured animal, palms held up gently. "Steady," he says. "I won't touch it if you don't want me to."

Isabella is desolate and uncertain. She feels as though her edges are dissolving, as though she is made of sand and the wind is eroding her. "I'm so hungry," she says.

He nods, then stands and moves to the cooker. She stares at her bandaged hand, and can't remember how she cut it. She strains her memory. Flashes come to her. Eating lizard. Hunting berries. Pushing her feet up the beach. Then she remembers that she cut her hand just hours ago, climbing up the rocks. The fact that a hole seems to have opened up in her memory makes her panic. What is happening to her mind? She shoots out of her seat again and begins to pace.

The lighthouse keeper turns to her with a plate of steaming soup. He watches her pace and he stands very still, as though his stillness can infect her. Eventually she stops, blinking at him in the growing dark.

"My name is Matthew Seaward," he says.

"I'm so hungry," she says again.

He nods towards the table, and she sits. The lighthouse cottage smells oily and hot: trapped air, old seaweed, moldy wood. She doesn't mind. She breathes in the present, and it fills her lungs brightly. She is safe, for now. The soup is salty and thick. Her mouth and her stomach are in heaven. She eats her fill, then washes it down with a cup of clean, cool water. Her mind slowly seems to reassemble itself. She settles.

"I have nowhere to stay," she says. "I don't know what to do."

He leans back on his sink, his gaze traveling from her hair to her dress to her hands and then finally to her eyes. "Your eyes are haunted. What have you seen?"

She shakes her head. "Please don't ask me." She sinks forward onto the table and puts her face on her outstretched arms.

The lighthouse keeper allows the silence to stretch between them, and then finally he speaks. "The town is just a half-mile from here. I'm sure somebody will take you in."

"I can't go looking like this."

"There are clothes in the bedroom, left over from the previous keeper's wife. And shoes. There's a big house at the nearest end of the main street. Pale pink boards. Mrs. Katherine Fullbright. She will take you in."

Isabella's stomach drops with disappointment. She doesn't want to go to town. She wants to stay here, completely still, on this stool. The ordeal is supposed to be over, but clearly it is not. And now she considers it, the ordeal will never be over. She was broken before the ship went down, now her pieces have become muddled.

When he speaks he is infinitely gentle, despite his size and obvious strength. "Mary, you can stay here tonight. Tomorrow, you can bathe and make yourself presentable. Mrs. Fullbright stands on ceremony and a torn dress and dirty face won't do. You cannot stay here for longer than a night. It isn't right."

Isabella struggles to comprehend him in her addled state. It finally sinks in that he is trying to preserve her reputation. She no longer cares about her reputation, but she nods because she sees he will be immovable.

"Thank you. Thank you."

She eats, then returns to the rough bed. The mattress sags. The room is unmistakably male: no fancy cushions, no curtains, no tablecloth, no cut-crystal decanters or vases for flowers. It smells of tobacco, papers, oil and dust. Matthew Seaward's things. And in Matthew Seaward's bed she sleeps, dreamless.

Nine

2011

Libby devoted a week to getting her life back in order, creating some kind of routine. She felt like an ant whose tracks had been washed away and who had to create a new path through a new place. She shopped at the local greengrocer and got to know the owner's name as he boxed her vegetables. She had her electricity and phone connected and her windows cleaned. She registered to borrow at the nearest library. She scrubbed her cottage from top to bottom. She avoided her sister: the cool reception had told her that Juliet still harbored nothing but ill will for her. She swam every afternoon in the sea, as the evening closed in and the bright lights of Noosa to the misted south blinked into life. And she sketched, spending long hours in the well-lit art room, curled in a rocking chair with her sketchbook on her knee, with a plan to paint something very soon.

Between each activity she had to stop, rest and fight the tears. The grief weighed on every thought, every action. She pushed herself to keep going, keep setting up this new life. It was what Mark would have wanted for her.

A week after she arrived, Libby bought a new SIM card with a local number for her mobile phone and, before inserting it, charged the phone to see if there were any last messages on it. She expected nothing, so she was surprised to hear the familiar voice of Cathy, Mark's secretary, on her voicemail.

"Oh, good morning, Libby. It's Cathy here from Winterbourne Jewelers. I wonder if you might call me back. I have some mail here for you and I need your forwarding address."

Libby listened to the message again, confused. It was one in the morning in England now. She would have to endure eight hours of curiosity.

She glanced up at the view through the sparkling windows: a wide wedge of blue sea, golden sunlight on its white caps. Mark was on her mind again now. Sometimes, she forgot about him for a blissful five or ten minutes. Her body still felt bruised from the inside, but sometimes she forgot just how devastated she was. Then it came tumbling back, and she hated herself for having stopped remembering him, even for a little while.

She got through the day, absorbed by her drawing and cleaning and swimming in the sea. After her shower, while another dish of frozen lasagna heated in the microwave, she called London.

As the phone rang at the other end, her heart thumped hard. The last time she had called this number, she had said what she always said: "Hello, Cathy, it's Libby Slater. May I have a word with Mark, please?" She would have to find a new sentence.

"Winterbourne Jewelers, Cathy speaking."

"Cathy. It's Libby Slater, returning your call." There, not so hard after all.

"Oh, hello, Libby! You've left Pierre-Louis. We couldn't find you."

"I'm back in Australia."

"That was sudden." Cathy was the only person whom Libby suspected of knowing about her affair with Mark.

"I'd been unhappy at PL for a long time. I got your message.

Something about mail?" Libby realized she was pacing, so she forced herself to stop and lean against the kitchen bench. The smell of the lasagna began to fill the air.

"Ah, yes. Bit of a mystery. I've been going through the papers in Mark's office. As you can imagine, it's terribly sad."

"I'm sorry. That must be difficult." Libby swallowed over the lump in her throat, wishing she could be there in London to go through Mark's papers; to have any keepsake of him, even a scrawled sample of his handwriting.

"We all miss him terribly, Libby."

"His family . . ."

"I haven't seen either of the girls, though I understand the eldest is pregnant. Emily is doing well, I think. Obviously she's devastated, but she's been in at work every day since the funeral, and it looks like she's going to take over Mark's job, at least in the short term. But let's sort out this mystery with the mail. I found six letters, all addressed to you care of Mark's post office. Mark hasn't opened any of them, just shoved them in a drawer."

Libby was both thrilled and terrified. Why would anyone write to her care of Mark? Was this some secret surprise Mark was keeping from her? Or was it blackmail? "Do they have a return address?"

"They're all from the same place. A company called Ashley-Harris Holdings in Australia."

A company. So not blackmail, and probably not a secret surprise either. "I have no idea who that is, or why they are writing to me at Mark's address, Cathy, but can I ask you to pop them in the mail to me?"

"Of course," she said.

Libby gave Cathy her new address, reluctantly realizing that as soon as the phone call ended, her connection to Mark would be severed again.

But then Cathy said, "There's one other thing, Libby, and I don't know what you'll say, but Emily said I must ask you."

Libby's stomach clenched. Twelve years of keeping their affair secret had taught her to be afraid of Mark's wife's name. "What is it?"

"Pierre-Louis called looking to secure our account again, but when we discovered you were no longer there we didn't sign for this year. Emily was very keen that we ask if you'd be happy to design our catalog again as a freelancer. Now, I know perhaps you have reasons for not doing design work anymore, but—"

"Yes!" Libby said. "I would love to."

"Splendid! Emily will be so pleased. She's a great admirer of your work."

"She is?" Mark had never mentioned Emily's name if he could help it. She felt strangely exposed.

"Twelve years on the same job, Libby. You were highly regarded at Winterbourne Jewelers. Now Mark is gone, we'd like to continue the association."

"I'm so flattered. I . . ." Libby remembered she had no computer, no Internet connection, no e-mail address. "Can you give me a week? I'm just setting up my new office over here and . . ."

"Certainly. Call us when you're ready and the account is yours."

They said their good-byes just as the microwave beeped, but Libby didn't retrieve her dinner. She stood in the kitchen, staring out the window at the darkening sky, feeling the distance between her old life and her new. Mark was, and would forever remain, a million light-years away. But then she straightened, and told herself to stop being maudlin. What would Mark want for her, if he were here? To make up with her sister? Well, that hadn't gone well so far, but she had hope. Solve the Winterbourne family mystery? It didn't seem likely she could do that, and yet he would definitely want to drive up to Winterbourne Beach to see it with his own eyes. Tomorrow, then.

*S*he left just after eight. Paris traffic had never been like this at rush hour. In fact, there was no rush hour at Lighthouse Bay. A couple of cars queued on the roundabout and a few cyclists on the beachfront road, but nothing else. Libby recalled the packed platforms on the Metro, choking on somebody else's cigarette smoke or strong perfume, the constant beeping of car horns as mad Parisian drivers tried to make their way around each other on narrow roads. She put her window down and breathed in the sea air and sunshine. The drive north took just under an hour, along a straight highway hemmed by cane fields.

Winterbourne Beach was smaller than Lighthouse Bay, a tiny village surrounded by bushland, a vast deserted beach and a general store that doubled as the tourist information center. She stopped to buy a chocolate bar and a juice, and picked up a brochure about activities in the bay.

Want to find a lost treasure? Dive the Aurora*!* Libby flipped the brochure over and scanned it. The owner of the dive company lived four houses down, according to the map. Her phone was out of range up here, so she decided to visit him. Libby followed the map in the hot sunshine, and soon stood outside a weather-board house with a large motorboat on a trailer out the front. If the boat was in, he'd be home.

She started up the path when a shirtless man with an enor-mous belly emerged from behind the boat and called out gruffly, "No diving today."

Libby smiled. "I don't want to dive, I just want to ask you a few questions," she said. "Do you have a few minutes?"

He rubbed his hands on a greasy cloth. It looked as though he'd been working on the boat's engine. "What do you want to know?"

"History of the shipwreck?"

He nodded. "Look, love, my boat's been out of operation for a week. I've lost a lot of money. You pay me fifty bucks and I'll make you a cup of coffee and tell you everything I know. Fee for service."

Libby spread her hands. "Of course. But it had better be good coffee."

The man grinned and held out a meaty hand for Libby to shake. "I'm Graeme Beers."

"Libby Slater. A pleasure to meet you."

He took her upstairs and through a bright, airy living room, then sat her at an outdoor table on a wide verandah that looked over the scrub to the ocean. The sun was on Libby's shoulders, and she cursed herself for not putting on a layer of sunscreen. She backed her chair as far as she could against the wall, flinching out of the sunshine.

Libby couldn't imagine enjoying morning coffee in the damp heat with the sandflies everywhere, but when it arrived it was superb. Exactly the right strength, served in a large white cup with creamy milk, with mango-flavored shortbread on the side. Every now and again a stiff breeze rose off the ocean, cooling her skin and lifting her hair. It was vastly different from coffee with Mark in Paris, but it was pleasant in its difference.

Graeme had put on a blue cotton checked shirt. He slapped a plastic folder on the table and sat with her.

"So, you're new to town?"

"Not really. I grew up at Lighthouse Bay. So I've heard of the Winterbourne treasure. But I was never much interested in the shipwreck when I lived here."

"What changed your mind?"

"I worked with the Winterbourne company for a number of years." A twinge. Why couldn't she just say it out loud? *Mark Winterbourne and I were in love.* Still a secret. Always a secret.

Graeme nodded, looking suitably impressed. "Right, then, the wreck of the *Aurora*. It was April 1901. There was no township here then. Miles of empty coastland, a few Aborigines and plenty of wildlife. *Aurora* was a three-masted iron barque . . ." Here he flipped to the first plastic sleeve in the folder, which held a blurry photograph of a magnificent sailing ship. ". . . a cargo ship built in Glasgow but privately owned by Captain Francis Whiteaway of Bristol. He was never off the water; back and forth between here and England, making a killing. Brought tiles and curtains and fancy nonsense from England to all the rich people living here, took back wool for all the cold people living there. He was forty-three at the time of the wreck." He stopped to slurp his coffee noisily, then resumed.

"This time he had precious cargo aboard. Queen Victoria had commissioned a parliamentary mace as a gift for the Australian government for federation." He turned to another picture, this time a watercolor, perhaps a copy of the mace designer's sketch. "The mace was made of gold, and set with four emeralds, eight rubies, four sapphires and a single diamond at its tip. Arthur Winterbourne, eldest son of the Winterbourne jeweling family, designed it and oversaw its production. Then he wanted to take it to Australia himself. Winterbourne and Whiteaway had gone to school together, so Whiteaway was happy to have him on board." Another slurp of coffee, another plastic sleeve, this time with a meteorological photograph of a cyclone.

His voice grew dark; he was no doubt used to milking the drama out of the story for his clients. "They were due to leave cargo in Brisbane before sailing to Sydney, but they hit cyclonic conditions as they approached the southeast coast. Cape Franklin lighthouse reported seeing them on the evening of April the seventh, but Lighthouse Bay lighthouse, the next one along the coast, never saw them. God only knows what they were trying to do coming into the beach here: maybe they were taking on water and thought they could beach the ship. In any case, they struck a submerged reef." He gestured directly out to sea. "The conditions were horrific, it was late at night, the ship was broken to pieces. Nobody survived. When the ship didn't reach Brisbane, the local police sent out a search party. Debris washed up just here on the beach alerted them to the ship nearby. Over the next few weeks they recovered a lot of the cargo and a few bodies. The younger brother, Percy Winterbourne, came to see it with his own eyes. Wandered around between here and other places on the east coast, sure somebody would know something. He searched, but never found anything. Died suddenly in a hotel room in Tewantin one evening."

Percy was Mark's great-grandfather. "Died suddenly? Suspiciously?"

Graeme shook his head. "Not according to local knowledge. Just dropped dead."

Libby thought about Mark's aneurysm.

Graeme was still talking. "Upshot is, nobody's ever found the mace. So, people still like to look for it. Which is why I have a business." He flipped to another photograph in his book: a half a ship, lying on its side underwater, encrusted with barnacles.

"Do you think the mace is still out there?" Libby asked.

"Don't know. It's a mystery. That wreck has been combed over by many hands, and nobody's ever turned it up. People still like to dive it—who can resist a treasure hunt?—but I think most of them realize they're not going to find anything. You should come out one time, have a look for yourself."

"I don't know that diving is something I'd be terribly good at," Libby said. The thought of being so far underwater made her nervous.

"If you can swim, you can dive. It's easy."

Mark would do it. He would tell Libby to do it.

"I'll give you a mate's rate," Graeme continued, seeing her wavering. "You really should take a look."

She shook her head. "Sorry. Why don't you show me some more pictures?"

He flicked the pages of his folder, showing more images of recovered cargo, talking about the centenary celebrations of the wreck and offering titbits of local knowledge. But he didn't mention the Winterbourne family again, and Libby found herself sipping coffee and gazing at the horizon, wishing Mark were here to take her hand and lead her under the water, and bring her back safely.

Libby turned on the fan over her bed when she got home and lay down to rest, only to wake hours later disorientated with a pounding headache, her cotton dress damp with perspiration. It was late afternoon and her stomach growled with hunger. She microwaved some fried rice and went to her art room. The photograph Graeme had shown her of the *Aurora* had intrigued her. She was an artist who loved depth and detail, and those old ships were crisscrossed with ropes and rigging. She flicked through her Turner book and found one of his ship paintings, then sat with a sketchbook on her lap copying a detail of the rigging. Hours passed, dusk came.

She put aside the drawing and decided to go to the library

the next day and borrow some books about ships. Eventually, she wanted to paint the *Aurora*, as a way of remembering Mark. But she'd have to work carefully first, relearning the skills she'd left behind at art college.

She pulled on her flip-flops and let herself out of the house, then took the path down to the beach, where she realized the night had fallen quickly. One sand crab running over her toes was enough. She headed back up the path.

That's when she saw the figure of a man, near the door to the lighthouse. He had fair hair and broad shoulders, but she couldn't make out any other features. She shrank back around the side of the cottage. He was fiddling with the lock, then he opened the door. He looked around furtively, then went in and closed the door behind him.

So, somebody was at the lighthouse, and he knew he shouldn't be there. Libby went inside her cottage and locked the door carefully. She felt a long way from civilization.

Libby woke some time in the night, from under deep layers, and lay for a moment wondering why she was awake.

A sound.

Her senses were suddenly on high alert, her ears prickling.

Heat flashed across her heart. Somebody was lurking around outside her window.

She couldn't move, she was so afraid. She wanted to be asleep and oblivious again. Then she heard footsteps, moving off, around the side of the cottage. Libby thought of the man she'd seen at the lighthouse. She pulled back the covers slowly and slunk out of bed, half-crouched, and hurried through to the kitchen to find her phone.

She had put it down somewhere—she fumbled across the benchtops—but it was small and it eluded her. Should she turn the light on to find it? Would that scare the intruder off, or encourage them to burst in and . . . what? What did they intend?

Libby stifled a groan of fear. She was so far from town, tucked up here at the end of the road. Her hand hit a teaspoon she had left out after making coffee, and it clattered to the floor. She froze, holding her breath. She heard nothing outside but the wind and the sea.

She decided to brazen it out, and switched on the kitchen light.

She heard the footsteps speed into a run. A car engine burst into life, and she realized that there was a car parked in her driveway. She went to the front door and threw it open in time to see bright headlights flash on, blinding her. A dark figure—too big and square to be a woman—got into the passenger's seat, and the car roared away, leaving Libby with the ghost of the headlights in her eyes. The car backfired once in the distance.

She stepped back inside and locked the door, then called the local police station.

"Sergeant Scott Lacey." He sounded sleepy.

Libby breathlessly told him where she was and what had happened.

"And they've gone now?" Sergeant Lacey said.

"Appear to be."

"I don't think you should be too worried. Living at the beach . . . People are always down there at odd times."

"He wasn't visiting the beach. He was lurking around my house."

"That place has been vacant a long time. He probably thought it was empty . . . but I'll come by in a car to check in a little while, and if you like I'll make sure we include you on our beat most nights this week."

Libby's ribs unclenched. "Would you? I'd really appreciate that."

"Sure. You didn't tell me your name."

"Libby Slater."

"Libby? Juliet's sister? You don't remember me? I was in your math class."

Libby scoured her memory. Scott Lacey. Wild surfie curls and a firecracker in every pocket. "Ah, yes. Scott." She wasn't reassured that he was in charge of the police station.

"It's good to have you back in town. Juliet's an old friend."

Libby realized that if Scott was an old friend of Juliet's, he would also know about Libby's past, and she felt a sudden flush of shame.

"Don't worry, Libby, we'll keep an eye on you."

His words were meant to comfort her, but all she could feel was the distance between her and the safety she craved. Sometimes, when Mark stayed at her Paris flat, she would fall asleep with her head on his chest, breathing in the warm, male scent of him. On those occasions she felt safe; more than safe. She felt as though there was an impenetrable bubble around her. Inside was love and light. The idea that she would never feel that again made her feet tremble. She pushed them hard onto the floorboards. "Thanks," she managed to say to Scott Lacey. "Good night."

Libby went back to bed. After half an hour she heard the police car come and go, but she didn't sleep until dawn came and nothing could hide in shadows.

Libby kept telling herself she didn't care that Juliet hadn't called, but she did. Libby had taken the first step; surely it was Juliet's turn to take the second. It was Saturday afternoon before she realized that she hadn't left a phone number and Juliet might not be comfortable just dropping by.

Damn, why was she so *bad* at this family stuff?

So, with a heart that fluttered slightly, she phoned the tea room. Juliet answered on the third ring.

Libby became very aware of the words she chose. "It's Libby," she said. "Is this a bad time?"

"I'm just locking up."

"I'd like to see you." Did that sound too bossy? Too soppy? Libby remembered the last time they'd met. The messy tables. Juliet's harassed air. "I can help you clean up if you like."

If anything, this offer made Juliet cooler. What had she said wrong? "No, no, I can manage by myself. I always have. Why don't you come by around seven? I'll make us some dinner."

"That sounds great."

"I'll leave the side gate open for you. We have a lot to discuss."

Libby's heart ticked away like a bird's as she showered and dressed. *We have a lot to discuss.* What did Juliet mean by that? Why did she sound so somber when she said it? Or was Libby's guilty conscience getting the better of her? Libby knew she'd been a rotten sister. She knew she'd missed twenty years' worth of birthdays and Christmases; she'd even missed their father's funeral. She'd missed everything. She'd become a stranger to her closest living relative. Accidentally? Deliberately? But there was more to it than that; there were wounds so deep they may not have healed. Perhaps they could never heal.

She pulled up outside the tea room at seven, and rounded the steps to the apartment she, Juliet, and their father had lived in twenty years ago. There was a smell of approaching rain on the night air. Juliet called to her down the stairwell.

"Over here," she said. "I converted our old place into B&B rooms."

And then they were standing, face to face, at the door to Juliet's apartment, while the evening sea breeze rattled the fronds of the palms that lined the street. Libby didn't know whether she should hug her sister. What was the protocol after half her life? Her arms seemed heavy and awkward all of a sudden.

"Come in," Juliet said, turning her shoulder away.

"You're living on the side overlooking the street?"

"There's not much traffic at night. I can still hear the ocean." Juliet sounded a little defensive.

"It looks lovely." This was an easy, truthful statement to make about the apartment. Juliet had decorated in shades of sea blue and pale yellow, the couch was covered in lots of checkered cushions, and the space was lit softly by lamps. It was inviting. Homey. Libby felt the corner of a feeling: of the comfort and acceptance and warmth that only comes from family.

"Sit down," Juliet said, sounding a little distant and tired. "I've made a risotto. It's almost ready."

"Thanks so much. I know you're busy."

"You've no idea," Juliet called from the kitchen.

While Juliet served their meals, Libby glanced around the room: a computer nook with a desk piled high with paperwork, a bookshelf with a lot of battered paperbacks and . . . Libby's heart sped. A picture of Andy. Juliet still kept a picture of Andy. She looked away quickly, studied her nails, the piping on the cushions, then stood up and said, "Can I help with anything?"

"Nothing to do," Juliet said, emerging from the kitchen. "Let's eat on the couch, it's more comfortable."

They settled. They ate. The silence was awkward, but the food was wonderful.

"You are a fabulous cook," Libby said.

"Why did you come back?" Juliet asked, at the same time.

They laughed uncomfortably about the sudden clash of their words, their intentions.

"It was time," Libby said, hoping the enigmatic answer might satisfy.

It didn't. "What does that mean?"

Libby sighed. "Things went . . . badly for me. I was . . ." No, she couldn't tell Juliet that. She couldn't say she'd been having an affair with a married man for twelve years. "A close friend—the one who bought the cottage—he died." It was awful to demote him to "close friend," but she'd kept Mark a secret so long, it wasn't hard to pretend to the outside world that he meant little to her. It was her inside world that spasmed with pain at the thought of him. "And I was tired of my job. I felt dislocated. I hoped that . . . I hoped that coming home would be a good idea."

Juliet visibly tensed, her knuckles blanching as they gripped her fork. Libby wasn't sure what she had said to invoke this reaction.

"So, you'll be staying, then?" Juliet asked.

"I don't know. I'm in a transition phase, I guess. I'm just living moment by moment."

"And you want your half of the business?"

"My half of the . . ."

"Dad left it to both of us. Your name's still right there on the paperwork."

"No! Oh, God, Juliet. No. This is yours. I've never wanted it and I certainly wouldn't take it from you. I'd never even consider it."

Juliet, though still wary, relaxed. "I see."

"Put it out of your mind. I have no desire to take anything from you." Libby squirmed. Her sister's opinion of her was so low. But then, why should it be any different? Juliet knew nothing about her but what she remembered from their youth. And there was little from that part of her life that flattered her.

"I feel bad about it," Juliet was saying. "I don't know what your financial situation is, but I've worked so hard here. It's a very different business from the one I inherited. I've put some money aside for kitchen renovations, but I could give it to you if you—"

"I don't want your money. You don't need to worry about me. The keeper's cottage is mine."

Juliet's eyes rounded. "Really? Your friend left it to you?"

"Yes," she lied. No point in saying she'd owned it for six years and been too afraid to face her past.

"Do you own the lighthouse too?"

"It's not on the title deed. I think the government still owns it. It doesn't operate anymore, does it?"

"No. It was decommissioned in ninety-nine. They built a fully automated one off the tip of Maroona Island instead." Juliet pulled her feet up under her on the couch. "There was a preservation society that stopped the old one from getting knocked down. It's pretty unsafe. But they couldn't raise enough to restore it, and then the man who was in charge of it all died and I don't think anything much has happened since."

"There's a danger sign on the door."

"Is there? I'm not surprised. Melody, the young lass who works with me, told me she went in with a couple of friends. They climbed in a window. The stairs inside are dodgy, and she nearly broke her ankle."

Libby supposed that answered her question about who was in the lighthouse. Curious teenagers would always find something mildly dangerous to do in a small town.

"So, fill me in on the last twenty years," Juliet said. She was much more relaxed now Libby had reassured her about the B&B.

They talked for a long time, but Libby didn't tell Juliet every-thing, and she suspected Juliet didn't tell Libby everything either. There were no problems talking about work, about travel, about world events. But nothing went deeper. Neither mentioned love nor lovers, children nor their desire for children, hopes or dreams for the future. And they certainly didn't discuss what happened twenty years ago.

It was only as she was leaving, standing at the door after the "Good-bye, I'll see you soon," that Libby finally found the courage to say, "I'm really sorry I wasn't here. I'm sorry for . . . everything." She thought of the photo of Andy.

Juliet reached out and rubbed Libby's forearm lightly, seemed about to say something, then recalled the words. Finally, she man-aged, "It's okay."

Then they stepped apart, and Libby hurried back to her car, half-hopeful and half in despair. She told herself it was only early days. If she could just do everything right from this moment on, she could surely patch up this rift with her sister. And then, just maybe, there would be a time to discuss the past and make amends.

A fresh wind off the sea had picked up by the time she pulled up at the front of the cottage. She had her front door key in her hand when she glanced up and saw the lighthouse door standing open and candlelight flickering in the very top window.

Libby realized she was holding her breath. She badly wanted to go and look inside. She could knock. Or, she could just go inside her house and forget about it.

But she wanted to see if there was anybody there.

She withdrew her mobile phone from her handbag and clutched it in her hand like a knight taking a sword into battle. Then, with purpose, she walked up to the lighthouse. The sign on the open door read: DANGER: PARTS OF THIS STRUCTURE ARE UNSOUND. She knocked lightly.

"Hello?" she called.

All was dark within. She could make out two large cabinets on the bare floor, and the curve of the staircase leading up. The smell was one of oil and fish and seaweed.

"Hello?" she said again.

No answer.

She switched on her mobile so it gave a little light, and moved inside. The two cabinets were glass-topped, and inside them were collections of shells and sea creatures pinned to boards, like a science exhibit. Beyond the cabinets was another door, boarded over. Libby stood at the bottom of the stairs in the dank darkness and looked up. Twenty feet up, the stairs disappeared into a closed hatch. She entertained the thought of going up there for a few moments, then realized she hadn't the stomach for it. Especially if the stairs weren't safe. She took one last look around and then went back out the door, then home.

The next morning when she looked, the lighthouse door was firmly shut.

Ten

Libby hadn't worried about money in twelve years. Even though most of her salary was eaten up in rent, Mark had never let her want for anything. He paid for all their meals out, all their clandestine holidays, he bought her shoes and handbags and clothes. His generosity had allowed her to save a lump sum, but she hadn't been careful with it. She hadn't invested. She had lived, as most mistresses do, on a day-by-day basis. She couldn't plan for the future if she refused to acknowledge the future would come. Her long relationship with Mark had been a series of present moments. In fact, he had said it over and over: "Let's be in the moment. Let's simply be in the moment."

The moment had gone. The car had been expensive, as was the computer equipment and software she needed to complete the Winterbourne catalog. Without a steady income, she would run out of savings by Christmas.

Libby sat in her new chair and gently swung it in a semicircle. She had spent the day installing software, connecting to the Internet, downloading security and back-up programs and setting up an e-mail account. She was very pleased with herself. All these years she'd relied on Mark to do computer-y things for her.

Thoughts of Mark: instant rain. Time to get on with work so she didn't feel it so acutely.

The old dining table wobbled when she leaned on it, so Libby wadded up a piece of paper and jammed it under the uneven leg. She reassured herself that her clients never needed to know that she was working on a wobbly table in the corner of an ugly lounge room. As she dialed London to let Cathy know she was ready to receive the brief for the Winterbourne catalog, she tilted her chair back and put her feet on the table.

"Winterbourne Jewelers, Cathy speaking."

"Hello from Australia, Cathy, it's Libby Slater again."

"Oh, I'm glad you called, Libby. I'll just put you on to Emily so you can sort things out."

"I—" But the phone had already clicked. She was on hold with a Chopin waltz. And any second Mark's wife was going to speak to her. *Mark's wife.*

"Hello, Libby?" She sounded cultured, of course, but also a little unsure.

"Emily, hello. It's nice to . . . er . . . meet you."

"Likewise. I've heard so much about you."

"You have?"

"Oh, yes. Mark was very enthusiastic about your work for us. When I heard you'd left Pierre-Louis, I was adamant that Cathy track you down. Things are in . . . Things are changing and I . . ." She faltered. Libby's heart stung. "I want things to be the same as much as possible. You designing our catalog is part of that."

"I understand," Libby said, but she felt as though she were watching herself from a long way outside herself. *This is Mark's wife.* The rival. The enemy. The person Libby had needed to believe was cold or shrill or vain. It was clear, in the few seconds they had spoken, that Emily was none of these things.

Not even a little. She suddenly remembered what she should say. "I'm so sorry for your loss. Mark was a wonderful man." Was that too warm? "Or he seemed that way to me, whenever I worked with him."

"He was just a man, Libby. Sometimes he was wonderful, sometimes he was a pain in the neck." She laughed lightly. "I've never learned to deal with his perfectionism."

There. Emily had slipped into present tense. Libby felt strangely comforted: she still thought of Mark in present tense too.

"But for all his faults, I loved him dearly and I miss him more than I can say."

Libby blinked back tears. "Are your daughters well?"

"Oh, yes. They have their own lives. And I'm looking forward to becoming a grandmother in July. I take each day as it comes. Oh, listen to me! As if you want to hear all my nonsense. I've been blubbing to strangers and people who don't care since the moment he died."

Libby licked her lips, choosing her words carefully. "I'm not a stranger and I do care," she said.

Libby heard a drawn breath on the other end as tears were withheld. Then Emily collected herself. "Still. Business first. Work is keeping me ticking along. So, how does this work? We send you the pictures?"

"Mark commissioned the photographer and sent me the files, yes. Then we'd sit down together and talk through the season's theme, how he wanted the brochure to look, which pieces he wanted to feature and so on."

"He did all that? No wonder he was gone to Paris so much. Libby, I've no idea, but you worked with Mark for twelve years. Can you do it alone?"

"Of course."

"I'll pay you extra."

"There's no need." Libby kicked herself. Winterbourne Jewelers was a huge business. But she couldn't bring herself to charge Emily, because Emily was Mark's wife, and Libby had spent the last twelve years—*be honest*—wishing Emily didn't exist.

"Can you commission the photographer too?" Emily asked.

It was getting tricky now. "I know a few good people in London and Paris, but I'll need to see the new collection first. Can you send me some photographs? They don't need to be high quality. Just take them with your phone and I'll sort through them and send you some ideas."

"Yes, I think I can manage that. It will keep me busy. Now you don't mind if I call you directly, Libby? I'm going to rely rather heavily on you for this."

"Any time," Libby said. She gave Emily her phone number and new e-mail address and then hung up the phone. She shot out of her chair and pulled her flip-flops on, and headed straight for the beach.

It was dark; cool but not cold. She walked down to the water's edge and stood there, the waves licking and sucking around her ankles. What was this unpleasant lurking feeling that had driven her out of the house? Grief: yes, that was still there. Anxiety: that was normal, but she would be able to coordinate the job easily once she'd found the right photographer.

Guilt.

It wasn't that she'd never felt it before. She'd felt it for twelve years, vaguely, stirring from time to time, like a coil of nausea that never quite develops enough to purge the stomach. But this was a different kind of guilt. Mark had a wife. Her name was Emily. She loved Mark. If she'd known that Mark was seeing Libby, it would have ruined her happiness.

Libby would have ruined her happiness.

She still could. And suddenly she was desperate that the secret never, *never* come out. In the past, she'd sometimes secretly hoped it would, forcing Mark's hand. *Leave her; be with me!* Now it seemed impossible that it could stay a secret forever. Cathy already suspected: those letters would have seemed greater proof. Who else had suspicions? Who else might let down their guard now Mark wasn't around to urge them to be silent? *Please, no, never let it come to light. Never let anyone know what a selfish human being I am.* Libby stood on the beach for nearly an hour, while the tide came in around her legs, and the sea roared, drowning out her sobs of shame.

*L*ibby arrived outside Graeme Beers' house at four o'clock the next afternoon. She'd spent the day sketching, enjoying getting the detail of ropes and sails right: their complex crisscrossing, texture and shadows. Mostly she'd been copying pictures out of books, but she had become determined that it was the *Aurora* she wanted to paint. The only image available online was too small to be useful, and she hoped Graeme could give her a copy of the picture he had in his folder. So, on a whim, she'd driven north to Winterbourne Beach.

No boat out the front. Still, she climbed out of her car and went up the stairs to knock. No answer.

Libby sighed. She should have looked up his number and phoned first, perhaps. Then she thought, he must have taken a diving group out. It was growing late, so he had to come in soon. She got back into her car and drove towards the beach.

A sign pointed her towards the boat ramp and car park. There she found Graeme, strapping his boat to his trailer.

"Hello!" she called, waving.

He looked up. It was obvious he didn't register who she was, but he waited for her to approach all the same.

"Graeme, I'm Libby. We met—"

"Yep, I remember. Changed your mind about coming diving with me?"

"No, I'm after something much safer. You had a picture in your folder of the *Aurora*. I wonder if I could have a copy. I want to paint it, you see."

"Ah, I see," he said, tightening a strap and moving to the other side of the boat. "You're an artist, are you?"

"I'd like to be."

"Meet me round at my place in ten minutes. I've got something for you."

Libby was curious as she waited out the front of Graeme's house. Soon he rattled up with his boat on the trailer and parked his car. He gestured for her to follow him up the stairs, and let them into his house.

"Wait right there," he said, indicating the couch.

She sat down, feeling the first misgivings. Here she was alone, in a strange man's house, and nobody knew where she was. But then he returned with a gift of such generosity that she felt ashamed of herself for doubting him.

He sat next to her and handed her a photocopy of the photograph. Then he spread out an old roll of musty paper on the coffee table before them.

"What is it?"

"Ship's plans."

Libby's eyes rounded. "For the *Aurora*?"

"Yep."

Her gaze traveled over the page, and then the one below it.

Every measurement, every detail was drawn in. "How did you get these?"

"Stealth and cunning," he said with a grin. "These were Percy Winterbourne's. He brought them with him from England, no doubt so he knew where to look in the wreck. As far as I can tell, when he died at that hotel, some chambermaid or other got her hands on all his papers, then probably felt so guilty she stuffed them into the back of her wardrobe. I picked it all up a couple of months ago at a garage sale. I like a good garage sale. The old duck selling them had no idea what they were, so I got 'em pretty cheap."

"And have you used these to go looking for the mace?"

"Of course."

"But you don't show your divers?"

"That would defeat the object of having my business. If somebody actually finds the mace, that out there is just an old wreck. At the moment, it's a potential treasure."

"And you'd let me borrow these?"

"As long as you don't make copies and as long as you give them back when you're done. I can loan them to you for fifty dollars. You'll have to give me your address so I know where to find you if you don't bring them back."

Libby had to stifle a laugh. Still, he wasn't going to part with them if she didn't pay him. "All right, Graeme. You have a deal."

He saw her off at the front door, catching her at the last minute to say, "Now when you bring those back, are you sure you wouldn't like to come for a dive? I've had a drop-out on the third."

"I've never dived before."

"Doesn't matter. I have lots of first-timers. It's beautiful down there. An artist like you would love the colors. I won't charge you for gear hire. Up and down for two hundred."

She couldn't fault his salesmanship. She was about to say no again when she thought, *Why? Why am I saying no?* Mark wouldn't have said no. And in that moment she missed him so fiercely, so viscerally, that there was no other answer than, "Yes. All right, then."

He winked. "You won't regret it, love. I'll see you in a couple of weeks. Be here by nine. And don't forget to return the plans."

*W*ednesday, late afternoon, as Libby was coming back from her swim, she saw him. A man, lurking around near the front of her house. Her heart froze, but then anger burned through it.

She'd had a rotten day as a result of a rotten night. The car engine outside her window at 1 am. Not being able to get back to sleep. Falling in and out of half-dozing bad dreams about Mark, about people trying to break into her house. Spending the day tired and strung out. And there he was, bold-faced, out in the open.

There was still enough daylight to make her brave. Why shouldn't she just march up to him and tell him to leave her alone? Why should she cower in her own house at night? She forgot that she was dressed only in a wet bathing suit and a striped towel, and she hurried up the slope. But he was already moving away, up towards the lighthouse. So, she wasn't imagining it: there *was* somebody living there. And she bet it was the same person making the noise with the car at night that kept waking her up. Libby broke into a run. He fiddled with the lock and was just about to disappear inside when she called out, "Hey! You!"

He glanced up, alarmed, and tried to get inside the lighthouse before she reached him, but then he dropped his key outside and had to stop to scoop it up.

Libby stopped in front of him, panting, hair dripping, feet caked in wet sand, and grasped his forearm. "Stop," she said. "Who the hell are you?"

The man looked at her closely, his eyebrows twitching. He had green eyes, sandy hair tied in a curling ponytail at his nape, and a neat goatee beard. Libby's heart hammered, trying to read his expression.

And then he smiled and said, "Elizabeth Slater?"

Libby dropped his forearm and searched his face, but try as she might, she couldn't identify him.

"Your sister Juliet used to babysit me." He held out his hand for her to shake. "Damien Allbright. Do you remember?"

Yes, she remembered. Last time she'd seen Damien, he was eight. That would make him twenty-eight now. But she couldn't match up the skinny child she'd known with the tall man who stood in front of her. And none of it explained why he'd been hanging around her house. "What's going on?" she said. "Why have you been outside my house at night?"

"You're living at the cottage?"

She nodded.

"I haven't been outside it at night, unless I'm coming or going from here."

"There's been a car. A man . . ."

"I've heard the car too, but it's not mine. I don't have a car. I don't have . . . Look, Elizabeth, you've just come back from the beach. Do you want to come by later and talk? You must be getting cold."

Libby was suddenly cruelly aware that she was wearing so little. She crossed her arms over her breasts. "Everyone calls me Libby. You live in the lighthouse?"

"It's a long story."

Libby's curiosity grew. The breeze off the sea coaxed goose bumps on her arms. "All right."

"See you soon." He nodded, and slipped inside, leaving the door open.

Libby hurried off, her mind whirring. So Damien Allbright was squatting at the lighthouse. Should she overlook the fact that this was suspect, if not illegal, just because Juliet had once babysat him? He had come to their apartment every Friday night and Juliet had read to him and played games with him while Libby put on her make-up and headed out to the surf club to drink with friends. He'd always seemed a sweet kid: thoughtful and clever. But that didn't mean she should trust him now.

She showered, dressed and ran a comb through her hair. When she arrived back at the door of the lighthouse, the sky was on the brink of dusk.

"Hello?" she called into the dark.

"Wait there. I'll come down," he called. A weak light descended, and Damien emerged from the bottom of the stairs, holding a lantern with a candle in it. "Sorry, there's no electricity," he said. "Hold on to the railing as we go up the stairs. They're a little wobbly."

The stairs were narrow and steep, almost like a ladder. She held tight to the rails on either side as she followed Damien up and through the hatch to the next level. Here, Damien had arranged a dozen of the candlelit lanterns around the circumference of the room. On the floor was a mattress and blankets, a large backpack, a battered wooden cabinet and two boxes overflowing with papers.

Damien indicated the mattress. "That's the only place to sit, I'm sorry."

Libby perched on the edge of the mattress, gazing around the candlelit room. "I don't understand, Damien. You live here?"

"Not permanently. Not even for very long, I hope."

"Where do you cook? And shower?"

"There are plenty of public toilets and showers along the beach, and I eat really simply. I sometimes use the gas barbecues at the park behind the surf club. It's a pity they had the original keeper's quarters knocked down. When I was a kid, you could go through that boarded-up door to two little rooms." He shrugged. "It's okay. I manage."

She turned to look at him, now. He sat on the floor about three feet away, with his knees folded under his chin. "I barely recognize you," she said.

He held out his right arm, palm turned over to catch the light. "Remember this?" He indicated a deep, white scar on his forearm, and at once Libby remembered. He'd been mucking around in the kitchen one night and crashed into the pantry, shattering a jar of honey. One of the glass shards had embedded in his forearm. Juliet didn't have a license then, so Libby had had to drive them both to the hospital.

"Oh, yes," she said. "The night of blood and honey. I never got the stains out of my car seat."

He wrapped his arm around his knee again. "How's Juliet?"

"She's . . . ah . . . I've only just come back to Lighthouse Bay after a long time. She seems well."

"Did she end up marrying Andy Nicholson? I remember the night she told me she was engaged. It broke my heart. I had such a big crush on her. But that was right before Mum and I left Lighthouse Bay, so I never heard what happened after." He was smiling at her, but as he took in her expression his smile faded.

"Andy died," Libby said.

"Ah. That's horrible."

"The day before their wedding. He . . . he drowned. Just outside the surf club."

"What a nightmare."

Nightmare. Every part of it was a nightmare. Twenty years in the past and still she could remember it as though it had just happened. "They were crazy in love, those two. I mean, who else gets married at nineteen? But she and Andy had been together since they started high school and Dad was fine with it and Juliet . . . Juliet loved Andy so much." Libby's voice caught in her throat as she felt a sick, guilty rush in her stomach.

Damien nodded solemnly. "But is she happy now? Did things work out for her?"

"She never married or had kids. But she owns and runs the tea room and B&B single-handedly. It's a big success." Libby's words sounded hollow and she knew it. All Juliet had ever wanted was a family. "Come on, then," Libby said. "Enough heavy stuff about Juliet. Tell me why you're here."

"There are two reasons," he said, leaning back on his forearms. "The first is, I have nowhere else to go just now. I've just been through . . ." He shrugged. "Some difficult times, I guess you'd say. Things didn't go as I'd hoped, so I came back here."

"I can understand that. But why live here, with no electricity?"

"My money is tied up at the moment with some legal issues and I'm between jobs. I can't work just now. This is all temporary, though. Really it is. I want to be out while the weather's still warm."

Libby turned this over in her mind. She wondered what Damien's legal issues were. Was he a petty criminal? He was nearly thirty, had no job, and was squatting in a lighthouse. "So what's the second reason?"

"Do you remember Pirate Pete?"

"The crazy old lighthouse keeper?"

Damien winced. "Yeah. He was my grandfather."

"Pirate Pete was your grandfather? I'm so sorry, I would never have been so rude—"

"No, it's all right. I got used to people saying cruel things about him. And he was a little crazy, I'll admit. When I was a boy, he showed me all these secret cabinets in the room upstairs, where the light is."

"Secret cabinets?"

"Yes, built into the wall panels. There was nothing much of interest there to a little boy: old papers and so on." He indicated the boxes in front of him. "Only as an adult did I get curious again. After Granddad died—he lived till ninety, you know—I kept thinking about the history in the walls. Nobody else knew it was there. I came up here, but the cabinets are all falling apart now. There were papers spilling out everywhere. I just felt I should stay till I fix things up."

"I think it's the damp: it makes the cupboard doors swell. That's what's happening with my linen cupboard, at least. So, you've been reading through all this history? At night? By candlelight?"

He smiled. "Sometimes. But mostly during the day. At night I just sleep."

"And you've never been down at the cottage at night?"

He shook his head. "No, never."

"They've been around a few times. Late at night. A car outside for ages. It spooks me."

"I understand, but it's not me. I don't have my car at the moment. Hey, listen, I can keep an ear out for them, and I can come down. You don't have to be afraid."

Libby was touched. "Thanks. That's a lovely offer." She leaned back, resting on her elbows. "So, is there anything of interest among those documents?"

"Most of it is pretty boring. But there's a little bit of gold. The lighthouse journals are here, going back to the mid-nineteenth century. Some of the keepers just record weather events and notable shipping, but one of them talks endlessly about how beautiful his wife is. Look." He ploughed into the box, pulling out an old leather-covered journal. He found a page he'd marked with a Post-it note and read: "*December 18, 1878. Last night a storm blew in and rattled all the panes. My dear, delicate Eliza was quite alarmed and I had to hold her closely by me to still her fluttering pulse. This morning when I awoke, she had already been risen for half an hour and had made me my favorite breakfast of bacon pie, and said it was for gratitude that I had been such a comfort to her. I am so blessed in the love of my dear wife.*"

Libby found herself smiling. "That's sweet."

Encouraged, Damien found another journal. "This one from the 1930s is good too. I think the lighthouse keeper had some kind of mental disorder. *I go to town and I see them all watching me. I know what they want. As long as there is breath in my body, they will never steal my thoughts.*"

Libby's eyebrows shot up in surprise. "Any others like that?"

"That's the only one. There was a new keeper two weeks later. And this one is very mysterious, listen. It's from April 1901. This guy, Matthew Seaward, usually writes very plainly, then this: *I was surprised yesterday evening by the appearance of a strange woman, barefoot and bleeding, who has appeared at the door of the lighthouse looking for refuge. Her clothes are in rags but her manners speak good breeding. I gave her food and found an old dress left here by the previous keeper's wife, and sent her in to town to find a more appropriate place to stay.*"

"April 1901?"

"That's what it says."

"Is there anything more about her?"

"I don't know. There could be. I haven't read them all."

"In rags, injured, barefoot." Libby's mind was ticking over. "The *Aurora* was wrecked in April 1901. Could she have been a survivor?"

"Surely she would have said?"

"Maybe she did and he didn't write it down." Libby's imagination whirled with the possibilities. "Let me know if you find anything?"

"I sure will."

Libby hesitated, then said, "If you want to come down for a hot meal, one night . . ."

"I'd like that," he said quickly. "How about one night this week?"

"Great. Thursday at seven? In the meantime, see what else you can find about the 'strange woman.'" Libby stood and stretched.

"Here, I'll see you down the stairs," he said, reaching for a lantern.

At the lighthouse door, she looked back to the cottage. "I hope they leave me alone tonight."

"What do you think they want?" he asked.

Libby was stumped for a moment. She had never even thought of it; she had been too busy being afraid and angry. "I don't know. To scare me?"

"But why? And if they wanted to scare you, they could do it more effectively."

Libby thought a little harder, then her skin started to crawl. "Maybe they're looking for something." And if that were true, perhaps they wouldn't stop until they found it.

"Maybe. But don't worry. I'll listen out. And if you're ever frightened, just come knock on my door."

"Thank you so much."

"Can I just ask, though, that you don't tell anyone I'm here?"

Libby shrugged. "Of course. I have nobody to tell."

"Well, not Juliet. You know."

"Ah, I see. Okay."

"It's not forever, and I will eventually send all these papers to a museum or a library."

Libby opened her mouth to ask for more details about his life, about why he was squatting in a lighthouse, but then she closed it again. "Sure," she said. "Your secret is safe with me."

That night, she dreamed she was on a ship. The waves were rolling up sickeningly high beneath her, and she was convinced that somehow Mark was in the water and she had to rescue him. But every time she got near the side of the ship to try to winch down the lifeboat, a huge wave would boil up and throw her backwards, until the deck was almost vertical and she had to drag herself along with aching fingertips.

Her own sobs woke her in the deep of the night. The sound of the sea in the distance. Emptiness walking her ribcage. Mark long gone from her reach.

Eleven

Libby got an early start on her e-mail the next day. At last, a swag of material came through from Emily. Eighty photographs that looked like they'd been taken on a mobile phone. Libby recognized many of the pieces as classic Winterbourne designs, but there were a handful of new and surprising designs among them. She flicked through them, then turned to the e-mail Emily had sent.

> *I want the catalog to honor Mark and the Winterbourne history, but I also want it to reflect new hope, a way forward. I think you'll agree that some of our new designs are very forward-focused, so I would like to make those the centerpiece of the catalog. But I will be guided by you. What do you think?*

Libby realized that Emily was using the catalog, the new line, as a way of pulling herself out of grief and towards whatever came next. Mark would never have made such an artistic decision. Winterbourne, in Mark's eyes, traded on its history, as stuffy as it sometimes made them seem. New designs, especially experimental ones, were always hidden at the back of the catalog. Libby felt a pulse of real affection for Emily for being able to see beyond tradition, and for finding the positive in overwhelmingly negative circumstances. She shot back an e-mail with enthusiastic support for the idea, and started to sketch ideas in her notebook. Then she sent off e-mail enquiries to some of the photographers she'd worked with in Paris and London, and began to draw up a schedule for the catalog's production. She was mad: she should have let Emily pay her extra for coordinating the project. It was going to be a lot of work.

The sound of the postman's motorbike roused her, and she realized she hadn't stretched her legs for hours. She rose and went outside, taking deep gulps of the sea air. The work, she realized, was making her feel better. She still missed Mark, of course, but, because of Emily, she knew today that there was something beyond sorrow. She didn't know what it was, but she would never find out unless she began to move in that direction.

She flipped open the mailbox and pulled out a large yellow envelope from Winterbourne Jewelers in London. She peeled it open as she walked back to the house, and found inside the unopened mail for her that Cathy had discovered in Mark's office.

Libby sat at her desk and sorted the letters into date order: all from Ashley-Harris Holdings. They dated back two years. She opened the oldest one and read it. It opened with the line, *Thank you for your correspondence. We do understand the reasons you won't sell. I would like to introduce myself still . . .*

So, this wasn't the first letter. Mark had intercepted one previously, in which they had offered to buy the cottage, and he'd knocked them back. She quickly tore into the other letters. Over two years they wrote again and again, asking to meet with Libby, offering to fly to London, wanting to send plans and drawings. They were all signed by the same sender: Tristan Catherwood. He was persistent but not pushy. The last one was dated four months before Mark's death.

Libby sat back and turned all this over in her mind. A small part of her, not a part she was proud of, was irritated that Mark had never passed these letters on. Of course she never would have sold the place, but he had passed everything else on: the rates bills—after he had paid them, of course—and the yearly land valuations. Did he suspect she would sell to the first developer who offered? But then, could she blame him for being wary? She had been so reluctant to come here. She had probably seemed ungrateful. He had bought her a house and she had seen it as a burden rather than a blessing.

She was curious too. Why did Ashley-Harris Holdings want her cottage so badly? There were plenty of other places to build hotels.

Still, Tristan Catherwood had been waiting for a reply for a long time, so she sat down to write him a letter of refusal. Then she realized the number on the bottom of the letter was local. Ashley-Harris Holdings was based in Noosa. So she phoned him instead, on his mobile.

"Tristan Catherwood." He had a soft voice, not deep and brash as she'd been expecting.

"Oh, hello. My name is Elizabeth Slater. I—"

"The cottage by the lighthouse! How lovely to hear from you, Elizabeth."

"Look, I'm sorry that you've had to send so many letters. I didn't get the last six until just now, for reasons too complicated to explain. But I just wanted to say that I'm not interested in selling, so you needn't send any more. I'm very happy here now and I'll be staying."

"You're living in the cottage?"

"Yes, I've been here a few weeks."

"It's a beautiful part of the world. The view from the lighthouse makes my heart stir. Elizabeth, seeing as you're in town, let me take you to lunch. Are you busy at one tomorrow?"

"Tomorrow? I . . . I don't know what I might be doing tomorrow."

"Today, then. It's just after twelve. I can swing by and pick you up at one, bring you back down here to Noosa. There's an Italian place down on Hastings Street that makes the most incredible puttanesca."

Libby was being schmoozed, she knew it. But she was drawn to the idea of being chauffeured to an expensive lunch, and she was curious about Tristan's plans for Lighthouse Bay.

And Juliet never needed to know.

"All right," she stammered. "I guess it can't hurt."

He arrived in a black Audi right on the dot of one. From the crack between her bedroom curtains, Libby watched him walk down the front path. He was not at all what she expected. For one thing, he was younger than she'd imagined: around her age. For another, he was casually dressed in an untucked button-up gray shirt and a pair of washed-out jeans. He knocked, and she took her time going to the door. She didn't want him to think she'd been waiting for him, even though she had.

"Hello," she said.

He took off his sunglasses and smiled warmly. He had deep brown eyes that were soft and friendly and Libby found herself smiling back just as warmly. "So, you're Elizabeth?" he asked, extending his hand.

"Libby," she said, shaking it. He smelled wonderful, of some musky, woody cologne.

"For some reason I thought you'd be older."

"Likewise." She was glad now that she had put on her deep red blouse. She knew how it flattered her pale skin. She was enjoying his appreciative gaze.

"Let's head off, then, shall we? I'm starving."

Libby followed him up to his car and settled into the cream leather seat. He started the car and soon they were following the beachfront road south. Past Juliet's tea room. Libby shrank into her seat for a few moments, and Tristan didn't seem to notice. Then they joined the traffic on the main road.

"So, you were in London?" Tristan asked.

"Paris, actually. The address in London was a friend's address. He didn't pass on your mail."

"He did in the end."

"He died."

"I'm so sorry," Tristan said, his voice dropping gravely, then he moved on smoothly. "And how long have you been in Australia?"

"A few weeks. I'm from here originally. My sister owns the B&B."

"Juliet? Of course. I should have realized. You have the same surname."

"I'm surprised you know Juliet."

"I know a lot of people in town, but for all the wrong reasons, I'm afraid. I've been the person who's had to read through the community submissions when we've gone for approvals, so I know how much some of them hate me." He grimaced, but then laughed. "It's not much fun being the grim reaper."

"Why do you persist, then? If you know the town *really* doesn't want a high-rise?"

"A high-rise is off the cards," he said with a sweep of his hand. "The people have spoken. The community doesn't want it, and we're an ethical company. We won an award for ethics in property development last year, actually. We take pride in it."

"Then you don't want to buy the cottage?"

"I absolutely do. But look, let's wait and talk about this over lunch. I don't want to come across like a pushy salesman, and I'm more interested to hear about you and Paris and why you came back."

Libby gave him a brief history, leaving out all the most important things—the twelve-year affair, the long feud with her sister—but still proudly letting him know that now she was freelancing for Winterbourne Jewelers when she wasn't painting.

"I've always admired creative people," he said. "I've done nothing creative since writing bad poetry in high school. My background is geotechnical engineering."

"And is there no poetry in that?"

He pressed his lips together, thinking. "I suppose there is. The geology of building foundations, finding a point of harmony with the earth. Though I'd never thought of it as poetic. And mostly I work in an office these days. Not much poetry in working with money."

He talked a little more about his personal history—it turned out his high school and her high school had been mortal rivals for soccer trophies in the late 1980s—and soon they were driving into Noosa and parking outside an Italian restaurant that gleamed with chrome surfaces and was tastefully lit.

"Ah, Mr. Catherwood!" exclaimed the head waiter. "Your usual table? For you and your lovely guest?"

"Please, Mario. And a bottle of my favorite wine."

Soon they had settled and ordered, and Tristan was pouring her a glass of wine. He reminded Libby a lot of Mark, with his easy confidence. The staff were certainly fond of him, and she found herself drawn to him too. He wasn't doing the hard sell on her. He was relaxed and upbeat. A few mouthfuls of wine and the soft jazz made her relax and feel light, and soon she realized she was enjoying herself.

As they ate, he finally got down to business. He'd worked for Ashley-Harris Holdings for ten years, and had worked his way up to co-manager of development. His dream was for a boutique eco-resort at Lighthouse Bay, on the promontory where the lighthouse cottage stood. If they could buy the cottage, they would invest money in buying and restoring the lighthouse, to add to the distinctiveness of the resort and, in his words, "give something back" to the community. He pulled out of his briefcase photographs of a similar resort he'd built in Tasmania, and Libby had to admit it was impressive.

"This resort caters to a particular kind of clientele," he said. "We charge nine hundred dollars a night, and it's rarely empty. Even in winter."

Libby nodded. "Why do you want my cottage?"

"Because it's my last chance. The shire council and public opinion have stopped me building anywhere else. But there's only scrub across the road from you: nobody to reasonably complain about blocked views. And it's out of the central business district, so those by-laws won't apply. I'll admit we were too ambitious at first. A fifty-room complex won't work here, nor will a high-rise. But a boutique eco-resort with only eighteen rooms? Lighthouse Bay is made for it. It will be good for business. Good for tourism. Good for everyone. It will put Lighthouse Bay on the map."

Everyone? She tried to imagine what Juliet would think.

"I can tell by that expression that you're still not going to sell."

"Thanks so much for taking the time to show me all this," she said. "But perhaps you should look elsewhere."

"Lighthouse Bay is perfect for it. It's going to be the next to develop. It has to be." Then he put his hands up, a defeated gesture. "I understand. Will you at least let me put some sums together and e-mail you an offer?"

Again, Libby was curious. But a little current of fear ran through her. With the money problems she was facing, it could be too tempting.

"Please?" he said.

She looked at him. He had such a genuine smile. "It can't hurt. But please do brace yourself for disappointment."

"Of course. Once you've refused a formal offer, I'll leave you be. I'll still get my gold star for meeting with you. That's some-thing my boss has been trying to achieve for years."

She smiled back. "Thank you for lunch."

"The pleasure was all mine." He caught her in his gaze a mo-ment, then looked away almost shyly and, inexplicably, Libby's heart lurched. "I have a three o'clock meeting. I'd best get you home."

That evening, she checked her e-mail and the offer was waiting, attached to a message from somebody named Yann Fraser. Tristan's name wasn't anywhere in evidence. Libby felt strangely let down. Then she opened the file and her heart stopped.

They were offering her two and a half million dollars.

Twelve

1901

Matthew gravitates towards the woman, again and again. He works the lamp, he times the signal, he cranks the weights, he listens to the mechanism make its familiar clunking noise as it turns the prism that sends the pattern of light out across the sea. In the telegraph room, he writes in his journal by the light of the lamp and he fills out the forms the government and the shipping companies require. But in between these tasks he returns to the side of the bed and looks down on her, and a sadness stirs inside him. No, she is not Clara, but she is so very like her. The fair hair, the soft bow of her mouth. But more than that. The wildness in her eyes, the sense that she is somehow a trapped bird who requires kindness and the gentlest handling, and eventually—inevitably—release.

A trapped bird, but a very pretty bird.

But perhaps he is a fool. Twenty years alone can bend a man, even if the isolation is chosen by him rather than thrust upon him. He knows nothing about this woman. Where has she come from, barefoot and bleeding? How far has she traveled? From one of the inland gold-mining towns? Then why not simply take the train to Brisbane? Why is she here, and what has she left behind?

The long wooden chest—and the way she leaped on it like a wildcat defending her young—makes him curious too.

Matthew pulls up a stool a few feet from the bed and watches her in the flickering lamplight. She looks peaceful now, her chest rising and falling softly. Tomorrow he will have to coax her out of the lighthouse before anyone knows she was here. He rises and goes to the window, looks out at the sea. The light from the big prism above him flashes out across the waves, running from north to south, then going dark again, but the sea is quiet tonight. No ships, no storms, no high winds. Light, then dark, light, then dark, the familiar pattern in which he has found comfort these many years at Lighthouse Bay. But even though the light still runs to its rhythm, he can feel that his own has been disrupted. And he both longs for his familiar loneliness and dreads it in equal measure.

Isabella wakes in the gray before dawn. The room is filled with the aromatic punch of tobacco smoke. Matthew stands by the narrow window. He puffs on his pipe and it illuminates his face momentarily. She blinks rapidly, adjusting her eyes to the dark. There is something peaceful about his countenance. Matthew means her no harm. He is her beacon in the dark.

"I'm sorry," she says, "I left you nowhere to sleep."

He turns. "I don't sleep at night. I sleep during the afternoon," he said. "I'm very busy at night."

The horrors of her recent past come back to her, but a good night's sleep in a warm bed has taken the edge off their cruelty. The future hasn't come yet, the past is behind her. Just now, she is safe.

He withdraws his pipe from his mouth and taps the ashes out into a clay saucer on the table. "Sleep a little longer, Mary," he says.

"My name isn't Mary," she replies, though she doesn't know

why. It is as though she cannot stand Matthew to be fooled in such a way. "My name is Isabella."

"I see."

"Please don't ask me to tell you anything else."

He presses his lips together, and it makes his face look grim in the dark. Then he says, gently, "And so I shall not. Not of your past. What I do need to know, so I can help you, is what you intend next."

What does she intend next? Just a week or so ago she had been so sure: escape her husband, sell her jewelry, find her sister in New York. Now she has already escaped her husband. Back in England there is a house for her, wealth, a life of ease, but those things would come at a high price: continuing attachment to his family. Old Mrs. Winterbourne would be there at every opportunity, looking for a way to make Isabella's life a misery. Percy . . . Well, what wouldn't he do? Given how he had treated her when his brother was still alive.

"I'm running away," she says. "I'm running away to America to find my sister." And as she says it, she is filled once again with purpose. "I have escaped a loveless marriage. I lost an infant, and my husband sought to punish me for my grief. I am running away to New York, where I can find some comfort, and be of some use to my sister Victoria, who is expecting a child of her own. And I will be free to feel . . ." Isabella realizes she is sitting up, fists clenched on the blankets in front of her. Her voice has become shrill. "I will be free to feel whatever is in my heart," she finishes in a whisper.

She glances up at Matthew's face. The darkness in the room is dissolving. She sees the softness in his eyes. He moves to the side of the bed and kneels next to it. He takes her hand: her fingers in his, his other hand encircled around her wrist. "Isabella, I am so sorry for your loss. What name did your child go by?"

"Daniel. His name was Daniel."

"I am so sorry you lost Daniel. That is a great sorrow for any-one to bear, but especially a mother. Your heart must be heavier than the ocean."

A fist of grief pushes its way up Isabella's throat. Nobody has ever said this to her before. She has been told that Daniel is smil-ing at her from heaven, that she will have another child to replace him, that if she works very hard the sun will shine again, that if she doesn't get over her sadness she will lose friends and vex her family. But nobody, in almost three years, has simply said, "I am so sorry you lost Daniel." Most of the time, other people won't even use his name, though she doesn't know why. As though one mustn't say the name of a dead child because it will make mat-ters worse. Fifteen days alive is hardly alive at all. Better to lose him before he became a real human being, with a name and a personality. She knows they think it. She knows they think she is nursing her loss self-indulgently or refusing to get better.

Matthew doesn't think that.

He stands and moves away, and she feels the warm after-impression of his touch on her skin. He comes to rest at the window again, looking out over the sea. The waves roll and crash, but today the sound is soothing. Faraway chaos, while she is safe and still. It occurs to her for the first time since the wreck that she is back on solid ground.

"I need to bathe, Matthew," she says.

He nods. "Of course." He shows her where the bath is, and fetches her a pale yellow gown and a pair of brown shoes; she can see immediately that the latter will be too small. When she is clean and dressed, he is nowhere to be seen. She cautiously surveys his cottage. The main room, the tiny bedroom, and another room full of wires and metal objects and reels and other unrecognizable equipment.

"The lighthouse is also the telegraph station," he explains, making her jump.

"I didn't know you were there," she says.

"I was upstairs, extinguishing the light. My shift is finished now."

"Do you operate the telegraph? Or does somebody else work here?"

"No, only me. Lighthouse Bay doesn't have a post office. I receive and send telegrams for the town here."

"Lighthouse Bay? Is that where I am?"

"You are."

"Am I near Sydney?"

He shakes his head. "No, but a little farther south there's a port that might be able to take you there. Certainly, if you want to go to New York, you have to get yourself to Sydney first," he says in a practical tone.

"It will cost money for a trip to America," she says, thinking of her jewelry, lying at the bottom of the ocean. "I have nothing of value I can sell." Trying to sell the mace would be like setting a dazzling beacon for the Winterbournes to locate her.

"Mrs. Fullbright was lately expecting a new nanny for her child, a little boy named Xavier. I took the telegram to her just a week ago: the young woman engaged for the position decided not to come. There is honest work there for you, I'm sure, if you're willing to ask for it."

Mrs. Fullbright again. Matthew was determined she should go to town, and now, after a night of sleep has restored her senses, she understands that he is right. She cannot wait here at the lighthouse for things to change on their own. She must make a move even if it means working as a servant to a woman who probably isn't as wealthy as she is. There, in the chest, is an object of such immense value that it could buy Mrs. Fullbright several times over. Gold. Gems. Then she thinks of Daniel's bracelet on its modest black ribbon, buried in the bottom of the chest, and she is seized with the sudden knowledge that everything bad happened *after* she took it off.

The argument with Arthur that saw her confined below deck, unable to say her prayer to the sea.

The unrelenting stormy weather.

The shipwreck. The struggle to survive. The injuries.

The bad luck wouldn't stop until she had that bracelet back on her wrist. "I need you to help me open the chest," she says, her voice shaking.

"Do you not have a key?"

"No." She is already on her way to the main room, where the chest is still by the door.

He frowns as he crouches next to her, in front of the chest. "Is this . . . ?"

"Stolen? No. Not . . . not really stolen." A creeping fear. Now Matthew's kindness will run out, the last few grains of sand through an hourglass.

A moment of uncertainty. Then he nods. "I said I would ask no further questions and I will keep to my word."

"Thank you."

"Come," he says. "I keep the small axe up on the deck."

He hefts the chest and starts up the stairs. Isabella hesitates on the first step, gazing up at the nautilus swirl of the staircase. But Matthew is clattering ahead of her, and she makes her way up and up, past long dangling chains, through a hatch and up into the top of the lighthouse. An immense lamp, surrounded by a box of prismatic lenses, golden and glass concentric circles, takes up most of the space. There is an oily smell, not unpleasant. Matthew opens a small door and fresh morning air pours in. Then she is stepping out onto a round deck, high above the world, with a view for miles and miles to the distant dark horizon. The deck is peppered with dead moths and beetles, and one dead seagull. Matthew scoops it over the edge with his toe and drops the chest to the metal floor with a clang.

He opens a wooden box, full of tools, and pulls out a small axe.

"I will try to do this without doing too much damage to the chest," he says.

"I don't care. I will be ridding myself of the chest and most of its contents as soon as I can. It is a burden I wish never to see again." Her heart is beating fast, so fast it makes her head feel light.

Matthew raises the axe, takes aim and then brings it down on the first lock. Wood splinters, the lock clatters to the ground. Then another, and another blow. Five in all, one for each of the wretched locks. Then he stands, moves back and makes a show of turning away. "I'm better off not knowing what is in there," he says.

Isabella can't breathe, she is so grateful. She quickly flips open the lid. High sunlight dazzles off the gold and gems. Her hands are already moving underneath it, lifting the velvet, finding the ribbon.

She withdraws it and lets the lid fall closed. Her thumbs move over the coral beads on the bracelet, and a strange calm settles on her nerves, untangles the knots in her brain. All is simple: she will work for Mrs. Fullbright for as long as it takes to earn her passage to America. With Daniel's bracelet around her wrist, she can endure anything.

"You can turn around now," she says.

He turns. She holds out her wrist. "Will you help me tie this on?"

"Of course." He gently and quickly ties the ribbon around her wrist.

"This is the last memory I have of Daniel," she says softly, and her voice is nearly carried away on the wind and the sunshine. She looks at the chest. "And I should get this far away from me. Somewhere nobody can ever find it." Her eyes go to the sea. That's where it belongs: at the bottom of the ocean.

Matthew follows her gaze. "I can row it out a little way and drop it in the water."

"Is it deep?"

"I'll take it out as far as I can, while the ocean is still relatively calm."

She nods. "Do it."

They take the chest back inside, wrap it in Isabella's torn, bloodstained dress, and then Matthew leaves to take it out to sea, away from her. She clatters back up the stairs and out on the deck to watch her last link to the Winterbournes severed forever.

Matthew tells himself over and over that he won't look. He won't look. He doesn't need to know what is in the chest. And yet . . . here she is, asking him to dump it at sea. She is tired, confused, crushed by a grief that has clearly bent her mind. What if she regrets it? What if she regrets sending the contents of this chest to the bottom of the ocean? He remembers the time Clara charged him with burning a letter from her mother before she had read it. He did as she asked, only to be berated tearfully later.

So he must look. He must be the rational brain that she cannot be. If he looks, and it is a collection of old books, or clothes, or bottles, or clocks or . . . anything worthless and random, then he will dispose of it. But if it is something that signifies, something that she may later wish she had kept, then he will preserve it for her secretly.

The door to the lighthouse closes behind him. He rounds the corner of the cottage and finds the tin cabinet that keeps his woodpile dry. In the shadow of the cabinet, he unwraps the chest and, quickly so he can't change his mind, flips it open.

"Oh, my. My, my, my," he mutters. For in the chest is a thing of such beauty and value that he cannot comprehend at first. Its gleaming stem, its ornate head, carved gold. Jewels: red, green, blue. He doesn't know what the object is, but it is not something worthless and random. And he knows he cannot let her dispose of it. She will regret it. He is certain.

He pulls a log from the woodpile—about the same length as the chest—then wraps it in the dress. Then closes the chest and hides it carefully among the woodpile. He makes his way down the narrow path to the sheltered side of the rock wall, and down the mossy stairs to the rowboat. He glances up. Isabella is watching from the deck. He waves to her, and she waves back, the black ribbon around her wrist. A moment's guilt, then he is rowing against the waves. This task would be impossible in the afternoon, when the wind is fresh and the sea wild, but mornings are often calm. He rows as far out as he can before the rip catches him. The sun is on his forearms. He makes a show of hefting the log and plunging it into the water. She will be watching. Will she already be regretting? It matters not. If she changes her mind, he will have it somewhere safe for her.

Whatever it is.

*M*atthew insists she takes the day to rest before heading to Mrs. Fullbright's. Her wounds are still healing and her feet are still sore. She spends the morning in bed, then when Matthew needs to sleep at noon she sits up on the deck watching the ocean and letting her mind drift. She is apprehensive about approaching Mrs. Fullbright, and still doesn't know if she will be welcomed. But Matthew seems confident, and she trusts Matthew. She trusts him even though she doesn't know him. There is something familiar about him, something comforting in his presence that awakes a primitive feeling in her, a long-buried sense of safety. She is loath to leave him, but understands she must. She knows how society works: a young woman cannot stay with a single man in a house with one bed. She needs to do what society dictates if she wants the job with Mrs. Fullbright, if she wants to earn honest money and find her way to her sister.

The afternoon deepens. It will soon be dusk, and Matthew will be awake, ready to work. She takes a few last breaths up here on the deck, above the world, then returns down the deep spiral staircase and into the cottage.

Matthew is up, in his trousers and undershirt and braces, lighting his pipe. He turns as she enters the room, smiles with only one corner of his mouth.

"I suppose I must go," she says.

"It's for the best. You will find your way."

She nods and moves to the door to pull on the shoes that are too tight. Matthew has packed for her a small bag: two more dresses, both too large for her. But at least she has clothes. Her heart is beating in her throat, she feels helpless.

"I am here if you need me, Isabella," he says, then smiles and corrects himself, "I mean, Mary Harrow."

"Thank you," she says. "For everything."

Then the door closes quietly behind her and she stands on the path that will lead her down to the town.

Despite her stinging feet, she moves with deliberate sure-footedness. The path is sandy, bracketed on both sides by thick, sharp-smelling vegetation. She recognizes the edible berries, but she doesn't need to pick them. She has eaten three solid meals today, and Mrs. Fullbright will have more for her. The path opens up, and the town comes into view. On the other side of the forest verge that protects them from the ocean winds sit wooden buildings with tin roofs. There are, perhaps, twenty houses. A pub. A large shed that might be to do with the sugar and timber trade Matthew has mentioned. A plain little church with plastered walls.

From the hill, she looks for the big house at the near end of the main street. Pale pink boards. Two stories high with a large verandah all the way around. It sits on a square of green grass, with tidy garden beds. This is where Mrs. Katherine Fullbright lives with her son, Xavier, and presumably a husband and other hired help. Before Isabella saw the house, she had been half-hoping that Mrs. Fullbright wouldn't take her in. She could return to the safety of the lighthouse. But now she has seen the lawn and the flowers, she wants to be there. She wants to put her feet in grass. She wants to be in a real house with carpets and curtains. It has been months since she has known such ordinary comforts.

Isabella walks with purpose down the path and over the grassy shoulder of the dirt road, then through the gate and right up the steps to Mrs. Fullbright's front door. The windowsills are painted white. There are lace curtains. She likes Mrs. Fullbright already.

Isabella pulls her hair over the cut in her neck so she doesn't alarm Mrs. Fullbright. Gloves borrowed from the former lighthouse keeper's wife cover the scabs on her hands. She can do nothing about the sunburn, but she turns her face out of the full lamplight in any case.

She rings the brass bell and waits.

At length, the door opens a crack, and a dark-haired, sloe-eyed, full-lipped woman peers out.

"Hello," Isabella says. "I am here to see Mrs. Fullbright."

The door opens fully. "I am Katarina Fullbright," says the woman with a slight accent that Isabella cannot place.

Isabella had thought a maid would answer the door, and is now trying to understand that this impossibly beautiful young woman, with smooth olive skin and slightly flared nostrils, is Mrs. Katherine Fullbright. She had been expecting a middle-aged Katherine, English of course, fussy about manners and laced into a conservative gown, not a crimson-clad Katarina.

She remembers her purpose, offers Katarina her hand. "I am Mary Harrow. I heard you require a nanny. I am a nanny and in need of employment."

Katarina's perfectly arched eyebrows shoot up. "You are?"

"I am. Though I have lost my references . . ."

"Do come in, Mary," she says, unperturbed, leading Isabella into a sitting room with a high ceiling and wood-paneled walls. A large sofa with a crocheted throw on it sits next to two leather armchairs. Bookshelves and a sideboard cover one wall. Isabella can see through to a small dining room and beyond to a kitchen. The house is clean and smells like lemon-and-oil furniture polish. It is lit only by two fat candles. "Sit down. This is a welcome surprise," Katarina says.

"Thank you," Isabella says, perching on the sofa with her bag between her feet.

"I had thought I would have to advertise again, wait for months," Katarina says. "It's hard to find anybody willing to come so far and Xavier is . . . He is a difficult child. You don't mind a difficult child?"

For the first time, Isabella fully realizes that she will have to work for this honest money she wants. Back in Somerset, her days were consumed with needlework, cutting and arranging flowers, organizing high teas, accompanying her husband to town. She has never worked in her life. "Of course I don't mind," she says, and she wonders at the distance between what she is saying and what she is feeling. She should have stayed a few more days at the lighthouse. She shouldn't have decided so rashly to come here. She is not thinking straight, she can't think straight. The feeling of helplessness is back, a dark sob in her brain.

"Xavier, he is not here now," Katarina is saying. "He has gone away with Mr. Fullbright for a few days."

"Do you want me to come back then?"

"No need. You are here now. There is nowhere to stay in town except the pub, and that's not fit for women. Cook has finished for the night, so you have missed dinner. If you are hungry, there is bread and dripping in the kitchen."

"I'm not hungry. I . . ." Isabella touches her own forehead. "I am terribly, terribly tired."

Katarina smiles. "Ah, a long journey? I see you are sunburned from being on the cart. Down from the gold fields? Is that where your last job was?"

Isabella nods.

"Come, Mary, I'll show you the bathroom and nursery. You will sleep in the same room as Xavier. You have an early night tonight, and tomorrow we will work out details, yes?" Isabella has the impression that Katarina is itching to be away. Perhaps that explains the glorious gown.

Isabella nods, and Katarina leads her down a carpeted hallway: rooms lead off left and right. At the final set of doorways she stops, indicates right, "Bathroom," then left, "Nursery. There are sheets in the large chest at the end of the bed. I am going out this evening, you must forgive me."

Then she is off in a whirl of red fabric and dark hair. Isabella goes to the bathroom. In the half-light, she can barely see her face in the mirror, but what she does see alarms her. She is, indeed, sunburned: glowing, with blisters on her nose. Her face is hollow, the shadows beneath her eyes dark and long. Her hair is lank and unbrushed. Compared to Katarina's fresh beauty, Isabella is a hag. She has seen too many horrors and it shows on her face. She looks away. She splashes water on her face and washes her hands, then heads to the nursery.

Lanterns sit in brackets on either side of the doorway, so she lights them with the box of long matches that sits on the dresser. There is a cot pushed against a wall, and a small bed. Against the other wall is an adult-sized bed. Between the beds is a large blue rug and a box of toys. Isabella picks up a dropped teddy bear and places it on the small bed. She hasn't even asked how old Xavier is. Again the feeling overwhelms her: what is she doing here? It's too fast. She needs time to get used to the fact that they are all dead and she is on her own in a foreign place.

But last night she felt overwhelmed too, and after a good sleep she recovered. Her ordeal has exhausted her, deep down to her soul. She drops her bag beside her bed and slides out of her dress.

The front door bangs shut. Footsteps recede down the stairs. She is alone in a strange house. Curiosity prickles. She opens the nursery door and listens out, hard. Nothing. She pads to the end of the hallway and tries the door through to the sitting room. It is locked.

Isabella bristles, even though she knows she hasn't a right to. Katarina had met her for the first time less than an hour ago: of course she isn't going to have free rein to explore the house alone. She is hired help.

Isabella returns to her room and sinks down on her knees on the bed, with her elbows resting on the windowsill. She can see the top of the lighthouse above the trees. Its beam has flashed into life and is making a pattern out to sea, across the miles and the raging ocean that separate Isabella's old life from this new, strange one. She watches it while the night deepens and the dark closes in.

It is 3 am and Matthew is burying a large object in the forest. It is not a body, but he would feel just as guilty if it were. He has cranked the weights so the signal will keep flashing, but he has never left the lighthouse during operation before. Leaving the light unattended briefly is not forbidden, of course, but it is flirting with risk, and Matthew does not like risk. Nor does he like the fact that he lied to Isabella about this precious object that he has sealed carefully in its walnut coffin with oilskin, in order to bury it here among the buttonwood trees.

He finishes digging and stands, with his hand on his back. He is not as young as he once was. Then, when the twinge of pain recedes, he drops the box in the hole three feet deep and begins to cover it with soil. As he works, he wonders why he is doing this. Why is he neglecting his duties, toiling in the darkest hour of the night, hiding something precious that was probably gained illegally, for a woman he has known barely twenty-four hours? Is he such an old fool that anybody who reminds him of Clara can crook his moral compass?

No. He is helping a person in need, that is all. She came to him, desperate and bleeding, without so much as a pair of shoes. Now she has the precious token of her lost baby, and she has a place to stay and an honest job. Burying this chest is as good as dropping it in the ocean: it just allows her to change her mind, should she decide to go back to where she came from one day.

Matthew pats the soil so that it lies at the same height as the surrounding area. Finally, he arranges some deadfall on top of it, so it seems as though nobody was ever here, burying treasure. It is time to go back to the light.

Thirteen

Percy Winterbourne can't read. Of course he has been taught. Of course he isn't stupid. But when he looks at letters and numbers, they sometimes turn to hieroglyphs: twist themselves upside-down and backwards. With a little concentration and some clever tricks—covering some letters while deciphering others, looking at them with a pocket mirror, then again without—he can usually get by. But the best way to get by is never to sit at a desk, never to open a book or a ledger, and never to be in company in those moments when he is forced to read something.

And when Arthur finally returns from his journey, Percy will hand all this paperwork back to him and never look at it again.

He sits, at his brother's big mahogany desk, under the window that looks out onto the chestnut wood. The catkins are all blooming, and wildflowers glow golden on the ground in the late-afternoon sunshine. How he would love to be out there, with his dogs, tramping or hunting or just whistling a merry tune. Not in here trying for the fourth time to make the numbers at the bottom of the column match the sum of the numbers at the ends of the rows. He swears that now the numbers are jumping between columns and rows just to spite him because he has cursed them so often today.

A knock at the door. Percy pushes the ledger under a pile of jewelry orders. He doesn't want anyone to know that he is still struggling with March's figures, given it is nearly May.

"Come in," he says, making sure that he doesn't sound frustrated or weak or defeated.

The door opens and Charles Simmons, head of trade, stands there. He is as white as a sheet. Apprehension tingles in Percy's gut. "My Lord, I . . ."

"Close the door, and sit down," Percy says. It is bad news. Nobody looks like that if it's not bad news.

Charles crosses the thickly carpeted floor and sits in the leather chair opposite the desk. He folds shaking hands over his knees.

"Spit it out," Percy says.

"I had a telegram earlier today from an angry businessman in Brisbane, Australia. He was expecting a shipment. It seems the *Aurora* has failed to reach Brisbane."

Percy is confused. "Where is Brisbane? I thought Arthur was going to Sydney."

"Brisbane was the last port before Sydney. They were due to drop off a load of carpets and wallpapers." Charles glances at the flocked green wallpaper in the office.

"Then they are late. Lateness is not a thing to be so pale-faced about."

"I have telegraphed the port in Townsville. *Aurora* left a shipment there on March twenty-nine, just before a spell of very poor weather. That was nearly a month ago, sir. Townsville to Brisbane is only a handful of days."

Percy tries to stop the rising tide of panic. A disaster! The priceless mace, the item that has finally brought them a Queen's commission. And Arthur: how will he tell Mother if Arthur has been lost at sea? Since Father's death, she worships her firstborn son. So much so that Percy has long since turned cold towards his brother and his mad sister-in-law.

Then a thought jolts his heart: if Arthur is gone, will Percy be stuck in this office with numbers and letters forever?

He leaps out of his seat. "Don't tell a soul," he says. "They might yet turn up. Telegraph the light stations along the coast. Contact the constabulary in this Brisbane port. Do everything you can to locate the *Aurora*. We aren't to assume the worst. Not yet." The thought of the priceless mace deep at the bottom of the ocean with only his dead brother's hands to protect it makes Percy's stomach itch. If it is lost at sea, then anyone brave enough to dive under the water for it can have it.

"I will, sir," Charles says, standing. "I won't rest until we know what happened. And I regret being the man who brought you the fear of losing something so precious."

"So precious," Percy repeats. "The most costly thing we have ever made."

Charles clears his throat. "I meant your brother, sir."

The short, awkward silence makes Percy angry. "Go on. Away with you. Let me know what you discover."

*I*sabella wakes very early, but the door at the end of the hallway is still locked. She rises, washes and dresses, then sits on the end of her bed to wait. She is not the mistress of her own house. She is a servant. Servants wait on the whims of others. This is not so different to the general condition of being a woman, so Isabella hopes she will grow accustomed to service quickly. Surely it will take her only a few months to earn the money for her journey.

Isabella rubs her fingers lightly over the black ribbon on her wrist. She can endure it.

As the sun hits the window, she hears the sound of others stirring in the house. Tentatively, she rises and leaves the nursery. The inner door is now open, and the smell of cooking fruit and cinnamon beckons from the kitchen. She rounds the corner, passes through the dining room and sees a full-hipped woman standing at the wood stove, stirring a pot. Isabella clears her throat softly.

The woman turns. "Oh, good morning, miss," she says, with a tight smile. "Mrs. Fullbright told me to expect you."

"Is Mrs. Fullbright about?"

"She's just downstairs. She'll be up for breakfast shortly, but if you're hungry you can eat here with me." The cook gestures to the small, round table in the middle of the kitchen. "It's where we staff eat."

Isabella pulls out a chair and sits down. It is stiff and hard. "I'm Mary," she says.

"I'm Bessie, but everyone just calls me Cook." She spoons out a bowl of porridge with stewed apple on top and places it in front of Isabella.

"Are there other staff?"

Cook glances around and drops her voice low. "The Fullbrights aren't as well-off as they were. She let the maid go two months ago, and hasn't advertised for another. You and I will have to do most of the dusting and cleaning."

Dusting? Cleaning? "I see."

"There's not much, love. We'll get it done in a jiffy, and when Master Xavier's back you'll see he's little trouble. Can entertain himself for hours quietly."

"Really? Mrs. Fullbright gave me reason to think him a difficult child."

"Aye, but not noisy or demanding. He doesn't speak."

"How old is he?"

"Oh, three or four by my reckoning. Should be talking his head off by now, but hasn't said a word. Not even *Mama* or *Papa*." Cook turns back to the pot. "But you mustn't mention it directly to the Fullbrights. They are very sensitive about it. Can't bear the idea that he might not be normal. Mr. Fullbright has formed the opinion that the boy is quiet simply to be naughty."

Isabella lets this knowledge sink in. She is curious to meet Xavier, and Mr. Fullbright. She is curious too to see Katarina again in the light of day. Her memory is of a glamorous beauty, gleaming darkly by lamplight. Perhaps she looks more like a real woman now. But Isabella is also afraid: she hasn't looked after a child since she lost her own.

Cook sits down across from Isabella with a bowl of porridge and eats noisily. Isabella hears footsteps on the stairs and then Katarina's voice: "Is Mary awake yet?"

"Here, ma'am," Isabella calls back, pushing back her chair and meeting Katarina in the living room.

Katarina's hair is pulled back tightly today. Without the mane of dark hair she lacks the cloud of lush sensuality that Isabella remembers from last night. She is not in red, but in dark blue serge. Still beautiful, yes, but not distractingly so. Isabella wonders where Katarina went last night, without her husband, in such unabashed glamour.

"Ah, Mary. Your face is not so pink today and you have brushed your hair. I'm glad. You should terrify Xavier should he meet you looking such a wreck. Come, let me show you around the house and we'll talk about your engagement."

Katarina points out all the rooms Isabella has already seen or passed, including the two next to the nursery. One is a sewing room, the other a guest bedroom. On the far side of the sitting room is a sumptuous bedroom, which belongs to Mr. and Mrs. Fullbright. Isabella is led downstairs, then through a wooden gate to the lower floor of the house.

"Here is Cook's room and sitting area," she says, indicating a door on the left. "Here is where the maid sleeps, though she has returned to Scotland and we haven't replaced her yet." Then she indicates, with a nod of her head, a narrow hallway ending in a door. "You aren't to go down there."

Isabella opens her mouth to ask why, then remembers she is staff and must not ask. "Yes, ma'am," she says instead.

"And don't take Xavier near it either." She opens another door. "Laundry. Cook's doing laundry at the moment until we find a new maid. I want you to take care of upstairs. Make the beds every morning, beat the mats on Saturdays, keep up with dusting and polishing. Cook will show you where everything is. You can start today while Xavier is still away."

"Yes, ma'am," Isabella says again, glancing back to the forbidden hallway, the forbidden door.

"Through here is the garden, though you can also get there down the stairs off the kitchen." Katarina opens a door onto a sunlit garden.

Isabella smells the grass, the flowers. It has been so long. Without thinking, she steps out ahead of Katarina, slips off her shoes, and buries her toes in the grass. The heartbeat of the world thunders up through the soles of her feet.

"Please, Mary, keep your shoes on," Katarina says with a frown, then starts up the back stairs.

Isabella startles out of her reverie. Shoes. She presses her feet back into them and hurries up the stairs after Katarina.

*   *   *

$\mathcal{M}$atthew is on his way down the spiral stairs when he hears the telegraph machine clatter into life. It is just before eight in the morning, and he has been idly sweeping the dead bugs off the deck, wondering how Isabella is today. Mooning like a lad. He is grateful for the distraction of the Morse code. He pulls out a blank telegram and begins to decode the signal. Because he must transcribe telegrams that are not intended for him, he has become adept at writing down what he hears without really listening to it. It is only when he has transcribed the first line that he realizes this message is intended for him.

Lost ship Aurora. Three-masted barque last seen March 29th Townsville. Expected in Brisbane April 12th at latest. Reply urgently with news of any sighting.

In his time as a lighthouse keeper, he has witnessed the unfolding drama of two other ships being lost. It is a slow disaster for those left behind, though for those on board it must be fast and brutal. Families and traders and police, however, experience it at one remove: first the suspicion of something astray, then the growing certainty, then the sinking realization that a cruel death has long since taken important men from them. It is horror in increments. And while Matthew hopes for good news of the *Aurora* for the sakes of all those involved, he has already readied himself for what comes next.

He finishes transcribing the telegram, looking sadly at the name of the man who has sent it: Charles Simmons on behalf of Percy Winterbourne. He wonders if either of these men are family, if they are pacing anxiously with hot hearts waiting for news of loved ones.

Matthew turns to his station records, where he logs every ship that he sees and on which date. It is possible that *Aurora* passed a long way out to sea, beyond his view, but if she was coming to Brisbane she would likely be no more than three miles off the coast. He checks the date. *Extremely bad weather.* He shudders. He would not have wanted to be out in that weather. He prepares to telegraph back the truth, that he has no record of seeing *Aurora*. Perhaps another light station has seen her. But then he pauses, his hand frozen in the air.

Isabella.

If *Aurora* went down, it would have been in the past three weeks. Isabella had arrived, out of nowhere, dragging that chest, her clothes in rags. The burned skin on her face and arms, the swollen blisters on her feet—how far had she walked? Had she walked away from a shipwreck?

Matthew sits back. He mulls it over awhile, then, instead of telegraphing Charles Simmons in England, he sends a message to the next lighthouse north, to Clovis McCarthy at Cape Franklin. Within half an hour he receives a reply.

Yes we saw her April 7th. Have let Simmons know.

On 7 April *Aurora* had passed Cape Franklin. By any estimation, she should have been in Brisbane long ago. She has gone down; Matthew is sure of it. He is also sure that Isabella was on the ship, and that the treasure buried in the woods was on it with her.

But he will not say anything. Not yet. Perhaps not ever. She said she is running away. He sends a return telegram, giving them all the information they have asked for and nothing more. No, he has no record of seeing the ship. They have heard from Cape Franklin, they will figure the rest out for themselves. *Aurora* is lost. There are no survivors. At least, none who wants to be found.

*   *   *

After five days of living in shoes, with a roof over her head, Isabella is healing well physically. The deep cut on her neck is not so bruised; her hand is marred only by a few dry scabs; the sunburn is peeling away and revealing white skin beneath. She has been busy polishing brass and silverware, sweeping and mopping, dusting and sorting. In the afternoons she helps Cook prepare food, sending out an enormous meal to Katarina, who only picks at its edges. She eats well, she sleeps well, she settles into a groove in this, her new temporary life. It reminds her a little of the plays she and her sister put on for their family as children. She is wearing a costume of sorts: she is performing the role of Mary Harrow, nanny and maid. And but for the occasional slip—when she reveals she has never polished silverware before or doesn't know how to take curtains off the rails to wash them—she is performing it admirably.

A horse and carriage pull up in front of the house in the bright of the afternoon and Katarina immediately goes into a flurry of orders. "It's Mr. Fullbright," she gasps to Isabella and Cook as they sit at the kitchen table shelling peas. "I want an afternoon tea brought within half an hour."

Although this seems impossible, Cook nods and beckons Isabella out of her chair. Katarina has gone to the door to greet her husband and child, but Isabella is too busy to indulge her curiosity and peer out to the sitting room. Mr. Fullbright has a deep, booming voice, but little Xavier has no voice at all. Isabella only presumes he is there: she has no proof yet.

She and Cook recover the rest of the fruit loaf from breakfast, cut up apples and cheese, brew tea, toast bread and drizzle it with honey. Then Cook bustles out with it all on a tray, to set it on the dining table. Isabella hangs back in the threshold, waiting for instruction.

"Mary, will you come to meet Xavier?" Katarina calls.

Isabella goes forward. Mr. Fullbright pauses in spreading butter on his fruit loaf to frown at her. "Who are you?" He has a thick black mustache that curls over so deeply that it looks as though he has no top lip at all.

"This is Mary Harrow, our new nanny. Mary, this is Ernest Fullbright, my husband."

Ernest Fullbright prods little Xavier. "Go on, lad, greet your new nanny."

Xavier, who has been shrunk against his father's side, takes one look at Isabella and begins to cry. Isabella, sensing the importance of a good first meeting, kneels in front of him and takes his hand gently. "There, child."

Xavier is so shocked by this direct contact that he stops crying, and fixes her in his gaze. His eyes are very dark. Isabella can see fear in those deep pools. She doesn't try to cheer him out of it. Instead, she respects it. "My name is Mary and I shall be very good to you," she says.

Katarina reaches forward and removes her hand from Xavier's. "No hugging and so on."

Xavier is looking at his own hand, turning it in front of his face as though seeing it for the first time.

"She stopped him crying, at least," Ernest mutters into his mustache.

"That is what nannies do," Katarina says. "That is what we pay Mary for."

Isabella remains crouched in front of Xavier, holding his gaze. "How old is he?" she asks.

"He will be three in July."

July? Isabella's heart picks up a rhythm. "Which date?" she asks, thinking, *What shall I do if it's the eighteenth?*

Katarina says, "The eighteenth."

Isabella holds her face very still, but Xavier sees the change in her eyes and he begins to blink rapidly as though he might cry again. The eighteenth of July. Xavier was born on the same day as Daniel. Standing in front of Isabella is a model of what her child might have been. Not the dark hair and eyes, perhaps, but the plump fists and sturdy legs, the liquid gaze and poreless skin. He is Daniel's living twin and she is frozen a moment, but the child looks frightened, so she takes a piece of apple from the table and hands it to him. Distracted, he relaxes again.

"He's a difficult child," Katarina says. "He refuses to talk, though it's clear he understands what is said around him."

"Don't spoil him," Ernest adds. "Make sure he learns his letters and numbers."

"And he's not to suck his thumb."

Isabella climbs to her feet and beckons Xavier. "Shall we go to the nursery, Xavier?"

Xavier rises to follow her. She closes the door at the end of the hallway and immediately offers Xavier her hand again. He takes it quickly and willingly—his fingers are soft and slightly sticky—and she knows that he feels what she is feeling: somehow, they were meant to find each other.

Isabella wakes, blinking in the dark. Voices, shouting. She lies very still in her narrow bed, listening. Outside, it is windy and trees are shushing against the night sky, casting moonlit shadows through the lacy curtain. She cannot hear what they are saying, but she can tell it is Katarina and Ernest. Katarina is shrieking, Ernest is booming. Back and forth the accusations go. Isabella rises, and pads past Xavier's bed. He is breathing softly and steadily, untroubled by the voices. She opens the nursery door and listens in the hallway, catches a few words, none of them harmless: *drunkard, whore, liar, bastard*. Then comes a deafening bang, and the whole house shakes, as one of them storms out and slams the door with murderous brutality. Isabella withdraws quickly into the nursery, closing her own door, but it is too late. Xavier stirs, begins to whimper.

"Sh, sh," Isabella says, kneeling next to his bed and stroking his brow. She picks up his little hand and puts it near his lips. Sure enough, he finds his thumb and begins to suck hard. The whimpering stops; sleep returns. She stays by his side a few minutes, making sure he is settled. Then she returns to the hallway.

Now she can hear sobbing. It is Katarina, sobbing as though her ribs might break. Isabella approaches the door at the end of the hallway and tries it. It is locked. She knows this is none of her business, but she remembers sobbing like that herself and nobody ever coming. She knocks softly on the door.

The sobbing stops. Isabella hears light footsteps, then the door opens. Katarina stands in front of her, face tear-stained in the lamplight. "What is it?" she asks, and Isabella can see she is desolate and trapped. Isabella knows exactly how it feels.

"Let me make you tea, ma'am," Isabella says.

Katarina shakes her head, but Isabella is already on her way to the kitchen. Katarina follows, sinks into a hard chair at the kitchen table and puts her head down to cry some more. Isabella lights the stove and boils the kettle, scoops tea into the pot, fetches milk from the icebox. Finally, she sets the tea tray down in front of Katarina. Steam rises from the cups as she pours.

Katarina lifts her head. "Thank you, Mary," she says. "Did the child wake?"

"He did when the door slammed, but only briefly. He is fast asleep now."

"I am so unhappy," she says.

"I know," Isabella replies.

"How could you know?"

Isabella doesn't say that she too has been trapped in a marriage where hate filled her heart instead of love. She doesn't say that just a few short weeks ago her husband died and she hasn't cried for him once. She simply says, "I just do."

"He is jealous. He thinks I look at other men. He thinks I court their attention and make a fool of him." Her voice drops low. "Sometimes I wonder if he'll hurt me. He'll get the idea in his head that I have taken a lover and he'll kill me."

Isabella stares back at her, remembering the times she had seen Arthur so angry she had wondered if he would raise his fists against her. The anger of men is a frightening thing, indeed. Katarina is sobbing again, and Isabella's heart stirs. She slides out of her chair and bends to put her arms around Katarina. Katarina clings to her, sobbing all the louder.

"Hush, now," Isabella says.

"I hate him."

"I know, I know."

"How can I live? How can I go on?"

"You will. Hush now." Isabella stands back. "Drink your tea. It will make you feel better."

"Nothing will ever change."

"Drink your tea." Isabella sits back down.

"You are a strange one, Mary," Katarina says, sniffing back tears and reaching for her tea.

They sit in silence, drinking their tea, then Katarina says, "He will come back later. He will be drunk, but he is a merry drunk. Keep the nursery door closed so Xavier doesn't hear." Then she stands and, without another word, heads to her bedroom.

Isabella finishes her tea, then empties the pot and cleans the cups. She isn't tired, so she opens the back door and sits at the top of the stairs. The night smells soft and fresh; the breeze lifts her hair. The lighthouse is alive, and she thinks about Matthew. Is he angry like other men? Would he ever look at a woman as though he wanted to break her bones? Would he be dismissive, or cold or cruel? She cannot imagine it, but perhaps she is a fool. Perhaps women make men wild simply by mattering. Perhaps the way to be with a man is never to matter. Like Percy Winterbourne's wife: popping sons out with as little complaint as other women bake scones. Isabella drops her head to her knees. No, Matthew is not like other men. She knows it in her bones. She hopes she can see him again one day soon.

At breakfast the next morning, Xavier is happily eating his toast fingers and tea when Katarina flounces into the kitchen and says, "Mary, Xavier eats breakfast with his parents in the dining room."

Isabella notices a coolness about Katarina. Cook is downstairs in the laundry, so she takes the opportunity to say, "Are you feeling better?"

"Better? I'm sure I don't know what you mean." She yanks Xavier from his chair, and he is pulled out of the kitchen without protest. "Ensure Xavier is ready for breakfast with his parents every morning in the dining room," she says over her shoulder. "Family and staff should not mix."

Isabella has the distinct feeling she has been put in her place.

Fourteen

Matthew recognizes Clovis McCarthy's horse and carriage outside the Exchange Hotel on Shore Road, and guiltily realizes he is late. To meet with Clovis this afternoon, he had to sleep between ten and three. Sleep wouldn't come under duress. When it finally did, it was too deep and too long. He had woken half an hour late, dressed quickly and hurried down the road to the drinking hole, with only one hopeful glance towards the Fullbright house.

He opens the painted green and glass door to the Exchange, and is greeted by the smell of wood paneling, beer and cigar smoke. He scans the dim room. Ernest Fullbright stands at the bar with Abel Barrett, the sugar-mill tycoon: those two are as thick as thieves. In the far corner, under the Queen's portrait, sits a noisy group of five itinerant workers, wearing dirty caps and boots laced with string. Behind the bar, pretty Eunice Hand wipes glasses dry with the cloth attached to her waistband. Eunice has always had a shine for Matthew and she might have made a good wife, but despite her good heart Matthew finds her a little dull-eyed: Clara spoiled him for all other women. By the window, at a dark wooden table with two tall beers waiting, is Clovis.

Matthew approaches with a smile. Clovis rises from his seat, stiff in the joints now, having become an old man since Matthew last saw him, just three years ago.

"Old friend," Clovis says.

"I'm late."

"I have all the time in the world." Clovis has been the lighthouse keeper at Cape Franklin for sixteen years. He is on his way south, now, to Brisbane, to retire.

After a firm handshake, Matthew sits and sips the top off his beer and watches as Clovis props his cane against the wall and lowers himself to his seat.

"The stairs have finally defeated me, Seaward," he says.

"What's the new man like?"

"Young. Smart. Has a young family: a plump wife and three little boys. Already talking about replacing the oil with acetylene tanks. I resisted it myself. Always worried the damned things would blow up."

"I feel the same. My last shipment, they sent me an acetylene tank instead of kerosene. I have it sitting around the back for them to take, but I think even the delivery service is wary of carrying it."

Clovis raises his eyebrows. "There's worse. His wife knows the code. She'll be taking the telegraph."

Matthew smiles. He knows what Clovis thinks of women. "Is that right?"

"Shouldn't give a woman a job like that. They're too prone to gossip. She'll know all the town's business and start interfering. You mark my words." Clovis shakes his head. "Times are changing too fast for me, Seaward."

They drink as the afternoon shadows outside lengthen. One beer. Then another. Clovis offers to buy Matthew a third, but he refuses. In less than an hour, he needs to fire up the light. He knows his limit, and he never exceeds it.

Matthew has been assiduously avoiding talk of the *Aurora* because he doesn't want to speak untruth directly to anyone, especially Clovis. But it is, in the end, unavoidable.

"I've had the police up to talk to me about the lost ship," Clovis says, starting his third beer. "I shan't miss working with them. The local constable is a sorry fool. Couldn't find his own feet, let alone a ship."

"You mean the *Aurora*? So they've started a search?"

"It was full of cargo, some very expensive. And an important nobleman on board. Arthur Winterbourne and his wife."

"His wife?" Matthew's ears ring faintly. "Do you know her name?"

Clovis shakes his head. "No idea. They're all dead now, though. Must have had an imbecile for a Captain. Why he didn't shelter farther north is beyond reckoning. The weather was appalling."

"Have they found anything? The police?"

Clovis shrugs. "More than a hundred miles of coast between my light and yours, Seaward. The constable thinks they've found some debris just to the south, but I would have seen her if she was that close. Probably some old junk dropped off the side to lighten her load if she was taking on water." Clovis drops his voice. "I overheard something I shouldn't have."

"Go on," Matthew says, wishing he'd had that third drink.

"On board was a gift from Queen Vic to the Australian parliament." Clovis indicates the portrait of the Queen. "Priceless."

Matthew's heart rate rises. "What was it?"

"A ceremonial mace. Can you imagine? Gold and gems, out there somewhere in the sea, being shit upon by fish."

Gold and gems. Good Christ, Isabella had handed him a box-ful of problems.

"The family of the jeweler who made it, the Winterbourne fellow, is very keen to have it back."

"I would presume so."

Clovis keeps talking, speculating, then he's off on another topic, but Matthew doesn't quite manage to get his cheer back. The mace wasn't Isabella's. It should be given to the police. But how is he to do that without alerting them to her presence? It is clear now that burying the mace was foolish. Illegal.

"Nearly dusk, my friend," Clovis says, indicating the long shadows and golden light outside.

"Time to work," Matthew replies.

"I envy you," Clovis says. "I wish I was young again."

But at this moment, Matthew feels very old and tired. He bids his friend farewell and walks home up the hill. He takes a short detour off the track to where he buried the mace, and looks down at his boots. Beneath him, a priceless object, belonging to a noble family, or the Queen, or the parliament, or all three. People far more important than he is. If only he had never looked. If only Isabella had never brought it. Or never come at all.

But it is too late now. What has happened, has happened. And what comes next will surely come.

It has been a week and two days, and Isabella doesn't know when she will be paid. Weekly? Monthly? At the end of her service? How can she trust the Fullbrights? She didn't even talk to them about how much she would be paid. They are providing her room and board, so her earnings won't be much, but she needs them. Matthew has an electric telegraph in his cottage: she wants to send a telegram to her sister to say she is coming. She secretly hopes that her sister might convince her husband to send Isabella money, so this long slog of work can end more quickly.

Though she would miss little Xavier.

He sits across from her now in the kitchen, helping to sort wool. The child is fiercely bright, for all that he doesn't speak. She has seen him follow along with her when she reads to him at night, pulling her up with a peremptory point of his index finger if she misses a word or turns the page too soon. He is sorting the yellow three-ply wool scraps from the four-ply without any difficulty, his dark eyes focused sharply in front of him, his thumb jammed firmly between his lips. She keeps her ears pricked for the approach of Katarina, who is determined that he oughtn't suck his thumb, that the habit is to blame for him not talking.

"Very well done, Xavier," she says to him.

He doesn't meet her eyes, but she can see the corner of his smile. She suspects Xavier is beginning to like her.

Footsteps. Isabella quickly but gently removes Xavier's thumb from his mouth. He seems to understand that they are complicit in this deception, and wipes the saliva from his thumb on his pants.

"Mary?" Katarina says, pausing in the threshold to the kitchen. "Mr. Fullbright is having a guest for lunch today and has requested Xavier join us without his nanny. You can help Cook here in the kitchen."

"I have been here more than a week, Mrs. Fullbright. I see Cook has an afternoon off a week. Might I not also?"

Katarina blinks at her. "I suppose so. Cook will likely manage alone. It is only one extra guest."

"And, Mrs. Fullbright, when might I be paid?"

"You are very blunt," Katarina says.

Isabella isn't sure if this is a criticism or a compliment, so she says nothing. This is the first time she has ever had to ask for money.

"We are a little short this week, Mary," Katarina says. "I can give you two shillings now, but Mr. Fullbright will pay you at the end of the month, when his own debtors have paid him." Katarina glances away, as though talking about money embarrasses her. "In future, you should talk only to him about your wage."

The house is soon in an uproar as Cook is instructed to prepare a roast for the guest, a very wealthy friend of Ernest's named Abel Barrett. Isabella helps her with the vegetables and the Yorkshire pudding batter in between playing with Xavier and his wooden horses in the nursery.

Ernest seeks her out in the nursery just before midday.

"You need money?" he says, his mouth turned down disapprovingly.

She wants to say, "No, you *owe* me money," but she knows that will only inflame him. She must pretend to be the supplicant; after all, that is what she is. "Yes, sir. And Mrs. Fullbright says I might take the afternoon off."

"Ha. A woman loose about town with money and nothing to keep her occupied is a dangerous prospect. Still, if Katherine has promised it to you . . ." He fishes in his pocket and pulls out a few coins to offer to her.

"Thank you, sir," she says, taking them.

He folds his hands behind his back and leans down to speak to Xavier, who hasn't looked up from his wooden horses. "Come on, young man. We have a guest."

Xavier looks longingly at his horses, then casts a gaze towards Isabella, who smiles at him encouragingly. "Go on, Xavier. I made the pudding batter especially for you. I will see you this evening."

Then they are gone, and Isabella goes to the bathroom to wash before going up to the lighthouse. It will be the first time she has seen Matthew since she left. An aeon seems to have passed, although it has been little more than a week, and she doesn't completely understand why she should be so keen for him to see her washed and groomed. She has never been vain, but Matthew has only ever seen her battered and sunburned. Once in her life, she was considered beautiful.

To leave the house, she must cross the sitting room. She pauses near the front door and casts a glance back towards the dining room, where Abel Barrett is in deep conversation with Ernest. Abel looks up, catches her eye. She sees him turn to Ernest and knows he is asking about her. She hesitates: should she wait to see if she is summoned to greet him? But then Katarina comes into view, and makes a theatrical shooing-away gesture. Isabella slips out of the house and down the stairs.

The sky is gray today, a leaden blanket between earth and sun. Despite its weight, she feels the lightness of being free of duties. Once she lived her whole life like this, never knowing how sweet it was to be unencumbered. She is tempted to go to town, to look in the shop windows. But there is likely nothing there she can afford. So instead she takes the overgrown road up the hill to the lighthouse.

She raps hard on the door, then waits. A few moments pass and she suddenly remembers that Matthew sleeps in the afternoon. She is both mortified that she might have woken him and disappointed that he won't wake and she won't see him.

Footsteps inside. The door opens. "Isabella?" he says, wiping a hand over his beard.

"I'm sorry. Did I wake you?"

"No. I was just finishing some paperwork."

"I need to send a telegram to my sister."

"Then come in," he says. "Come in."

The smell of the place overwhelms her: she associates it with the safe haven she found after days of hardship, and one sniff of it makes her feel safe and somehow sad, as though a good time has passed. She goes straight past the staircase to the round table and sits down.

Matthew brings her a form and a fountain pen. "Here," he says, sliding them in front of her. "Fill out the address and the message."

"How much will it cost?"

Matthew shakes his head. "I won't charge you."

Isabella fills out the address, then hesitates. What is she to write? Then her heart starts: what if her sister contacts the Winterbournes?

Matthew sees her hesitate and says, "What's wrong?"

"Perhaps it's not safe to tell her where I am."

"Do you trust her?"

Isabella thinks about this, then nods.

"Do you trust her husband?"

"I've only met him once. But he seemed a lovely fellow."

Matthew shrugs. "Only you can decide."

Isabella shakes herself. "I'm being foolish. If I intend to go to her for safe haven, then I must trust her." After all, she trusts Matthew. As the rain begins outside, hammering on the tin roof of the cottage, she writes: *Coming to stay with you as soon as I can. May be some months. Have left Arthur and have no money. Contact me via the light station at Lighthouse Bay in Queensland, Australia, but don't tell a soul.* Then she puts the pen down and hands the form to Matthew. He takes it to the telegraph room; she follows him and stands in the threshold to watch. She wonders if he has heard of the wreck of the *Aurora* but is keeping his "no questions" promise. He begins to tap out the message.

She hears the clacking of the tapper, and the reel starts to turn. Isabella doesn't understand how it works, or where her message has gone now, but when Matthew is finished he turns to her and hands her back her form.

"No, I can't take it with me. You dispose of it for me."

Matthew tears it in half and drops it in a wastepaper basket.

"How long will it be before she gets it?" Isabella asks. "Can I wait?"

"Oh, no. It may take some time for your message to arrive. It's not instant. For all its innovation, this is a primitive form of communication at its heart. A medieval lighting of beacons, from one hill to another. It takes only one lookout to miss the flare and the message can sit at somebody's desk for days, unread."

She fights disappointment. "And you will let me know if she telegraphs me in return?"

"I will deliver the message to you at Mrs. Fullbright's."

"But don't give it to anyone else. They mustn't know. Mrs. Fullbright thinks my name is Mary."

"I'll be discreet." He smiles. "Have you been well?"

"I've been too busy to be unwell," she replies. She wants to stay a little longer, she wants to sink into the comfort of the lighthouse. Outside the rain is cold and heavy. "Could I trouble you for a cup of tea? It's too wet to walk home yet."

He hesitates.

"I'm sorry," she says, realizing she is interrupting his day. "You must get to sleep."

"It's not that . . ." he says, and she knows what he is thinking: it won't do. If anyone sees her staying here for longer than is necessary, people will talk. But Isabella doesn't share his fear. Nobody has seen her arrive, and they are unlikely to see her leave. She hasn't brought an umbrella, so he can't turn her out. She finds his concern endearing. He is clearly a man with a responsible nature, and he is protective of her.

"Please? I will drink it quickly and go as soon as the rain stops."

This makes him chuckle, and his eyes crinkle up sweetly. "A pot of tea, then," he says. "Please, make yourself comfortable."

He lights the stove and puts on the kettle. "How do you find living with the Fullbrights?"

"A little exhausting. I'm not used to service. But the little boy is a delight." She hesitates, then plunges forward. "His birthday is the same day as Daniel's."

Matthew half-turns, raises an eyebrow. "That must be . . ."

"I thought it would be difficult. I thought I would always be looking at him, thinking about Daniel. But he is his own boy. Do you not think it strange, though? A coincidence? Their names have only a few letters different, just the consonants. Of all the people I should meet, after all the miles I have come . . ." She trails off. Dimly, she is aware that she sounds a little mad; but she is used to being considered a little mad.

"But he is his own boy. As you say," Matthew finishes for her. "He isn't Daniel."

"Of course," she says, and an unexpected desolation washes over her, as though a window has been opened in a warm room, letting in the first edge of a bitter wind.

The kettle boils and Matthew wordlessly makes the tea. Isabella sits and waits, wishing for something she cannot articulate. She had been feeling fine and light, just half an hour ago. Now the dark network of memories is closing around her again, just as the dark clouds outside are pressing out all the light.

But the tea helps. Hot and sweet.

"Tell me about your sister," he says gently. "Are you close?"

Isabella smiles, thinking of Victoria: as dark as she is fair. "We were terribly close as children. We grew up on the north Cornish coast, though Papa and Mama were from London—Papa the son of an MP—so we didn't speak like everybody else. Father was a jeweler. Oh, he was quite mad. He'd work late into the night, with his hair all stuck up." She gestured to her own hair. "He had the strangest clients: barons and so on from European towns I'd never heard of. He was terribly popular. All his jewels were made with cold connections. Do you know what that means? Without solder. Every clasp bent and wrapped into shape by hand. His hands were so strong he could crush a tea tin with his fingertips. After Mama died, he let us run wild. We'd spend all day down at the beach collecting shells and stones, then come home and make brooches and bracelets." Isabella drops her eyes, thinking of Arthur. Once in her life, she'd mistakenly thought that she and Arthur would have so much in common. But Arthur never took joy in making jewels, not the way Papa did. Everything Arthur did was passionless. Bloodless.

"Do you not think it strange," she asks, after a few silent sips, "that I haven't missed my husband at all?"

"No. I presume you left him because he didn't treat you well."

"Sometimes I worry that there is something wrong with my heart."

Matthew doesn't answer. He seems comfortable simply to sit and wait for her to continue.

"Perhaps it is broken," she says. "Not a broken heart in the usual sense, not a simple crack down the middle. But broken like a clock that has been taken down from the mantel, disassembled by a rough hand, then left in pieces on the floor. Broken so it cannot work right again." She checks herself. She is talking too much about nonsense. If Arthur were here, he would admonish her for drawing attention to herself with her wild ideas.

But Arthur isn't here, he's dead at the bottom of the sea.

"My husband is dead, Matthew," she says softly.

"Then what have you run away from?"

"His family."

He nods, seems about to say something, then thinks better of it. "You don't have to tell me anything. In fact, it's probably better if you don't."

She tries to be bright. "Then you shall think me too mysterious. A secret keeper. Perhaps even a liar."

He holds her gaze in his a moment, another moment, time winding out. She is acutely aware of his masculine presence, the oil-and-sea smells, the darkness of his eyes.

"I couldn't think ill of you," he says at last. "Put it out of your mind."

Something flares into life inside her, something she has never felt properly before, so at first it puzzles her. A warmth, down low. A tide of longing to press her whole length against his. This is desire. She desires Matthew, the lighthouse keeper. It surprises her, but not unhappily. She doesn't know what to do, so she stays where she is. It's unlikely he feels the same, and he would not think it proper for her to express her feelings. She finishes her tea. The rain has eased. It is time to go.

"I have stayed too long," she says. "It was terribly selfish of me."

"I've enjoyed your company," he says, and she thinks she detects discomfort. No doubt he has seen her desire and it has embarrassed him.

She pushes back the stool and stands. "I wish you a good rest."

"And I will let you know the moment your sister responds."

They stand like that a moment, regarding each other. Then Isabella is heading for the door and down the damp path to town.

*   *   *

$\mathscr{A}$ week passes with no news from her sister. She tries to make sense of it. Perhaps she will receive a letter instead of a telegram, with money in it. Perhaps her sister is away and hasn't yet received her message. Perhaps she is busy with her new baby and it has slipped her mind. Or perhaps . . . perhaps her sister doesn't want her to come. Isabella goes on hoping, day after day. It will be some time before she has saved the money anyway. She works hard, she tries to stay cheerful for Xavier, and she waits.

Katarina and Ernest argue every night. Isabella puts Xavier to bed at six, helps Cook clean up until seven, then goes to the nursery and collapses into her own bed exhausted. Within an hour, perhaps when they think she is asleep and doesn't hear them, they start. She can't hear their words, just their voices, so she doesn't know how or why they start. But it is as predictable as nightfall. Most of the time it is just a little shouting. Sometimes it is slamming of doors. Sometimes Katarina shrieks as though it would make her throat bleed. Isabella has learned not to interfere. Her job is to keep Xavier safe. She is happy to be behind the locked hallway door at night.

Tonight she is lying in her bed in Lighthouse Bay, but her imagination is away in America with her sister. They are drinking tea together. Victoria's infant coos softly on Isabella's lap. She builds the scene in such detail that she wonders if she could ever bear to open her eyes and see where she really is. But slowly noises filter into her furtive imagining. Voices within the house. The argument starts and she barely notices. But it escalates rapidly, and within a few minutes there is the sound of smashing glass or crockery. Each smash is punctuated by a devilish shriek from Katarina, so Isabella knows it is Ernest on the receiving end of the storm. Xavier stirs and Isabella shoots out of bed to smooth his hair.

But this time he doesn't go back to sleep. He sits up and his little face is working hard not to fall. Ernest is shouting at Katarina so loudly that they can hear the words. "Whore! Hellcat!"

Xavier finds Isabella in the dark with his eyes and starts to cry.

"Sh, sh," she says, stroking his hair.

Xavier launches himself into her arms and she presses his warm body against hers and holds him firmly. The argument continues. It sounds as though everything in the house is being thrown. Isabella presses one of Xavier's ears against her breast, and covers the other with her hand. He sobs against her for a little while, then seems to settle.

The shouting has died down. There are sounds of shards being picked up, angry talking but no more murderous fury. Isabella gently lifts Xavier and brings him back to her bed. Katarina would never condone it, but Katarina thinks it well enough to frighten the child with her anger, and barely touches Xavier. A child needs comfort, and Isabella has so much comfort to offer.

They curl together on their sides in bed, his compact body tucked inside the curve of hers. She clasps her arm around him, sniffs his hair, feels his soft heat, and the tick-tick of his little heart. "Don't worry, don't worry," she says, "I will keep you safe."

His pulse begins to slow, he settles into her. She can hear him sucking his thumb rhythmically. After a few moments, he is fast asleep.

But Isabella lies awake a little longer. In the dark, she can imagine this is Daniel. Her own child. He would come to her for comfort, and, oh, she would give it to him. She would live to be all his comfort. She would love him so well, make him feel so safe and treasured . . .

She begins to drift off, and the veil between reality and fantasy lifts and she is with Daniel, curled together in bed while the night deepens towards midnight, and all is well in the world.

*P*ercy is afraid of his mother. Many men are afraid of his mother. The only man who wasn't was his father, and he has been dead for several years.

Mother still believes Arthur may be alive. She refuses to accept that the ship is not just late, it is sunk. She believes that even if it is sunk, Arthur has somehow clung to a piece of wood and has now, no doubt, made a hut for himself on the beach and is eating coconuts and awaiting rescue.

"They are incompetent fools!" she rages, as Percy tells her the local constabulary at Cape Franklin cannot say with certainty whether debris they have found belongs to the *Aurora*. "A good British marine officer could tell in a heartbeat. Arthur would have been found by now! The mace would have been recovered! I do not want our family name forever associated with losing a gift from the Queen!"

It is late on a Sunday evening. Sundays tire Mother out terribly, what with church and then Sunday roast for dinner. Percy sits opposite her in the conservatory, and lets her rage against the Queensland marine authorities. He knows his moment will come. Last week, he made a terrible error. He sent the wrong figures to the bank and cost the business five hundred pounds. Mother hasn't discovered yet, but he knows if he plays her right this evening he can be a long way away before she does find out.

"You know what would be best?" Percy says, in a gap in her tirade. "If somebody who represents the family could go and try to find him."

"Like who? Charles Simmons? He wouldn't last a moment on

a ship, let alone on a desert island." Mother thinks Australia is a small place with one palm tree and a lagoon.

Percy waits a moment, then says, "I am willing to go. Simmons can take over from me. I'll find Arthur and the mace, and bring them home safely."

Percy does not believe Arthur will be brought home safely, but he is certain he wants to get to the mace before somebody else does; somebody who would think themselves so far from law and civilization that they would steal it. He cannot bear the thought of some hairy savage, with the mace in his hut, using the jewels to decorate his loincloth. Or a lowly sailor saving it from the wreck, only to take it home and melt it down and laugh at the Winterbourne family.

"We can't spare you, and your wife and children certainly can't spare you," Mother says, but Percy hears in her voice she is almost wavering. Arthur means a great deal to her; Percy doesn't. "It will take too long."

"A steamer can have me there in seven or eight weeks. Mother"— he drops his voice low so she has to sit forward to hear—"who else would show the care and attention to detail necessary to find a lost brother? Who else can we trust? Nobody. I am Arthur's flesh and blood."

Mother considers, knitting and unknitting her plump fingers in the lamplight. Finally she says, "You are right. You should go."

Percy breathes a sigh of relief. Out and away. No more office, no more numbers. "Very well," he says, "I shall organize it in the morning."

Fifteen

For a month, Xavier has slept in Isabella's bed at night. They both take comfort from the practice, so it continues. Isabella knows that Katarina would be displeased, but Katarina locks them in this part of the house alone together every night; she won't know. And it isn't as though Katarina lavishes the child with physical affection: she barely touches him. She has no right to be jealous of the embraces Isabella takes. A thing that isn't valued cannot be stolen.

Isabella thinks herself safe from discovery, but she hasn't reckoned on the most unreliable of vessels: the bladder of a three-year-old child. Early one morning, before the dark has lifted, she wakes in a warm puddle.

"Oh, no," she says softly.

Xavier wakes, whimpers.

"All is well, little one," she says, lighting a lantern and scooping him up. He is soaked. Her nightgown is soaked. The bedding is soaked. "Let's get you clean and dry."

She takes him across to the bathroom, strips off his sodden clothes and sponges him down as he blinks in the lamplight. Goose bumps rise across his skin, and she rubs his arms briskly. She is growing cold as the wet nightgown sticks to her legs. "There," she says. "A pair of fresh pajamas and you can go in your own bed."

He shakes his head and puts his arms up. He wants to sleep with her.

"The bed's all wet now. You have to go in your own bed." She leads him back across the hallway, dresses him and puts him to bed. He clings to her hand, so she kneels next to him, cold and wet, while he falls to sleep. Gently, she extricates her hand and strips off her own clothes, her own sheets. The mattress is wet, so she sponges it uselessly. She needs to get it outside in air and sunshine. She needs the laundry, and she needs it when Cook isn't around to catch her.

But of course she is locked in this section of the house. Isabella brings her lantern and holds it up to the keyhole. Katarina has left the key in the lock on the other side. All she needs is a sheet of paper . . . one of Xavier's drawings does the trick. She slides it under the door, then with the long end of a paintbrush pushes the key out of the keyhole. It lands with a soft clunk on the paper and she pulls it under to her side, then unlocks the door. Quietly, she takes her damp load through the kitchen and down the back stairs to the laundry.

She lights the copper and waits for it to fill with water. Through the floorboards she can see the first flush of dawn. Birds sing, but these are the harsh-voiced birds of Australia. Not robins and blackbirds. One, which Katarina calls a kookaburra, makes a noise that sounds exactly like maniacal laughter. Isabella is so busy listening to birds and the flow of water that she doesn't hear Cook come up behind her.

"Mary?"

Isabella turns with a guilty jump. "Oh, Cook. I'm sorry. Did I wake you?"

"No, I always get up at this time. But you don't. And you've never heated the copper before." Cook surveyed the heap of laundry. "Your sheets?"

Isabella knows she must protect her secret. "I . . . I soiled them."

Cook glances away, embarrassed, and mutters, "Well, I expect it can happen to anyone." She reaches down and gingerly pulls up the corner of the sheet. As she does, Xavier's sodden pajamas plop down on to the dirt floor. Both women look at the pajamas, then look at each other. Isabella holds her breath.

"This is wrong," Cook says. "You mustn't get so close to the child."

"It was only the once," Isabella says. "He had a bad dream."

"If Mrs. Fullbright finds out, she'll send you away and you won't see the child at all."

"Please don't tell her."

Cook presses her lips together tightly, and they form an upside-down horseshoe.

"Please," Isabella says again, quickly throwing the pajamas, her own nightgown and the sheets into the copper. "No harm is done. Xavier gets no affection from his parents and I—"

"Don't think to judge them. Have you never been in service before?"

Slowly, Isabella shakes her head.

Cook narrows her eyes. "I might have guessed it, I suppose. So, where are you from?"

"It doesn't matter. I'm in service now and I want to do the right thing and earn money. And I want to do what's best for Xavier."

"His mother and father decide what's best for him. All you have to do is follow instructions. Mrs. Fullbright doesn't want the likes of us holding her child, and she sure as sure doesn't want you sleeping in the same bed as him. I won't tell her, not this time. But make sure it doesn't happen again."

"Of course. Of course."

Cook softens, touches Isabella's sleeve. "Mary, don't get so close to the child. Not just for his sake, but for your own. Nannies don't last long in this household. Eventually they get the blame for Xavier not speaking and the Fullbrights let them go. If you do need the money, keep your head down and don't give them an extra reason to get rid of you. Don't let him in your bed. No good will come of it."

Isabella nods, but she isn't persuaded. She intends to do exactly as she has done. She wasn't secretive enough, that is all. If it happens again, she will know better. They won't stop her sleeping with her boy.

Isabella waits, crouched behind the sofa, smiling too hard. She hears footsteps, soft and uncertain. Xavier is looking for her. He draws closer, she holds her breath . . .

"Boo!" she says, springing out from behind the sofa.

He jumps, then cackles loudly, banging the wooden spoon on the saucepan lid that he carries around during hide-and-go-seek. It is his way of saying, "I found you," without words. Laughing and clattering, he runs away, his feet thundering on the wooden floorboards. She runs after him, laughing too.

The door to Katarina's bedroom opens.

"Mary!" she says sharply.

Isabella turns, immediately quiet. Xavier hesitates in the kitchen, looking back towards her with big, frightened eyes.

Katarina gestures towards the child. "Why must he make that noise? Take the saucepan lid from him."

"It's how he lets me know he's found me."

Katarina's face works: Isabella thinks she sees anger, shame, perhaps a fleeting trace of sadness. Then she composes herself and says, "He should use words."

The silence draws out. Isabella won't speak of Xavier's perceived deficiencies in front of him. His thumb has gone to his mouth.

"Get that thumb out of your mouth," Katarina shouts at him. "And both of you go outside. I have a headache. I have no desire to hear such noisy nonsense."

Isabella bristles. How heartless must this woman be to speak to a small child so sharply? But she also bristles for herself: told off in such a fashion. If Katarina knew who she was, how rich her husband's family was . . .

But they are not her family. She doesn't want them to be her family. And alone in the world, she has nothing.

"Come, Xavier," she says to the little boy. "Let's play hide-and-go-seek in the garden instead."

They walk quietly down the back stairs and, for a little while, play prudently. But Xavier loves hide-and-go-seek, and is soon squealing with laughter and happily banging his saucepan lid. The sun is shining from somewhere very high. The seasons are all backwards: it is May, but autumn is here. The sky seems cooler and the leaves on the birch at the bottom of the garden are turning brown. There is a smell of sea salt and wood smoke on the air, and Xavier's laughter seems to ring all the way to heaven. They hide, they seek, they chase, they catch. Grass stains on their knees, faces flushed.

Then Isabella counts to ten, her face hidden in her hands down at the back fence. She turns—Xavier has disappeared. She looks at the last hiding space, but he's not there. She tries the other trees and bushes, but he's not there.

She leaves the sunny garden for the laundry: not there. But she sees that one of the floorboards is missing on the far side of the laundry. She approaches and finds the board right next to it is broken and loose. It can be pushed aside, leaving just enough room for a little boy to squeeze through and round to the side of the house. Isabella squeezes too, barely making it through, and finds herself in a part of the garden she has never seen before. Behind the laundry, down the side of the house, Xavier is squatting and playing with something on the ground. The grass on this small strip of garden is patchy, covered in weeds. A high fence cuts it off from the front garden. It is a non-place, and yet Xavier has found something very interesting.

"What have you got there?" she says, kneeling next to him.

He holds up two cigar butts, one in each hand.

Isabella quickly but gently brushes them out of his hands. They fall to the ground, and she sees that there are dozens of them, right under a window. She goes through the downstairs floor plan in her head, and realizes they are outside the forbidden room. There will be trouble if she is found here. She pulls Xavier to his feet. "No, Xavier, those things are very dirty. Must not touch."

He holds his hands out, the signal that he wants her to wash his hands. She quickly but quietly leads him back to the laundry, pushes an empty barrel against the broken board so he can't make his way through again, and takes him to the tub to soap up his hands. As she tends to him, she considers what she has just seen. A collection of cigar butts just outside the window, as though they have been thrown there by somebody inside. Is this Katarina's terrible secret? That she enjoys smoking cigars? It isn't a sin, but Isabella can imagine if Arthur had discovered she had such a habit: he would have given her the cruelest edge of his tongue. So, perhaps she can understand the secrecy.

She dries Xavier's hands briskly and looks down. His little face is turned up to hers, shining with happiness. She smiles and the words are on her lips before she has the wisdom to recall them. "My little boy," she says. He throws himself at her, wrapping his arms around her legs and burying his face in her skirt. He is hers, just as she is his. They belong to each other.

*I*sabella tries not to think about Matthew during the day, but at night she sometimes lifts the corner of her restraint and lets thoughts of him in. It has been so long since she has seen him that he has almost become a fictional character in her world: the dark-eyed, musk-scented man who rescued her, who holds her at arm's-length for her own good. She is almost surprised, when she sees him at the greengrocer's one morning, to find that he is real.

Xavier's hand is warm in hers as she approaches him, thoughts of buying potatoes for supper forgotten. "Matthew?"

He glances up and sees her, smiles almost as though he cannot help it. "Mary," he says carefully. "And this is little Master Fullbright."

"Xavier," she says, a protective hand on the child's shoulder. "Xavier, meet Mr. Seaward, the lighthouse keeper."

Xavier is shy or frightened or both, and hides his face in Isabella's skirts. Isabella rubs his back softly. "There, darling, don't be afraid."

"Hello, Xavier. It's a pleasure to meet you," says Matthew, crouching to be at the little boy's level.

Xavier risks a glance, responds to Matthew's warm smile with a shudder and buries his face again. Matthew stands, chuckling. "Children never much like me on first sight."

"You are rather tall and foreboding," Isabella says, then regrets it. Will he take it as an insult? She changes the subject quickly. "You haven't yet heard back from my sister, Mr. Seaward?"

His forehead crumples in concern. "No. No telegram. I hope

that she has sent you a letter and it is taking time to get here. I will alert you the minute I know."

"Yes, a letter will take time to come, I expect. It has only been six weeks."

He nods. "Yes. It feels longer since . . ." He doesn't finish his sentence and she knows why. *It feels longer since I last saw you* sounds romantic, not pragmatic. And Matthew Seaward, she knows, is a pragmatic man. Isabella can tell he is thinking about saying something more, but his eyes go to Xavier and he remains silent. The silence lingers. She doesn't want him to go, but she knows he will.

"I must get on," he says.

"It was lovely to see you." She wants more. She wants him to invite her for tea. Invite her to stand on the deck of the lonely lighthouse at dusk and watch the night roll over the sky, with her hand in his. But where do these errant thoughts come from?

"Farewell, Master Fullbright," Matthew says, and Xavier risks a slight nod.

Then Matthew is gone. She squeezes Xavier's hand. "Come, little one," she says. "Cook needs a few things for supper."

*M*atthew paces.

On the stairs. Around the deck. Through the cottage. Finally he comes to a stop in the telegraph office, his long blunt fingers making delicate patterns on the desk. Night has fallen, the light is working, he has a little spare time.

Isabella hasn't heard from her sister. Matthew knew this, but seeing her disappointment has woken an itch in his belly. Isabella is still stuck here in Lighthouse Bay, and she calls the Fullbright child "darling" as if he were her own.

That's the point that troubles him the most. She looked so happy with Xavier. She looked like a mother, proud of her child. But Xavier isn't her child; Xavier belongs to the Fullbrights, who are as volatile as they are wealthy. Matthew should have realized that taking care of another woman's child was no fit task for Isabella, who had lost her own. He should never have recommended the position to her. Isabella needs her sister; she needs a reason to get away.

He has kept the address, of course. This time, he sends the telegram from himself, a single line asking whether or not Mrs. Victoria King is still at the address. He also sends it because he cannot be sure the original message made it. Every telegrapher relies on the next in the chain.

He pushes back his chair and walks up the steep spiral staircase, to stand alone on the deck awhile. The sea has been his only companion for twenty years; this view for the last six. But tonight her ceaseless movement cannot comfort him. Seeing Isabella is no good for him, no good for him at all. Her wild sweetness gets between his skin and his bones. It makes him feel bruised from the inside.

In the distance, the light picks up the ghostly shape of a ship at full sail. Fewer and fewer ships now come to Australia under sail. Lumbering steam ships beetle along the horizon more often now. He feels the passing of one time into another; the passing of elegant might into ugly practicality. He thinks about Clovis McCarthy, descending the lighthouse stairs for the last time. One day that will be Matthew, too old to manage the light anymore, a relic from the past. And what then? What loneliness and emptiness lie beyond that date?

Now he is getting sentimental. He gathers himself, goes back down the stairs and busies himself with his usual night duties. As he does every night. And it is after three more nights like this that the return telegram comes to him: *No longer at this abode. No forwarding address given.*

Matthew closes his eyes and rubs the bridge of his nose. Isabella's sister has moved. That is why she hasn't responded. She doesn't know Isabella needs her. Matthew feels Isabella's helplessness in the world. What will she do if she can't get to her sister's? Go back to the family-in-law she despises? Stay at the Fullbrights' until they throw her out for getting too close to Xavier? She is as fragile as a bird. These things might break her. The vision of her, collapsing at the door that first night he met her, comes to mind. And while he knows that her collapse was due to the hardship of her journey on foot, he can't help but see it as a signifier of her nature: she can only go so far, and then she will simply stop, crumple, disintegrate.

Matthew sighs, opens his eyes. He has at his disposal a telegraph machine. Whatever he can do, he will do to track down Isabella's sister.

The sky burns blue above Isabella and Xavier as they walk hand in hand along the beach collecting shells. It is only recently that Isabella can set foot on the sand without cold dread creeping through her: the memories of her long trek are still shadowy nightmares in her mind. But it helps that Xavier loves the beach and the sand, and so before the heat of the afternoon sets in she helps him pull on his hat and shoes and bag, and off they go.

Xavier particularly loves the slender dark pink shells. Isabella is always looking out for perfect white ones. Together they walk on the hard sand near the shore line, occasionally disappearing up to their ankles as the waves wash around them. The big blue-green rollers lift and curl, white horses on their backs, then crash and echo against each other. The sun is warm but not harsh. Xavier finds a long stick of driftwood and shows it to Isabella. Its end is worn down to a point, like a pencil.

"That is a wonderful stick," she says. "Good lad."

Xavier pushes the end into the sand, then turns around slowly, drawing a circle around him. Isabella claps, then goes up the beach for seaweed to arrange at the top of the circle for hair. Xavier watches as she makes eyes from shells, then finally a big grin from a collection of moss green pipis. Xavier finishes it off by drawing two uneven ears.

The sea roars on. A seagull flaps past overhead, crying loudly.

They smile at each other in the sunshine. Isabella remembers Daniel's face, and tries to imagine what he might have looked like, had she been smiling at him now rather than at Xavier. But his baby features were not yet distinct enough, and she finds herself imagining that he would simply look like Xavier. That somehow Xavier and Daniel, having shared a birthday, were the same person. Dimly, she is aware that this is not rational, but in her heart she feels it is good sense. There is a rightness about her and Xavier being together, alone on the beach in the sunshine, while the world and all its petty mundaneness ticks along on the other side of the pandanuses and wattle trees.

Then Xavier points at the drawing and says, as clearly as the seagull's cry, "It's a smiling face."

At first Isabella cannot believe what she has heard. Xavier, nearly three, has never spoken. *Never.* Not "Mama" nor "Dada" nor "supper" nor "play with me." And here, now, he has said a complete sentence. She is so shocked that at first she doesn't answer, then suddenly realizes she *must* answer or risk discouraging him from ever speaking again.

"Yes," she says. "He must be happy." Then for good measure she adds, "As happy as I am when I'm with you."

"He must be happy," Xavier echoes, then his thumb goes back in his mouth.

"Are you happy, Xavier?" she asks.

He nods silently; then, as if nothing astonishing has happened, he continues up the beach looking for more pink shells.

Isabella gathers herself. She knows she should take him home and tell Katarina, but she relishes being the only woman to have heard the child's sweet voice. She is special to Xavier: this surely proves it. He didn't speak to his mother, he spoke to Isabella.

She knows, then, that she will not tell Katarina. Let her spend enough time with her son that she finds out herself.

Isabella hides a smile: perhaps Xavier won't talk to anyone but her. The bright sun shines just for her.

"Xavier, wait for me, my love," she calls after him, as a wave runs onto the beach, washing away their sand picture.

Sixteen

Isabella is on the floor, on her stomach, pretending to be a worm. Xavier giggles madly, as sweet as a little chiming bell. He is supposed to be the bird but cannot stop laughing long enough to play his part. From here, Isabella can see the pieces of a jigsaw puzzle under her bed and knows that it won't be long until Cook or Katarina or perhaps even Ernest tells her she spends too much time playing and not enough time cleaning up. But when she is with Xavier, tidy doesn't count. Just the present counts, and holding on to it for as long as possible.

"Worm," says Xavier, pointing at her. "Worm."

She is used to him speaking now, although it has only been a few words each day. He still hasn't made a sound in front of his parents. She points back at him. "Bird. Come along. Your turn."

Footsteps approaching make him shrink and pop his thumb back in his mouth. Isabella sits up, brushing dust from the front of her dress. The door to the nursery opens and Katarina stands there.

"I'm sorry if we're too noisy—" Isabella starts, but Katarina holds up her hand to silence her.

"Mr. Seaward from the telegraph office is here to see you."

Her words suggest she is puzzled, perhaps disapproving, but mostly irritated.

Isabella leaps to her feet. It must be news from her sister. She doesn't want anyone to overhear anything, so she says to Katarina, "Would you mind sitting with Xavier while I talk to Mr. Seaward?"

Katarina glances at Xavier as though she might be frightened of him, then forces a smile. "Why, no, I don't mind." Then as Isabella leaves the room she adds, "Don't be long, will you?"

Matthew waits at the door, two steps down. Isabella doesn't know whether Katarina didn't invite him in, or whether Matthew refused to come in. Probably the latter. He speaks without greeting her. "I haven't a telegram for you. I'm sorry."

Isabella realizes he is managing her anticipation. She deflates. "No word?"

He shakes his head, spreads his hands and speaks quietly. "I'm sorry, but your sister isn't at that address anymore."

Silence. No, not silence. She can hear the sea in the distance, the wind in the tops of the tall eucalypts, the crows in the garden. Above it all, she can feel the loud thrum of her blood coursing around her body. But there is a pause in life, as everything she believes becomes something new. "Not there?"

"She must have moved house."

"But why would she not tell me?"

"Perhaps she did. Perhaps she sent a letter to you in England."

Yes. That was it. And even now that letter is waiting for her back in the house she once shared with Arthur. "But how am I ever to find her now?"

Matthew moves to touch her hand, then pulls back at the last moment. She tastes the regret in the space between them. "I am doing what I can to find her."

"If you don't find her . . ." A wave of desolation rises up, crashing over her. What is she to do? Where is she to go? Her hand flails out, reaching for the doorjamb to support herself. She loses her balance, but he catches her hand, grasps it firmly. He steadies her with his grip, and she can see his forearm flexing against the cotton of his sleeve. She is on her own feet again and he doesn't let go. He doesn't let go. Still he doesn't let go. His heat travels through her fingers to the rest of her body. She flushes. He tries to pull his hand away, but she clasps his fingers in her own. "Don't let me go," she whispers.

"I will find her," Matthew says. He gently tugs his hand away and this time she releases it. "Be patient, Isabella, and don't lose heart."

Isabella thinks of Xavier waiting for her in the nursery. She tries to warm herself on the thought of him, but even this is tainted because when she finds her sister, when she has saved enough, she will have to leave Xavier. She feels lost in the world. She closes her eyes, feels time flowing through her, knocking her feet from under her.

"Isabella? Are you well?"

"I should get back to my little boy," she says, half-turning away.

"*Your* little boy?" he says.

Irritation itches her. "What do you mean by your tone? Xavier loves me and has come to rely on me." She drops her voice and leans forward. Even though Matthew is standing two steps below her and his face is level with hers. "He has spoken. To me. Nobody else."

Matthew seems about to say something, then stops himself. It is too late; she knows what he is thinking.

"He is my responsibility. That is all I meant," she finishes. "Why should I not call him 'mine'? No harm is done by it."

"I'm sure you are right," he concedes, dropping his head. "Good-bye. I will let you know the moment I hear anything."

She watches him move off down the stairs, then across the lawn and out the front gate. He doesn't look back.

Isabella stands a moment, collecting herself. Her joints feel loose, as though they might bend the wrong way. A flash of memory comes to her, of being at home with Arthur, sitting by the fire on a chill February evening. Arthur reading his paper, Isabella sewing, her round pregnant belly serving as a table for her embroidery ring. Such an ordinary time. Everything so reliable. Certainly she wasn't happy, but nor was she unhappy. The nightmare was still to come. The ground was still stable beneath her feet.

"Mary? Is everything well with you?"

Isabella turns to see Katarina emerging from the hallway, her hand firmly around Xavier's wrist.

"Yes, yes," Isabella says. "I am expecting a telegram from my sister. Mr. Seaward was simply letting me know the communication has been delayed."

Katarina thrusts Xavier towards her. "Take him out for some fresh air. I've given myself a headache entertaining him. I must go and lie down."

"Shall we collect some leaves in the front garden?" she says to him. She longs to press him against her and take comfort in his warm little body, but not while Katarina is watching.

Xavier nods solemnly and Isabella leads him from the house on unsteady feet, out into the strange warm winter so far from her home.

The horse and carriage rattles up the mountain path. Xavier sits between Isabella and Katarina. Ahead of them, leading the way in another carriage, is Ernest, his friend and business partner Abel Barrett and Abel's wife Edwina. The sun is bright, and the unfamiliar smells of the Australian forest surround them: Isabella now recognizes the sharp, medicinal smells of eucalpyt and tea tree, but there are other smells she cannot place. Birds chirp deep off the track. It is Sunday and they are going for a picnic. The basket of food is between Isabella's feet. Cook packed it this morning, looking relieved that she didn't have to come.

Katarina brags that she is a fine horsewoman, that she won prizes in her youth in Costa Daurada. She certainly handles the whip and reins well. She wears a frothy white dress and a large white hat. Isabella wears the yellow dress she took from the light-house. She has tried to tie the waist so it doesn't swim on her, but it is of little use. She thinks about the blue muslin gown in her trunk at the bottom of the sea, then reminds herself that she has no need to keep pace with Katarina's beauty. She surreptitiously squeezes Xavier's hand. There is no competition.

They have been traveling for an hour, and they are still only on the low slopes. The men's cigar smoke wafts back towards Isabella. She can hear only snatches of conversation and thinks Ernest and Abel terribly dull men. Abel's wife cackles occasionally, trying hard to keep up with their boorish jokes. Every time Edwina laughs, Katarina's jaw tightens and Isabella wonders if Katarina wishes she were in the carriage with the men, rather than stuck here with the child and his nanny.

"Is it much farther?" Isabella asks.

"No, the path runs out soon. One can only make it to the top of the mountain on foot, and we'll hardly be doing that today. There's a little clearing on the northern side where we like to lay out our food. You can see the ocean and the mountains. It's very beautiful."

Isabella is taken by the idea that Katarina finds this place beautiful. She had suspected that Katarina, like herself, missed the familiar landscape of home. "More beautiful than where you come from?"

Katarina glances at her, smiling tightly. "In Spain I was not rich. I think money makes things more beautiful." She turns her eyes back to the path. "Men, for instance."

Isabella doesn't answer. She wonders that Katarina can speak in such a way in front of her son. But she suspects that Katarina underestimates Xavier: perhaps she has forgotten that although he doesn't speak he can hear and understand.

"Where are you from, Mary?" Katarina continues.

"Cornwall, ma'am. Southwest England."

"Do you miss it?"

"Sometimes."

"Do you dream of going back?"

"I'll never go back." The finality of her own statement makes her sad. Where will she go? Is her sister even in New York still? She could be on the next street over or she could be on a different continent, anywhere in the world.

"Good." Katarina smiles, but this time it's a little cruel. "All my other nannies leave me, so you'll forgive me for being wary. It's good to know that your heart is here with you."

But where is Isabella's heart? She puzzles over this for a moment, then chides herself for forgetting. It is in Daniel's grave. As she thinks this, a cloud crosses the sun and for one superstitious instant she wonders if she has caused the brief chill that follows. But then the carriage carrying the men pulls off the path and climbs over a hump and down the other side to a grassy clearing. They follow and soon come to rest. They are perhaps halfway up the northern side of the mountain—not a very high mountain, more of a volcanic hill rising out of the flat coastal land—where there is a broad rocky plateau. There are no trees to block the view of the ocean. It is even more vast from high up; the breakers, silenced by distance, seem to move more slowly, thoughtfully. The air is clear and cool. Isabella helps Xavier out of the carriage, then kneels to button his jacket. Katarina has already disappeared to talk with Ernest, Abel and Edwina. She adjusts her own bonnet, then leads Xavier to the others.

"Would you like me to set up your picnic here, then?" Isabella asks.

"Yes, that would be capital," says Abel Barrett with a sniff of his nose. He has a strong jaw, bright blue eyes and thick curly hair. His wife, Edwina, is far less attractive than he is—a peahen— and her eyes rarely leave his face. She wears an expression of mild astonishment, as though she can't believe this terribly handsome man is hers to keep.

Xavier hangs about Isabella as she lays out the picnic rug and sets it with plates and cutlery and cups. The others have moved off a few yards to take in the view. She hears Abel explain that Lighthouse Bay was so named because one of the early explor- ers saw, from this very position, that the first beams of the dawn sun illuminated the point before any other place in view: the point where the lighthouse now stands. Isabella likes the idea that Matthew is greeted by the sun before everyone else. She glances over her shoulder and can see the white needle of the lighthouse, and wonders what Matthew is doing right at this moment.

Cook has prepared cut sandwiches and fruit, and baked an apple pie. Isabella lays it all out neatly. Ernest has brought with him a bottle of whiskey and a bottle of wine, and Isabella is star- tled to see how quickly the women drink. She has drunk one glass of claret in her life, and didn't much like the way it made her stomach feel. Xavier hangs about her, helping her unfold napkins and polish silverware. The others are rowdy already, drunk on the promise of being drunk later.

Katarina calls, "Xavier. Little one, come here to Mama."

Xavier looks alarmed. He glances at Isabella as though for reassurance.

"Go on," she says. "Do what Mama says."

Xavier edges towards them, and Isabella watches from the corner of her eye as she shoos away a fly. Katarina crouches with her arms spread for Xavier. Isabella has never seen her do this. Nor, it seems, has Xavier, who stops in his tracks. Isabella cannot see his face, but she suspects he is frightened by Katarina's sudden show of affection.

"Come here, darling. Give me a big kiss," Katarina says to the child. "Don't be shy." Then she turns her face to Edwina and rolls her eyes. "He isn't very bright, but Mama still loves him."

Isabella's stomach clenches with anger. She understands, now, that Katarina is showing off for Edwina. Edwina is older, childless. Katarina is playing the part of an affectionate mother, perhaps to be one up on Edwina, perhaps even to be cruel. Xavier hesitates, and Isabella fears he is going to run right back to the picnic rug in a moment, so she marches up to him and gives him a gentle push on the shoulder. "Go on, Xavier."

Xavier takes a few more hesitant steps and Katarina swoops forward and encloses him in her frothy sleeves. Isabella sees his chubby hand close over Katarina's forearm and the bolt of jealousy is so hard and so steely that she takes a step backwards. Edwina is cooing over Xavier now, while the men drink whiskey and stub out their cigars on the grass. Isabella is outside it all. She doesn't belong here. Xavier doesn't belong to her.

"Lunch is ready," she announces, and a moment later Katarina is handing Xavier back to her, telling her to take him somewhere he won't bother them and give him something to eat. Isabella ushers Xavier ahead of her, grabs the little paper bag

Cook made up specially for him, and takes off into the bushes.

"I can hear a creek," she says, taking his hand as soon as she's confident they are out of sight of his parents. "Shall we see if there are any fish in it?"

Xavier nods and they make their way down through the scrub. She shows him the berries that are safe to eat, and he doesn't question her on how she knows this. Nor does he show a particular fondness for the berries, which taste nowhere near as sweet as the banana packed in his lunch. Together, she and Xavier sit on a large rock with their bare feet in a shallow stream, listening to the birds and warming their shoulders in the sunshine as they eat honey sandwiches.

"Xavier," she ventures, "why won't you talk to Mama?"

He looks at her and shrugs, returns to eating his sandwich.

"Do you love Mama?"

He doesn't answer. His free hand creeps out and clasps hers. Isabella realizes her heart is thudding hard in her throat. She is in so deep with this child, too deep. "I love you, my little boy," she says.

"Mary," he replies, and he pronounces it like his mother with a soft, round "a": Mah-ry. And she can almost hear how he would say, "Mummy."

She opens her mouth to tell him her name is Isabella, so he knows who she really is, but she stops herself. He is too young to understand, surely. He happily munches on his sandwich, unaware that he has made her heart sing.

After they have eaten, they play near the creek's edge, sticking to the shade where they can. There is mud, but that is easily washed off in the cool water of the creek. There are sticks, but they can be left behind before the return to their picnic party. Isabella sinks into the pleasure of being with Xavier, of loving

Xavier and having him love her in return. When they hear Ernest call them, they quickly wash their hands and feet, and reluctantly return to the clearing.

The others are drunk now, their faces flushed from alcohol and sun. The food is all gone, and Abel Barrett dozes on his back in the grass. Edwina, made bold by wine, races over to pick up Xavier and caress him. Katarina stands back magnanimously, reveling in her superiority as the woman who produced such a beautiful child. Xavier begins to cry and Edwina immediately puts him down.

"I'm sorry, little one," she says.

In a moment, Xavier has raced away from her and is clinging to Isabella's skirt, his face pressed against her hip. Isabella strokes his hair. Katarina's eyes narrow.

Ernest looks up and says, "Look at that. He treats Mary as another boy might treat his mother."

And there it is. Isabella can hear it. The false note in the beautiful symphony. It has been played, and its echo will shadow them all now. Katarina strides over, tears Xavier from Isabella's hands and says, "Mary, you can travel with Ernest and Abel. They are both drunk and need a pair of sober eyes to guide them home. Edwina, be my guest in my carriage with Xavier and me."

Xavier is still crying, but Katarina doesn't seem to hear him. Isabella quickly packs up the picnic while Ernest wakes Abel with his toe. Isabella reassures herself. Katarina isn't interested in Xavier. She'll get past this slight. If Isabella just keeps her head down, all this will blow over.

*E*rnest and Abel are drunk, and she is squeezed up against the side of the seat, choking on their tobacco smoke and their male sweat. Ernest is next to her, but his back is half-turned, and they talk as though she isn't there. Abel complains about his wife: she is too meek. Ernest complains about his wife: she is too wild. Isabella wants to interrupt and ask them precisely how much spirit a wife should have to keep them happy, but senses they wouldn't reply readily. They clatter back down the mountain too fast, and Isabella clenches her teeth to stop them rattling. Isabella gleans from their conversation that much of Abel's money comes not from his business dealings but from his wife's family; and that Ernest was so smitten by Katarina's beauty that it took him a full year of marriage to realize she was a harpy. Isabella glances back at the other carriage. Xavier sits quietly, ignored, between Katarina and Edwina. This precious child, surrounded by such vanity and venality.

And the first thought of it creeps in: Xavier would be better off with her, in New York with Victoria.

She banishes the thought straightaway. It is madness. She has frightened herself, though, and it has made her indignant. Why should she not reach such a conclusion, when she loves the child so dearly and all around him seem incapable of love? She doubts Katarina would even miss him; Ernest certainly wouldn't. And if Xavier stays with them, he will become just like them. It is inevitable. He will learn that money is more important than people; he will become a cold, hard man.

Would Daniel have become that way too? No, surely not. For Isabella would have been a guiding hand in his life, her love would have shaped his values and softened his contours. She can do the same with Xavier, at least while he is under her charge.

She turns back again and catches Xavier's eye, waves to him brightly. He beams and waves back. Katarina sees her and puts a protective arm around Xavier, distracts him with a word in his ear. But Isabella doesn't mind. She knows whom the child really loves.

*   *   *

𝒾sabella knows she shouldn't, but sometimes she thinks about it: the long journey across the ocean with Xavier. Just the two of them. The things they would see when they reached the other side. His hand in hers, forever. She tells herself she'll think about it for only one minute every day, but the one minute always bleeds into five minutes, and soon her idle thoughts take a detour down the same path. She tries to stop herself. She knows she will never do this. She loves Xavier, and because she loves him she will not remove him from his parents and his home and thrust him into a world of uncertainty as a fugitive. But the fantasy becomes a familiar pleasure to roll between her fingers when other, darker thoughts come to hand.

Ernest leaves early one morning the following week for a business trip to Brisbane, a large city many miles to the south. Xavier has been awake half the night with a mild fever and a cough. Isabella is consumed with keeping him warm to sweat the fever out: a child's illness is a terrifying thing for her; it makes her stomach loose. She keeps Katarina updated throughout the day, but Katarina appears indifferent. The weather has turned wild and the rattling of the eaves intensifies Isabella's anxiety, as though nothing in the world is secure.

"He had the same thing about three months ago," Katarina says. "He'll be better in a day or so."

Isabella doesn't know whether to interpret Katarina's dismissal as callousness, or as simply the calm wisdom of a mother who has known her son his whole life. She returns to the nursery where she sits with Xavier until the afternoon shadows grow long outside, then leaves him awhile to help Cook with dinner.

At the end of the hallway, the door is locked. Already. Isabella missed lunch and her stomach is grumbling. It isn't nighttime, so why has she been locked in? It doesn't matter. She knows how to get out now. She pops the key out and drags it under the door on a piece of paper, and heads to the kitchen.

Cook is not about, though, nor is Katarina. The rest of the house is in quiet darkness, except for the sound of the carriage clock ticking on the bookshelf. Isabella strains her ears for any sound of them, but hears only the faint ring of silence in the house, a contrast to the rushing wind outside. She lights a lamp in the kitchen and goes to the icebox. Xavier is sleeping and shouldn't eat while feverish, but surely nobody will mind if she cuts herself some bread and cheese.

She eats in silence in the dim flickering lamplight, then returns to Xavier.

Her hand, almost without thought, goes to his forehead. It is clear immediately that his fever has broken. Her hand comes away damp with cool sweat. The weight lifts off her heart and she realizes she has been holding back a tenth of every breath all day. She sits on the edge of the bed and gently strokes his hair away from his brow, talking to him softly under her breath. He stirs but doesn't wake. She feels ridiculously happy.

Then she hears a thump from downstairs—a door closing?— and remembers Katarina. She will want to know that Xavier is well again. Isabella decides to slip downstairs to see if the thump was Katarina, or Cook, who might know where Katarina is. If it is neither of them, then she will keep the news to herself and feel all the more special for being the only one who knows.

She takes a lantern and makes her way down the back stairs. The grass is wet with the day's rain and the air is chill. A rough wind shakes the branches in the tall eucalypts, and they make a rushing sound to rival the crashing of the sea. She goes into the laundry and stops, listening. Nothing . . . nothing . . .

Then something. A woman's voice. Low and soft. Isabella's skin prickles. Is it Cook or Katarina? She sounds as though she is in pain.

Isabella presses on into the dark under-house area and realizes the noise is coming from the forbidden room; realizes at the same moment that this isn't the sound of a woman in pain. It is the sound of pleasure.

The cigar butts outside the window. Ernest away in Brisbane.

It all falls into place quickly, and Isabella knows she should turn around and go back upstairs to the nursery and forget what she has guessed. That is what staff are meant to do. But Isabella is not staff. Isabella is a woman just like Katarina, and Isabella already suspects Katarina is not a fit mother. Or rather: Isabella *hopes* Katarina is not a fit mother, because that would legitimate all her fantasies.

Her fingers are on the door handle before she can withdraw them. Of course it is locked. But she has the key still, in the front pocket of her apron. Isabella hears a rough male voice. She must know who it is, how many of them there are, what foul things are taking place in that locked room. She must know it *urgently* if she is to keep Xavier safe in the world. She cares nothing for being quiet now; her heart is thudding too hard in her ears for her to hear the reasonable voice saying, *Stop, no good will come of this.*

The door swings inwards. The room is dimly lit, but she can see there is only one man, and nothing more sinister is taking place than the oldest act of love in the world.

Katarina lets out a half-shout, half-screech. Abel Barrett pulls the bed covers over his head too late. Isabella feels herself freeze:

the ice moves from her feet, up her veins to her knees, thighs and so on, finally reaching her heart and shoulders and head. Katarina is screaming at her to get out, out, out.

Isabella has lost it all. She has lost Xavier. There will be no going back to the quiet nursery to lie curled on her side and dream of being in New York with him. The fantasy is unraveling faster than she can comprehend. Katarina has wrapped herself loosely in her dress, retrieved from the floor, and prods Isabella away, shouts at her to pack her bags and be gone.

Isabella cannot move. This is not happening. Reality billows around her.

Then Abel is there, miraculously dressed while Isabella was paying no heed. He hauls her by the arm, out into the garden.

"You have five minutes to pack your things and go," he says. "Or I will call in the local police constable, who is my very good friend."

Self-preservation galvanizes Isabella. She runs up the stairs and to the nursery, clattering in so loudly that Xavier wakes. She folds him in her arms and sobs, "I have to go. I will find you. Don't be sad. I can make things well again, I'm sure. We are both still alive." She realizes she is rambling and stops.

Katarina, dressed now, is standing at the door. "Get out! Get your hands off my boy! Get out and never come back!" She begins to slap and punch Isabella, raining down the blows with all the intensity of her fear and anger.

Xavier scrambles out of bed and tries to seize Isabella, but Abel intervenes, picking up the child under his arm and telling him to be still. Xavier starts to scream, and it is a noise to tear Isabella's heart. White heat flashes through her. If she thought she were capable of it, she'd kill them both and take the child and . . .

Isabella gathers herself. It will be easier on Daniel if she just leaves . . . No, not Daniel. It will be easier on Xavier if she leaves quickly and quietly. Somehow she can make it well again. Surely. *Please, God, surely it isn't over. Surely it isn't over.*

"I'm sorry," she says, to Xavier, Katarina, Abel, but mostly to herself. For she is very, very sorry that she acted blindly.

Xavier starts to scream, "Mary! Mary!" Katarina looks at him, startled to hear him speak. Isabella leaves as quickly as she can, with the child's voice following her all the way down the stairs and out into the evening shadows.

"Mary! Mary!" The wind and the sea distorts the name, and it sounds like "Mummy! Mummy!" And she has to walk away. There is nothing for her to do but to walk away. There is nothing she can do. Nothing at all. He is gone. It is over. Her knees shake.

She heads for the lighthouse.

It seems a million miles, although it is only one. Rain begins to sheet down. Clouds cover the stars. All around her comes the roaring of the wind, the roaring of the sea, the roaring of her sobbing heart. Matthew's light is shining through it all, clear and bright, reaching out to sea. She stumbles up the path, mud in her shoes, cold rain and hot tears, and hammers on his door.

Waits.

She hears his footsteps clattering down the stairs. Then the door swings in and he is there, and she collapses into his arms. He hesitates. She says, "I have lost him." And Matthew's arms fold around her tightly and his hand is in her hair and he is kissing the top of her head. "My pretty bird," he murmurs. Desire ignites as it never has before in Isabella's body. Matthew reaches over her to close the door, shutting out the wind and the rain. Her clothes are dripping, so she begins to unfasten them: the buttons on her wrists, the laces at her throat. Matthew's hands are moving in tune with hers, stripping the wet clothes from her. They gather in a pool on the floor and Matthew's warm fingers are running over her cold collarbone. Her skin prickles into goose bumps, her nipples harden to tight peaks. He reaches down and picks her up as though she weighs nothing, takes her to his bedroom and lays her gently among the covers. The familiar smell of them—his smell: man and soap—overwhelms her and she closes her eyes. His lips touch her throat. She arches. Tears are still running from her eyes, skidding onto the pillow. He kisses her face, licks the tears from her cheeks. She feels his desire in the hot tautness of his body. When she opens her eyes, she sees he is naked in the lamplight. She reaches for him. His heart, her heart, in faultless rhythm.

In the dark, much later, he says, "I will find your sister. You can't stay here with me. You have to go to her."

"I have no money. I've lost everything that's dear."

"I kept the mace."

She sits up, looks down at him. His eyes seem black.

"Are you angry?"

"No," she says. "I am tired of doing the right thing. If necessity dictates, why should I not take something that isn't mine?" And while she says this, she is not thinking simply of the mace. She is also thinking of Xavier.

Seventeen

2011

A light shower moved in after the afternoon-tea rush and Juliet hesitated before going out. But the clouds were only pale gray, and at least the beach would be deserted if it was raining. She hated it when she went down there to think and dogs or children kept running into her.

She left Cheryl and Melody in charge of cleaning and locking up, something she rarely did. Once a year now. At first, in the early years, it had been once a week, then once a month she came down here. But grief can't hang on forever and now she only really came because it seemed wrong to *not* remember the date.

Twenty years since Andy died.

Juliet found the spot on which she always sat, up on the grassy part of the dunes looking down on to the soft white beach. She put her umbrella up and sat down, crossing her legs. She took a deep breath and closed her eyes. The breeze coming off the water was soaked in the scent of rain and salt. Her hair caught in it and flicked across her face. She gently pushed the strands back.

If she had been sitting in this spot twenty years ago tonight she would have seen it all unfold. She would have seen the headlights shining down from the park onto the sand. She would have heard the emergency sirens. She would have seen herself down on the beach, frantically pacing and crying, while friends tried to hold her still. She snapped her eyes open. There was no point reliving old misery.

For a long time, she'd come down here to talk to Andy, as though his spirit might have soaked into the sand and sea when he died. Juliet had no firm ideas about the mysteries of life and death, but she had long ago released the idea that Andy was here in any way. But today she found herself wanting to talk to him because he knew Libby. He knew what had happened. So he was one of the few people who could give good advice.

What was she to do about Libby? The short time since her unexpected arrival had been tumultuous. On rare good days Juliet managed not to think of it at all: her life was busy and she was used to Libby being out of it. Some days she remembered with a jolt that Libby was in town, just a five-minute drive away, and guilt shook her and told her to make amends. Family, blood, all that. Some days there was panic, some days anger and some days an inexplicable sinking dread. Life had grown quickly and unmanageably complicated the day Libby arrived. Granted, life wasn't easy before, but it was predictable. Time ticked away: twenty years since Andy died. Twenty whole years lived between breakfasts and morning and afternoon teas, between stripping beds and making beds. She had kept her head down, she had kept life simple. But then Libby had come back.

Guiltily, she hoped that Libby might leave again just as quickly. Libby had always been confident; in her youth she had even been conceited. It would be unsurprising if she decided—once again—that Lighthouse Bay was too small for her and were to head off to whatever exotic destination she felt suited her best. If Paris had lost its gloss, perhaps it would be London or New York next. If Libby went, then Juliet could get on with living her quiet life.

But instinctively, she also knew that her quiet life was slowly crushing her. Juliet sometimes woke in the middle of the night with a white-hot fear under her ribs: *You haven't lived.* She usually managed to push the feeling down, make a joke of herself, but Libby's arrival had made the fear hang around all day. Because it was true: she hadn't lived. She'd lost Andy and she'd decided just to skim over the top of life.

Juliet dropped her head to her knees. "Libby's back, Andy," she said, her voice barely audible over the crash of the waves. "Do you think I can forgive her?"

Andy didn't answer, but he didn't need to. He was a thought-ful man, wise beyond his years. She knew he would have said something like, *Just spend a little more time with her and don't rush anything and don't expect miracles.* And maybe he also would have said, *You really should have moved on by now.*

"Hey, Juliet!"

Juliet lifted her head and opened her eyes. Down on the sand, in his board shorts and a white T-shirt, was Scott Lacey. He made his way up to her.

"Afternoon, Sergeant," she said with a smile.

He grimaced. "Don't call me that or I'll ask you if you're sitting there waiting for Romeo." His standard joke, usually delivered in good humor except for the tense weeks after she turned down his offer of love. "I thought I might find you here. Twenty years today, isn't it?"

"Yes. Twenty years today."

KIMBERLEY FREEMAN
211

"And your sister back in town too." Scott lifted his gingery eyebrows. "That's got to hurt."

"I don't think she realizes. I think she was a lot more able to let go of the past than I've ever been."

"Yeah, well, you and I are like the old-timers around here now. Preserving local memory." He turned to look at the sea, saying wistfully, "Andy was a great guy." Then he returned his attention to Juliet. "So, your sister's a bit jumpy. Called me the other night saying there were footsteps outside her house, a car engine, that kind of thing."

Juliet was surprised to find she was concerned. "Really? She didn't mention it. Or perhaps that's why she asked if anyone used the lighthouse anymore."

"I've been past a few times but haven't seen anything. I'm hoping she might feel grateful enough to go on a date." A broad wink.

Juliet had given up trying to be sure when Scott was joking or serious. He had been married three times and didn't want for female company, so perhaps this was just a joke. She could only imagine how Libby would look down on somebody like Scott, who had spent his whole life in one place. Just as Juliet had.

But perhaps that wasn't right. Perhaps she was getting the old Libby confused with the new Libby. Her sister still had the glamour that came from aspiration, but she had seemed genuine, even sweet, when she'd come for dinner.

"Do you think she'd say yes?" Scott was saying. The rain intensified, but he didn't seem to notice.

"I have no idea," Juliet replied. "She's become a stranger to me."

"You ought to do something about that," Scott said.

"Yes. Perhaps you're right."

*   *   *

𝒯irst thing Monday morning, Libby phoned Ashley-Harris Holdings, gave her name and asked to speak to Tristan. A few moments later a man's voice was on the line.

"Tristan?"

"No, Elizabeth. I'm Yann Fraser. I'm handling this part of the project now."

"I understand that, but it's Tristan particularly I want to speak to." She and Tristan had connected. She'd felt it, and she knew he did too. She didn't want to talk to a stranger. She wanted to pose her questions to somebody she trusted.

"Tristan is in Sydney this week. But I'm happy to help."

Libby paced in frustration. "No, I'll work it out," she said. "Good-bye."

She hung up. Was Tristan just a smooth-talking charmer sent in to soften her up? She certainly felt disinclined to do business with Ashley-Harris now.

But the money.

Libby was about to return to her art room when the phone, still in her hand, rang.

"Hello?" she said, realizing too late that there was still impatience in her voice.

"Libby? It's Tristan Catherwood."

Immediately, she softened. "Tristan! I'm so glad you called."

"Yann just texted me to say you were looking for me. I'm in Sydney for a few days. Look, I need to explain something to you and it's potentially awkward, so be kind to me."

Libby frowned and said slowly, "Okay."

"I know I've handed you over to Yann. He's my equal in the business, and he's more than qualified to handle any property

agreements we make. But there's a reason I handed you over."
He fell silent.

"Go on," she prompted.

"I don't think business and pleasure mix very well," he said
softly.

"What do you mean?" But she suspected she knew what he
meant, and flushed warm at the thought.

"I mean," he said, "that I felt very strongly about you when
we met. I was reluctant to see you go. And I can't ask you out for
dinner if we're in the middle of a property deal."

Now it was Libby's turn to fall silent. It had only been two
months since Mark's death. She was in no way ready to date.

"Libby?" he said with a nervous laugh. "I just asked you out
for dinner."

"I'm sorry," she blurted. "I . . . The man who died. He was . . ."

"Oh, I see. He was your partner?"

No. He was never her partner. He was never her husband. He
was her lover. They saw each other one weekend a month and the
occasional stolen week away in an exotic location where nobody
knew them. They never had dinner with friends or family. She
never met his mother. She had loved Mark, but he was not her
partner. She took a deep, shaking breath. "I'd love to have dinner
with you, Tristan," she said.

"Really? I mean, I do understand if it's too soon."

"I'd love to," she said again. "When are you back from
Sydney?"

"Friday morning. How about I pick you up on Friday night
at six?"

"That sounds wonderful."

She regretted it as soon as she hung up, but it was too late.
The future was coming. It had to.

*   *   *

$\mathscr{L}$ibby forgot that Damien was coming for dinner until half an hour before he was due. She scrambled around in her pantry and refrigerator, and was relieved to turn up enough ingredients for pizza. She set about tidying the house, especially the desk where she had been working feverishly the past twenty-four hours on the catalog, trying to distract herself. Her last bad decision had resulted in twenty years of consequences; who knew how many decades she might feel the reverberations of this one? To take the money and regret it; to refuse the money and regret it.

Libby was in the bathroom, brushing her hair, when Damien knocked at the door. She opened it to find him standing there with a tool kit and a cat.

"This is Bossy," he said. "I hope you don't mind."

"I don't mind, but I don't understand," Libby said, as the fine-boned ginger cat slid past her ankles.

"I don't want to leave her alone at the lighthouse. Too many places for her to get stuck or lost."

Libby bent to scratch the cat under the chin. "She's beautiful. Did you just get her?"

"No, I've had Bossy for years. It's complicated and I don't really want to talk about it, except to say that this week I managed to get my cat, my utility belt, and"—he lifted up his tool kit—"my tools. You said you had some problems with your linen cupboard."

"You can fix it?"

"Yeah. I'm a carpenter. It's the least I can do, considering you're making me dinner."

"Oh, I thought . . ." She trailed off, realizing it might be an insult if she said, "I thought you didn't have a job." Instead she said, "I didn't know that."

He was already in the hallway, testing the door on the linen cupboard. She watched him a little while. Where had his cat been? And his car and his tools? He must have gone to get them this week, but why? She was dying to ask, but it was clear he wasn't going to tell her.

She cooked while he took the doors off, planed them down, then refastened them on their hinges. He was very at ease with her and it made her feel at ease with him, and they chatted about the past and people they'd known. While the pizza was cooking, they sat outside on the mismatched outdoor furniture. She was tempted to tell him about the offer from Ashley-Harris and the potentially disastrous situation with Juliet but decided he wouldn't be much help. He had no money; he didn't even have a job. Big property deals were probably beyond his scope.

In any case, he had other things on his mind to talk about. "I kept looking at the 1901 lighthouse journal," he said, pulling it out of his tool box. "I found something interesting in the final few pages."

Libby leaned forward. "Go on."

"At first I thought there was nothing. I thought maybe the keeper—his name was Matthew Seaward—might have been foreign because there were a number of sentences with very odd grammar. Things like, *Brought home some fresh apples for I,* or *I very down today.* But then I realized he's not saying 'I' as in himself. I think it's somebody's initial." He flicked through the pages, looking for an entry.

"Oh? So he means Isaac or Ivan or something like that?"

"No. It's a woman. Because there was one entry . . . Ah, here it is: *I anxious. Not sure what is wrong with her.*"

"Was he married?"

"The records say no. And I looked back through his journals

from when he started in 1895, and there is no mention of another person, no mention of 'I' until after the diary entry I read you. About the strange woman."

"And is she there with him until he finishes?"

"I don't know. I haven't found all of his journals yet. This one ends in July 1901."

Libby turned this over in her mind. "Just because a strange woman turns up—one he sends to town to find a more appropriate place to stay, remember—that doesn't mean it's necessarily the same woman that he starts talking about later in the journal, does it?"

"Well, no. We're working with possibility rather than probability. But it's fun to imagine, isn't it? She gets shipwrecked, he takes her in, they fall in love. It doesn't matter if it didn't happen; it's all in the past now."

Libby let this idea sink in. Yes, eventually it all becomes the past. Like her love affair with Mark. Time erases everything. Did Mark know that? Is that why he always urged her to live in the moment? She tried to feel the moment now. The soft breeze, the beat of the ocean. Happiness was almost there. But there was still too much sadness lying on her heart. If she could, she would wish Damien away and put Mark in his place. She could have had that. She could have sat here with Mark with the breeze and the ocean, but she had been too stubborn and now it was too late. Time had passed.

But it also meant that her decision about selling the cottage would disappear into the past one day too. Did that mean it didn't really matter what she did? She furrowed her brow, trying to make it not matter.

"Are you okay?" Damien said.

She glanced up, tried a smile. "Yeah. Yeah, I'm fine. Do you think I could hang on to this journal? I'd like to read it for myself."

"Sure." He laid it on the side table. "Shall we check on the pizza?"

Damien wanted to eat inside, on the couch. He said he hadn't sat on a couch for a long time and Libby found this both funny and puzzling. But neither of them probed each other's secrets. It was much more comfortable to eat pizza, talk about the locals and construct an elaborate story behind their lighthouse mystery.

"I'll come back during the week and check your other cabinets, if you like. Anything else you need done?"

"It wouldn't be right. I'm not really in a position to pay you and—"

"I have an ulterior motive."

For a second her heart fluttered: he wasn't going to make a move on her, was he? He wasn't her type and she was a lot older than he was. But then he said, "Is there any chance I could leave Bossy here with you?"

The idea delighted Libby. "Of course."

"And if you can make me a meal once in a while, I'll pay you back in odd jobs. There are . . . problems with my bank accounts. I can't even get hold of the bits of paperwork that would make it easy for me to get a job. I need cash jobs and in-kind trades. If you know of anything . . ."

"Damien, why—"

"It's too raw. I can't talk about it."

She nodded. "You should go and see Juliet. She says she needs some work done in the kitchen of the tea room."

"Really? Perhaps I will, then. Could you let her know I'll drop in?"

Libby's mind whirled. No, she wasn't going to speak to Juliet again until she'd made up her mind. If she told Damien she was considering abandoning any chance of a relationship with her sister for two and a half million dollars, he would judge her. Everybody thought that family relationships were priceless.

"Sure, I'll let her know," Libby said. The lie was harmless. "She'll be glad to see you."

Later, after Damien had gone home, Bossy was waiting on the end of the bed when Libby came out of the shower.

"Hello, puss," she said, switching on the lamp and climbing into bed with the lighthouse keeper's journal. Bossy stretched and came to lie at her side, purring softly.

At first, Libby found it difficult to decipher Matthew Seaward's writing, but then she got the hang of it and flicked through, looking for mentions of "I." Damien was right that most of them were in the last few pages of the journal, recording events in late June. Mostly very mundane things. But then she flicked backwards and found an interesting entry from April. *I returned to telegraph sister.* I returned. Was he speaking of himself, or of the mysterious woman whose name began with "I"? Curious now, she began to read more closely, as a storm moved in off the sea and made the eaves shake. A list of telegraphs received. At the end, squashed against the bottom margin: *Still no reply from I's sister.*

It sounded as though Matthew Seaward had become invested in the mysterious woman and her sister. A little further in, a longer entry caught Libby's eye. *I has not heard from sister. Best for I if we find her soon. She needs family of her own to love and guide her.*

Libby read these lines over and over. The mysterious woman—possibly a shipwreck survivor—had tried to find her sister. Libby's imagination toyed with this idea while Bossy slept on beside her and the rain lightened and lifted. In the direst of circumstances, this woman had needed a sister "to love and guide her." Libby found herself acutely and unexpectedly jealous. Such a relationship didn't exist in her world, least of all with her sister. And nor would it ever. Since she had become an adult, the only person who had ever loved and guided her was Mark. Somebody else's husband.

Bossy stood and stretched, lightly leaped off the bed and padded away, no doubt in search of nocturnal adventures. It was getting late. Libby put the journal aside and switched off the lamp, but lay awake for a long time.

By Friday, Libby had been enormously productive. She had booked a photographer for the catalog, roughed out three designs to run past Emily, and blocked out her painting of the *Aurora*. Anything to keep her mind busy.

She could be rich. Juliet would hate her forever. Two and a half million dollars. Thirty days to respond.

The decision had a bearing on everything she did. When she worked on the catalog, she thought about how she wouldn't have to worry about how quickly or slowly she gained new clients for her design business. When she painted, she thought about how she could do it full-time for at least a year. When she researched photographers on the Internet, she slid over to a French real estate site and looked at luxury apartments in Paris. She had missed Paris: its pace and sophistication. And when Juliet phoned to see if she would come over for dinner one night on the weekend, she'd had to refuse because she knew she couldn't look Juliet in the eye until she'd made her decision.

Libby suspected that Juliet was wrong in her fear of Ashley-Harris: their eco-resort wouldn't be competition. Nobody paid nine hundred dollars a night for a room at a B&B. It was a completely different kind of business.

But then all her rumination would start to feel very much like an elaborate justification for choosing money over family.

The nights were the worst. She could normally get to sleep, nurturing herself with guilty fantasies about painting in the light-flooded sitting room of her dream apartment in Montparnasse, but at 3 am the hot reality of her dilemma would prickle her awake and she would lie until dawn, unable to sleep. Meanwhile, the thirty days had become twenty-three days.

Libby was pacing the living room in her high heels and pencil skirt when she heard the Audi pull up. She waited until he knocked, then took a deep breath and opened the door.

"Hi," she said.

"You look beautiful," he said. He was dressed in a charcoal gray blazer and jeans, and smelled of expensive aftershave.

Her heart thudded. A date. She was going on a date.

Bossy slinked out of the hallway and froze, looking at Tristan.

"What's wrong, Bossy?" she asked.

Tristan crouched and rubbed his fingers together, trying to coax Bossy over for a pat. But Bossy flounced straight past him and headed for the couch instead.

"Cats usually like me," he said.

"Don't worry." Libby laughed. "I won't read anything into it."

Tristan stood again. "Are you ready?" he asked. "I'm keen to get going. I'm taking you somewhere really special."

"Bye, Bossy." She locked the door behind her and followed him up to the car. Once she had her seatbelt on, he started the engine and drove up the road past the lighthouse, onto the gravel shoulder, and then stopped the engine.

"We're here."

Libby smiled curiously. "Here?"

He got out of the car and came round to open her door. Then he popped the boot and pulled out two folding chairs and a picnic basket. "I wanted to impress you by taking you somewhere with great food, great ambience and a great view." He put down the picnic basket and straightened out the chairs, gesturing to one with a sweep of his hand. "My lady."

She grinned. "Why thank you, sir," she said, imitating a posh English accent not unlike Mark's. "And what shall we be dining on this fine evening?"

Tristan opened the picnic basket and withdrew a plastic tablecloth, which he laid on the bonnet of the Audi. Then he pulled out a white paper bag of fish and chips, a bottle of champagne and two plastic champagne flutes. "Only the best. From the village."

"The Salty Sea Lion?"

He poured her a glass of champagne. "Yes. Best fish and chips on the Sunshine Coast."

They clinked their plastic glasses together.

"Here's to the most beautiful view in the world," he said.

Libby looked around. The sea at dusk was gray-blue. Sea mist obscured the headland to the south. The sky was soft blue and purple. "You might be right," she said softly. She glanced up at the lighthouse. No candlelight in the window.

"Where do you live?" she asked Tristan, suddenly curious.

"I have a flat at Noosa, and a country house in the mountains behind Sydney. I don't get there much these days."

"Do we have knives and forks?" she said, searching through the white paper bag.

"Near my Audi? I don't think so," he said, laughing. "It tastes better with your fingers anyway."

Libby pulled off a piece of crumbed fish and popped it in her mouth. Divine. Mark had never taken her on a date to eat fish and chips off his car bonnet. For a while, with the champagne bubbles going to her head and the novelty of the setting to distract her, she forgot about her problems. They chatted about work and weather and lightly about their pasts and futures.

But then her mobile rang. She pulled it out of her handbag and the screen said "Juliet."

She'd already turned down two calls and felt bad turning down a third, but she hit the mute button and slid the phone back into her bag.

"Anyone important?"

"My sister."

"Ah. Juliet?"

"Yes."

"You're frowning."

"I've got a big decision to make."

"I know. I'm sorry, but you can't talk it over with me."

"Really? I can't talk it over with anyone else."

"Libby, I have handed the project over to Yann precisely for this reason. My business decisions and your personal decisions have to be completely separate. I know Yann has handed you a dilemma, but I can't help you with it."

"It's only a dilemma because Juliet will think wrongly that she'd lose her livelihood."

He made a motion, zipping his lips, and shook his head.

Libby sighed, refilled her champagne glass and sank back into her chair.

"All I'd say is that you are lucky to have such a decision to make," he said softly. "You have great financial opportunities, and a family bond that means a lot to you. Some people have neither."

She opened her mouth to ask him more questions, but then swallowed them. He was right. She was on her own.

The sea cooled around ten, and she hadn't brought a jacket. He dropped her home, and walked her up the front path. She didn't know if she should ask him in. In her champagne-fueled state she found him devastatingly attractive, but reason told her to wait until she knew him a little better.

He made the decision for her. "I'd best get going. I have an early flight in the morning."

"Away on business again?"

"Two weeks in Perth."

Two weeks? She felt deflated but forced a smile. "That sounds like fun."

"Can I call you?"

"Of course." By the time he returned, she'd only have nine days to make up her mind. "I'd like that."

He caught her cheek with his right hand, softly. Stroked her chin with his thumb. Her heartbeat drowned out all other sounds. Then he leaned forward and kissed her gently on the mouth. Her body responded by pressing against his. His tongue was between her lips.

It was the strangest feeling, to be kissing somebody else after all these years. Familiar but different. She couldn't lose herself in the moment because she was too busy watching herself from outside, kissing somebody who wasn't Mark.

Then came the sound of a car engine.

Libby snapped away from Tristan. Was it the men who had been hanging around her cottage? No. It was a police car. And here was Scott Lacey—a little softer around the middle since high school, but still instantly recognizable—climbing out with his hand on his belt. He stood there, hesitant now that he could see Libby was with Tristan, who had his arm around her waist.

"Scott?" she said.

"Libby? Is that you?" He strode forward now, offered his hand for her to shake. "You haven't changed."

Libby introduced Tristan, but he said immediately, "Yes we . . . ah . . . we know each other."

Libby looked from Tristan to Scott and her stomach dropped. Scott was on Juliet's side.

"I've been driving by every couple of nights, like I said I would," Scott said. "I saw the car here and thought . . . ah, well. You're okay."

"I am. I am okay."

"I'll leave you to it, then."

Libby and Tristan watched him go, Libby's heart thudding dully. She groaned, leaning her head on Tristan's shoulder. "He's going to tell Juliet."

Tristan looked as though he was about to say something but changed his mind. "I'm sorry I can't help," he said. "And I really do have to go. Dinner when I get back?"

"I'd love that."

A quick peck on the cheek and he was gone. She went inside and eased off her high heels. She intended to shower, but somehow found herself curled on the couch with Bossy, drifting off. Her head spun, a cocktail of champagne and guilty thoughts.

Eighteen

The Saturday morning breakfast rush meant the smell of frying bacon and brewing coffee. Juliet always hit the ground running on Saturdays. Taking orders, making orders, clearing plates away, welcoming new customers where the old ones were sitting just a few minutes before. Her breakfasts were famous in town, famous enough for her to hire four staff on Saturdays to cope with the demand.

She was making coffee when Scott Lacey came in, in civilian clothes. At first she barely paid attention. She presumed Melody would find him a table and take his usual order, but then it became apparent he was hanging about near the coffee machine, trying to get her attention.

"I'm super busy," she said to him over the hiss of the milk steamer.

"I can wait."

"Go sit down. I'll bring you something. Cappuccino and raisin toast?"

"Take your time."

She was curious, but busy enough to put it out of her mind. In the first lull, she took his breakfast over and sat with him.

"Thanks, Juliet," he said, spooning three sugars into his coffee.

A slanted beam of warm sunshine through the window lit up the gingery hairs on his knuckles.

"You're always welcome, Scott. But what's up?"

He shrugged. "I saw something you're not going to like."

A small, hot flick of adrenaline. "Really?"

He sipped his coffee, and it left a thin line of cocoa on his top lip. "I went past Libby's place last night, as I've been doing since she called. And there was somebody there, so I got out to look."

"Is she okay? She hasn't returned my calls."

"I think I know why. She was cuddling up with Tristan Catherwood."

A coiling feeling in her stomach. "Cuddling up with . . . What do you mean by *cuddling up*?"

"I mean cuddling up. Kissing him. Passionately."

"How does she even know him?" Her voice seemed to come from a long way away. Scott must surely be mistaken. It simply couldn't be possible that her two biggest problems—Libby and Ashley-Harris—had somehow become entangled. This must be a bad dream. Scott considered her across the table, his green eyes steady and sad.

"I don't understand," Juliet said softly, helplessly.

"You don't?" Scott asked. "She owns a property. And they need one."

"But why . . ."

"I don't know, Jules. You'd better ask her yourself."

Juliet climbed to her feet. Rage flooded her hands and her stomach. She wanted to punch something, even if it meant breaking all her knuckles.

Scott grasped her wrist gently. "Hey, are you all right?"

"No," she snapped, then realized she had said it too loudly. Several patrons had glanced up curiously. She drew the rage back into her body, into a hard ball under her ribs. "No, I'm not all right," she said softly. "I'm an idiot. I should have known she'd never be any different."

$\mathcal{I}$t was simple: Juliet would pretend she had no sister—then she couldn't get hurt. Admittedly, this was difficult when Cheryl asked her, "Have you seen your sister again?" on the breakfast shift the next day, but Juliet found that responding with, "Can you please take this teapot to table six?" shut down the conversation swiftly. It was also difficult at night, as she lay in bed after the world had gone quiet except for the sound of the beating ocean, when her thoughts swirled around in an unhappy whirlpool.

But the most difficult time to pretend she had no sister was when her sister turned up, right on closing time, in carefully faded jeans and a lace shirt, and with her dark hair pulled back in a loose bun. Juliet noted that she had taken the time to put lipstick on to come down here and explain, and for some reason the fact hardened Juliet's heart, as though the time taken primping herself was time taken away from feeling guilty.

But then, the twenty years in Paris was also time taken away from feeling guilty. Juliet tried to squash this feeling. She tried to be in the present, deal with the present.

Libby stood in the doorway a few moments, then said, "We should talk. I can see from your expression that Scott Lacey has spoken to you."

"There's nothing to talk about. You're an adult. You'll make your own decisions." Juliet's voice was very loud in her own ears.

"You're really angry, aren't you?"

"No," Juliet said, vigorously wiping down a table.

"Yes you are. You're going to wear a hole in that table."

Juliet straightened her back. "Okay, we'll talk." She strode to the front door of the shop and shut the bolt, switched off the lights so that the only light was coming from the kitchen. She didn't want a visit from customers looking for a late takeaway coffee while she was having it out with Libby. She indicated the table closest to the kitchen and Libby sat down. Juliet took the last tray of dirty cups to the kitchen, then returned. For a moment, she considered her sister in the late-afternoon light. Libby had her face half-turned away, but Juliet could detect the guilt and the anxiety in her brow. Something troubled her, something big. And Juliet grew frightened, because perhaps there was more to this Tristan Catherwood business than a date.

She owns a property. And they need one.

Libby must have sensed she was being watched. She looked around and tried a smile that didn't quite make it to her eyes. Juliet sat. They were silent a moment while the fridge hummed, the dishwasher swished, the clock ticked. Juliet knew that if she spoke first, it would be ugly, so she held her tongue.

"I think it would be a good idea if we took my name off the paperwork for the business," Libby said, surprising Juliet.

"Why?"

"Because you assumed I'd want to take my half and I don't. I don't want to take anything from you." Libby swallowed hard.

Juliet's skin prickled lightly with suspicion. Was she being softened up for some fresh horror? Libby had said she wanted no money for her half of the business; had she changed her mind? She had no job, so perhaps she needed the money quickly. "I see."

"So, can we do that soon? I want that out of the way. Otherwise

I don't think we have a hope of rebuilding this . . ." She indicated the space between them with a loose wrist.

"And will you want payment?"

Libby shook her head. "No, no payment. I can see with my own eyes that this isn't the business Dad left behind. I wouldn't dream of taking advantage of your investment of time and energy. Juliet, I want you to feel you can trust me," she said softly.

Juliet smiled, and the bitterness made it a hard smile. "Trust you?"

"I came to reassure you. Look, Tristan is off the Lighthouse Bay project now. I'm seeing him entirely independently of all that."

"But you know who he is, right? He's the man who's been fighting for years to bring something unwanted into this town. For *years*." Juliet kept her voice steady. "Libby, he's the enemy."

"He's not. He's just a man. He's very nice."

Juliet's brows twitched with irritation. "It's none of my business who you see or where you go. You don't need my permission to do anything."

"I don't want things to be so tense between us. I want us to get along. To be family. That's why I came back."

Juliet struggled with her words, then finally said, "For twenty years, Libby, you haven't been family. Family are there. Family phone or e-mail. They send letters, not just random Christmas cards. Family share the ups and downs. They don't turn up unannounced and blithely say that the years of struggle against a big greedy business that wants to take everything from local traders *don't count*!" Juliet balled her hands into fists and cursed herself for displaying her anger so openly. Deep breaths, now. In . . . out . . .

Libby sat silently, her big eyes blinking back at Juliet slowly. "You can't forgive me, can you?"

"For Tristan Catherwood?"

"For anything." Libby's eyes darted away. "God, there's so much to forgive. Maybe I can't forgive me either. You must think I've ruined your whole life."

Juliet opened her mouth to deny it, but the truth was that sometimes she had thought it. She truly had. But then she thought deeper about Libby's comment and grew irritated. "My life isn't a ruin," she said hotly. "My life is fine. I've been happy. Right up until you showed up."

"Would you like me to leave again?"

Yes. *Yes.* "That's your decision."

"I'm trying to . . . Is there any point? Can we fix things? Or will you always hate me?"

"Hate you?" Did she hate her sister?

Libby must have grown tired of being apologetic. She scraped her chair back. "Look, let's just get that paperwork out of the way soon. If you want to talk to me, you know where I am. I'll sign anything, whatever you need."

Juliet watched her go, heart thudding. Was she allowing anger to cloud her judgment? Perhaps Libby really did want to hand over her claim on the business; perhaps her date with Tristan Catherwood really was innocent. But Libby was a stranger to her, and before she'd become a stranger she had been an enemy. Juliet simply wasn't ready to trust her.

At nine on Wednesday night, as Juliet was finishing up sorting invoices and thinking about a pot of tea, the after-hours doorbell rang. Ordinarily, she would just assume it was a guest who had forgotten their key, but it was a rare night when all her rooms were empty.

Curious, she left her apartment and walked down to open the

after-hours gate. Standing on the other side, a yellow streetlight reflecting on his face, was a tall man with long hair.

"Hi, Juliet," he said.

Juliet frowned, puzzled. There was something familiar about him, but she couldn't put her finger on it.

"Ah. Libby didn't tell you I was coming."

"Libby?" What was her sister up to now? Suspicion hardened in her veins.

The man smiled. "I'm so sorry. She said she'd call you and tell you I was going to drop by." He stretched out his hand. "Damien Allbright."

At the mention of his name, the feeling of familiarity solidified. Damien. She had babysat him as a boy. Only he wasn't a boy anymore. He was a man, dense with muscle, with a shadowy beard across his jaw and warm, firm hands around hers.

"Oh, my. You grew up," she said, then realized she sounded like an idiot and withdrew her hand. "What's this got to do with Libby?"

"I ran into her up at the lighthouse and . . . Can I come in? I know it's out of nowhere, but it's all a bit complicated to explain out here on the street."

"Of course. Where are my manners? Follow me up. I was just about to make tea."

He sat on her couch, his long legs taking up a lot of room in her small apartment. She brought tea and scones and he fell on them hungrily as he and Juliet chatted around easy topics including the weather and the tourists.

"Those scones were amazing. No wonder your business is booming."

"It's not really booming."

"Libby said it was."

"She did?" Would that prickle of irritation at the mention of her sister's name *ever* go away?

"Yes. She fed me the other night. I'm . . . ah . . . in a difficult situation at the moment. I'm squatting at the lighthouse." He couldn't meet her eyes. "Sorry."

"Why are you apologizing to me?"

"Because your opinion always meant something to me." He smiled. "Twenty years later, it's a hard feeling to shake."

For some reason, this confession made her smile. "So, why are you here?"

"I'm a carpenter. You need a new kitchen. There are problems with my bank accounts, my documents . . . It's really complicated. So Libby thought you might be interested in a deal. I can take cash or in-kind."

At all of this, Juliet bristled. The nerve of Libby, assuming she could make such an offer to Damien. But then she softened. She had four empty rooms and winter was coming. And it was true that she had put up with the old kitchen cabinets for decades.

She must have been silent a long time, because Damien said, "No pressure. Even if I could come and do some measurements for you, make some suggestions and draw up some plans. Knock a few things out . . ." He trailed off, and a silence grew. Juliet knew she should answer. It was all so confusing. Did she really want to refit the kitchen now, when all of this business with Libby was going on? Or had she already put it off too long, afraid that she couldn't afford it, always counting every cent in fear of a hostile future?

And then there was Damien. Yes, she could still remember his pirate-ship pajamas and his love of *The Very Clever Engine*, so the shock of his masculinity—*admit it: his very attractive masculinity*—had made her awkward, unsure. Did she really want him around, in her kitchen, when she was sweaty and stressed and wearing a food-spattered apron?

But this was not a handsome stranger. It was Damien Allbright, a person she had known in a happier past. All of a sudden, she wanted to cling to that idea: somebody who knew her and liked her before the bad stuff happened. "Sure," she said at last. "Why don't you do that?" Then, doubt kicked in, so she added, "Why don't we say you can stay here for a week at the B&B for free, if you give me a week's worth of preparatory services. In-kind. Then after that, we'll see."

He smiled broadly, but Juliet could see a kind of desperate relief in his eyes and she wondered what had happened to put him in this situation. She sensed, though, that it was too early to ask. Instead, she said, "If you've finished your tea, I can take you down to your room now."

He leaped to his feet to help her clear the plates and teapot away. "Did Libby tell you about our lighthouse mystery?" he asked.

Juliet smiled evenly over the top of her discomfort. "No. We haven't actually talked much."

He cocked his head to the side. "Really? But you've been apart a long time."

"Yes, that's true." She kept her head down as she slotted the plates in the dishwasher. "Come on, I'll give you the side room. You'd have to sit right at the window to see the sea, but you'll be able to hear it while you go to sleep. I always think that's the best thing in the world."

She grabbed the key out of her desk drawer and led him out of her flat and down the hallway to Room 2. She showed him which key was which, where the security light was, and let him into the room. He flicked on the light. Room 2 was the smallest but it was the first she'd redecorated, so she had a soft spot for it.

Pale blues and sand colors. He collapsed on the bed on his back, spreading out his arms and legs.

"Ah," he said, "a real bed. I'm going to sleep well tonight."

"Breakfast is between seven and nine," she said, not really able to look at him lying on the bed. "Just order it with Melody. You're welcome to take it back to your room. I'll be too busy to talk about the kitchen until the afternoon, so perhaps if you come down around four?"

"Sure." He propped himself up on his side. "Hey, thanks so much, Juliet. I can't . . . I can't tell you what this means to me."

Her pulse flickered. She was looking forward to talking to him tomorrow afternoon more than she should. She nodded and withdrew, closing the door behind her. So what if he was attractive and kind and a bit mysterious? He was a decade younger than she was and he wouldn't be interested. She was a fool to get herself all worked up. A deep breath, and she headed back down the hallway to her flat.

Nineteen

Tuesday—dive day—dawned with perfect weather. All through Monday, Libby had secretly hoped for the kind of bad weather that would mean she could call the dive off. She didn't want to go. She felt discouraged, frightened, preoccupied. She felt like anything but a woman who dives shipwrecks. She wished for somebody to talk to: somebody who really understood her and her situation. But who was there? Her relationship with Mark had been necessarily isolating. She'd had work colleagues for movie nights and picnics but nobody really close, because right at the heart of her life was a secret affair.

Nonetheless, it was Tuesday. It was dive day. She would go because if Mark were alive he would never have stopped teasing her if she chickened out.

Libby pulled a light summer dress over her bathing suit and got in her car for the drive up to Winterbourne Beach. She noticed her hands shook on the steering wheel as she backed out into the street. Her stomach twinged. She tried to cheer herself with the idea that she'd see the actual ship she'd been sketching and painting these last few weeks. Yes, it would be in pieces on the ocean floor, but she imagined it would feel like touching history. Mark's history.

Graeme had told her to meet him down at the boat ramp, and he was waiting when she arrived, squinting in the bright sunshine. She handed over the boat plans she had borrowed, and he took them with a wink.

"Did you get what you needed out of them?"

"I did, thanks," she replied. Then she remembered Matthew Seaward's journal. "Graeme, to your knowledge, were there any women on board the *Aurora* when she sank?"

"Whiteaway's wife. Margaret."

"No others?"

"A ship like that wasn't a place for a woman," he said. "Ah here, this is my son, Alan." They were joined by a slight man in his twenties with coarse ginger hair that stood up at wild angles. "He's going to be your dive buddy seeing as how you've never dived before. He's really experienced and he'll keep an eye on you."

Libby's stomach flipped. "So, it's okay to go down there without any training?"

He wouldn't quite meet her eye, which should have made her turn and run. "Yeah. It's only a little dive. Training is costly and it takes a lot of time. We'll have you in and out with the minimum fuss."

Libby regarded Alan, who had turned away and was in deep, hushed conversation with his father, and her panic grew. He looked like thin comfort. She wanted a big man with her, somebody with courage and strength and honor. She wanted Mark. She never seemed to stop wanting Mark.

Another couple pulled up in a black BMW, and then when everybody was on board, Graeme started the motor and they moved out into the bay.

The sun was bright but gentle, the water deep blue-green beneath them. Libby sat on the starboard side of the boat, watching its wake over the low railing. The couple were obviously experienced divers, talking to Alan in confident voices. Graeme stood in his half-cabin, steering the boat out towards the reef. After a ten-minute journey, he cut the motor and they slowly came to a dipping-and-bobbing rest.

Graeme came out with a wetsuit and fins, and Libby changed quickly. Then he spoke to her rapid-fire while harnessing her into a vest that he called a "BCD," air tanks with tubes leading everywhere, a belt and a diving mask that pinched the skin around her cheeks. She listened carefully as he explained how everything worked, as the other couple splashed into the water, leaving her behind. Her brain whirled frantically. It wasn't simple. Not at all. And she was going to have all that water on top of her. This wasn't like swimming laps at the health club, it wasn't even like taking an afternoon paddle in the ocean. She would be a long way under.

"Look, love, nothing's too complicated. Breathe through here, and if that doesn't work breathe through there. Alan's going to be beside you the whole time."

Libby nodded, apprehensive despite his reassurances. Soon, she was sitting on the side of the boat, about to splash into the water.

She was a good swimmer. She hadn't always been, but Mark liked to go to the beach for holidays, so she had practiced laps up and down the narrow pool in the health club a block from work back in Paris. Mark would tell her she was being silly. Mark would tell her just to get in.

But Mark didn't know everything about her.

She popped the regulator in her mouth, steeled herself and then tumbled into the sea.

Alan gestured that she should follow him, but she took a moment to get used to breathing through the regulator. At first her chest felt constricted and anxious, but soon she had the hang of it, and she began to swim down into the blue. The light penetrated softly, lending everything a smoky haze. She could see the wreck already, barely recognizable as a ship. It seemed both manmade and organic: carefully wrought and now overgrown with mad, woolly sea life. The hot colors on the spectrum disappeared the deeper they swam, until everything was smoky blue. Libby gazed around her in wonder. Rays and turtles and schools of silvery fish. She felt free and light and alive, and so incredibly glad that she'd come. How Mark would have loved this. How proud he would have been for her to put aside her fears and come down here. Alan pointed down towards the wreck and indicated she should go ahead. She swam down towards the *Aurora*.

Libby gazed in wonder at this ship, this mysterious vessel she had been sketching and painting for weeks. It was as though a mythical being had sprung to life in front of her. After having only seen it in her imagination, its physical presence electrified her. It was in two clear parts on the ocean floor, divided by rocks and weed, sloping at impossible angles. Only part of the main mast still stood, like a jagged tooth emerging from the deck. She checked that Alan was close by, then swam towards it and around it, then along the deck through the warm blue water. A large ray shadowed her underneath, slipping over the side of the ship and into the dark below. Libby saw a hatch up ahead and put on speed to get to it.

She stopped above it, treading water a minute, looking down into the hatch. It was dark, but she had a torch attached to one of the cords on her BCD, so she fumbled for it and pulled it out. Its beam lit the inside of the hatch, which bristled with weeds and barnacles. A set of stairs, debris on the floor. She thought she saw a shard of broken crockery and slowly made her way into the hatch to investigate.

It was cramped, and immediately she wanted to turn around.

The space made it difficult, but she managed, only to notice that she was surrounded by tiny bubbles. She watched them all around her face, frowning. Was that normal? She emerged through the hatch again, only to be buffeted by a warm current. Bang. Her right elbow hit the edge of the hatch hard. Instinctively, she put her hands out to steady herself, remembering too late that Graeme had warned her not to touch anything with bare hands. She hardly felt the sharp edge of the barnacle slice into her hand, but she certainly saw the blood smoke into the water, a dull green color.

Libby looked around for Alan but couldn't see him. She was alone.

She pressed her hand against her thigh to stop it bleeding and made her way out of the hatch. She tried to regather her happy feelings of freedom, but she was disorientated now. The angle of the wreck made it difficult for her to work out which direction she'd come from, and she could see neither Alan nor the other couple, nor had she any idea where Graeme's boat was. And all of this was made worse by the veil of bubbles in front of her eyes.

She decided just to swim upwards.

That's when her air stopped flowing.

One second she was breathing, the next there was nothing.

Cold panic hit her heart. Not just panic for the situation now, here in the present, but a terrible dark memory, dredged like a childhood nightmare from her brain. *I am underwater and I can't breathe.*

Her throat seized up. She remembered she had a spare regulator, somewhere on her vest. She felt around for it, but her hands were suddenly made of clay. She couldn't move them properly, couldn't find anything with them, and stars were spangling around the edges of her vision.

The weight of her body.

The lead in her lungs.

Her arms reaching out for help.

The light going out in her brain.

Then, suddenly, her regulator was ripped from her mouth and replaced with another. She opened her eyes to see Alan, holding his spare regulator to her lips. She breathed greedily, letting him swim her slowly up to the surface. Grateful, so grateful to break the surface and breathe real air. Alan was shouting something at Graeme, who hauled her into the boat like a prize fish. He took off her mask and she blinked water out of her eyes. The sunshine was blinding.

"You all right, love?"

"I think so. What happened?"

"Alan said your reg malfunctioned."

"My . . . what . . ."

"Don't worry, you're okay. Do you need to go to hospital?"

"I . . . No, I'm fine." Libby sat up. "It was more panic than anything else." She swallowed hard. "I nearly drowned when I was younger. It brought it all back."

Graeme squinted off into the distance, as if afraid he was being watched. "Yeah, yeah. I see. Well. Let's not . . . Ah. I won't charge you for today, hey? So you don't need to tell anyone."

It took Libby a moment to realize he was worried she was going to report him for faulty equipment. And probably for letting her dive untrained. She shook her head. "I won't. Don't worry. It's the last thing on my mind."

He fussed about her a bit longer, then the other couple came up and they headed back to shore. Libby sat watching the water again, but without the lightness on her heart that she'd felt going out. Everything seemed too bright now; overexposed and raw.

Today had brought it all back: the reason she'd never wanted to return, the reason Juliet had never forgiven her. Twenty years ago, she had done something terrible. And she would never be able to escape it.

*J*uliet was sitting at one of the tables in the tea room, with invoices spread about her to sort out. It was late afternoon, just after closing time. She normally did this upstairs at her desk, but Damien was still in the kitchen measuring cabinets. A knock at the locked front door caught her attention, and she looked up to see the elderly couple who had been staying in Room 1.

Juliet rose to unlock the door, and they handed her their room key.

"Have a safe journey home," she said.

"Thank you for the late check-out," the man said. "We really appreciate it."

"It's fine. It's the start of the quiet season now and nobody else was using the room." She heard a thump from the kitchen and wondered what Damien was doing.

The elderly man nudged his wife, who reached into her basket and pulled out a bottle of red wine.

"This is for you," she said. "We had a lovely stay and your breakfasts were superb."

Juliet beamed. "Oh, thank you." She tucked the bottle under her arm and shook their hands. They said their farewells and Juliet locked the door again, placed the wine on her table and went through to the kitchen.

"Are you okay?"

Damien was crouched on the floor with his head in a cupboard.

He looked up when she came in. "Yes, sorry. I dropped one of your drawers. It's back in place now." He stood, stretched out his leg. "Though it did land on my foot."

"Ouch. You need ice?"

"I should be fine."

She leaned closer to look at his foot. A red lump swelled on it. "No, you need ice. And you need work boots, not flip-flops."

"I do have some. But . . ."

"Yes, I know. It's complicated. You've said that a few times now."

"I don't mean to be mysterious." He glanced around. "I'm done with measurements. Want to talk through some ideas?"

Juliet hesitated, then swallowed hard and ploughed ahead. "I've got a bottle of wine out there. Would you like to share it?"

He smiled. "I would love that."

She found a bag of frozen peas for his foot and they sat in the locked tea room by soft lamplight, drinking wine out of tea-cups. She opened the side windows so they could hear the sea. They talked through the first cup about his ideas for the kitchen, through the second cup about how she had managed the business these last fifteen years, and by the third her curiosity overrode her politeness.

"You'd better tell me what's going on. Why don't you have access to your bank or your boots or anything else?"

Damien shook his head. "A very, very bad relationship break-down." The pain on his face was momentarily visible but then carefully hidden. Juliet had a flash of memory from twenty years ago: Damien frightened by a bad dream. In childhood, the night-mare situations usually involved monsters. In adulthood, night-mares were far more mundane. Broken hearts, money worries, family problems.

"We owned a lot of stuff together," he continued. "She's locked me out of all of it. Bank accounts, our house . . . I had to break into my own garage to get my car. I swiped the cat while I was there. Left her with Libby."

"I'm really sorry to hear it."

He shook his head. "Wow. This is the first time I've talked about it to anyone." He laughed. "I don't know if it's the wine or if it's just because I've known you so long. Trusted you with my feelings . . ."

Her heart felt warm. Or perhaps she was just a little drunk.

"You know, I haven't even told my mother. She didn't like Rachel and she warned me about her." Damien shrugged. "Sorry. I guess I sound pathetic."

"Not at all. But you shouldn't just let her . . . Rachel get away with it. Can you call a lawyer?"

"I'll get there. Eventually. Time will help, I hope. She'll cool off and . . ." He trailed off. "Well, nobody knows what the future holds. I'm trying to be optimistic, but it's been a little hard sleeping on a mattress in a lighthouse. So, now you can see how much it has meant to me to have a proper place to stay."

Juliet considered him by the lamplight. The sea roared in the distance. She had a sensation of the familiar and the strange, the past and the present lying on top of each other: she knew Damien, but she didn't know him; she knew her sister, but she didn't know her. Why was this all happening at once? It was as though the twenty-year anniversary of Andy's death had brought to the surface matters that had long been buried.

"Anyway," Damien said, shifting in his seat and rearranging the frozen peas on his foot. He looked very comfortable and at ease. "In-kind. I told you my dark secret. What's yours?"

She smiled. "I don't have one."

"Yes, you do. What's going on with you and Libby?"

"Nothing," she said, a reflex.

"Come on. It's written all over your face that something's wrong. You practically flinch when I say her name."

Juliet sighed. Libby. Inescapable Libby. "The short version is that I haven't seen her for twenty years and now she's shown up and is making life difficult for me."

"Difficult? She just sent you a free carpenter." He spread his hands.

She laughed. "Well. I suppose I'll send her a thank-you card."

"You're lucky to have a sister. I always wished for a sister or a brother."

Juliet remembered all the times she'd wished she didn't have one. "It's complicated."

"Why did she go away for twenty years anyway?"

"Lighthouse Bay wasn't enough for her."

"But not even to visit? To maintain contact with you?"

Dark feelings. She wished she hadn't drunk so quickly. Her head felt crowded.

Damien seemed to read her mood. He dropped his voice low. "Juliet? Are you okay?"

She shook her head.

He was silent a moment, then he said, very softly, "What happened?"

"Andy drowned," she said.

"Libby told me that much. What *really* happened?"

Juliet took a deep shuddering breath, the horrible truth— voiceless for years—about to be spoken aloud in the world. Was she really going to say it? But then the words were falling from her lips and she couldn't recall them. "Andy drowned and it was Libby's fault."

Damien was stunned, wordless for a few moments. "Okay," he said, "you're going to have to tell me everything."

So she told him. Everything.

*J*uliet and Andy were meant to be together, and everybody knew it. She'd made a space next to her in Year Nine math class for the new boy with the sandy hair and the deep brown eyes, and he'd occupied it willingly from that moment on. They were like an old married couple by their final year. Other relationships around them came and went. Libby, with her head-turning looks and coquettish teenage vanity, chewed through boyfriends in a week or two; but Juliet and Andy were steady.

But not boring. Never boring. He had a unique intelligence. He saw things from such interesting perspectives. She loved to talk to him, for hours and hours, about everything: the natural world, the social world, history, philosophy, cooking, painting, anything. He had something to say. And just when she thought she wasn't interesting enough or clever enough to keep him, he would laugh at one of her jokes and she would be reminded that it would always be easy with Andy. He loved her easily; he was easy to love.

Then there had been a pregnancy scare. A false alarm as it happened, but they'd started thinking, *Why wait?* They knew they wanted each other, they knew they wanted a family, a future. Dad had given them his blessing: he adored Andy. A beach wedding— she would wear something simple and pretty—then a life together full of as many simple moments as adventures. Soul mates.

It was Libby who suggested the night-before party. Juliet had turned down the idea of a hen's night, just as Andy had little interest in a boys-only night on the town. So Libby invited a dozen old school friends out to the surf club. Juliet didn't want to be hungover at her wedding and, besides, she was never much of a drinker, and Andy kept her company in sobriety. But everybody else drank way too much, the way only young adults do.

Libby drank the most of all. Juliet had seen her wild before, but tonight something was different. She had on her usual bright red lipstick, her dark hair was teased up high, and she wore a tight blue dress. Every man in the surf club was stealing glances at her. But it wasn't just her looks that were attracting attention. She was laughing loudly, flirting with everyone, tossing her hair and making lingering eye contact. Juliet often wondered if Libby was jealous of Juliet getting married: she was, after all, used to being the center of attention. Or perhaps she was just happy and excited that night.

It was definitely Libby who suggested they all go skinny-dipping at the beach. There were murmured agreements, but it wasn't serious. They flowed out of the surf club and down onto the sand, laughing and chatting and splashing about, but nobody really thought they would go in for a swim.

Until somebody dared Libby. It was one of the boys, no doubt inflamed from a night watching her vivacious show.

"Double dare me!" Libby shouted. And then, "Triple dare me!"

This went on for a while and Juliet had started to feel tired. She squeezed Andy's hand and leaned into his warm shoulder. The April breeze was soft on her skin. "Time for bed," she said.

"And when we wake up, it will be tomorrow."

She turned her face up for a kiss, and his warm mouth closed over hers. But a sudden screeching made him break off. A hundred meters down the beach, Libby was wriggling out of her blue dress. The others were hooting and laughing. Juliet and Andy stood back.

"She's gone crazy," Juliet said.

"She shouldn't go in the water like that," Andy said. "She's too drunk."

The first stir of unease spread across her skin.

There was Libby, wading into the water in her black bra and knickers. Then diving under and emerging, hair flat now, make-up streaming, laughing and laughing. "Come on!" she called. "The water's fine."

She dived again.

And time grew elastic. Juliet's breath went hard in her lungs.

"Where is she?" Andy said.

A white limb, flailing, a long distance from where Libby had disappeared. Panicked shouts down near the water's edge. Andy running for the water—the only one sober and strong enough to save Libby—peeling off his shirt and diving in.

And never coming out.

Juliet heard the silence that followed her voice—it had seemed to go on for a long time—and she couldn't meet Damien's eye. Inexplicably, she felt embarrassed. For talking too long, for getting choked up, for not being able to forgive and forget after twenty years. For loving too hard. For not getting over it. For telling this young, attractive man who probably saw her as a pitiful case, past her prime, on her way to terminal, bitter spinsterhood. The wave of self-loathing was so enormous that it crushed her.

But then, Damien's hand crept over hers. He took her fingers in his own and squeezed firmly. "I am so, so sorry."

She watched his hand on hers. His tanned, strong fingers. But then he withdrew the contact and sat back in his chair, and she was forced to look up and meet his eye.

"How did Libby get out?"

"Andy managed to get her on the sand bar before the rip pulled him under."

He paused a moment. "I'm sorry for Libby too," he ventured. "That's a big burden she's had to live with."

Juliet fell silent, anger and grief and her own guilt making her mute.

He smiled, held up his cup.

Curious, she raised her own cup. "What are we toasting?"

"That we lived long enough to see such miserable complications in our lives."

She blinked back her tears, laughing. "Yes, I suppose you're right. At least we're still out here, getting buffeted by the ill winds."

"And the wind can change any moment. Fairer weather. Yes, at least we're still out here." He drained what was left in his cup. "So, Juliet, are you going to let me rebuild your kitchen?"

"Yes, I am," she said. "I'm glad you're around."

*L*ibby abandoned the idea of sleeping properly. She kept busy day and night with work on the catalog and on her painting. Slowly, the cogs in her mind turned, and her decision became clear.

Juliet was never going to forgive her. A reconciliation between them was impossible, so there was no reason not to take the money. Selling the land to Ashley-Harris wouldn't hurt Juliet and she would see that in time.

Six o'clock came. Perhaps she'd slept two hours, not consecutively. Blinking made her head hurt. She could hardly focus on the tiny keys on her phone as she typed the text message to Tristan. *I've decided to sell.*

Her thumb hovered over the send button. Her heart skipped a beat. Then she sent it.

Her phone rang within minutes.

"You didn't check the time zones." He laughed. She could hear interference on the line. He was outside, somewhere windy.

She squirmed with embarrassment. "What time is it?"

"Four in the morning in Perth."

"I'm so sorry."

"Luckily I'm not in Perth. I came back yesterday. Finished business early."

Libby sat heavily in the armchair in her art room. The rising sun made her eyes ache. "You're in Noosa?"

"You want me to come by?"

"I want that so much." Did that sound desperate?

"You know I can't talk business."

"I just want somebody to hold me. This is the hardest decision I've ever had to make."

"Will you make me breakfast?"

"Of course."

They never got to breakfast. The moment he arrived she drew him inside and he turned her and pressed her against the door. Clothes were shed in a trail behind them. She lost herself for a while in the hard, passionate lovemaking, forgetting everything but the searing pleasure in her body. Then, after, they drifted off twined around each other, her body collapsing gratefully. Sleep at last.

Even if she was sleeping with the enemy.

Twenty

1901

The pre-dawn light is soft and blue. Isabella still isn't used to the sharp, fresh smells of the Australian landscape: moist earth and pungent foliage and tangy sea. The air is damp with humidity and salt mist. From the deck of the lighthouse this morning, she was able to see the deserted sea and beach: places it seemed no man or beast ever visited. But down here in the woods, there is activity: birds waking and animals creeping out of their burrows. It comforts her to know that other creatures are busy too. As busy as she and Matthew. A humid chill clings at her cheeks.

Matthew turns over soil with his spade. Under the ground here is the mace. The idea that it still exists in the world is both awful and wonderful. Awful because as long as she is near it she is in danger from Arthur's family. Wonderful because if she is clever and careful it will pay her way out of this dreadful place and into her new life.

But she has to be clever and careful.

She stands by and watches as Matthew works. His bodily presence is fascinating to her. His rough hands on the spade, the clench and release of his shoulders, the strong steadiness of his legs. Just a few hours ago, those hands and shoulders and legs were

gently yet unstoppably involved in pleasuring her body, and she
can't quite believe it. In the past, her body had seemed only on
loan to her: more properly the property of husband, child, family.
But Matthew has made her feel that she belongs in her limbs and
organs and skin. The desire for him ignites again.

He glances up, as though he can tell she is thinking of him.
He smiles and her heart lurches.

"What are you thinking, pretty bird?" he asks.

She smiles in return but doesn't answer. Through the trees, the
first finger of orange-gold dawn creeps. Birdsong intensifies. He
continues to dig. Finally, there is a *thunk* as his spade hits the chest.

Matthew falls to his knees, abandoning the spade. Hands in
the soil. Isabella joins him, brushing clumps of dirt off the box.
Matthew has one end of the walnut box, and he hefts it out of
the hole with a grunt.

Then he stands, grasps the box and says, "Come along, Isabella."

They return to the lighthouse. Matthew takes the mace up the
stairs to the middle deck and places it on the ground next to the
cabinet in which he keeps his tools. It would be easier to work at the
table in the telegraph office but, Isabella knows, Matthew is worried.
If somebody comes by to send a telegram, they will see the mace.

He opens the box and stands back.

Isabella lowers herself to the floor, her fingers brushing over
the jewels. Eight rubies, four sapphires, four emeralds and one
diamond: seventeen gems, each held by a carefully handmade claw.

"I'll need a set of pliers," Isabella says. "The smallest you have."

"Everything you need is in the cabinet there." He sits down
on the floor with her. "I'm sorry you have to work on the floor."

"I want as much as you to go undiscovered," she says.

"That diamond alone might fetch enough to pay your passage
to New York."

Two passages. She needed two. "It's a long journey. I need to be comfortable, in a cabin. I'll also need clothes, shoes, money for the other side. I haven't even found Victoria yet. I'll need a place to stay. No, I will sell them all."

"But surely it will create too much suspicion if you have these gems out of nowhere. I don't know how it can work, Isabella."

The plan is forming slowly, and any doubt that Matthew expresses is like a dull ache in her head. It is true that she, Mary Harrow, lately a lowly nanny, would draw much attention to herself if she suddenly started offering for sale the gems, especially seventeen gems in the same configuration and cut as they were on the mace. She must disguise them, and she certainly cannot sell them here in Lighthouse Bay. Quite apart from the fact that it would be too suspicious, there are few, if any, here who have enough money.

"Let me think about it," Isabella says, refusing to be discouraged.

Matthew goes about his morning chores. Isabella finds a fine-tipped pair of pliers and gently loosens the first sapphire from its setting. Gold is a soft material, but still it makes her hands ache. She is aware of Matthew's presence, here then gone, as the morning brightens. She is tired, so tired. She barely slept, so wound up from losing Xavier and so shocked by the fact she allowed Matthew to make love to her. But finally, she has all the sapphires in her hand.

Matthew crouches next to her. "It's going well, then?"

"I will make them into pieces of jewelry," she says. "I have always loved to make jewelry, and being married into the Winterbourne family has taught me much. No man will buy a sapphire, but he may well buy a sapphire brooch for his wife."

"But where will you sell them?"

"I am still thinking," Isabella says. "I have not stopped thinking." She trails off into a murmur.

Matthew looks closely at her face. "Are you well?"

She shakes her head. "No. I am tired and I cannot believe what life has handed me. But I know what I must do, and that gives me heart."

He touches her hand, and the flame ignites again. She gazes into his eyes. His pupils dilate, then his lips are on hers again. Isabella gratefully loses herself in instinct and pleasure. She is tired of thinking. Thinking frightens her.

Matthew walks up the road from town, a string bag full of potatoes and beans in his hand. It is strange to him how this walk up the road from town has become so significant, so laden with promise and anxiety. Once, he would take this walk and think nothing of it. He would be lost in thought, barely noticing his surroundings. But now, he is going home to Isabella. The path is no longer a neutral place: it is a happy place, made musical with birdsong and the crash of the wild ocean.

His heart is glad. So glad.

Yes, there is the dark thread of doubt. But it is a long way deep. Isabella is determined to sell as many of the gems as she can by making them into items of jewelry. This will take time. She isn't going tomorrow, or the next day. He knows he can't keep her—he knew that the moment he saw her—but he will be blessed with her in his life for a little while. And that is more than he ever thought he would know again.

For a week she has been working. There have been trials and there have been errors. She sometimes grows so frustrated that she flings a precious gem away from her so that it rattles against the ground. Then she stands, walks to it, picks it up and quietly starts again.

Matthew unlocks the front door. He is not greeted by empty solitude, as he has been all these years; there is another warm body in here. The thought makes him flush. Her softness makes him hard.

"Isabella?"

"Come and see!" she calls, and her voice is bright with excitement.

He moves up the stairs. She has continued to work here on the floor, right next to the tool cabinet. Her bits and pieces are spread everywhere around her. Every morning she eats and returns to her spot, fair hair falling over her face, focusing with the kind of desperate intensity that must have carried her through the long walk down the coast to the lighthouse. This time, however, she is standing, waiting for him, when he emerges through the hatch. She is beaming, holding out her hand.

In her palm is a brooch. Her resourcefulness delights him. A shell from the beach, a satin ribbon from her dress, the fine gold chain that held the walnut box's lid in place. Glinting darkly blue at the center of the piece, a sapphire. It is pretty, unusual. Just like Isabella.

"Very nicely done, Isabella," he says.

"Isn't it, though? Victoria and I used to make shell brooches together when we were girls. Though we never had sapphires to work with." She frowns. "I will need more things. Silver wire to make clasps and chains. I want to sell this one and use the money to buy what I need for the next."

He almost doesn't hear. Her cheeks are lightly flushed and her hair slipping loose. The stirrings of desire nearly unseat him. He forces himself to focus. "Where can you get such things? Not in Lighthouse Bay. Not even in Tewantin. Timber and sugar, yes, but silver wire . . ."

"Brisbane."

"You are going to Brisbane?" It is an overnight trip by paddle-wheel steamer. His gut clenches at the idea of Isabella alone that far from him.

But she is already shaking her head. "No. But I know some-body who goes there a lot, somebody who knows rich people who might want to buy jewelry."

"Who?"

"Abel Barrett."

Matthew is puzzled. "You know Abel Barrett?"

"I know more of Abel Barrett than most people," she says with a sniff. "I have a plan."

"Do not put yourself in any danger, Isabella. It's best if nobody in Lighthouse Bay knows you're still here. Mrs. Fullbright will no doubt have poisoned the well by speaking ill of you, and . . ." He trails off, suddenly ashamed. Isabella sleeping here with him in the lighthouse also needs to be kept secret. He cannot reconcile the fierce protectiveness he feels at this thought and the shame that he is the one who has placed her in this position.

But she is waving him away. "Don't concern yourself. I am not reckless."

He hesitates. He wants her nowhere near Abel Barrett. But then he says, "Don't go to his house. His wife is a friend of Mrs. Fullbright. He drinks at the Exchange every afternoon, usually with Ernest Fullbright, but Ernest is out of town at the moment. Your best chance of catching him alone and unseen is on Shore Road just after sunset."

She beams at him. "We are a good couple, are we not, Matthew?"

Even though he knows she means something different—that they are partners in crime—the thought of them as husband and wife comes to his mind. But there will be no marriage. Isabella

cannot stay in Lighthouse Bay forever, and he . . . he cannot leave.
It is too late in his life to leave. Sadness seeps into his bones.
"Yes, we are a good couple," he replies somberly. "A good couple
doing bad things."

Isabella dismisses him with a wave of her hand. "I see no crime
here. All I have taken from the Winterbournes is gold and gems.
They took from me my freedom and happiness without blinking.
Arthur would have gladly taken my life to save his own out there
on the sea. He pulled that oar so hard, I truly believed he wanted
me to be in the water with him." As she says this, a peculiar kind
of cold touches her voice and Matthew feels a niggle of alarm.
"Don't torture yourself with guilt," she continues, touching his
hand lightly with her soft fingers. "The end will justify the means."

*T*he wind off the sea is cold and heavy with salt. Isabella shelters from it by pressing her back against the sturdy trunk of a
mango tree, waiting in shadows and watching the front door of
the Exchange Hotel. A few people have entered the building,
but nobody, as yet, has left it. She is wearing Matthew's dark
overcoat, and her hair is under a scarf. The sun has set and the
evening hides her. Her heart beats dully in her throat. Sometimes
her scheme seems all too impossible, but she reminds herself to
take one step at a time. She has made the first piece of jewelry:
the first Winterbourne gem is ready to rejoin the world. That is
enough for now.

She looks at the sky. Stars twinkle between scudding clouds.
She has been so consumed with prizing the gems off the mace,
with making and remaking this brooch, that she hasn't stopped
to think. But thoughts come now. Thoughts of Daniel and Xavier
and Arthur and Matthew. Thoughts of Victoria, whom Matthew

is trying to locate in America. Isabella would say she feels a long way from home, only she isn't sure where home is anymore. She is adrift in the world. Perhaps she is destined to be the kind of woman who only touches certain spaces at certain times. For now, home is the lighthouse, but she knows it cannot last. Matthew knows too.

But she wants very much to be a different kind of woman: one with family and roots and bricks under her feet that will be there when she dies. Melancholy washes over her, but she tells herself there is no time to be melancholy. All she must do now is sell the jewels and make enough money for a comfortable, safe passage into her new life.

The door swings open, and there he is. But he is not alone and Isabella's heart falls. She must be alone with Abel Barrett, or this will not work. He is lighting a cigar and chatting to another man. She slumps against the tree.

Then Abel Barrett waves the other man off, and he is alone, walking in her direction. She straightens, pulls the coat tight about her, and waits for him to pass.

"Mr. Barrett," she calls softly.

He stops, turns, peers into the dark. "Who is there?"

She leaves the shadow of the tree, but not by much. "Talk with me," she says.

"Mary Harrow? Why should I? What are you even doing in town still?"

"Talk with me," she says again, "because I know things about you that your wife does not."

He hurries over, anger on his brow. She braces herself. He might grow violent. He is a rich, arrogant man used to having things his own way. But he does not strike her. He is, after all, also a man whose wife keeps him wealthy. "Now you listen," he spits, "you are nothing. Nothing. Nobody will believe anything you say so—"

"Stop," she says. "Listen to me."

He puts his cigar up to his mouth, folds his arms and glares at her. The rich smell of his cigar smoke catches in her throat. It reminds her, inexplicably, of her childhood. Perhaps her father smoked cigars. She takes a deep gulp of the smell.

"Go on, then," he says. "I'm listening."

"I need your help."

He lifts an eyebrow.

"I need things from Brisbane. You go there all the time."

He breaks into a grin. "So you intend to blackmail me? I haven't any money of my own, you know. She watches every penny that leaves my bank account."

"No. I don't want any money from you. I want only your time." She fishes in the pocket of the coat for the brooch. "Here, do you see this?"

He peers at her hand, then withdraws a match from his waist-coat and strikes it. It flares into life, catching the dark gleam of the sapphire and making her palm glow amber.

"It's one of the few items of value I have," she says. "I want you to sell it for me and bring me back some things I need."

She senses he is both puzzled and relieved.

"This is highly irregular," he says gruffly.

"I am not asking much. And I will pay with my continued silence."

"So it is blackmail?"

"Bribery," she said. "It's a prettier word."

He puffs on his cigar, bright eyes hard on her face. Then he scoops the brooch from her palm. "I'm off on Friday. I'll be back within a week. This will be the only thing I do for you. Nothing else. No more 'bribery.'"

"I agree." She hands him the list of items she needs. "There will be money left over, I hope. Please bring it in cash."

He reads through the list, looks as though he might ask what she needs silver wire and a jeweler's glass for, but thinks better of it. He wants this transaction to be discharged and over with minimal fuss. Instead, he examines her face again and says, "Who are you?"

"Mary Harrow," she answers, without blinking.

"You are more than that," he says. "Katarina always felt so."

"I am only what you see in front of you."

"It is dark. There are shadows. I don't see you well at all."

Isabella bowed her head. "When can I meet you again?"

"Friday and one week. Here, same time. I will have your things, and then any relationship between us is dissolved."

She lifts her head. "One more thing," she says. "May I have a cigar?"

He pats his pocket, finds a cigar and bends to light it for her. She coughs and chokes and he watches her, bemused.

"You need to know that Katarina has put the word out that you stole from her," he says.

"Has she?"

"It was the only way to explain your sudden departure. I would be careful about town if I were you."

"I will be careful. Thank you."

Isabella sits on the beach later, finishing the cigar. The coughing and choking have passed and her throat and lungs have settled. A warm, pleasantly distant feeling swims into her head. She hopes Matthew is busy enough at the lighthouse not to worry about her. She is enjoying being outside, rather than locked up in the lighthouse hiding from the eyes and opinions of others. She smokes her cigar and watches the ocean, and dreams of what might come.

* * *

They share a bed but do not sleep at the same time. Matthew sleeps in the afternoon, they are up for a few hours together for supper, then she goes to bed. She works while he sleeps; he works while she sleeps. They make love in the morning when she wakes, when he has finished his long shift and needs the comfort of her body.

She rattles around in the lighthouse by herself when he is in bed, trying to be quiet, feeling bored and lonely and on the edge of desperation. Now she can do little but wait for Abel Barrett to return with her supplies, she finds the afternoons long and empty. Matthew has given her books to read, but she has never been bookish. Sitting still for hours on end makes her impatient. She thinks too much: long unfettered fantasies of how life might be on the other side of the ocean. Sometimes the fantasies are pleasing, but sometimes they terrify her. Winterbournes turn up and throw her in prison, she is forced somehow to marry Percy, Xavier dies of a fever on the long crossing.

This afternoon, however, she is neither reading nor thinking. She stands on the upper deck, outside, surveying the world from up high: miles and miles of white sand, green coastal woodland and sparkling blue-green ocean. The wind is strong, tangling her hair in knots and jumping down her throat, but there is something so exhilarating about being up here. It is as though she is part of nature, a bird perhaps. She spreads her arms in the warm sunshine and lets the wind roar over her.

Finally, it becomes too much and she rounds the lighthouse to find a sheltered spot. Now she is looking down towards the beach, and she sees two figures on the sand. A large one and a small one. She is reminded of her visits to the beach with Xavier, his sweet hand in hers. She feels the space between her eyebrows crease into a frown. Perhaps it is Xavier down there. With Katarina? No, Katarina would never go near the sand.

A new nanny? Already?

Isabella's heart feels hot. What if the new nanny is kind and soft? What if he grows to love her just as he grew to love Isabella? Surely he wouldn't. Surely he too felt the special bond between them.

She is pacing. She stops and holds on to the wooden railing, peering down through humid sea mist to the beach. It is an adult and a child, without doubt. Of course there are other children in Lighthouse Bay; it need not be Xavier. But Isabella is desperate to know.

Inside the lighthouse all is quiet and still. Matthew only sleeps a few short hours a day, so he sleeps hard. She tiptoes down the stairs, then lets herself out.

The wood between the lighthouse and the beach is thick with tangled plants and uneven beneath her feet. She picks her way carefully, emerging eventually on top of a sandy dune covered with long spiky grass. Here she pauses, scanning the beach. They are, perhaps, a quarter of a mile away, and it is definitely Xavier. He stands with his thumb in his mouth: a familiar pose. The woman's back is turned, but it isn't Katarina. It is a matronly woman who has crouched to build a sandcastle while Xavier watches.

Isabella aches to hold him. This other woman, this new nanny, does not touch him. She does not pull him into her lap and stroke his hair and whisper close to his ear. Surely he needs all of these things to be happy.

But then a darker thought: perhaps he is happy. Perhaps he is happy *without Isabella*. This new nanny may not be affectionate, but she may be calm and practical and safe—things Isabella knows she is not. On the one hand, the idea that Xavier is not suffering is a relief. On the other, the idea makes Isabella desolate. If he doesn't need saving, then what is her purpose in life? She does not want to go on the long journey to America alone across the hollow miles.

Isabella creeps along the edge of the wood, hoping to get close enough to see better. Something about the hunch of the woman's shoulders is familiar to Isabella. On closer view, she realizes it is Cook. Cook is looking after Xavier. Of course. Katarina would not have found a new nanny so quickly. She is relieved because she knows not only that Cook will be kind to Xavier, but also that she will keep her distance. Cook is intently focused on the sandcastle. Xavier scans the horizon.

Isabella holds still, willing him to look her way. He doesn't.

She moves back into the hem of the wood and picks her way down towards them. Cook will not want to see her. If what Abel Barrett says is true, and the town thinks she is a thief, it is not safe to speak to anyone.

They are playing hide-and-go-seek now, Cook and Xavier. Cook stands on the sand facing the sea, with her hands covering her eyes, and Xavier hurries up the sand and into the wood. He won't go far: he is afraid of snakes. But Cook turns and makes a fuss of not being able to see him, finds him in the edge of the wood. Then she returns to the sand and they are off again.

Isabella's heart thuds. Dare she find him before Cook?

She dashes through the trees, clumsy over roots, scrambling over a gully. A low-hanging branch whips her face. Cook has found Xavier again, but there may be another turn. *Please let there be another turn.*

This time she can hear Cook's voice on the wind. Counting to twenty.

"One . . . two . . . three . . ."

And now Isabella is within calling distance of Xavier. Only she dare not call. She closes the space as quickly as she can. He hears her footsteps and looks up.

Isabella holds her finger to her mouth to indicate he must not speak. She grasps his hand and he squeezes her fingers hard enough to bend them.

"Quickly. Come with me," she whispers, pulling him farther into the trees. She hurries him to the gully and ducks down, gathering him onto her lap.

"I'm sorry," she says, tears on her face. "I'm so sorry. But you mustn't tell anyone you've seen me."

He shakes his head, indicating he won't. Has he stopped speaking again?

She stands him up in front of her and surveys him, feeling along his limbs as though not quite believing he is real. "I miss you so much," she says. "Are you happy?"

He cocks his head as though listening for the answer, then shakes it slowly.

"Is Cook treating you well?"

He nods.

She nods back. "You should go. I don't want to get you in any trouble. And you mustn't let on you've seen me. But I'll be watching over you, Xavier. And I still love you."

He nods again. Cook's voice in the woods: "Where are you, child?"

He touches Isabella's face once, his dark eyes huge and liquid, then he dashes off.

Isabella hunches down among the foliage, breathing deeply. All will be well. Surely all will be well. Just as soon as she is out of Lighthouse Bay.

*   *   *

*O*n the Friday she is due to meet Abel Barrett, Isabella's stomach churns all day. Her imagination, always prone to frightening her, pictures Abel turning up with the police, or denying she ever gave him a sapphire, or not turning up at all. If any of these things happen, would she dare to go through with revealing his affair to his wife? And would his wife believe her?

She need not have worried. Abel waits for her under the mango tree just after dusk. It is a clear, mild evening and the smell of his cigar smoke is strong and aromatic. He sees her approaching and moves into the shadows.

"Here," he says, thrusting a brown paper bag at her. "It's all in there. Your supplies, the rest of your money and the jeweler's address."

"The jeweler's address?"

"He surmised from your purchase of equipment that you made the brooch. He's interested in seeing more." He holds up his hands. "I don't want to know."

Isabella peers into the bag but can't see anything clearly in the dark.

"Don't ask me to take anything else for you," Abel continues. "That's it. We are square."

"Yes. We are square."

He is visibly relieved. "And now, I can't linger. I can't be seen with another woman."

"How is Katarina? And the boy?" Isabella asks quickly. "Is there any news of them?"

"I don't know. They are both away."

"Away?"

"Two or three months in Sydney. She is taking the boy to

a specialist who can get him to speak." He stubs out his cigar against the tree.

Complicated feelings traverse her heart. It will be so long before she can put her plan into action. And Katarina has taken him. Is this the sign of a loving mother who wants what is best for her child? Or is Katarina simply trying to fix him so that she needn't feel embarrassed about his difference? Isabella can probably convince herself it is the latter, but doubt has tainted her fantasy.

Abel Barrett thrusts his hands in his pockets. "So it is goodbye, and now I do not know you."

"Don't worry," she says. "You have never known me."

She watches him stalk off purposefully towards the Exchange. Clutching her brown paper bag against her, she heads for the lighthouse. She has at least two months, so this time she won't make just one piece and sell it. She will make half a dozen, or more. She will travel to New York comfortably and arrive a rich woman.

Twenty-one

For three weeks Isabella has not left the lighthouse. What would be the point? She will only run into trouble in town; Xavier is away and not likely to be on the beach; and she is busy, so busy, making brooches and bracelets from her dead husband's treasure. She works to stop herself thinking about the future, the past, even the present—for Daniel's and Xavier's shared birthday comes and goes and she feels too far from them both. She works so hard that sleep does not stop her: ghosts of ribbons and shells and gems arrange themselves on the insides of her eyelids. Her hands ache so much at the end of every day that she has to soak them in the icebox.

But she has made beautiful things. She is almost embarrassed about her first brooch now, the one she already sold. These are much more tasteful and pretty. Unique without being odd. Opulent without being ostentatious. Matthew has been asking her for weeks how she intends to sell them, and finally she tells him that she will take the paddle-wheel steamer to Brisbane from the wharf down in the Noosa River. He blanches.

"By yourself?"

"Yes."

He is afraid, but he lets her go.

And so now she stands on the wharf at Tewantin with her one-pound ticket, in a dress she sewed newly—and rather poorly—for going to town. She holds tightly a small case full of precious jewelry and one spare dress as she waits to board the *Plover*, a ninety-foot paddle-wheel steamer. Dusk is moist and cool. The smell of sawdust and animal droppings hangs on the air. Carts and horses and men carrying barrels move up and down the wharf. She tries not to stand out, but she notices she is the only woman traveling alone on the deck. She hears women's voices from the saloon, which has already boarded, but Isabella's fellow passengers are men in faded clothes making their way between their failed dreams of the gold fields and the security of employment in town.

It seems they stand waiting in the late-afternoon sun a long time, but finally she is ushered up the gangplank and on board. The deck is covered by a large, striped canopy, but the sides are open and it is a cool day. Some men unfold chairs and sit to read their papers in the last light. A number of the rougher-looking men gather towards the stern to smoke cigarettes. Isabella is not sure what to do, where to sit or stand, so she stands near the railing and watches the river disappear under the big wheel amid the smell of coal and the hiss of steam. They slowly pull away from the wharf. The evening air is chill and the wind makes her ears ache.

They won't arrive in Brisbane until tomorrow morning, and then Isabella has a room in a boarding house that Matthew organized for her over the telegraph. He was solicitous when he bundled her into the hired carriage that morning—telling her to keep her bonnet down low and glancing about all the time to see if anyone had spotted her—and then when he'd dropped her at the wharf he'd said she must be terrified of traveling alone. But she is not. Yes, there is a prickle of apprehension, but mostly she is excited. Her plan is unfolding. There is even a small, vain part of her that enjoys making jewelry and selling it. She is good at it. She has never really been allowed to be good at anything.

The *Plover* moves very slowly through the calm water of the river, then out through the mouth into the sea. She is reminded of the day she left England—it seems a million years ago now. She was surely a different person then. Night settles in and the coastline is too dark to see anymore, so she unfolds a chair and sits back. A purser brings her supper in a brown paper bag: a wizened apple and some bread and cheese. She puts hers under her chair and pulls her legs up next to her.

The smoking men pass around hip flasks, and start to grow rowdy. At first, Isabella finds it easy to ignore them, but then they start to sing in rough voices: songs with dirty lyrics. She is keenly aware that she is a woman, alone. She puts her feet back on the deck, an ankle on either side of her case.

She leans her head back and closes her eyes, trying to let the rocking water soothe her, but their voices are hard and loud and she understands this will be a very long night.

Then a woman's voice breaks through the rough sounds. "Do you mind?"

Isabella opens her eyes and sees a beautifully dressed woman in her late thirties standing at the top of the stairs between the deck and the saloon. She is pleasingly curvaceous in the way only wealthy, well-fed women can be, with dark auburn hair and a pretty mouth. She wears a well-cut shirtwaister with a large collar and full sleeves, and carries a silver-tipped cane. The authority in her voice is enough to make the men stop and turn, open-mouthed.

"I can hear every dirty word you're singing downstairs, and I am *most* unimpressed," she says, pointing her cane at them. "Let me ask you, what would your mothers think if they could see you now?"

Sheepish looks, mumbled apologies. The woman scans the deck and sees Isabella, lifts a curious eyebrow and flounces over. "You there," she says. "Why are you up here alone? Do you not have a father or a husband?"

Isabella is taken aback, searches for words. "I have neither."

"Why are you on this journey alone?"

She doesn't want to say that she has a case full of jewelry, so instead she says, "I am traveling to Brisbane for a . . . business meeting."

"Business? What business?"

Isabella thinks quickly. "It's private . . . personal."

Despite her plain answer, the woman softens. "A business-woman, eh? And all you can afford is a seat up on deck with those ruffians?"

Isabella nods.

The woman offers her a soft hand, which Isabella takes curiously. A moment later she is hauled to her feet.

"Come," the woman says. "You can join me and my entourage in the saloon."

"I haven't the right ticket."

"A minor matter. Let me take care of it. I'm Berenice. Well, I'm Lady McAuliffe, but you may call me Berenice."

"Mary Harrow," she says, picking up her case and following.

"Mary Harrow, I hope you have learned your lesson. The twenty-five extra shillings for a saloon ticket are *always* worth it."

Isabella is led down the stairs and into the saloon. It is lit with dozens of candles. A semi-circular leather seat is built into either end, with a large table covered in food: roast turkey and potatoes and china bowls full of peas and gravy. Well-dressed people play cards at small, round tables. It is quiet and calm.

The purser pounces on them the moment they set foot on the carpeted floor. "She can't be here."

Berenice waves him away. "Nonsense. I know you have a free berth back there, and Miss Harrow is going to sleep in it. She's going to share the food my friends and I have paid for, and you're not going to say a word about it."

"But her ticket is for the deck."

And now all Berenice's lightness is gone. Her voice is made of iron. "Yes, and there are a bunch of monstrous, noisy men up there whom I had to go and silence because you aren't doing your job."

When it looks as though he might speak again, Berenice presses a finger against his mouth firmly. "This young woman is traveling to Brisbane *alone*. I won't have her sitting among ruffians. Now do not speak to me of it again or I shall think you less than a gentleman."

The purser, angry but resigned, leaves them be. Berenice turns a twinkling smile on Isabella. "I always get my way," she says. "Now, something to eat?"

Isabella helps herself to a small plate of food as Berenice introduces her to her friends: two women and one portly man with a mischievous grin. They greet her easily and continue talking and laughing as if she has been their friend her whole life. Isabella deduces from the conversation that Lady McAuliffe is a rich widow whose husband, son of a London MP, owned a lucrative gold claim in Gympie. Now Berenice runs the business and lives the high life in Brisbane. She is an extraordinary woman, imbued with the energy and glow of the sun. Her friends hang on every word she says as she offers her opinions, thinks aloud through her philosophies and tells jokes far dirtier than the ones the men on the deck were singing. Isabella is fascinated by her.

And Berenice is fascinated by Isabella. Isabella, guilty for lying about her name and intentions, tries not to answer any of Berenice's questions directly. But somehow it slips out that her husband is dead, that she has a sister in New York whom she hopes to reach very soon, and that she owns only two dresses, one of which she is wearing.

"How long will you be in Brisbane?" Berenice asks thoughtfully, after hiding her shock at the idea of owning only two dresses.

"I'm booked to return three days hence."

"And where are you staying?"

"A boarding house in New Farm. I'm told it's clean and it takes women and children."

Already Berenice is waving her hand dismissively. "New Farm is *miles* from Eagle Street, where the steamer docks. You mustn't stay there. You must come to stay with me."

"Truly? That is too generous an offer."

"Yes, yes, you must. Then I'll send you in my carriage to your business meeting. A pretty, well-bred girl such as you shouldn't have to rough it."

Isabella realizes that she cannot say no: Berenice is not a woman to whom people say no. "I will happily accept your offer of a place to stay, but you must allow me to be free to make my own way between appointments."

Berenice momentarily withdraws her dazzling smile. Her friends watch carefully to see what she will do with this resistance—they look almost frightened—but then she smiles again and rubs Isabella's wrist. "You remind me of me at your age," she says. "You know what you want. An independent spirit."

The purser approaches them and hands Isabella a pillow and a blanket. "For your berth," he says. "It's the last one on the starboard side."

"Thank you."

He glances at Berenice, then back to Isabella. Nods once and heads off. She is suddenly very tired.

"I'm very sorry," she says, "but I'm exhausted."

"Of course you are, you poor dear. We will see you at breakfast." Berenice kisses her cheek. "Dream beautiful dreams."

Isabella makes her way to her berth, a fold-down bed in a shallow alcove concealed by a thin curtain. She climbs into it and curls on her side under the blanket. *Dream beautiful dreams.* She tries, she really tries, but the moment she is alone the melancholy comes back and her dreams are a confused jumble of images: water and steam and coal and thunder, and a little boy slipping away from her forever in a dark wood.

$\mathscr{I}$sabella holds the address of Maximillian Hardwick the jeweler in her left hand, her case in her right. She is tired in her body and her mind. Berenice continued to probe her with questions over breakfast. The more Isabella deferred and demurred, the harder Berenice prodded. She wonders if she'd have been better at the boarding house.

A well-dressed man on a bicycle speeds past, his warning bell jolting Isabella out of her thoughts. It is a busy town, with flat roads and new buildings. A horse-drawn tram rattles along in the middle of the unpaved road. She notices all the women have parasols, and with the bright sun full on her face—even in this cool season—she understands why. She tries to cling to shade as she finds her way to Queen Street and looks out for the jeweler's sign. Finally, she spots it in an upper-story window. Isabella pats her case for good luck and walks up the stone stairs and into the jeweler's store.

It is a small shop with a strong smell of wax and polish. The only light comes through a narrow window with the jeweler's name painted on it: from the inside it reads backwards. In glass cabinets sit jewelry and watches and decorative clocks. An elderly man with a thick mustache sits behind the counter at a table where jewelry is spread out to be cleaned. He looks up as she enters, his eyes crinkling in a smile. "Good morning, madam," he says in a deep voice. "How may I help?"

"I am Mary Harrow," she says, extending a gloved hand.

"Max Hardwick." He takes her hand and gives it a brief squeeze before dropping it. "I know your name. Abel Barrett was in here several weeks ago, selling a brooch to me that I suspect you made."

"You have a good memory, sir."

"Am I right? It wasn't a family heirloom. Far too modern."

"Yes. I did make it, and I have brought more in the hope that you will take them too." She lifts the case onto the counter. "Would you like to see?"

"Well, then," he says, wiping his hands on his apron. "Open it up."

She opens the case and pulls out three brooches and three bracelets. They are a tasteful concoction of dazzling gems and natural materials, made feminine with lacquered ribbon and lace. He pores over them with his jeweler's glass to his eye.

"The wire wrapping is most unusual."

"My father taught me the method, as a girl."

"Where did you get these rubies and sapphires?" he asks.

She doesn't show that her pulse has quickened. "I bought them with the small inheritance my late husband left me," she lies smoothly. "I had always wanted to make jewelry, and he had always encouraged me. I create these pieces with him in my mind and it makes me feel close to him still."

The jeweler nods sadly. As he looks over the jewelry, Isabella glances around the room. She notices an entire cabinet of Winterbourne jewelry.

"They are lovely and I do want them," he says at last. "However, I haven't the money to buy them all from you. I've not yet sold the first one. But if you want to leave them here I can sell them for you and take a small commission."

Isabella's heart sags with disappointment. "No money?"

"Eventually there will be money, dear. Where can I contact you to let you know they've sold?"

This is not the plan. The plan is he buys them all, for as much or more than he paid for the last piece; that she leaves here a rich woman who needs to wait only a little while for her young charge to accompany her to New York. Who knows how long it will take to sell all the pieces? Dare she leave them here with him? What if he is not honest? What if the gems are recognized?

Her brain is full of blackbirds now. She cannot decide what to do. The desolate feeling, repressed under so fine a veil, has returned. What will become of her?

She imagines Matthew is here. What would he advise? A warm calm steals over her.

"I will leave you half the pieces," she says, pushing forward two bracelets and a brooch. "You may contact me via the telegraph office at Lighthouse Bay."

He hesitates. She knows he is wondering what she will do with the other pieces, but then he relaxes and says, "As you wish. Now, may I sell these under your name? I will have more luck if I promote them as an exclusive handmade line."

"I can only trust your judgment," she says, enjoying the small thrill of knowing her jewelry will compete with the Winterbourne pieces on display.

Her jewelry, made with their gems. A fine jolt of heat to her

heart. Stolen, all of these gems are stolen. And here she is bringing them into the world so publicly.

But it is too late now. Wheels are in motion. She says her
good-byes and returns to the sunny street, curious but excited
about spending more time with Lady McAuliffe.

"*I* thought you'd never get here, dear," Berenice says, grasping
Isabella's arm and drawing her into the sitting room. "I have such
a surprise for you. Meet Adelaide. She's my dressmaker."

"Hello," Isabella says curiously, removing her gloves. She has
been lost for a good half-hour, unable to follow the hastily scrawled
map that Berenice gave her. She notices that the long, overstuffed
couch is strewn with dresses.

"These are all old dresses of mine that no longer fit. Adelaide
is going to measure you up and take them all in for you."

Isabella is already shaking her head by the end of the sentence.
"I can't possibly accept such—"

"Oh, nonsense. Of course you can. I'm not ever going to wear
them again and they are just sitting in the cupboard gathering dust."

Isabella gapes. There must be a dozen dresses. "I can't. I
would feel too obliged." But she wants them. She wants them
so much. She has been wearing the same old dress for months,
and the one she made for going to town is already falling apart
at the hems: she never was taught to be a seamstress. "I would
be so grateful for a new dress."

"Choose three or four, then," Berenice urges. "I don't want
to make you feel uncomfortable, but a beautiful young woman
needs more than two ill-fitting dresses."

Isabella cannot hide her smile as she searches through the
dresses. She can see herself on the ship to America in some of

these: elaborately trimmed tea gowns, shirtwaisted dresses with flouncing trains, gauzy white summer dresses with wilting sleeves and white embroidery. Then Berenice locks the door behind them and has Isabella strip off to her chemise for Adelaide to measure her. Berenice chats the whole time as Isabella is pinned and turned and stripped and re-dressed four times. Finally, she climbs back into her own clothes and Adelaide leaves with arms full of expensive fabric.

"I'll need them by tomorrow morning," Berenice says in a warning tone.

"Yes, ma'am," says Adelaide. "I won't let you down."

Berenice turns to Isabella. "We're having tea tomorrow with some friends. You're invited, of course. I'd love for them to meet you."

"I'd be delighted." The inkling of a plan. Berenice's friends are all wealthy and all do what she says. If she wears a Mary Harrow bracelet and brooch, she might be able to persuade somebody to buy one of the pieces she has left.

Berenice turns her head on the side, smiling her pretty smile. "There's something so sweet about you, Mary Harrow. I can't put my finger on it."

Isabella smiles in return.

"Come. Let me show you about the place." She folds Isabella's arm in hers and they leave the sitting room and head down the parquetry corridor. "My husband collected paintings," Berenice explains, pointing out the row of elaborately framed portraits that line the corridor. "I don't much understand the appeal myself. Painted people are never as interesting as real people."

"Are these people known to you?" Isabella asks.

"They were friends and relations of my husband," Berenice says. "I've forgotten who most of them are. Though come with me and

I'll show you the best one." She leads Isabella through two heavy wooden doors and into a library. One wall is dominated by an enormous portrait of a sweet-faced man with a half-smile on his lips. "There he is," Berenice says. "My dear departed husband."

"He looks kind," Isabella says.

"Oh no, he was a rascal. Hadn't a kind bone in his body. He frightened children. But I did love him and I still mourn him. How about you? Do you still mourn your husband?" Berenice fixes Isabella in her gaze. "No, don't answer that. I can tell."

Isabella's face burns with shame. "We each mourn in our own way," she mutters.

"Indeed. I miss my husband every day, but truthfully I am better off without him. He was terrible with money." Berenice grows quiet a few moments, studying the portrait. "I don't think I'll remarry, Mary. I think I'm better off alone."

"You're hardly alone. You have so many friends."

"Do you think you'll ever remarry?"

Isabella thinks about Matthew.

Berenice has a gleam in her eye now. "There is someone, isn't there?" she says with a smile. "I can see it on your face."

"I'm not sure what the future holds," Isabella replies.

"Another of your enigmatic replies."

"I don't mean to be enigmatic," she says.

"Well, whoever he is, he will have his faults. And you, as a woman, will have to overlook them. He'll be angry, or vain, or he'll treat your body as though it belonged to him. None of them are different, dear. None of them."

Isabella considers Berenice's words, and knows that she is wrong. Matthew is different. He is good. He is too good. He is so good that she will have to leave him secretly one day soon, because he cannot ever know about her plans. The thought makes her sad, but then Berenice is chatting again and Isabella is distracted enough to forget it, at least for a little while.

The lighthouse is empty without Isabella. Before he met her, he never realized how empty it was, or how lonely his existence: sleeping, working, eating. Easy and comfortable, yes, but empty. Matthew finds himself moping, something he has never done. The smell of her imprinted on the pillow is enough to make him sit still for a full ten minutes, his face against the pillowslip, breathing deeply.

Matthew sits out on the deck, looking at the moon and smoking his pipe. He is in love. He admits it and he knows he is a fool. Isabella cannot be held in one place. He has known from the moment he met her that she would leave him. But still he has gone and fallen in love. The thought of her alone in Brisbane makes him ache. It is so far away, it is such a big place. She cannot possibly be safe.

And yet, she does as she pleases. He knows better than to try to control her. The moment he tries to control her, disaster will come. That was how it was with Clara. He draws on his pipe as he remembers her shouting at him, running from him. He can't even remember the argument that sparked it: something about attending a neighbor's party without making it obvious she despised them all. She hid for four days in the woods outside town, returned bedraggled and grubby, laboring with a cough that sank deeper and deeper in her lungs until, six weeks later, it finally claimed her. For a very long time he had blamed himself for her death. Taking his first lighthouse post was a way of punishing himself: he didn't deserve society. But the prolonged isolation also allowed him to reflect and settle his guilt. She had said herself, in her dying moments, that he wasn't to be sad, that being sad was pointless, when the sun kept shining and the sky brightened every morning.

Matthew exhaled forcefully, leaning his head back against the outer wall of the lighthouse. Out there, across the ocean, Isabella's new life waited. And he would be here long after she was gone, as quiet and enduring as a statue, wishing he had never let her go.

Twenty-two

$\mathcal{P}$ercy stands on the beach, wondering if his eyes will ever adjust to the light in this empty place. It dazzles off the sand and it bites his lily-white skin. The constable stands a respectful distance away. He thinks Percy has come here to grieve his dead brother. Perhaps he has, in a way. But after nearly three months, the sting of losing his brother is fading. He is now more interested in scouring through the wreckage. Barrels and boards have been washed up by a high tide and left on the beach. There is nothing of value here, but Percy is very interested in the upturned lifeboat on the bar of rocks farther up the beach.

This hasn't been washed up as these incompetent colonial police told him. This has been deliberately placed by human hands. Which means the police are wrong, and not everyone is dead.

Percy flips the boat over and drops to his hands and knees, sifting through the sand with his fingertips. The ocean draws and falls in a constant rhythm behind him. First he turns up a shred of white lace, and he knows that whoever escaped in the lifeboat was a woman. Either Meggy or Isabella.

His gut tightens. Meggy Whiteaway was a seagoing woman. Had she survived, she would have known whom to contact and what to do. It was Isabella. He knows it was Isabella and the thought inflames him. He takes a moment to breathe.

Was Arthur with her then? Had Arthur survived? If so, where was he now?

Percy beckons the constable to come forward. "This lifeboat indicates somebody survived," he says. "Why did your lot tell me the opposite?"

"Because nobody has reported themselves. Certainly, somebody may have made it to the beach in the storm, but between here and civilization there are snakes and wild dogs and vicious natives. And none of these things put together is so dangerous as sun, exhaustion and thirst." The constable's eyes go to the bushland that hems the beach. "He may as well have walked into the mouth of a monster."

Percy turns this thought over in his mind, still on hands and knees, still tracing fingers in the sand. He considers the piece of lace in his hand and tries to imagine Isabella walking into the woods, looking for civilization. It has taken hours in a horse and carriage to get here, in blazing sun. Would she survive?

Damn it all. He *can* imagine it. There is something about her—a core of overweening self-regard that some might mistake for nobility—that gives her strength. She thought herself better than them and she would survive just to spite them: he knows it. How he longs to crush the arrogance out of her.

"Did you search in the woods?" he asks the constable.

"Yes."

"Nothing?"

"Nothing. I'm terribly sorry, sir." And as the constable moves out of the direct sun, something glints under a fine layer of sand. It is in his hand a moment later. The brass clasp from the walnut box made for the mace.

He feels his face flush and turns it away so the constable doesn't see it. In a flash, his mind has built the picture. Isabella escaped with the mace. Perhaps she caused the shipwreck. Perhaps she pushed his brother overboard. The conviction that somehow all this is true clenches in his guts. And the idea that she somehow got away, that she is free somewhere in this empty country with infinite places to hide, causes him physical pain.

"I'm sorry," the constable says again. "I'll leave you alone with your thoughts." Percy watches him trudge back up the beach. What now? Look in the woods for her? Go home and do nothing? She has the mace. He wants it back.

Percy knows he won't survive wandering in the woods, but he absolutely cannot return home empty-handed. No, if Isabella survived, she has been *somewhere* and met *someone*. If he puts the word out that she is missing, the beloved daughter-in-law of a powerful family, she will turn up. It may take time, but he will find her.

Isabella stands before the long looking glass, wearing a blue shirtwaisted dress the exact shade of her eyes. It has been so long since she has dressed well. She has no corset, but luckily her natural body shape is very small at the waist. She has her hair fastened loosely at the nape of her neck with a blue ribbon, with fair wispy strands framing her face. And pinned to her collar, she has a sapphire brooch that she made.

A swift knock at the door, and Berenice comes in. She takes in the sight of Isabella, dressed appropriate to her breeding, and pauses. "You look wonderful, dear," she says. "Shall I burn your old dress?"

Isabella laughs.

"I'm not joking. Not even a little," Berenice says, straight-faced.

She stifles her laugh. "No," she says, "I had best take it home with me."

Berenice spots the brooch, moves in and gently turns Isabella around. She fingers the brooch delicately. "This is divine."

"I made it."

Berenice's eyebrows shoot up. "You did? Well, aren't you full of surprises."

"I bought a few gems with a small inheritance from my husband," she says. She has told the lie twice now, and wonders if on the third telling she will start to believe it herself. "I have always wanted to make jewelry."

"It is no bad thing for a woman to have work that pleases her," Berenice says, beaming. "And this is gorgeous. A real sapphire, then?"

"Yes, it's real."

"But this would be worth something? Why do you only have two dresses?"

"I haven't sold any pieces yet."

"I'll buy one. What do you have? Bring them down to morning tea. My friends will love them. Handmade from things you found on the beach: I love it!" Berenice's face shines with enthusiasm.

Isabella shows her the other brooches and bracelets. "I will only make ten more pieces," she says, mentally counting the gems she still has at home.

"But they're wonderful, dear. You must continue to make more. You could start your own jewelry-making company, like that Winterbourne family."

At the sound of their name, heat jolts Isabella's heart. Any appeal from the idea of founding a jewelry-making dynasty of her own immediately vanishes, and she tells herself she must sell all the gems quickly and get to America before they find her. Xavier must come home soon.

Berenice has fastened a bracelet around her plump wrist and is admiring it in the light coming through the deep window. "Very fetching," she says. "I shall buy it. How much?"

Isabella names the price the jeweler paid for her first piece, but Berenice is already shaking her head. "Twice that, dear, twice that. People won't value something that doesn't sting. I'll show my friends. I'd be surprised if they didn't all want one. Then you can come back when you've made some more. Come."

Isabella can smell tea brewing from the upstairs hallway. This time, she is not brewing the tea, or laying out the scones and cream, or slicing the currant teacake into perfectly even portions. She is restored once again to the status of a lady who enjoys tea without having to serve it. She smiles and nods at the maid as she enters the room, because she understands now how tedious it is to wait on others.

Berenice has invited five friends for tea, and Isabella cannot keep all their names in her head. There is a Margaret and a Margery, but while trying to differentiate them in her memory she misses the names of the next two and then cannot hope to catch up. She smiles and takes a cup of tea and remains quiet and close to Berenice. For her part, Berenice is full of her usual vigor and enthusiasm, the center of every conversation, exploding into musical laughter without warning. The other women seem as dull as peahens in her company. Isabella presumes she seems equally dull, stuck here at Berenice's side.

But she remembers how to do this: how to make small talk and smile along while another person talks for too long or too loudly. She sips her tea and carefully eats a scone and wonders at how different this world is from her world at the lighthouse with Matthew. Where his place is dark and rough, smelling of wood and oil and sea, this place is light and polished, smelling of wax and lemon and sweet food.

After an hour, Berenice clears her throat and ting-tings a spoon on the side of a crystal glass until she has the attention of everyone in the room. She grasps Isabella's hand and pulls her up in front of the group.

"Now, you've all met the lovely Mary Harrow," she says, "but what I've not told you about Mary is that she is actually a jewelry maker. In fact"—here she brandishes her wrist—"Mary made this delightful piece and the pretty brooch she is wearing. She makes them from precious gems and things she collects on the beach near where she lives." Berenice turns to Isabella and gives her a reassuring smile. "And this morning she has told me she will only make ten more pieces. I have tried to convince her otherwise, but I don't think she'll change her mind."

There are approving mutters, raised eyebrows. Isabella holds her head high and smiles as brightly as she can.

"So, do come and talk to Mary, because I'm sure she'll be back for the spring ball in September, and if you want the chance to own a rare and special piece of jewelry, she might be persuaded to take orders."

As the morning wears on, every woman in the room comes to speak to her, to coo over her brooch. She is pressed upon to fetch the last unsold brooch from her room, and Margaret or Margery—she still can't tell them apart—buys it on the spot. This causes enough anxiety among the remaining guests that another woman—a petite one with curling red hair—offers to buy the one Isabella is wearing. Now she has sold all three pieces, she wishes she could go back to Hardwick's and reclaim her other three, because with the room in this mood she almost believes she could sell them all.

Berenice parts the crowd then, her plump arms spread like a saint, promising everyone that Mary Harrow will definitely be at the spring ball and that she will bring her jewelry to a high tea here the afternoon before if anyone wants a piece. "Spread the word." Murmurs of excitement pass from lip to lip. Isabella knows that if she can make ten pieces between now and then, she can sell them all and be on her way.

Berenice turns to her and says in a low voice, "And of course, you must bring your gentleman friend."

Isabella splutters. "No . . . I . . . He's not . . ."

Berenice winks. "You will find a way. Next time you come, you should be accompanied. You are young. Love again."

Then Berenice is off, chatting and laughing, leaving Isabella to contemplate how she might make ten pieces good enough to satisfy Berenice's friends and their friends too, with only six weeks to do it.

*M*atthew is waiting for her at the wharf in the morning sunshine. She steps off the gangplank as light and fair as a dove, in a frothy white dress, and his heart lurches. *Isabella.* The idea of her bubbles happiness in his soul. She sees him and smiles, hurries over and spreads her arms to hug him, but he steps back, fearful of the opinions of others.

The awkward moment irritates her. Her temper is on her lips in a half-moment. "There is no one watching us," she snaps. "More importantly, there is no one who cares anywhere in the world."

"I am known, Isabella," he says, soothing her with a touch to her white wrist.

Isabella sighs. "I want so much to hold you."

"And so you will, just as soon as we are home."

He has hired a horse and carriage for the day; was up before dawn to begin the two-hour drive up here. She immediately launches into a tale of meeting a rich woman on the steamer who took Isabella under her wing, of selling jewelry and having more cash tucked into the lining of her case than he earns in a quarter-year and of a planned return trip to see Lady McAuliffe again. As she speaks, his ribs appear to soften and sag. She has found others of her class. She has tasted once again that glittering life that she knew before coming to the lighthouse.

"Why do you look so sad, Matthew?" she asks him, as they rattle over a rock on the road.

"I'm not sad."

"You stopped nodding and smiling at my nonsense a good five minutes ago," she says.

"I'm sorry, my dear. I am only thinking of how simple and raw the lighthouse will seem to you after Lady McAuliffe's house."

Isabella thinks about this proposition for a moment, then she slides her soft hand around his elbow and presses her body close against him. "Simple and raw are not necessarily bad things, my love."

His body responds immediately to her closeness, her sensual tone, but most of all to her words. *My love.* She calls him Matthew, or dear, but she has never called him her love before. They do not use the word. They talk around it, even though their lips and their bodies profess love every time they connect.

And now, something has ignited between them. She has let down some guard that he hadn't been aware she was holding up. The journey home cannot pass quickly enough. She clings to him, her sweet breasts pressed against his upper arm, her warm breath on his neck and ear. She only lets him go when they approach Lighthouse Bay, and sinks low in the seat with her bonnet pulled close about her ears and eyes. Outside the lighthouse, he leaves the horse still in harness because an urge so great it cannot be denied a second longer has gripped him. She sits him on the edge of the bed, turns and kneels so he can unfasten the long row of buttons down her spine. Then she stands and the dress falls to the floor. She pulls off her chemise and is only in stockings now, her tiny waist curving out to round white hips and buttocks. Then she turns and sinks into his arms, fair hair falling about her soft breasts, which are marked with faint pink lines from her past pregnancy. He catches her and hears her say the words he has been longing to hear.

"I love you, Matthew."

"And I love you, my pretty bird," he says, through a mouthful of hair. "I love you more than I can say."

And for the first time he thinks, *Perhaps, perhaps, I can keep this one.*

*I*sabella can't sleep. A sad, strange sickness has gripped her. She dozes and wakes all through the night, longing for Matthew to be in the bed next to her so she can take some comfort in lying on his hairy, muscular chest. Is she coming down with an illness she caught on the steamer or in town? But no, it's more of a nausea of the skin than the stomach. She longs but doesn't know what she longs for. She tries to soothe herself on familiar fantasies, but they do nothing. The night goes on forever. Finally she falls asleep, just as dawn is lighting the room.

The sun is bright a few hours later when the bedroom door squeaks open and Matthew looks in. She opens her eyes, disorientated.

"Are you well, Isabella? You have slept so late."

"What time is it?"

"Ten o'clock."

And there it is back again, the feeling that her skin is heavy with unshed sobs. She should not feel this way. She is young and she has allowed herself to love again. Surely she should be waking to bells of joy, not a sick, cold dread in her hands and feet.

"I am not well," she replies, "but I don't know–" Then she does know. She knows and the pain is so sharp and hard that she sucks in her breath with a gasp, her fingers going to the black ribbon on her wrist.

He sits on the bed next to her and puts his arm around her. "My love?"

"Is it the second of August, Matthew?"

"Yes."

"Three years ago today, my baby died." Her voice seems a long way off, a rational sound in place of a horrified sob.

"Ah, I see," he says, and folds her into his arms.

She presses herself against him. "My body remembered before my brain did," she says. "Do you not think that strange?"

"Not at all."

"Arthur would have said it was nonsense."

"Arthur was a cruel man and now he is dead. You can always say what you feel to me."

"Then I will say to you that I feel desolate and remote from myself. That I may as well have died on that day and would have been three years happy in my grave."

"And I would never have met you."

"Perhaps you would have been better not to meet me."

He doesn't probe her statement, he lets it stand and holds her tightly against him, and she screws her eyes tightly shut and lets the tears flow. He doesn't pull away, he doesn't grow impatient and tired of her tears. But her skin does not fit her comfortably today and she eventually pushes him away gently and says, "I am not consolable."

"I do not expect you to be."

"I will go for a walk on the beach, to clear my mind."

"Do you want my company?" He is hopeful, and it makes her heart contract.

"No. I need to be alone."

She dresses and takes an apple from the kitchen to eat as she walks through the woods and down to the beach. Its flesh is sweet and crisp, and it fills the gnawing hole in her stomach, but the hole in her spirit is still there. Three years on and it is still there.

Isabella realizes she is half-hoping to see Xavier, that somehow he will be back early from his journey to Sydney. Perhaps his warm-eyed gaze could cure the creeping sadness that weighs her down today. But she looks along the deserted sand and he is not there. The wind coming off the sea is cold and the waves are flat like silver-gray silk. A seagull is riding an air current above her, its wings spread and curved but not flapping. An inclement day, so unlike the day that Daniel died. It had been late summer, a long day of warm sun and cloudless blue sky and bees skimming the grass outside as though they didn't feel Daniel's loss. They didn't feel it. Nobody felt it. Nobody except her, which made her the loneliest woman in the world.

She turns and looks back towards the woods. On the other side, and just a few streets in—surely she won't be seen—is the Fullbrights' house. Katarina still away in Sydney, Ernest probably off on a business trip, Cook busy in the laundry perhaps. If she creeps up the back stairs and into the nursery, perhaps she can find something of his to keep. A little toy that she can hold against herself just for today to bring a little comfort. She makes her way through the woods, picking over the uneven ground and then out the other side on to the path down the hill towards town. Carefully, carefully now. Some people think her a thief. Cook will not greet her warmly if she sees her. But surely, even if Cook does discover her, she can simply say, "How can you deny me a small memento of Daniel?"

Xavier. She means Xavier, not Daniel. Xavier is the living boy. Daniel is her son who is dead, who has not had a third birthday. Isabella stops in her tracks, heart hammering. Her moment's confusion of names in her mind has unnerved her, sent a bright, sharp shock to her heart. It is like waking up from a dream that has wrapped another dream. She had thought herself rational, but now she thinks clearly, perhaps for the first time in months. Xavier is not Daniel. But she knew that. Did she not know that?

She looks around her, as if seeing the landscape for the first time. She will not go to the Fullbrights' house and creep into the nursery. This would be the action of a madwoman. But is she mad to dream of taking him with her to America? Her fantasies have gone so far ahead now, she is not sure if she can pull back.

Isabella turns and heads towards the lighthouse. She has a month to decide. She does love Xavier, and the love is real, and she must do *something*. She can't leave a little boy she loves in a house full of cruelty and anger and stifling indifference. Surely love will find a way.

Twenty-three

Isabella discovers the romance of working hard. She discovers the delicious pleasure of pre-dawn industry, working while the sky is still dark blue outside, the pool of lamplight on her hands and the floorboards where she lays out her materials and works them together with nimble fingers. Making and remaking, while Matthew makes a wide circle around her on his journey up and down the lighthouse. She grows addicted to the work. In it, she forgets the unwise promises she has made herself about the future, she forgets her nightmarish anxieties about discovery, she forgets that she loves Matthew and must leave him in a month. There is only the delicate and detailed work in front of her, the early-morning silence, the reassuring light of the lamp.

Weeks pass. Her fingers get faster at wrapping the silver wires that hold gems in settings, the precisely even circles that form chains and clasps. But still she is pushing herself to have everything made in time for the ball. Some days, if her fingers are aching and her head is sore from concentrating, she wonders in horror whether Lady McAuliffe has forgotten her. She still hasn't had word from her. One morning, while she works, Matthew hands her a telegram and her heart lifts, knowing it is finally Berenice giving her the date and place where the ball will be held. But it is not from Berenice. It is from Max Hardwick, the jeweler.

Have sold all pieces. Please return to Brisbane soon to collect £120.

Matthew, who has transcribed the telegram and seen the figure, looks at her gravely.

"You have enough now. You have more than enough. Will you go soon?"

Isabella can see that he wants the answer to be no as much as he wants it to be yes.

"I have put so much work into these," she says, indicating the untidy mess of jewels and silver wire around her. "I will see it through until the end."

"You could take them to America with you."

"Berenice is relying on me."

Matthew nods once, hides his smile, then leaves her be. She reads the telegram again, then dreams a little. She could take this money and buy more gems. Collect more shells, maybe work in gold instead of silver for a while. She would love to try to make a pendant: the chain would take days, but how beautiful it would be. Imagine the things she could make, the prices she could charge. Her name—or rather, Mary Harrow's name—would be known across the world. She could spend her life making jewels, and employing other women to make them with her. She could have a house like Lady McAuliffe's, society teas, beautiful gowns. Isabella lets herself flow down this river of fantasy for a while. She is well used to living inside her imagination, for all that it frightens her half to death sometimes.

Then she adds something new to the fantasy: Matthew is there. Matthew is her husband, and every night they curl up next to each other and sleep that way for the whole night. He doesn't go to work while she sleeps. His body remains next to hers.

Isabella finds she is smiling, then tells herself that these imaginings take up far too much of her energy, and gets back to work.

Matthew has had a cold day out on the deck, buffeted by the sea while he sealed a window that had been letting in rain and draughts. He feels a desire to drink brandy at three o'clock. Just one glass, and he keeps none in the lighthouse. He feels guilty about leaving Isabella to go to town to drink at the Exchange, but she gives no sign of being jealous of his time away from her. She is in the galley kitchen, stirring a pot of pork-and-barley soup.

"Will you be back to eat?" she asks.

"Of course. I will be back at dusk to tend the light."

"Good, for I should hate to have gone to this much trouble for nothing."

He smiles at her and touches her hair. She finds cooking difficult and time-consuming, but can spend hours of every day immersed in her jewelry-making. "It won't be for nothing, my love. I am sure it will be the best soup I've ever tasted." This is a lie. The meals she cooks are universally bland.

She kisses his cheek, and he goes down the hill, the wind whistling in his ears but the imprint of her lips still warm on his skin. The fireplace at the Exchange, which spends more than three hundred and fifty days a year cold and unused, burns brightly. He is greeted at the bar, and then at his seat, where folks pass him and ask him about shipping and the weather, when what they really want to know is if there have been any juicy telegrams that he might divulge.

He never divulges. Yes, he knows the whole town's business. No, he is not in a mood to share it. Sometimes he believes himself to have the perfect temperament for a telegraph officer: he has never found anything remotely enjoyable about knowing other people's secrets. If anything, he feels mildly embarrassed to be the first person to know if somebody has become a grandmother, or has lost a fortune, or has unwelcome relatives determined to visit. He has long cultivated the ability to forget all of these things quickly.

Matthew settles at a table under the window where another patron has left a newspaper. He flicks through it idly, only noticing halfway through that it is a week old.

But then, something catches his eye. In among the advertisements, local news and gossip, he sees the small headline, "Missing Woman Sought by Husband's Family." His ears ring faintly as he reads: *Mrs. Georgiana Winterbourne, mother of late jeweler Arthur Winterbourne of Maystowe in Somerset, seeks news of her daughter-in-law, Mrs. Isabella Winterbourne, presumed to be living in a coastal area between Townsville and Brisbane. She is five feet and seven inches in height, of a slender build, with fair hair and blue eyes. She is twenty-three years of age, and may be living under an alias. A reward is offered for information leading to her discovery.* And then an address for Percy Winterbourne in Maryborough, a large town inland to the north.

They are looking for her. Certainly, they haven't a picture to run with the notice, nor even a particularly specific description—Matthew presumes that this is because, as Isabella so often said, they have never cared much about her—but they are looking for her nonetheless. Leaving his brandy half-finished, he goes to the bar and tries to appear calm as he asks Eunice Hand if she has this week's paper. She smiles sweetly and rummages under her counter to find it for him.

"Thank you," he murmurs, returning to his table, where he

flicks rapidly through the paper, page by page, his heart growing more relaxed as he doesn't see it. One notice. Once. By now a memory, kindling for fire.

But then he sees it again. Percy Winterbourne is running it every week. How many weeks has he run the notice? In how many papers? All of them between Townsville and Brisbane? Isabella says they are rich and they are ruthless.

He stands, downs his brandy in one gulp and folds the paper under his arm. He raises a hand in farewell to Eunice and any-one else who calls out to him, and hurries up the cold hill to the lighthouse.

Isabella is no longer in the kitchen. He rattles up the stairs to find her sorting through her materials on the floor. She looks up and says, "I think I have lost a clasp I made."

He hands her the paper, folded back to the notice. It is only two inches high, one narrow column's width. But she sees it and her pupils shrink to pinpoints.

"I will be gone in a month," she says.

"You should go now. Today." The thought makes his heart shriek with resistance.

"He won't find me. Not yet. This could be a description of anyone. Can you imagine? Any fair-haired woman who moves to a new town along miles and miles of coastland. He knows that. He is desperate and he is afraid that he'll never find me. With so many ports along this coast, he knows I could be anywhere in the world."

"What if Katherine Fullbright sees it? Or Abel Barrett? He must surely have suspicions about you."

"Abel Barrett won't say anything," she says, and she sounds very sure. "Katarina doesn't read well, and certainly not the no-tices in the paper."

"What if he decides to run a picture next time?"

"The only photograph of me is my wedding photograph, which sits on the mantelpiece in the house I shared with Arthur in England. He is hardly going to send for it and wait months for its arrival." She is less confident now, rationalizing his fears away as if to convince herself.

"You could be gone by the end of the week," he says. "On your way to America, to your sister."

"I am honor-bound to take these pieces to Berenice's friends," she says. "And besides, I have to travel to Brisbane again to get my money." She doesn't meet his eye and, not for the first time, suspicion stirs inside him.

"Matthew, my love," she continues, "even if Abel Barrett or any other person in town sends Percy a telegram, what will they say? That I was here, but then I stole something and was forced to leave town. Nobody knows I'm here. I am invisible."

He listens to her, and allows himself to be convinced for now. "We will be careful," he says. "And you will go the moment you have your money."

She is shaking her head. "After the ball. I have put so much work in now. I will be gone in little more than a month. You mustn't worry. We will be careful, as you say. *I* will be careful." She reads the notice again, and he sees a spark of fear in her eyes that makes him steely with protective instinct. Yes, even if Percy Winterbourne turned up at the lighthouse door asking if Matthew had seen her, he would do everything in his power to keep her hidden: lie, fight, send him on a wild goose chase to the other side of the country.

Deep down, he knows he has conceded because he wants these last few weeks with her. It is not like him to ignore the most practical solution, but he is in love and cannot be blamed. He hopes he won't come to regret it.

*   *   *

𝒥sabella wonders on which date Xavier will return. She dares not go into town to ask anyone, or even to hide by the mango tree outside the Exchange to wait for Abel Barrett. He said two or three months, and that was two months ago, so it must be soon. She often stands on the upper deck of the lighthouse and gazes at the beach to see if Xavier is there with Cook. *Please, not another nanny.* But he is never there. It matters little, in any case. She keeps telling herself she is obliged now to sell the jewelry she has made, just as soon as she returns to Brisbane. The truth is, though, she won't leave until Xavier is back and she can decide what she will do; or, indeed, how she will do it.

She is up on the deck one sparkling morning, her knees under her chin and her feet bare in the sunshine, when Matthew seeks her out.

"A package just arrived for you." He is frowning.

"What's wrong?"

"It is addressed to Mary Harrow, care of the light station. You ought not to have given your address, Isabella."

She takes the package from him and turns it over. The sender is Berenice McAuliffe. "Berenice will not give me away," she says, not feeling certain. What has Berenice sent her? Its size tells her it must be more than an invitation, which might have just as easily come by telegram and certainly wouldn't require wrapping in brown paper and string. She climbs to her feet and pushes past him inside, taking the ladder down to the main deck, where her work is cleared away until the afternoon. Here she sits on the floor, her customary position, and unpicks the knots in the string. She folds away the paper and finds inside a deep pink gown. As she unfolds it, a card drops out.

*My dear Mary, you are invited, of course, to my
annual spring ball to be held at seven in the evening on
September the fifteenth, at the Bellevue Hotel ballroom
on George Street. I insist that you bring your gentleman
friend. I have enclosed a dress (one of mine that Adelaide
has altered for you), which you may wear if you have
nothing else.*

*Mary, I have taken an apartment with two rooms for
you and your friend at the Bellevue Hotel, which is the
finest hotel in Brisbane. If you would be so kind as to be
my guest, I will ensure tea is brought to your private dining
room at four in the afternoon the day before the ball, where
more than a dozen lady friends of mine are keen to view
your jewelry.*

> *With much warm sincerity,*
> *Berenice*

"So, you are going away again?" Matthew asks lightly, although
Isabella knows he feels no particular lightness at the thought.

"*We* are going away," she says. She shows him the invitation.

Matthew is already shaking his head. "No, no. I cannot leave
the light."

"Nonsense. Even lighthouse keepers are due holidays, surely?
Can't somebody come and watch the light for a few nights?"

"No. Well, yes. If I apply to the government they will send
a locum, but we have only two weeks and . . . Isabella, this is
too dangerous. I am not fit for company. Less so are we fit for
company as a couple."

"Nobody knows you in Brisbane," she says, trying to keep the
heat out of her voice.

"But we are not married. We oughtn't travel together as though—"

"Berenice has taken rooms, not a single room or a bed to share. We will have separate berths on the steamer. People do woo each other, Matthew. They have a courtship and an engagement, and they are allowed to see each other during those times. Please try to remember this is the twentieth century. Women will have the vote soon, and then nobody will dare to judge a woman for traveling with whomever she wishes. Besides"—here she drops her voice low—"Matthew, we are living here without the blessing of marriage anyway. You know that. Why should you be afraid to be accused of something you are?"

She has gone too far, and Matthew colors from the roots of his hair down into his beard. Shame and anger. He turns away, mutters something gruffly, then heads down the ladder and slams the door to the telegraph office. Her heart beats hard, and she takes a deep breath and tells herself to be calm. It matters little if Matthew will not travel with her. She will survive. She will get on.

But there is part of her that so longs for his company, for him to dance with her as though they are in love and together, to show him off to Berenice, who would love his calm practicality and would surely appreciate his manly loveliness.

No, it is a silly fantasy. Matthew won't come. She stands up and shakes out the dress, holds it against her and admires the silk and expensive lace. But the thought of wearing it to Berenice's ball is hollow. She wants to look beautiful for Matthew, not for strangers.

She unfastens her dress and slips out of it, then pulls on the ball gown and laces it firmly. She unties her hair and lets it hang loosely around her shoulders, then turns once, trying to see her reflection in the glass cabinet. She catches a glimpse of her waist, the contrast of her white skin against the deep color of the fabric. Then she heads downstairs to show Matthew.

The door to the telegraph office is open, and he is not there. Curious, she moves to the bedroom door. He stands over the chest of old clothes he keeps at the end of the bed, his back turned to her.

"Matthew?"

He turns, sees her, and smiles. "You look beautiful."

She can see now that he is holding a jacket in his hands. "What's that?" she says.

"This is the jacket I was married in."

Her skin feels cool and hot at the same time. "You're married?"

"I *was* married. Many years ago. My wife died when she was only twenty. Her name was—"

Isabella quickly presses her fingers against his lips. "Don't. Not now. I will hear about her in time, but please don't give me a name just yet, lest I grow to resent it." She knew, of course, that he must have loved once. A man does not get to his age without loving; but the sting of jealousy she feels surprises her.

He presses his lips together, unhappy but compliant.

She touches the sleeve of his jacket. "Will it still fit?" she asks him.

"I presume so. I am not a man of much appetite, so my body has changed little. If you like, I could wear it to the ball."

Isabella smiles. "Yes, Matthew. I would like that very much."

He looks at the jacket sadly. "It is a waste to wear it only once, I suppose." Then he turns his eyes to her again. "I have already contacted the Telegraph Department. We will go away to Brisbane together for Lady McAuliffe's spring ball. You can't travel without my protection. Just in case . . ." He trails off, then gathers himself.

"Isabella, I don't know how much longer I have you, and I want this memory to hold on to."

She falls into his arms, pressing her face into his shoulder, breathing in his familiar scent. "I am so glad, my love."

They hold each other, both terribly aware that time is running out.

Twenty-four

The clattering horse-drawn tram drops Isabella and Matthew off outside the Bellevue Hotel on George Street. It stands on the edge of rambling gardens, opposite the parliament house, and is constructed of neat brickwork, wide verandahs and iron lace. Isabella clasps Matthew's hand firmly. She can tell he is overwhelmed but will not admit it. She squeezes his fingers, but he doesn't squeeze in return; he is still not comfortable with this open display of affection between them. But more than that, he seems to take no joy from their being in a bustling town where so many eyes can see her. The specter of Percy Winterbourne is on his mind. Certainly, it is on hers too, but she must not let it intimidate her. She needs to sell the jewels if she is to get away.

The entrance hall is large and busy, lined with pedestals that bear stone urns. Isabella can see through to the leafy courtyard past the reception desk. To its left, the huge double doors are open to a large dining room, and she wonders if this is where Lady McAuliffe's spring ball will be held. Staff dressed in white bustle about laying tables with crisp white linen. Isabella and Matthew sign in at the register and leave their luggage to be sent up in the lift, then find their way up the wide staircase to their apartment.

Matthew visibly relaxes when the door has closed behind them and they are alone. He removes his hat and holds it at his chest with crossed arms. "And your friend, Lady McAuliffe, has paid for all this?" he asks.

"She is very generous. Also, very rich," Isabella says, pulling off her gloves and laying them on the dining table. The furniture is made of darkly stained cedar. Two high-backed grandmother chairs sit on either side of the door to the verandah. A chaise lounge is pushed against a wall decorated with flocked wallpaper. Isabella opens the door to the first room to see a canopied bed and a cedar dresser with wing mirrors. She goes into the room and pulls the heavy curtains open to inspect the view across the treetops. This kind of luxury is familiar to her; she remembers it in her bones.

Matthew stands at the door. "We have a room each," he says. "I have discovered mine."

She comes to him, slides her arms around his middle. "Nothing will keep me from sleeping by your side all night, my love," she says.

He smiles diffidently and drops his voice low. "I am not used to so many people around. There may be guests just in the next room."

"They neither know us, nor care about what we do," she says to soothe him. "Come with me."

She takes him out onto the verandah, where two cane rocking chairs take in the view of the wide, sluggish river. Matthew runs his fingers over the ornamental ironwork while Isabella sits and rocks. "Is it not splendid?" she breathes.

"Rather too splendid for me."

A knock at the door makes him jump, and Isabella laughs lightly, touching his hand. "My dear, you worry too much. That will no doubt be Berenice." She returns inside and opens the heavy wooden door, and it is indeed Berenice, dressed in a silk tea gown.

She encloses Isabella in a warm hug, then releases her and stands back to consider Matthew, who hangs back shyly. He is not used to society, and certainly not used to the kind of lavish comfort surrounding him now. He looks out of place: Isabella notices for the first time that his beard needs trimming. She feels a pang for him so sharp and so deep that it almost takes her breath away.

"Berenice, I would like to introduce you to my friend, Mr. Matthew Seaward."

If Berenice notices his discomfort, she blithely ignores it. She shakes his hand warmly and says, "It is a pleasure to meet you, Mr. Seaward."

"And a pleasure to meet you, Lady McAuliffe."

She waves the title away with her cane. "Pish. *Berenice* will do me. And what line of work are you in, Mr. Seaward?"

"I keep the lighthouse and man the telegraph at Lighthouse Bay. I have been there six years, in service to the marine board for twenty."

Berenice inclines her head. "That is dedication," she says. "You are to be commended. Now, I am certain you won't want to wait here and suffer through an hour of women squawking over jewelry. May I recommend to you the reading room downstairs? It is a lovely apartment with writing tables and you may read newspapers or periodicals in peace down there."

Matthew smiles apprehensively, and Isabella is keen to know what has amused him. She supposes he hasn't had the company of many women, and Berenice is certainly a singular woman. Perhaps she terrifies him in her delightful way. "Thank you, Lady McAuliffe," he says, showing that he is determined to acknowledge the difference in their classes. "I will do just that."

When Matthew has slipped out, Berenice urges Isabella to show her the new jewelry. Isabella has kept her little case near to her the whole journey, and she lays it on the table and flicks open the catch. Berenice coos. There are six brooches and three bracelets. "So very beautiful, dear. We'll sell every piece. I've told them to bring their money with them, lest they go home empty-handed. The tea will be here in twenty minutes, so you go and wash your face and tidy yourself, and I will lay all of these gorgeous baubles out to best advantage."

Isabella slips into her bedroom, her heart thudding. At the end of this day, all of the Winterbourne gems will be gone. The sturdy rope that has kept her life tied to theirs is fraying. Soon she will be free.

She pours some water into the bowl on her dressing table and splashes her face with it. It has been a long time since she has seen herself in the mirror and she is surprised by how well she looks, how rosy her cheeks and bright her eyes. She can't remember ever looking this well back in England after Daniel's death. She had become a shadow, but now she is returning to three dimensions. A pull of panic: does that mean she is recovering from her grief? Please, no. She never wants to stop feeling it, in case it means she has stopped loving him.

A knock at the apartment door alerts her to the arrival of the tea. She quickly tidies her hair and her shirt, smooths over her skirt and returns to the dining room.

Two young servants are laying out the tea on the dining table. Berenice has folded out a card table and laid out the brooches and bracelets artfully. She smiles at Isabella. "You look beautiful, Mary," she says.

"Thank you. Thank you for all your help. I can never repay it."

Berenice nods once. "One day you may be in a position to help someone who needs it. Repay it to them."

Isabella thinks about Xavier, his loveless family.

Within moments, the maids are busy to and from the door, letting in a parade of society women in frothy dresses, who know and love—or know and fear—Berenice. They greet Isabella effusively, talk about how they have seen her pieces and "simply must have" one of their own, but their talk doesn't necessarily add up to action. They eat and gossip and drink tea, some of them spreading out onto the verandah, and Isabella worries that they have forgotten about her jewelry.

Then she finally sees two women at the card table, gently insisting that they each saw a ruby brooch first and therefore it is theirs to purchase. Something about this polite disagreement captures the attention of the others, and before long a crowd has gathered around the card table and Berenice presses Isabella forward to talk to them.

"How much for this bracelet?" one matronly woman asks her.

Isabella thinks of a figure in her head, then doubles it, as Berenice has told her to do. "Seventy pounds."

"I'll take it."

And so it goes, until all of the pieces are gone and she has enough money to take Xavier to New York and back two or three times. Her heart flutters, but her face is warm with excitement now, not anxiety.

Just as the last pair of guests are leaving and the maids are clearing off the dining table, Matthew appears at the door looking uncomfortable. "Shall I come back later?" he asks.

Berenice grasps his hand and pulls him in. "No, not at all. Would you like cake? We seem to have rather a lot left over. Everyone was more interested in Mary's jewelry." Berenice nudges her gently. "You really must make more. You could be a wealthy woman."

Isabella is aware of Matthew's gaze on her. "I have no desire to be a wealthy woman," she says. "I have a few, simple goals. I thank you for helping me achieve them."

Berenice's eyes narrow, but she is still smiling. "You are a mysterious one, Mary Harrow," she says. "I'm never quite sure whether or not to take you seriously. Nonetheless, you are a sweet girl and pretty to boot. I shall look forward to seeing you at the ball tomorrow night. Listen out for the dinner gong at seven." She nods to Matthew. "We will speak again."

"Of course, my lady," he says.

Berenice rolls her eyes good-naturedly. "Yes, well. If you're determined to call me so." Then she is gone.

Isabella and Matthew wait out on the verandah until the maids have cleared away and the apartment is once again their own.

"Did you enjoy the reading room?" Isabella asks him as they watch the sky turn dusky over the river.

"Yes, and there is an electric telegraph in the other reception hall. The hotel has its own."

"I think many of the parliamentarians stay here."

"I wonder who else comes here. Let us hope Percy Winterbourne isn't lurking, looking for you."

"Oh, pish, Matthew. You are seeing monsters where there are none."

"Still. There are a lot of wealthy people between these walls." He smiles across at her. "Am I to understand you are one now?"

Isabella nods. "I sold them all. I have more than enough for a new start in America."

"Then you should go. Tomorrow, maybe. Steamers leave for Sydney all the time, and from there you can get a passage to San Francisco or New York."

"Not tomorrow," she says guardedly. "I shan't miss Berenice's ball. Not just yet. I can travel to Sydney from Mooloolah Heads just as well."

"But—"

She leaps from her chair and presses her fingers against his mouth, then leans in and replaces them with her lips. "Matthew," she murmurs, "forget all of that for just a few days, please."

He does as she says, at least outwardly. But guilt is starting to dig the ground out from under her.

*S*tiff trousers, shirt, silk waistcoat, heavy jacket, dark cravat: one by one Matthew pulls the items on, wondering why he is here. He should have stayed home. At the lighthouse, he knows what he is. But here . . .

The trouble is Isabella. Back at home, he doesn't feel the difference between them. He is a capable, independent man of good birth and good intelligence. She is a warm, childlike, graceful woman, also of good birth and good intelligence. They are right for each other. It is only here among society that he truly sees what he has been trying not to see. Her breeding is apparent in the way she speaks, the way she takes a cup of tea from a servant, the way she holds herself. There is an ease about her that he could never have, even if he should live in this hotel for a hundred years.

Isabella is different from him. And he sees now that, despite those fond glimmerings of hope, they could never have been together. Sooner or later, he will disappoint her. It is right and well that she should go away. It is right that he will be alone again, though he suspects he will never be well again.

A soft knock at his bedroom door causes his heart to jump. Then it settles: of course it is just Isabella; not the police coming to round her up; not Percy Winterbourne with a pistol. She stands before him in a deep pink ball gown, with fitted bodice and puffed sleeves that are decorated with dark red ribbon. She wears long gloves and her hair is gathered loosely at the nape of her neck. He should tell her she looks splendid: a vision of feminine beauty. But he doesn't think it. All he can think is, *She doesn't look like Isabella. She looks like somebody else.*

If Isabella notices his lack of compliments, she doesn't appear to mind. Instead, she straightens the tips of his collar and brushes a piece of fluff off his shoulder. "Are you all right?" she asks him, not meeting his eye.

"I am perfectly well," he says, and he knows he sounds gruff but is unable to stop himself.

"Matthew, can you dance?"

"No."

Isabella laughs, and now she looks like the woman he knows and loves. All the artifice is swept away. "Well, won't we be a pair, then?"

"We can sit instead and listen to the orchestra."

She puts her arm through his. "I don't mind what we do. As long as we're together while we do it."

Arm in arm, they leave the apartment and descend the staircase. A small orchestra tunes up in the dining room, where beautifully dressed men and women move from table to table looking for their seating card. Isabella finds hers—*Mary Harrow and friend*—and Matthew is relieved to sit down. Already his suit has drawn a few disapproving glances. It is old and old-fashioned; he doesn't have a sleek tailcoat like everyone else he sees. He wonders if Isabella noticed his disappointing clothes and said nothing, or if he really is blind to them.

The room is lit by gas chandeliers. The light glints off glasses and plates. The orchestra plays a soft bourrée as people take their seats and the first course is served. The parquetry dance floor stands empty for the present. A very young man sits next to Matthew and greets him cautiously. Matthew wonders if Lady McAuliffe sat him with a young man, presuming that Matthew was a young man too. Isabella is only twenty-three. He is nearly twice that.

His unhappiness deepens. He blames himself for being a fool. An old fool. An old, uncouth fool.

And then she turns to him and smiles, and the light of love is in her eyes and he wonders what she sees in him. But it is clear she sees something and his heart stirs. How is he ever to let her go?

*I*sabella needs a break to breathe. Her face is sore from smiling. All evening, women and their husbands have approached her, asking about her jewelry, when she intends to make more, shaking their heads with disappointment when she says she will not. One gentleman tells her his cousin in Sydney is a jeweler who exports to the whole world, and he should be pleased to introduce her.

No thank you. She has known enough jewelers in her time.

She is glad Matthew can't or won't dance. The French kid Louis heels she bought this morning pinch her across the bridge of her foot. She had forgotten how very tiring society is. She has spent so long curled up inside the lighthouse, much as a sea creature might curl up inside a shell—exposed, its instinct is to flee for cover.

She leans in to Matthew, to tell him she is exhausted, and when she looks up she sees a beautifully dressed, very thin woman approaching. "Come on," Isabella says to Matthew, "out to the courtyard. I simply can't speak to another person."

Pretending she hasn't seen the thin woman, Isabella grasps his hand and pulls. He rises, throws his stiff napkin on the table, and follows her. The tables are half empty now as the guests take to the dance floor. It is mostly men who remain seated, drinking, and the occasional elderly woman with tightly set curls and tightly set expression to match. The orchestra plays a lively waltz, and the ladies and gentlemen in their fine clothes move in considered rhythm around the floor. Isabella and Matthew head for the big double doors to the hall, and breathe deeply once outside in the courtyard among the dense tropical plants.

"Oh, Lord," Isabella says. "I am exhausted."

He catches her in his arms and she takes comfort against the rough material of his jacket, listening to his heartbeat. He strokes her hair gently.

Finally she stands back and looks at him in the reflected light from the chandeliers in the hall. "You must be even more exhausted than I am."

"There's no value in competing," he replies, slightly gruff as he has been all evening.

Isabella looks up beyond the treetops to the stars. The night is cloudless, and the stars are like white dust spread with a careless hand across the dark blue. Soon, she will be looking at those stars from somewhere else on earth. For the first time she wonders what Matthew will do without her. Whether they will write to each other. Whether they will continue to love each other under the same stars, even though they will be apart. She has only ever seen this love as temporary: a short starburst of passion and color that would bloom and disappear just as quickly. But there will be an after, and she wonders what that after will feel like.

She reaches for the lapel of his jacket. "Tell me about the first time you wore this," she says. She hasn't asked about his wife, yet.

A mixture of jealousy and fear has held her tongue. But tonight she feels she wants to know all of him.

He softens, all gruffness evaporating. "I was twenty-four when I married Clara. She was twenty. She was the daughter of a tea merchant, I was the teacher at the village school. We fell in love." His voice catches in his throat. It is hard for Isabella to listen to this, very hard. When she speaks of Arthur, her voice doesn't catch on the word *love*.

"We were married in the local church one summer afternoon," he continues. "It was warm and all the windows stood open, and there was a frangipani tree in full bloom just outside the window. A rough wind came by at one stage and blew a few of the blooms into the pews. Forever I will associate the smell of frangipanis with my wedding. Waxy and sweet." He closes his eyes momentarily, as though he can smell it now. Then opens them again. "Clara was not like other girls. She had a wildness about her that was uncontrollable. Selfish. Despite her woman's body and her adult intelligence, she had the will and temper of a child. I was in love and my love was blind, and she quickly beat me down with her demands and her sharp tongue. If she was cruel to me, the next day she would be like sunshine, full of apologies and softness. We entered a cycle of contempt and forgiveness, until I grew tired and one day . . ." He takes a deep breath, runs his hand across his beard. "One day I said, 'Enough, Clara,' and I demanded that this time, just this once, she would do as I wanted rather than the other way around. She disappeared. For days. When she returned, it was because she was ill, and that illness claimed her life shortly afterwards."

"I am so sorry," Isabella says. She doesn't say the other thing she is thinking: *Clara sounds like a monster who would have eventually broken Matthew's spirit.* Then the thin anxiety roused by jealousy makes her say, "Do you still love her?"

He frowns as he thinks about this question. "It seems a lifetime ago," he says. "I don't *not* love her. But love seems to me to be something bright and present, and what I feel for Clara is neither of those things."

They both fall silent for a few moments. Crickets chirrup and the music from the ballroom wafts out to them. Matthew smiles at her suddenly, grasping her hand.

"Here," he said. "I have told you an untruth today." He takes her other hand and stands back, in dancing position.

"You can dance?"

"Very poorly. But it won't kill me to waltz with you in the starlight."

Isabella smiles, and kicks off her shoes. They begin to dance. It is a little uneven at first, but then they catch each other's rhythm and whirl quietly around the courtyard. Her heart thunders with excitement and love. His eyes are on hers, and she feels closer to him than she has yet felt. For this waltz, he is hers, her darling man.

"Ah, there you are!"

They stop dancing and turn to see Berenice at the courtyard entrance.

"I had rather wondered where you'd got to, Mary. The governor's wife, Lady Lamington, wants to meet you. Come along."

Reluctantly she drops Matthew's hands.

He nods at her with an encouraging smile. "I might stay here and enjoy the fresh air a little more," he says. "I'm afraid I'm not designed for crowds."

Berenice waits while Isabella refastens her shoes, and leads her back towards the ballroom.

"Now, if she says she wants you to make her a brooch or some such, you simply mustn't say no," Berenice instructs. "She is a

very important woman as I'm sure you can imagine and I . . .
Oh, where has she gone?" Berenice scans the crowd. "No mat-
ter, she will be back. Sit here with me for a few moments while
I catch my breath."

They sit at two spare seats at the main table. To Isabella's
right is a very drunk man with thin white hair. He is expensively
dressed, but he has gravy on his collar and the buttons of his
waistcoat strain against his belly. Matthew may have cheaper
clothes, but he is a hundred times the gentleman. Isabella turns
her shoulder to the drunk man so she and Berenice are not
interrupted.

"Your young man is not so young," Berenice says with an arch
of her eyebrow.

"I never said he was young. You just assumed," Isabella coun-
tered lightly.

"Is he good to you? Kind?"

"Oh yes," she says passionately.

Berenice looks Isabella up and down. "Mary Harrow, I have
been watching you all night. And I watched you at high tea yesterday, and I have watched you since I first saw you sitting there
with your back all straight and your knees just so on the upper
deck of that paddle-steamer."

Isabella's pulse flickers at her throat.

"And you are not what you say you are."

Isabella takes a quick breath. "I never said what I am, you'll
remember."

Here Berenice breaks into a loud laugh, dispelling the tension.
"Well, precisely. You dance around every question I ask you, which
makes me suspicious. What has she to hide, I wonder. I thought
you at first a banker's daughter or some such, thrown on hard
times. But your movements and your speech and your knowledge

of society prompt me to believe that you are born and bred much above the middle class. Much more like my class, dear."

"You flatter me, Berenice. Really, I am nothing special nor interesting."

Berenice seems about to say something when her eyes catch across the room. "Ah," she says, "there's Lady Lamington. Wait right here." She elegantly climbs to her feet and heads across the ballroom. Isabella watches her, then sees a flash of light from the corner of her eye. She turns. Two tables away, a photographer is taking a picture of a group of women.

Her heart bangs. A photographer. And she is fairly sure she is in the frame. He says to the assembled group, "Just hold still. One more for the society pages." And she knows she must leave. Now.

She shoots from her chair and hurries, Cinderella-like, away from the ballroom. Berenice sees her and calls out, but she runs, head down. Matthew is still in the courtyard. She calls to him, "We must leave. Now."

He hears the urgency in her voice and hurries to her side. Seconds later they are safely inside their apartment.

"What happened?" he asks, as she falls into a chair with her head in her hands.

"A photographer for the newspaper."

His grunt of disapproval tells her what he is thinking. He knew it, he knew she shouldn't have taken the risk of coming out so publicly, not when Percy is searching for her. And yes, she knew it too. She knew it, but she still did it because she wants saloon-class tickets to Sydney and New York for her and Xavier, and she wants to be able to take a lease on a good home when she gets there. She wants too much. And those who want too much are often foolish enough to risk everything.

*   *   *

$\mathscr{I}$sabella stands on Berenice's front doorstep in one of Berenice's altered dresses. Matthew waits across the road with their luggage. A maid has gone to fetch the lady of the house, and Isabella has no idea if Berenice will be angry with her for running off last night. But she has brought a gift and she wants to make sure Berenice gets it.

The door opens again and Berenice stands there, her pretty mouth is pressed into a line.

"Berenice. Lady McAuliffe. Please let me apologize for—"

"For embarrassing me in front of the governor's wife? By all means. Go ahead and apologize. I shall be living down that particular mortification for months to come, but there's no reason you shouldn't make yourself feel better with a simple 'I'm sorry.'"

Isabella swallows over her guilt. "I had to go, right at that moment and not a second later. And I *am* sorry. I would have saved you the embarrassment, but I . . . My safety was at risk."

"More mystery, Mary?"

"I'm afraid so. You've been so kind to me, kinder than I deserve. Please, may I come in just for a few moments? I have a gift for you."

Berenice wavers, but her heart is good and her temperament is naturally sunny, so she smiles a little and stands aside to let Isabella in.

"Come to the parlor, dear. I've just finished my tea, but there are some crumpets left over if you want one."

"No, no," says Isabella, untying her hat. "Your generosity has already been too much. I am here to give you something."

Berenice closes the parlor door behind them and invites Isabella to sit on the chaise. Isabella opens her silk bag and withdraws a pendant: the only pendant she has made. The links nearly killed off her fingers. A single diamond—the only diamond on the mace—hangs at the center of the pendant. At equal spaces on either side are two shining black stones, which she found on the beach in Lighthouse Bay: twins, exactly the same size and shape. For days she had looked over them again and again, unable to believe they were identical. Then she decided that these special stones belonged in a special gift for Berenice. The stones are wrapped in narrow pink silk ribbons. The diamond is held gently but firmly between tight coils of silver.

Berenice gapes at it. "You made this for me? But it's worth a small fortune."

"I have all that I need, now," Isabella answers.

"But so do I, dear. I'm a rich woman."

"This is not a gift of wealth," Isabella says. "It is a gift of gratitude and love. Every good fortune that has come to me of late has proceeded from you and your actions."

Berenice looks away. Her eyes are misty. "You continue to fascinate me, Mary Harrow. I presume this is the tenth piece? I had wondered why you only brought nine to the tea."

"This is the tenth and last piece. I have come to say good-bye to you, Berenice. I will soon go on a long journey, and I can't tell you where I'm going, so please don't ask."

"Mysterious till the end, eh? Well, I can't say I'm not a little offended. I would have kept your secrets." She puts her arms around Isabella and hugs her tightly. "Take care and be well, my dear. And do let me know, some day, if you are still in the world and well."

"I will try my best," Isabella says. "But rest assured I will never forget you."

"Nor I you," Berenice replies.

Isabella leaves the cool house and finds herself once again on the humid street. Matthew greets her as she ties her hat back on.

"You look sad," he says.

"I am sad," she replies. "I'm getting ready to leave everything behind."

He averts his eyes, and she realizes he is sad too. She thinks that if either he or Berenice knew what she was planning, they wouldn't be sad about her going. They would be glad. They would be angry. They would judge her. This thought makes her sadder still, and it is with a very heavy heart that she walks alongside Matthew to the wharf.

Twenty-five

The days grow increasingly warm and humid on Isabella's return to the lighthouse. Matthew tells her this happens every year as if to remind them what is to come: a few hot days in spring, cracking thunderstorms in the evening, then cooling off until Christmas. Isabella finds the warm, moist air enervating. She is tired deep in her joints.

Every afternoon, while Matthew sleeps, she goes down to the beach to let the ocean wind cool her. She collects shells and stones, still idly imagining pieces of jewelry she might make but never putting the thought into action. Matthew asks her daily when she intends to go, but she says she wants to wait just a week or so, until this hot spell has passed, because she is fearful of being at sea during a storm. Perhaps he thinks that she is reluctant to go because she does not want to say good-bye to him; this is partly true. But she knows she can and must leave him, if she is to live the life she has imagined for herself.

Although she finds lately that imagining that life leaves her with a sick guilt in her stomach.

When she trudges down the grassy dune and onto the firm

sand this afternoon, she knows it will be a short visit. Already clouds like gray anvils are rolling in on the horizon. She thinks about going directly back to the lighthouse, but then something catches her eye: a dark-haired boy in the distance in the company of a tall, thin woman.

Her heart leaps in her chest. Could it be? Has Xavier returned? And who is this woman? It is not Cook, and it is not Katarina. Perhaps she is mistaken. Perhaps it isn't Xavier.

She climbs back up the dune and, keeping close to the trees, makes her way down the beach to see more closely. Yes, it is Xavier, and her body flushes warm at the thought that the moment is coming, very soon. Not today, for he is in company and she is not ready. But soon she will be ready, and she will find a way.

How she longs to hold him in her arms.

He is searching for shells while his nanny keeps a wary eye on the storm clouds. Closer and closer Isabella creeps, worried they will hurry off before she gets near enough to see them properly, then realizes that she need fear nothing. This new nanny doesn't know her. Xavier does not speak. She can approach and say hello and perhaps even find out from the nanny how long they have been home, how long they intend to stay. She leaves the cover of the trees and walks down the sand directly towards them.

The nanny looks up. She is a young woman with a hard face and big square hands. Her expression becomes puzzled as she realizes Isabella is coming to talk to her.

Isabella smiles. "Hello!" she calls.

The child looks up. His brow twitches, then settles. He grasps his nanny's hand and moves behind her.

Isabella's blood goes cold. Is he afraid of her? Has Katarina taught him to fear her?

"Can I help you?" the nanny says.

Isabella stops before them, her eyes on Xavier's face. He won't meet her gaze. "I am an old friend of the boy's mother," she lies. She crouches in front of Xavier. "You're not afraid of me, are you, little one?"

He shakes his head, then says clearly, "I don't know you."

"You don't . . . ?" A rumble of thunder. The wind suddenly changes direction, coming cold and laden with the scent of rain from the south.

"You'll have to forgive the little master, ma'am," the nanny says. "We are just back from Sydney today, where he has been in much society. There are a lot of faces and names for him to remember."

Isabella cannot speak. He has forgotten her? After only three months? She has thought of him every day and he has forgotten her? Racking pains take over her body. She wants to crush him in her embrace. She longs for the nights breathing his scent in the narrow bed at the Fullbrights' house.

The nanny grows suspicious of her long silence. "Ma'am?"

"I . . ." Her mouth opens and closes, like a fish dying on the sand.

"What is your name, ma'am?" she says. "If you tell him, it might remind him."

But she can't say her name, not either of her names. She shouldn't even be talking to them. If the nanny goes back and tells Katarina, if Katarina deduces it's her, if she has seen the advertisement in the paper . . . Isabella stands. "I'm sorry to trouble you. Perhaps I have the wrong child."

The wrong child. Oh, yes. He was always the wrong child.

"Very well, ma'am. I need to get the little one out of the storm, now." The nanny gathers Xavier against her, and he goes readily and happily. Isabella watches them go, then tries to walk back up the beach. Her knees are like rubber. One step. Another. Then she can't go farther so she lets herself fall, on her side, on the sand. Her hair spreads out around her and across her face. She curls herself into a ball and sobs, sand and hair sticking to her mouth. The first cold, fat raindrop splats onto the back of her hand. She doesn't move. The trees in the wood go wild, whipped one way and then the other. The wind stings sand against her. Thunder cracks in the distance. She doesn't move. The rain descends, driving round divots into the sand, soaking her clothes. She doesn't move. She cannot move. Her dream has cracked open and inside it is the hard, blackened kernel of truth: Daniel died and there is no comfort. There will never be any comfort. She lies in the driving rain and wishes for the ocean to rise up and swallow her, as it should have done months ago.

Matthew wakes to the rattle of thunder. He turns on his side and flaps the sheet to let some cool air into the bed, then closes his eyes and tries to chase sleep. The rain is heavy. He cracks open one eye again. It is very dark. There are stormy seas. He needs to put the light on.

He rises wearily: maybe he can catch an hour or two after the storm. He pulls on his shirt and his shoes, and makes his way up the ladder. He pumps the pressure tanks and ignites the light, adjusts the weights and then comes back down. Isabella's jewelry-making things are all packed away now and he admits he misses seeing her sitting there working. She had seemed so happy in those times, focused and busy.

It is only then that he realizes he hasn't heard Isabella moving around anywhere in the lighthouse. Frowning, he returns downstairs, expecting to find her in the galley kitchen or even in the telegraph office. But she is nowhere.

She is not inside. This means she must be outside. In the storm.

Matthew tells himself not to worry. She goes every afternoon to the beach. Perhaps she was caught unawares in the storm and now shelters in the woods. Does she know to stay away from tall trees during lightning?

Underscoring this thought, a violent flash of lightning and a simultaneous crack of thunder makes him jump. Should he go out to look for her? Isabella is made of strong stuff: she survived a shipwreck and walked miles and miles to find him. But there are darker thoughts: he is always worried that her husband's family will catch up with her somehow, while he isn't around to protect her. He goes to the door, pulls on his raincoat and wellington boots, and trudges outside into the storm.

The wood is awash, the ground muddy, leaves and branches blown down. The rain is torrential, finding inlets behind his collar and inside his boots. His beard is dripping water before he has even reached the beach. He scans the gray distance and cannot see her at first, but that is because he is looking for somebody standing upright. She is, in fact, curled on her side in a drenched, pale blue dress in the distance. What on earth is she doing? His heart starts. Is she dead? He runs to her, stumbling over sand in his sodden boots. "Isabella!" he calls, but she doesn't lift her head. He falls on his knees next to her. Her eyes are closed and she does not acknowledge his arrival. He rests a hand over her ribs and holds as still as he can.

She breathes. She is alive.

"Isabella, what is wrong? Can you hear me?"

She shakes her head. "Leave me be," she says over the wind and the rain and the wide ocean. "The tide will come in and carry me away."

But he will not leave her be, no matter what she says. He lifts her into his arms and starts back up the beach to the lighthouse. She is limp and she still hasn't opened her eyes. What has happened to her that she should want to die? Lately she has seemed happy, interested in the world. He carries her home, and inside the lighthouse he lays her carefully on the bed. He strips off his rain gear and returns to her. She shivers and her lips are blue. A flash of memory: Clara returning from the woods, cold and with haunted eyes. Matthew unbuttons Isabella's blouse and skirt and drops them in a puddle on the floor. He strips her naked. Still she doesn't move. Still she keeps her eyes closed. It is as though by playing dead she can will herself out of life. He dries her and pulls the sheet up over her naked body, then sits next to her and waits. She cannot play dead forever.

Isabella plays dead for a very long time. After the first hour, where she neither opens her eyes nor speaks, he decides to get on with his work. He checks in on her periodically, and she remains unmoved. He offers her food at dinnertime, but she doesn't respond. He demands that she drink water, but she acts as though she hasn't heard. From time to time he wonders if she is sleeping, but her breathing remains shallow and her face remains unrested.

Then, much later in the evening, when he is upstairs cranking the weights into the top of the tower, he hears the downstairs door open. He clatters down the stairs to find Isabella, dressed again in her wet things, heading out the door.

"What are you doing?"

"I'm going back to the beach."

"Why?" But there is no point asking why. She is incapable of rational thought. Her pupils take up nearly her whole irises. So instead of asking questions, he blocks her way, slams the door shut and restrains her with his hands around her wrists. "You are not going out. You are not going to the beach and you are certainly not going to throw yourself in the ocean."

"And why should I not?" she spits, struggling against him. "What is there in this world but misery?"

He tightens his grip, fearful that he might hurt her but more fearful that she will escape and never come back. "Stop it, Isabella. You must tell me what has happened to make you feel this way."

"My son died. Is that not enough?"

"Your son died three years ago. You have lived this long. Why stop living now?"

Isabella stops struggling. Her weight falls into his hands. He is incredibly aware of her softness, her fragility.

"Come," he says. "Take off these wet things and back to bed."

She allows herself to be taken back to the bedroom, and leaves her clothes once more in a damp heap on the floor. He lights the lamp and sits on the bed, while she turns on her side, the sheet pulled up over her breasts. Her eyes seem enormous in the yellow lamplight. Outside, the storm has long passed, but behind it has come a steady rain. It thrums on the windows and the tin roof of the shed.

Her hand steals out from under the covers and grasps his. He strokes her hand with his thumb a little while, then says, "Will you tell me what happened?"

"I saw Xavier on the beach," she blurts. "And he didn't remember me."

"It has been a long time and he is young," he says. "Why does this bother you so?"

She pulls her hand away and places it over her forehead, lying on her back. He watches her awhile.

"Isabella?"

"You will hate me."

"It isn't possible to hate you."

"You say that now."

Another silence. He feels his heart beating, carrying the old blood around the old circuits as it has always done. Why should she care about Xavier remembering her when she had little or no chance of ever seeing him again? Then it dawns. He challenges himself to think not like a middle-aged lighthouse keeper but like a young woman who lost a baby who would have been the same age as Xavier.

"Isabella," he says softly, slowly, "had you planned to steal the child?"

"Not steal, no," she says quickly. "I had thought to . . . persuade him to come with me."

Matthew holds his tongue. Judgmental words will not help.

She melts into sobs. "I can see now it makes no sense. I can see now . . ."

"You hoped to replace Daniel with him?"

She sits up, shaking her head. "I don't know! Did I try to replace Daniel? I think of Xavier now and he is just a little stranger: somebody else's flesh and blood. But Daniel is a stranger too. I never knew him to miss him, Matthew." Her voice breaks and she takes a moment to recover. "But I miss him." She makes a fist and pounds it between her breasts. "I miss him."

Matthew folds Isabella in his arms.

"It's empty," she cries. "The world is so empty."

"Sh," he soothes. "Sh."

She cries and cries, shaking in his arms. But these tears, like the storm, eventually grow softer and pass, and he realizes she has fallen asleep.

He gently returns her head to the pillow, and covers her with the sheet. He sits for a little while to stroke her hair and softly caress her back. What has she been thinking? That Xavier is Daniel, just because they have a few similarities?

And it is like the light in the room suddenly burns brighter, because now he wonders what *he* has been thinking, just because Isabella and Clara have a few similarities. He gazes at Isabella's face. It is softer than Clara's. Everything about her is softer. She makes no demands on him. She is young and scared, but she isn't wild or cruel: she is simply damaged. For all Clara's protests and dramatic resistance, nothing bad had ever happened to her. Isabella has lost a child and never been allowed to grieve.

In fact, as he thinks it through, he begins to realize that they are not alike at all. Not even a little.

*M*atthew comes to bed after the night shift and Isabella is still asleep. He curls up next to her and holds her, drifts off. He wakes less than an hour later to see her vomiting out the window. He gets up and rubs her back. She says she feels ill and he tells her to come back to bed, that he will make her tea. When he returns, she is shaking and holding her stomach. The electric heat of fear spreads through his middle.

"Rest, pretty bird," he says. "You need rest."

"So do you," she protests. "I've woken you up."

"I will be fine. You're ill."

She drinks her tea, then lies down again. "I am so weary, Matthew."

He watches as she falls asleep, then he falls asleep next to her again. The day grows bright and warm.

When he next awakes, she is lying next to him staring at the ceiling. He rolls onto his side and strokes her hair. "Are you feeling any better?"

"No. My body feels as if it has been crushed in a vice."

He feels her forehead, but it isn't hot. "Stay in bed until you are better."

A day passes, two, and she doesn't feel better. She periodically vomits and complains of excessive tiredness, and all the while she is immobile with heavy grief. He helps her as best as he can between jobs, but he is growing tired too. Tired because his sleep is constantly interrupted, and tired because he cannot shake the awful worry. He doesn't want her to get sicker. He doesn't want her to die. When he asks her how she feels, where it hurts, she simply says that it is her heart that is sick. Her heart that has decided she cannot get up ever again. He doesn't push her, he doesn't remind her about New York or the threat of the Winterbournes. He waits and he makes her food and he goes about his life with lungs slightly compressed by fear.

On the third day he dares to leave her alone for an hour to go into town. He has a lingering fear that she will throw herself from the upper deck while he is not there, but they are out of food and he needs to collect the mail.

The mail is in a small bundle tied together with string, and it isn't until he gets home that he finds it: a letter addressed to Isabella, with a return address in New York. His heart starts. Victoria. Finally, they have found Victoria.

He goes to deliver it to Isabella, but hesitates. What if it is unwelcome news? What if she says, "Do not come"? Something like that might break Isabella.

Fearfully, guiltily, he picks open the envelope, unfolds the letter and scans it. Mingled dread and hope. What will this letter do to Isabella? Dare he show her?

Then he hears her awake in the next room, vomiting again. He tucks the letter under a pile of papers and tells himself he will give it to her another day, when she is feeling stronger.

*I*sabella has sunk under a gray cloud. It is in her ears and eyes and lungs and bones, and she feels a weary nausea that seems as though it will never withdraw. She stays in bed and cries and sleeps and refuses to think about the future. Matthew takes care of her and she lets him, even though she knows she is a burden. She lets herself be a burden and she keeps sinking. Where she thinks solid ground will be there are only more clouds. Down and down she goes.

After a week of this, she finally feels well enough to sit up and eat some soup and ask for the curtain to be drawn so she can look out the window. The sky is very blue and the sea air seems to wash away some of the nausea. Matthew draws up a stool next to the bed and looks at her closely but doesn't say a word.

Finally, she says, "What is it, Matthew?"

"You are feeling better?"

"Perhaps." She doesn't want to make promises she can't keep.

He nods, and seems to decide upon some course of action. "Four days ago, I received a letter for you, from your sister Victoria."

Victoria. At the sound of her sister's name, Isabella's heart lifts. She is reminded of what is possible. "Then why did you not tell me?"

"There is some bad news within the letter."

And now she sinks again. "She doesn't want me to come?"

"No, that's not it."

"Why did you read it?"

"I want, in all things, to protect you, Isabella." He hands her the letter. "I am sorry for reading it first. But when you read it yourself you will see why I do not regret it."

Isabella notices her hands are shaking as she unfolds the piece of paper.

My dear Isabella,

You have no idea how welcome your communication is, even though it has passed many hands to finally get to me. We moved in March and I sent you a letter to your old address in Somerset, but of course by then you were away on your journey. Sister, I believed you had perished in the shipwreck! A friend of my husband had read it in the newspapers. The Winterbournes did not deign to send me word of your fate themselves. I am amazed and relieved that you are alive, but curious about where you are and what you are doing. I will, as your original telegram urges, remain secretive, and hope that you will be with me soon to tell me all. You are so welcome to come to me and to stay for as long as you need to. I will list my address on the back of the envelope and you need only turn up, at any time of day or night. I suspect you are far away, but I will wait and hope. Knowing you are alive is enough for me.

Now, sister, I have some unhappy news to share. You may remember that the last time we communicated I was expecting my first child. You no doubt have imagined me many times with a small infant but alas, it is not the case. The pregnancy did not take properly, and a few months in I was very ill and lost the child. Even sadder, I fell again and lost the next in similar circumstances. I have now been told

*by a doctor not to try again for fear of risking my life, and
so I am to remain childless. Please do not be sad for me. I
have made my peace and my husband has bought me two
Pomeranian puppies who will have to be my babies instead.
They are adorable, and I know you will love them and they
will love you.*

*Oh, listen to me waffle on about babies that weren't even
born, when you had to endure the death of your Daniel
and, lately, the death of your husband Arthur. I have no
idea what you have been through, dear Isabella, but I pray
you come to me soon so that we may cry together and gain
some comfort.*

*With much sisterly affection,
Victoria*

Isabella finishes the letter, then reads it through again. Her
eyes sting with tears of relief and sadness. She folds the letter and
puts it down, and now she knows what she must do. It is as clear
as the day to her. It is her only way to be free.

"Isabella? Are you all right?"

She sniffs back tears, meets his eyes and lifts her wrist in front
of her face. "My sister and I made this when we were girls," she
says. "Whoever had the first child was to keep it. I got it. I had
hoped to take it to her for her own child. There will not be a
child. There are no babies to wear this bracelet."

Matthew doesn't speak. She can see he is trying to puzzle out
what she is saying.

"Matthew, I never buried Daniel. I never mourned him at a
graveside. I never wore a black dress and had somebody hold me

up while I threw a handful of dust on his tiny coffin. My husband's family made certain I wasn't there, because I grieved too wildly and they were afraid I would embarrass them."

He grasps her wrist and rubs it gently. "I am sorry."

"I want to bury it, Matthew. I want to bury *him*. I want to say a proper good-bye. Will you help me?"

Matthew gathers her in his arms. Already she is doubtful. Already she is afraid. How can she put Daniel's bracelet in the cold, loveless ground? What if he is frightened? What if he misses her? But these irrational thoughts flash across her mind and are gone. Daniel is dead. He has been dead for three years. He neither knows nor feels anything.

"Of course I will, my love," Matthew says. "If you are sure you want to."

"I am not sure at all," she says. "I am only sure that the future will not come until I do this."

*P*ercy Winterbourne is unhappy with the way his tea has been made, but the maid has already gone, so he can't call her back and berate her. He has changed hotels half a dozen times already since arriving in Maryborough, and not one of them seems to know how to make tea correctly. He has exhausted every decent option for accommodation in town, so he must now put up with the tea-making at the Oxford Hotel. He doesn't want to travel too far from the wreck of the *Aurora*, but nor does he want to stay in a tiny village where the gritty sand and ever-present flies will drive him mad. This bustling colonial town will do for now. He sips the bitter liquid and checks over the newspapers that have just arrived. He demands that every newspaper in which he has placed an advertisement sends him a copy so he can check that his money has not been stolen. One by one, he begins to comb through them.

The ad has had no success. A few crackpots have written to him, but none of the communications has led anywhere. He often wonders if he is wasting his time. Mother has already telegraphed him to tell him to leave it and come home, that his wife and children need him, but home now that Arthur is gone is not a place to be. He cannot fill his brother's shoes; he does not want to. As for his wife and children, he does not miss them particularly. He cannot wait for his eldest son to be of an age where he can hold a conversation, but until such time it is best for the nanny to raise them. He smirks, thinking about how he can barely hold a conversation with his wife either. They are all millstones around his neck, so why should he not spend his time here in Maryborough, staying in one hotel after another and enjoying all of the pleasure and freedom a man of his substantial wealth can enjoy?

It is while he is flicking through *The Queenslander* that the game changes. He is caught by a garish heading that reads: "Women's Department" and at first he sneers. Women are infiltrating everything these days. They want to vote and run about like wild cats. Why do they need a whole section in a newspaper? But then he sees the photograph.

Oh, the photograph.

It is not the wobble-chin dames in the foreground that capture his attention, but the familiar profile in the background. It is her. It is Isabella. He scans the caption. *Guests of Lady Berenice McAuliffe at her annual spring ball at the Bellevue Hotel.*

He has her. At last. He has her.

Twenty-six

2011

Before Libby woke, she could feel the warm happiness in her heart. She opened her eyes. What was it? Ah, yes. Yesterday with Tristan. She rolled over and reached out to the empty half of the bed. He'd slipped away around one in the morning after a day and night spent tangled in sheets and blankets. They'd talked, eaten, drunk a bottle of wine in bed. Made love, of course: his hands constantly searching her curves, her fingers drawn again and again to the stubble on his chin. He'd cancelled his meetings and then switched off his phone and left it on the bedside table, a mute witness to their pleasure. She'd longed to curl up next to him and sleep all through the night but, despite her requests for him to stay, he had pleaded an early meeting and not wanting to disturb her.

Libby checked her watch on the bedside table. Half past nine. He would already be in the meeting by now. Would he be wearing the same stupid grin as she was wearing?

She nestled on her back and flung her arm over her eyes. Her heart felt stretched to bursting point. What a joy it was to feel passion for a man again. A small part of her heart tightened at the idea that she had forgotten Mark; but she hadn't forgotten him. She hadn't even stopped loving him. Perhaps she had just finally accepted that he was never coming back.

Libby lay there for a long time, half-dozing, remembering the bliss of yesterday, then told herself she had far too much work to do on the catalog to lie in bed much longer. The photographs should be waiting in her inbox and she needed to start roughing out the final layout. She rose and went to the bathroom and turned on the shower, but before she could step in she heard a knock on the front door.

Tristan. It had to be. He'd finished his meeting and come back. She quickly pulled her robe back on and hurried to the door.

Not Tristan. Graeme Beers. The disappointment was acute. His car was parked up on the street, his son at the wheel.

"Sorry for not calling first," he said. "I didn't have your number and it was . . . um . . . urgent."

"Urgent?" She wrapped her robe closer around her, very aware that she was naked beneath it.

He held out a thin sheaf of papers. "Yeah, it seems I . . . ah . . . overlooked asking you to sign these before your dive."

Libby frowned, took the papers from him and glanced through them. It was some kind of a legal agreement protecting Graeme and his business from responsibility for any loss or injury his divers suffered. She almost laughed. He was afraid she was going to sue him over the incident on the dive the other day.

"Come inside," she said. "I'll find a pen."

"Yes, I just don't understand why I didn't remember to show these to you. I—"

"It's fine. I'm not going to sue you. Or report you." She found a pen on her desk, ticked the "I agree" boxes and signed it. "Here."

"Thanks. I'm . . ."

Perhaps he had been about to say, "I'm sorry," but that might have been admitting fault. She waved him away. "It's fine. I'm fine."

He nodded, backing out towards the door. She closed it behind him and turned to her desk.

Then she heard it.

The car engine. The one that had been idling outside at night. She raced back to the front door to see Graeme and his son speed off. And if she had any doubts remaining, the car backfired for good measure at the bottom of the hill.

No, no doubt at all: it was Graeme Beers and his son who had been creeping around outside her house. Her skin rose in gooseflesh at the thought. What did they want?

Still in her robe, she marched straight up to the lighthouse and hammered on the door. No answer. "Damien!" she called. But he wasn't there.

She made her way back down to the cottage. What should she do? Call Graeme and confront him? Go to the police station and report it to Sergeant Lacey? She checked the time again. Was Tristan out of his meeting and available to talk it through with her?

She tried his mobile phone and it went straight to voicemail. She quickly copied down the office number and home number he left at the end of the message, then called the office.

"I'm sorry, Mr. Catherwood isn't in today."

"Not in?" Perhaps his meeting was out of the office.

"Yes, he's on leave for the rest of this week."

She put down the phone and gazed for a long time at the home number she'd written down. After the intimacies they'd shared yesterday, surely it was acceptable to call him at home.

On leave. An early meeting. Libby told herself not to read anything into it. Tristan was ambitious: it wasn't inconceivable for him to have a meeting while on leave. She snatched up the phone before she could think better of it, and dialed the home number.

One ring. Two. Her heart began to slow: he wasn't going to answer. On the fifth ring, the line went live and a woman's voice said, "Hello?"

It took Libby a full two seconds to find her words. "Oh, hello. I'm looking for Tristan."

The woman's voice went hard. "Who shall I say is calling?"

"Elizabeth Slater."

"One moment." The phone dropped onto a hard surface. A few moments later, Tristan was there.

"Hi, Libby," he said evenly.

"Tristan, I need your help—"

"Look, can I call you back? Just . . . just give me five, okay?"

"Okay."

The line clicked. Libby threw the phone across the room. It landed with a rattle up against the leg of the couch. She wasn't stupid. She knew all the signs. He was married.

Just like Mark.

She went to the shower and turned it on hot. The phone rang, but she ignored it, sitting instead on the shower floor to let the water run through her dark hair and down her spine. She breathed deeply. The terrible fall from this morning's heights of happiness and hope was crippling.

But then she realized, it would all be fine. She would sell the wretched house and move back to France. All her problems would go away: Tristan, Juliet, Graeme. She would move into a luxury flat and lock all the doors and never have to open up her heart again.

The hot water eventually ran out. She climbed out of the shower and wrapped herself in towels. The phone rang again. This time she answered it.

"Libby, it's Tristan," he said.

"Are you married?"

A pause. "No," he said.

"Who answered the phone?"

"Look, can we have this discussion in person? Libby, please don't be jealous. Jealous women make life so hard for themselves. This relationship is only new."

The admonishment stung and her face flushed with guilt and embarrassment. What right did she have to question him? She must look like a crazy woman. "I'm sorry," she sighed. Then her skin prickled as she remembered. "How did your meeting go this morning?"

"Fine. It wasn't a work meeting. A legal thing. I have some real estate issues I'm sorting out."

Yes, she was behaving like a crazy woman. Worrying about his meeting had made her jump to conclusions about the woman's voice on the phone. A sister, a flatmate, even a cleaner. But not a wife. He had said so. Not married. It was just a hangover from her relationship with Mark.

"Let me take you to dinner Friday night. I'd love to see you again," he said. "I've got a busy week taking care of this legal business, but by Friday evening I'll be ready for a nice glass of Shiraz and a good meal."

"It sounds wonderful," she said, and she meant it.

His voice was calm and reassuring now. "So, you said you needed my help. I was worried when I couldn't get hold of you."

"Ah, yes. I think I've sorted out my problem. I know who's been hanging around my house at night, but once I've moved it won't matter."

"Who is it?" There was a frown in his voice.

"Graeme Beers. The dive director from Winterbourne Beach. I recognized the sound of his car."

"Why would he be hanging around your house?"

"I don't know."

A short silence. "I don't know, Libby. It sounds a bit . . . implausible. Surely a lot of cars sound the same."

"I am absolutely sure."

"Okay. Well, then, I believe you. And I don't like it, so call the police and let them know. Don't confront him yourself."

She was touched by his protective urge, and hoped it would mean he would offer to come and check up on her tonight, but it stopped there.

"I'm sorry, Libby, I have to go. I have a few other appointments today and I'm already running late."

"Sure, that's fine. See you Friday?"

"Can't wait."

She put the phone down and dressed, then decided to call Scott Lacey. Her stomach growled and she realized she hadn't eaten since yesterday afternoon. She switched the kettle on.

"Sergeant Lacey."

"Scott, it's Libby Slater."

"Oh. Good morning." Cool.

She quickly explained the situation, but she could feel his doubts harden on the line before he'd even uttered a word.

"I'm sorry, but that's just not enough to go on."

"Really, the sound of that car engine is burned into my brain."

"Perhaps it's exactly the same make and model of car, but that's a coincidence, not a reason to go knocking on his door and asking him to explain."

Libby fell silent a moment. Then said, "Is this because I've upset Juliet?"

"What? No. What a ridiculous thing to say. I am quite capable of doing my job regardless of how I feel about you."

Libby bit back a retort. "I'm sorry," she said, knowing it sounded forced.

"It's okay. You're worried about your safety. I understand that. Your house is still on our patrol list. We haven't forgotten you."

Libby thanked him and hung up. The kettle boiled and whistled and she switched it off, but stood for a long time gazing out the window at the sea beyond, feeling anxious and unsatisfied and not sure what to do next.

*D*amien worked in the kitchen every afternoon between lunch and afternoon tea, got out of the way between three and four-thirty, then came back to continue work when the tea room wasn't busy. Sometimes he worked until seven at night, always sensitive to the fact that Juliet had to keep the business running. Rather than rip the whole kitchen apart, he cleared one defined space at a time.

The cupboard doors were plain oak panels that he had begun to stain outside the building by the compost bin. Between lunch and afternoon tea, while she was waiting for scones to bake, Juliet hung about near the kitchen window to steal glances at him working in the sunshine: strong arms, tanned skin, gleaming hair.

Cheryl silently sidled up next to her. "Eye candy, isn't he?"

Juliet jumped. Embarrassment crept over her skin. "Oh. No, I'm not . . . I was just seeing what the stain looked like. He's chosen a lovely shade, don't you think?"

Cheryl doubled over with laughter, and Juliet's cheeks flamed.

"It's okay, Juliet. I've been eyeing him too. He's very tasty. Pity he'd never look twice at old birds like us, eh?"

Juliet's heart fell. *Old birds like us.* She was seven years younger than Cheryl, but still a full decade older than Damien.

Cheryl examined Juliet's face and frowned. "You're kidding. You haven't developed a crush on him, have you?"

"No, no. Of course not."

Cheryl lifted an eyebrow dubiously. "Well, I hope not. I want you to find somebody wonderful and stable who will love you when you're old and wrinkly. Somebody who has a bank account would be a great start."

"His ex has frozen their accounts."

Cheryl waved the comment away. "Don't be too trusting. And don't lose your heart on a young stallion." Then Cheryl was off with a bottle of disinfectant spray and a cloth, to clear up the dining room.

Juliet sagged against the sink, her back to the window now. She felt such a fool. It was true she was attracted to Damien, but not just because he was young and good-looking. He was kind. He spoke gently. He had a strong moral compass. These were important qualities in any man.

But Cheryl was right: she would seem old to him. She used to be his babysitter; he probably thought of her as a mother figure, or at the very least an older sister. The idea made her cringe. She remembered him holding her hands the other night. His hands were young and tanned, but hers were getting thin-skinned and veiny. Not to mention the lines around her eyes. And she hadn't stayed out of the sun like Libby had, so her arms and décolletage were unevenly colored. Suddenly, she felt like a hag, pushing middle age. The idea of young love and building a life together and babies was ridiculous, a fool's fond dream. It was already far too late for that.

That night, back on Datemate, she searched the profiles of men Damien's age: they were all advertising for women in their twenties, not women of nearly forty. Half-heartedly, she scrolled through men her own age or above, but not one aroused her interest. It was always this way, and for a long time she'd thought that it was simply because she'd never find another man as wonderful as Andy.

And after twenty years, perhaps she had. It depressed her to realize that he wouldn't see in her what she saw in him.

$\mathcal{L}$ibby worked long hours over the following days. She was getting used to talking with Emily from time to time. She even ventured to ask if Emily had any family insight into the wreck of the *Aurora*. Emily was delighted to know Libby had dived the wreck, and vowed to dig up anything that might be of interest.

The photographs came back from Paris and most were superb. She'd requested three be rephotographed and was waiting for an e-mail from her photographer, Roman Deleuze, with the new images. Until then she continued to rough out the pages, moving and refining images and design. Although she had done the Winterbourne catalog for years, this year it was exciting. This year, Emily wanted something different, not so stuffy. Libby enjoyed every moment of the job. She wished Mark were alive to see it. She wondered what he'd think, how his opinion of Emily might change when he saw what she was capable of.

The sound of the mailman's motorcycle roused her from her work. She leaned back and stretched; time for a break and a cup of tea. She let herself out of the house and walked up to the mailbox. For the first time, the touch of cool in the afternoon air let her know autumn was on its way. It hardly seemed possible: Lighthouse Bay seemed a place permanently locked in summer sunshine and warm sea air. She breathed in the freshness deeply, flipping open the mailbox and withdrawing a large envelope from Ashley-Harris Holdings.

This would be the contracts on the sale. She tore open the

envelope and saw pages and pages of legalese, clause after clause. She supposed to Ashley-Harris it was a standard contract, but to her it looked as though it was written in another language.

She needed legal advice.

Libby sighed. She just wanted it over with quickly, but a few thousand dollars on a solicitor was probably prudent in the light of such a big property deal. She let herself into the cottage and dug out a local phone book, called the first legal firm listed and made an appointment for Monday.

She made tea and returned to her desk—removing Bossy from her office chair—to see an e-mail from Roman Deleuze. She opened it and saw the new photographs, and quickly sent back a message saying they were fine and wishing him well.

A moment later, another message pinged into her inbox.

Miserable weather in Paris. I envy you.

She smiled as she scrolled down to see he had included a picture of peak-hour traffic outside his apartment window. Rain. People with their heads bowed under umbrellas, squeezed up against each other's raincoats. It looked utterly miserable and she had to laugh. On a whim, she grabbed her phone and went out the back door and through the bushes until she reached the beach: the wide white expanse of sand, the deep blue sky, the turquoise sea. She snapped a picture of it and returned home, hooked her phone to her computer and sent it back to him.

All this, and it's autumn.

They went back and forth for a little while, her teasing him about city life and bad weather; him teasing her for living her entire life on holiday. For the first time, she realized she was living in paradise. Because she had grown up here, she'd taken it for granted. But the beach and the sky and the sun were miraculous and beautiful. Choking traffic fumes and damp crowds in overcoats would eventually wear anyone down until they were dreaming of the warm ocean.

Would that be her, eventually? Would the luxury apartment in Paris one day not be enough for her? Would the tide of her longing reverse, and the Queensland coast call her back? Was she destined to be dissatisfied with wherever she was?

Roman went offline to go to a meeting and she began to think about making herself some dinner before the night shift. She was keen to have the brochure done, and working kept her mind off other things.

When Libby arrived at Azzurro ten minutes late and didn't see Tristan, she panicked a moment. Had he grown tired of waiting and gone home? Or worse, had he stood her up altogether?

The maître d' saw her looking forlorn and came over to ask if he could help.

"I'm meant to be meeting Tristan Catherwood," she said. "Is he here yet?"

"Ah. Mr. Catherwood is upstairs. Come, follow me."

Libby followed the maître d' through the restaurant, along a side path next to the kitchen, then up a hidden set of stairs. They led to a closed-off area and a huge balcony overlooking the river. On the balcony sat a single table, candlelit. Tristan was waiting.

She laughed. "Oh, my," she said.

The maître d' winked at her. "Mr. Catherwood insisted on something exceptional."

Libby walked over and Tristan rose to his feet to pull out her chair, kissing her lightly on the cheek.

"Sorry I'm late," she said, taking her seat.

"It's no problem. I'm enjoying the view."

Libby turned her eyes to the river, the bobbing yachts. "It's pretty special."

"So are you."

She turned back to him, unable to hide her smile. "Well now. This is a lot of trouble and expense you've gone to. Don't you know you've already won me over?"

He reached for her hand, and fondled it gently in his fingers. "You look beautiful, Libby. I've missed you this week."

"Same."

"Did the contracts come through?"

She was put off by his abrupt change of topic. "Yes. I've made an appointment to speak to a conveyance solicitor next week."

"Wise girl." He poured her a glass of wine and they fell to talking, picking up where they had left off the other night. She was reminded once again of what she liked about him. He was interesting, he had done so many things, but he wasn't arrogant or egotistical. He had a freshness about him that she found in-toxicating. They laughed and talked their way through the entree, but when he lifted the wine bottle to refill her glass, she covered it with her hand.

"I'm driving, remember?" she said, hoping he would invite her to spend the night at his place.

"Ah, that's right." He checked his watch. "Half a glass? We'll walk on the beach after, if you like."

"Sure," she said. Then ventured, "Or I could come home with you."

He smiled. He looked her directly in the eye. But he said, "No, not tonight."

"Okay," she replied, trying not to sound disappointed. She realized they had been talking for half an hour and still hadn't broached the topic of the woman who had answered his phone. She opened her mouth to say something and he stopped her with a gently raised hand.

"My flatmate. She's got a thing for me. It's a bit complicated. Just best if you don't call me there or come by until I've sorted it out."

"Okay," Libby said again, nodding, staring at the candle flame. But she knew—she *knew*—it was a lie. Or at the very least, a half-truth. Rich forty-year-old men didn't have female flatmates like that.

"Are you all right?"

She smiled brightly. "Of course. Why wouldn't I be? And weren't you going to pour me some more wine?"

He laughed, refilling her glass. She kept the brightness afloat, but her mind was turning over carefully. Tristan belonged to somebody else. The thought was disappointing, but then she reminded herself that no healthy relationship produces a partner who looks elsewhere. That's what Mark had always said.

At the thought of Mark, she realized that she had done this before. She had made these excuses before. She had done it all before. And for that reason alone, she was the last person to judge Tristan.

Twenty-seven

Libby had seen no signs of life at the lighthouse for more than a week, so she was surprised when Damien turned up at the cottage on Saturday afternoon.

"Hi," she said, standing aside so he could come in. "I'd tell you Bossy misses you, but I don't know she's even noticed."

Damien found Bossy on the sofa and crouched to tickle her under the chin. She stretched and went back to sleep. "Cats, hey?" he said. "Always so glad to see you."

"Where have you been?"

"At the B&B. I came to say thanks for putting me on to Juliet. I'm rebuilding her kitchen and I now have a nice soft bed to sleep in every night." He stood and gave her a mock-stern look. "Though you didn't tell her I was coming."

"Ah, no. We're kind of . . ."

"Yes, I know."

"Juliet's told you everything?"

"Juliet's told me some things. Cheryl has told me a few others. Now, dating Tristan Catherwood, known enemy of the whole town . . . That took some guts," he teased.

"Don't," she said, slapping him away playfully. "You don't hate me?"

"I don't hate you."

"You're not on her side?"

"I'm on both your sides. I think you should try to work it out. Family. What can I say? You don't throw that away."

Libby felt self-conscious suddenly, so went to the kitchen to switch the kettle on so she could hide her face. "Tea? Or would you like to stay for dinner?"

"I'd love some tea. You don't need to feed me tonight. Juliet's always plying me with leftover quiches and roast beef sandwiches."

She looked at him a little more closely. "Actually, you do look a lot healthier."

"A week in Juliet's care," he said.

Libby thought he sounded wistful. She busied herself making a pot of tea and then cleared Bossy off the couch so they could sit together. "So, does this mean you've taken time out from the lighthouse mystery?"

"Not at all. I've cleared out the whole place and taken the boxes of papers to my room at Juliet's. I've spread them all out and put them in date order, but there's a lot of dates missing. Dates I'd be really interested to read about."

She poured their tea and sat back with her teacup. "Go on."

"I reread the journal I loaned you. Where Matthew Seaward mentions this mysterious woman called 'I' more and more often. He never talks about her at length, nor does he talk about his feelings, but . . . I don't know, Libby, it sounds like he's in love with her."

"Really?"

"Perhaps I'm being mushy."

"Mushy. Great word."

"You know what I mean. Perhaps I'm reading things that aren't there. From time to time, he talks about 'my pretty bird' and I wonder if he means her or if he actually had a pet bird. And elsewhere he talks about her going away to Brisbane on the steamer, and it's just a single line that says it all. Something like, *The lighthouse seems emptier than usual.* He sounds lovesick." He sipped his tea. "I wonder if she knew he felt that way."

Libby considered Damien with a smile on her lips. "Damien, you sound a little . . . lovesick yourself."

He gave her a sideways look. "Your sister *is* pretty special."

His reply was so unexpected that her mouth dropped open. "Juliet? She's ten years older than you. She used to babysit you."

"I know, so she's never going to look at me and see anything but a kid, right? But we're both adults now. Do you think I have a chance?"

She wanted to reassure him, to encourage him, but she couldn't. "I honestly don't know," she replied. "How sad is that? I don't know enough about my sister to answer that question. I suppose she's a conventional kind of woman, so . . ." Then she smiled, unable to resist teasing him. "Is this why you want me to work things out with her?"

He laughed lightly. "Forget I asked."

"Your secret is safe with me. Besides, I don't know if Juliet will ever speak to me again, so I'll probably never have an opportunity to tell her."

They fell silent for a few moments. Bossy moved onto Damien's lap and the sound of the sea and the beat of the fan lulled Libby into a reverie. Then Damien said, "Juliet told me about what happened the night Andy died."

The guilt, the mortification, was crushing. All she could bring herself to say was, "Oh."

He let the topic hang there, scratching Bossy's ears.

Finally, she said, "I know I did it. But it seems as though it happened to another person now. Twenty years. Half my life ago. I felt like an adult then, but I see now I was practically a child."

"When Juliet told me, I felt terrible for her. And I felt just as terrible for you."

Libby looked at him dubiously. "You did?"

"We all make mistakes in our youth. Most of them aren't fatal. You were very unlucky. I told Juliet that."

She looked down into her teacup, and noticed that her hands were shaking. Memories of that night were washing through her. The salt water in her throat, the chill wind, the sirens, the growing dread. Worst of all, Juliet's screams like those of a wounded animal, not a person. "I was an idiot," Libby managed to spit out. "He'd still be alive if I hadn't gone in the water. He and Juliet would have married, had children. She would have been happy." Tears brimmed. She blinked them back.

"You don't know that. They were kids when they got together; it might have all gone wrong down the track. There aren't any guarantees."

"No. But I took away their opportunity to try to build that dream. I ruined her life."

"Her life isn't ruined."

She looked up. "She said the same thing. Exactly."

"Then it must be true." He smiled warmly, gently. "Is the accident the reason you ran away to Paris?"

"Yes. I mean, I always wanted to get out of town. But when it happened, I wanted to be as far from Juliet as I could possibly be. The guilt was crushing me. It helped that she told me she never wanted to see me again." Libby paused a moment, Juliet's words still echoing in her ears, making the sickening guilt fresh again. She wanted to close her eyes and sink into the floor and never have to think of it again, but Damien was waiting for her to finish. "My French was good, so I bought a one-way ticket. I ran away. Literally. And somehow one year turned into two, then four, then ten, then . . . I missed everything. Every birthday, every Christmas, Dad's funeral. I have no idea what Juliet did because I never asked her. I presumed she would tell me if she got married or had a child. Sometimes I wondered how her life was going, but it made me feel so guilty I . . ." Her voice shook and she had to take a deep breath to stop herself from crying. "I made myself forget about her," she breathed.

Damien rearranged Bossy on his lap and reached over to touch her arm gently. "It's okay."

And something about his touch, his voice, made her fire up with anger. Who was this kid to feel sorry for her? To reassure her? She flinched and pulled away. "I know it's okay," she snapped, and then immediately felt embarrassed. She stood and walked to look out the window. She could feel him in the room behind her, waiting patiently. It seemed he hadn't taken offense at her hot words. "Can we not talk about this?"

"Sure," he said. "I'm sorry I brought it up."

"So, our lovesick lighthouse keeper . . ."

"Yes, I'm missing some papers from 1901. His journal cuts off just when he's getting interesting and . . . Er . . . Lovesick. Then there's nothing more from him. The next journal I have is by the incoming lighthouse keeper."

Libby turned to face him, her back against the kitchen sink.

He was still pinned to the sofa by Bossy. "Where would those papers be?"

"I think I know. Somewhere I can't get them."

She tilted her head quizzically.

"At my house. With all my other things. My house that I can't get into right at this moment. When Granddad died, he left loads of boxes full of books and papers. Mum stored about half a dozen in my spare room, intending to go through them some time. I think she's forgotten about them. But I have a suspicion some of the old lighthouse documents are there, that Matthew Seaward's journal is there."

"And why can't you go and search the boxes? If they're at your house?"

He grimaced. "Because my ex is there. And she's furious."

His predicament began to make sense. "What did you do to her?"

It was his turn to be embarrassed and annoyed. "I didn't do anything to her."

"You said she's furious."

"Because I stopped loving her," he blurted. "She's furious because I stopped loving her."

Libby returned to the couch, sat next to him and reached over to rub Bossy's ears. "So, she's locked you out?"

"And changed all the passwords on our joint accounts. But, you know, she'll cool off eventually."

Libby watched his face for a moment. "You're afraid of her, aren't you?"

"She has a bad temper. It's a little intimidating."

"You can't let her get away with it. You need your things. You need to move on."

"I know."

She smiled. "And *I* need the last part of Seaward's journal."

He smiled in return, relaxing. "Maybe I'll call her again. Maybe she'll listen to me for once instead of screaming abuse and hanging up."

Libby couldn't imagine anybody treating gentle, affable Damien that way, and she felt suddenly protective of him. "Would it help if I called her? Or came with you to see her?"

But he was already shaking his head. "No, no, no. I have to do it alone." He took a deep breath. "Thanks for the tea. I'm at the B&B if you need me."

"It's hard for me to come down there. So don't be a stranger. Drop by any time."

It was only as she was saying good-bye at the door that she remembered to tell him she thought Graeme Beers was her midnight creeper. Unlike Tristan and Scott, Damien believed her immediately.

"What do you think he's looking for?" he asked.

"I've no idea."

"He's never tried to get into the house?"

"No. Thank God."

"It's something about your property. Maybe he thinks he has some claim on it? Does he have family down here? Is he looking at the property boundaries?"

"Or has he lost something here? And if so, how and what?" She leaned against the doorjamb. "Should I just confront him?"

Damien shook his head. "Don't. He could be dangerous. You never know."

Her skin crept with cold. "Sergeant Lacey doesn't believe me."

"Just make sure you lock up well and keep your phone handy if they come by again. I wish I had a phone you could call me on, but it's with the rest of my stuff."

For some reason, Libby found this funny. She repressed a laugh, but Damien caught the twinkle in her eye and he laughed too. It felt good to laugh at their twin predicaments.

"Can I offer you some advice?" she asked him.

"Sure, go on."

"If you want to woo my sister, you'd best make sure you're cleanly out of that other relationship first. I have no idea if she considers your age difference a problem, but I know she'd be wary about getting entangled with somebody who has that much ex-girlfriend baggage hanging over him. You need to sort it out now, not later."

He nodded. "Good advice. I'll think about it. And my advice to you?"

She bristled, and he smiled at her. "Come on," he said, "you have to take it."

"What, then?" she asked, making her voice even.

"Forget about what you did in the past. Think about what you can do now, here in the present."

She nodded slightly. "Thanks," she said. "I'll think about it."

*O*n Monday morning, Juliet came downstairs to find Melody hanging around Damien's breakfast table, laughing and flirting. Juliet's stomach clenched. Melody had just turned twenty, so she was technically closer in age to Damien than Juliet was. And, of course, she also had tight skin and coltish limbs. Juliet thought about sending Melody back to the kitchen to wait for the bakery delivery—that was her usual job, after all—but she relented. Cheryl had warned her. Datemate had confirmed it. She wasn't about to stop Damien finding happiness elsewhere.

"Morning," she called softly, then went through to the kitchen.

The bakery delivery arrived shortly afterwards, and she kept herself busy counting stock and checking off the invoice. The other B&B guest didn't come down for breakfast and morning trade was very quiet. She made a scone mixture and was cutting scones carefully on the floured bench when Damien came up behind her.

"Juliet?"

She jumped, hand over heart.

"Sorry," he said.

"I was miles away," she replied. "How was your breakfast?"

"It's always great."

She swallowed hard. "Melody does a wonderful job of the weekday breakfasts. I couldn't survive without her." She smiled encouragingly. "She's a lovely girl."

"Uh . . . yes."

"You two seem to get on well. You should get together some time. I bet she knows all the good night places . . ." She trailed off. *Night places? Really?* What did she know about what young people did?

Embarrassed silence fell between them. Then Damien said, "I have to go away. A week at most. Perhaps less. I . . . I've got to sort some stuff out with Rachel. It can't go on like this."

She nodded warily.

"I promise I'll be back to finish your kitchen."

"Don't worry. You've already done so much."

"No, no. I will be back. I promise."

But she could feel it. He was pulling away, withdrawing from her life. Probably for the best. This crush was silly anyway. Crazy. She was embarrassed for herself. "Good luck," she said.

Then he moved closer and opened his arms to hug her. She was so surprised that the hug was over before she had a chance to sink in and enjoy it. She had a brief impression of his warmth, his texture, his beating heart, but most of all his smell: spicy, fresh, the sea. He backed away and said something under his breath.

"Sorry?" she said.

"It doesn't matter," he replied. "I'll see you when I get back."

"I'll keep your room for you," she said.

He smiled, then headed out the door.

Everyone knew Juliet. It was one of the benefits of having lived in a small town her whole life. Everyone knew her and most wished her well. Some loved to gossip to her, though she didn't enjoy gossip much. Nobody loved to gossip more than Shelley Faber, the secretary at Anderson and Wright Solicitors on Puffin Street.

She was headed for the bank in the brief half-hour between the morning-tea rush and lunch rush, hoping to make a quick transaction. But Shelley, formerly Juliet's classmate in Year Eleven English, was smoking a cigarette outside her office and spotted her.

"Juliet! Just the person I wanted to see."

"Me? Why?"

Shelley blew out a thin stream of smoke and butted her cigarette on the footpath. "Your sister. What's she selling?"

Juliet groaned inwardly. Why did everyone assume she knew what her sister did? "I don't know what you mean."

"Bronwyn over at Pariot's said Elizabeth Slater had made an appointment to talk to a conveyance solicitor this week. Conveyance. Real estate."

The burn started low in her belly. "I know nothing. Libby and I are not close."

"Do you think—?"

"I said I know nothing," Juliet snapped. "I'm sorry, I have to go."

Bank forgotten, Juliet marched down to the beach, slipped off her shoes and waded into the water. *Breathe in. Breathe out.*

Libby. Tristan Catherwood. Real estate. There was only one way all of those things were related. For years, the community had fought Ashley-Harris Holdings. Juliet had fought hardest of all, not just for the survival of her business but for the good of the town, its occupants, even the wildlife. What did Libby and Tristan know about Lighthouse Bay? Nothing. What was at risk? Everything.

Juliet had not felt this desolate in a long time. All those years of struggle had used her up. She had tried so hard to secure her own future, only to find that future emptied out: no love, no family, and now for certain a dwindling business in a town irrevocably changed. And she wasn't young anymore; recent events with Damien had made that horribly clear. All of a sudden, her life felt so brief, so ephemeral. She dug her toes into the sand, but the withdrawing waves pulled the ground out from under her feet. She closed her eyes, dizzy for a moment.

But it was eleven-thirty. She couldn't stand here forever feeling sorry for herself. Melody and Cheryl waited for her: the too-serious, used-up boss. The customers would come for today at least. What happened tomorrow or the day after or next year, nobody knew. Least of all Juliet.

*L*ibby woke deep in the night. She'd kicked her blanket off earlier, but now her skin prickled with cold. Half-asleep still, she reached for the blanket.

Then she heard it. The car. The engine cut.

She sat up, inched the curtain aside and looked out. Its headlights were still on. She couldn't see the license plate.

As Damien had advised, she slept with the phone next to her bed. She quickly dialed the police station and got a young constable. Libby told her what was happening, then hung up.

It would take a few minutes for the police to get here. She watched out the window. A dark figure—she could easily map Graeme Beers' son onto it—left the car and headed for the northern side of the house.

Libby froze in indecision. She could confront him. She could demand to know what the hell was going on.

He could be dangerous. You never know. No, she wouldn't go near him. But she could creep around the southern end of the cottage and try to see the license plate from behind. With a license-plate number, even Scott Lacey would have to believe her.

She rose and, still in her short cotton pajamas, went via the art room to grab her torch. She couldn't go out the front door: if Graeme was in the car, he'd see her. So she quietly removed the flyscreen on the art room window. She pulled a chair up to the window and carefully climbed out, landing with a soft thud on the tangled garden bed. She stopped and caught her breath, her heart hammering so hard she could barely hear the beat of the sea, the clatter of crickets. She strained her ears for footfalls. Nothing. She crept around the southern end of the cottage and waited a few moments.

She could see the car up on the street. If she walked directly out in the open, he would see her coming. So she clambered over the old fence, knocking off peeling paint and scraping her knee. Then, keeping low, she made her way up to the street. She flicked her torch on and peered around the side of the fence. She shone her torch directly at the license plate, and memorized the numbers.

Then, running footfalls: Graeme's son had seen her. She switched off the torch and shrank back, heart thundering, tripping over a stone and landing hard on her backside. The car roared into life, and screeched off over gravel.

They were gone.

But this time, she had them.

She went back to the house, remembering only as she was trying to open the front door that it was locked from the inside. She rounded the house, intending to climb back in the art room window, then curiosity got the better of her. What *were* they looking for?

Libby shone the torch in front of her. His footprints were clear in the mud beside the dripping hose. Carefully, she picked her way through the long grass, shining her torch this way and that, looking for some kind of clue. But all she saw were rocks and plants and spider webs. She noticed some grass pressed down flat near the house and shone her torch directly on it. The cottage was on two-foot stumps. It looked like he had laid down on his stomach here and flattened the grass. She crouched low, sending the torch beam under the house, inhaling the smell of cold dirt. A mark in the dirt indicated he had slid a little way under the house and . . . She had to lean right under the house now . . . Here was a shallow hole, dug with a trowel.

The sound of a car engine made her get up too suddenly, whacking her head on the underside of the house. She saw stars, dropped her torch and managed to catch herself on the boards before she fell.

It wasn't Graeme's car this time. It was Scott Lacey in his police car. She met him out the front.

"They were here again," she said, rubbing her head where she'd struck it. "I got their plate."

"Are you okay?"

"I hit my head."

"And your knee."

She glanced down to see her knee caked in blood and dirt. She sighed.

"Let's go inside," Scott said.

"I'm locked out. We have to go in through a back window."

He touched her shoulder lightly. "Why don't you wait here and I'll climb in and open up for you?"

She nodded gratefully. A few minutes later she was turning the lights on in her lounge room while Scott sat down and pulled out his notepad.

"Tea?" she said.

"Nah. Let's just get this sorted."

She turned on the kitchen tap and inelegantly raised her leg to wash off her knee. She gave him the license-plate number and the make, model and color of the car.

She turned to see Scott surreptitiously admiring her legs in her short pajamas. Self-consciousness made her cheeks go warm. He quickly looked away.

"They're looking for something, Scott," she said. "They were looking under the house. You don't know anything? Any local knowledge? What might they be looking for?"

"I've got nothing," Scott said, tapping his pen on his notepad. "But when we identify them first thing tomorrow, I'll head out to ask them." He looked up and smiled. "And you'll be the second person to know."

She considered him, then said, "Are you still cranky with me on Juliet's behalf?"

"I was never cranky with you." He couldn't quite meet her eye.

"Don't worry. I'll be gone soon."

"Yeah?"

"I was never really welcome, was I?"

"You didn't really try," he said, climbing to his feet.

She watched him go, then locked the door. Far too wired now to sleep, she switched on her computer to work on the brochure. Outside the sea roared, the stars glimmered, and the breeze played in the trees that separated the beach from the town. Just as they had twenty years ago when she lived here. Just as they would long after she was gone.

*A*nother police officer, not Scott, dropped by the following afternoon to tell her that, yes, the car was registered to Graeme Beers as she'd suspected but that, no, they hadn't spoken to him. His house had been locked up, his dive boat gone, his car and trailer parked near the boat ramp. They'd left a card for him to call them, but there was nothing they could do in the meantime. Libby felt deflated, still uneasy and glad that she would soon be gone.

Twenty-eight

1901

The sun shines on the day Isabella has chosen to bury Daniel's bracelet. The sky is clear and blue. She wears a black dress. Matthew went to the village to buy a length of black cotton for her and she spent morning until evening for two days sewing it. Now, Isabella sits on the bed carefully unpicking the stitches that have held the bracelet inside the black ribbon for so long. One by one, the threads that bound him to her are loosened. Finally, the coral bracelet falls on the bed. Isabella wraps the ribbon around her wrist again, ties it with her free hand and her teeth. Then she picks up the bracelet and considers it in the morning light coming in through the window.

Each of the coral beads is smooth. Each silver link between them shines. It is a tiny thing, only big enough to circle a baby's wrist. She kisses each bead reverently. Tears run freely down her cheeks and drip off her chin, but these tears feel different. They feel right, as though they are cleansing her.

Matthew comes in, dressed in his wedding suit. He holds out the walnut box that once contained the mace.

"Yes," she says, "it's perfect. I can't bear to bury it just in the dirt. This is almost like a little coffin, isn't it?"

He lays the box on the bed and strokes her hair. She holds the bracelet in her hand one last time. It weighs almost nothing. Then she drops it onto the velvet lining and reverently closes the lid.

Matthew takes the walnut box and Isabella follows him. The sun is warm on her face. The sea air is light and salty. This place, which she had once found so ugly and strange, is a beautiful place for Daniel to come to rest. He will hear the roar of the sea every night in his dreams.

Isabella grasps her own fingers and pulls them hard. It won't do to keep thinking like this. Daniel's spirit is not in the bracelet any more than it is in the Winterbourne family plot back in Somerset. Daniel's spirit was long ago freed from worldly concerns. She is not sure if she believes in heaven, but perhaps she does and perhaps she can imagine Daniel is there watching over her, wondering why she is wearing a heavy black gown on such a warm day. She smiles, lets her fingers go, and follows Matthew into the wood.

He has prepared the same hole in the ground in which the mace was originally buried. This time, a treasure infinitely more valuable will rest here. Matthew has brought his bible and they stand by the side of the little grave while he reads Psalm Twenty-three. *The Lord is my shepherd, I shall not want. He maketh me to lie down in green pastures.* Her heart beats so hard that it aches. She lets the tears fall, she moans her grief, and Matthew does not look at her sharply or tell her to stop. She falls to her knees at the grave side as Matthew lowers the box into it, then she collects a handful of dirt and kisses it, then throws it on top of the box. Then, as Matthew fills the grave in for her, she puts her face in her dirty hands and cries. Matthew moves a large rock over the site.

When she looks up, the sun is still shining. Matthew is still there.

"It is done," she says.

"You have to go," he says.

"I know."

*L*ate at night, while she sleeps, Matthew is busy. The last thing that ties Isabella and him to the Winterbournes, the mace, has to go. To bury it or throw it into the sea may be simple, but both are reversible. Besides, the gold is worth a great deal.

He buys an old stone anvil at the mill on the edge of the village, gathers his pliers and his stone mallet and leans the spare acetylene tank on its side. Here, on the sea's edge behind the lighthouse, he sets to work. He knows he will not be able to make fine ingots, but gold is malleable; it melts enough to be hammered and cut under the acetylene flame. Every night he works, when he should be doing other things. He works as much to distract himself from thinking too much about her coming departure as he does to secure her future in America. One by one, he stores the uneven pieces of gold in the bottom of the suitcase he hasn't used in many years, ready to give to her on the morning she leaves.

On the fourth night, the mace is no more. The Winterbournes no longer have anything to reclaim.

*I*sabella decides to take her jewelry-making materials with her. She will be alone on the voyage and perhaps making bracelets and brooches for her sister will keep her occupied so she doesn't fall into a deep pit of mourning and sorrow. While Matthew is out picking up her ticket to Sydney from the post office she makes a last trip to the beach for stones and shells, then packs them all neatly in a box and places them with her folded clothes, ready to pack on the morning of her departure.

She is marking time now. She feels disconnected from the days and nights; the passing of time seems to make her nauseous. Her grief may be just ordinary grief now—not the tortured passions of a woman forbidden from mourning—but it is grief nonetheless and it must be felt and lived through.

Isabella looks around the room. She wonders if there is a memento of Matthew that she can take. But there is nothing. No portrait or photograph, no cuff link or watch. There is his pipe, but he will need that. She sits on the bed heavily. No memento could capture the lived experience of being with him, anyway. His smell, his texture, his heat. The thought of leaving Matthew behind has her sobbing into her hands. She is so *sick* of crying. When will all the pain end? Will it be any different once she gets to America? The long journey by boat fills her with dread. Alone with her thoughts, out at sea.

The door bangs open and she is happy for the distraction. She palms the tears from her cheeks and greets Matthew happily in the galley.

He holds up an envelope. "October the fifth. Two days away. The steamer leaves Mooloolah Wharf at nine in the evening. I've organized the carriage, and I will take you there."

Both are suspended a moment, caught on the aching thought of saying good-bye at the wharf. Then they resume. Isabella takes the ticket and looks it over, Matthew says she has to purchase her New York ticket in Sydney. "You have enough for a night or two's accommodation if you need it," he says. "It's been impossible to find out much at this end. You'll want to look over the ship and make sure it's comfortable and right for you."

Isabella bites her lip, looking at the ticket. "It's such a long way to go."

His warm, rough fingers are under her chin. "You've come so far already."

She gazes into his eyes. "It's such a long way from you. Will you not come with me?"

"Me? In New York society?" He shakes his head. "Your sister will not want me there. No, Isabella, we have known from the start that this love is not to leave the lighthouse. Out there, the world will interfere with us. It will frown, it will add pressures we mightn't withstand. You were always going to fly, my pretty bird."

"And you were always going to stay," she murmurs. Is he right? Would it be impossible for them to be together? America is a land of unlimited opportunities. Surely nobody would care who they were and what they did.

But she knows Matthew won't be moved. He has always been too sensitive about the opinions of the world. And she cannot stay. Sooner or later, if she stays here, the Winterbournes will find her.

Isabella wants to fall into his arms and press herself against him, but she realizes that holding him so passionately will change nothing. No, she must wean herself slowly from him over the next few days. So she brushes his hand away from her chin and steps back. His eyes are hurt and she almost relents, but then he too turns away.

The separation has begun.

*   *   *

$\mathscr{B}$risbane is a hot town. Stinking hot. Percy sweats hard under his waistcoat. He longs for a chilly English breeze to cool him. But there is no breeze, just a hot, hanging warmth that makes him perspire in places he didn't know perspired. He can only hope that the inside of Lady Berenice McAuliffe's house is a little cooler than the colonnaded portico.

Finally, an aging manservant answers the door. "May I help you, sir?" he asks in a slow drawl.

"I need to see Lady McAuliffe. Urgent business. My name is Percy Winterbourne."

The manservant looks back at him suspiciously. "She is expecting no guest."

"Hurry, hurry," he says. "I'm melting out here."

The manservant leads him into the entranceway and leaves him there. Percy considers the fittings. This Lady McAuliffe must be worth a lot of money. He wonders how she came by it. He lifts the corner of a brocade curtain and examines it carefully. *Much finer stuff than Mother has back home. These colonials have it made. Their rent costs nothing because nobody cares to live here, and they spend what they have left over on the things that matter.*

"Good day to you, sir."

He looks up to see an attractive woman, much younger than he'd imagined, standing in the doorway. He drops the curtain and advances his hand. "Lady McAuliffe, I thank you for seeing me. I come on most urgent and unsettling business, I'm afraid."

She takes his hand and shakes it firmly. "Unsettling? Well, then, I'd best sit down while you tell it to me. Do come in."

Lady McAuliffe leads him to a parlor, where she offers him a grandfather chair. She sits opposite on a velvet chaise and rings for tea.

"Now, Mr. Winterbourne, is it?"

"Yes, Percy Winterbourne. Of the jeweling family. We recently lost my dear brother to a shipwreck on the north coast."

Lady McAuliffe's eyes round with horror. "Oh, but that is dreadful! You poor man. What a terrible thing to have to endure. How can I help you?"

Percy reaches into his pocket and pulls out the folded news clipping from *The Queenslander*. "I saw this photograph from your ball."

Lady McAuliffe looks over it, a guarded expression on her face.

"See this woman?" He points at Isabella.

"Yes, that's Mary Harrow," she says.

"No. It's Isabella Winterbourne. It's my dead brother's wife."

A short silence. Then a maid bustles in with a tea tray and they sit considering each other while she lays it out.

"Enough," Lady McAuliffe says to the maid. "I'll pour. And make sure you close that door firmly behind you."

When she leaves, Lady McAuliffe says, "What are you saying? What do you mean by this?"

"She told you her name was Mary Harrow to hide the truth. She is a thief. She has stolen something of great value from my family and escaped. And tell me, how does a young lass such as Isabella become the *only* survivor of a shipwreck? I know she is a thief, but I suspect she may also be a murderer."

Lady McAuliffe pours tea and sits back to sip it. "I am shocked," she says.

"I need to find her."

"Will you call the constabulary?"

"No. I want to find her myself." Then, realizing he sounds too brittle, he adds, "She is still part of the family. Our hope is for her . . . rehabilitation. It will not look good for us if she goes to jail." He hopes the last is convincing. In fact, he has not written to Mother yet with the news that he has tracked Isabella down. He wants to find her first, and he wants to decide on her punishment on his own. His top lip is sweating.

But Lady McAuliffe is already shaking her head. "I'm sorry, I can't help you find her. I've no idea where she is. I knew her very briefly and not at all well. She was a friend of a friend, turned up at the ball at the last moment. Why don't you leave me your card, and I'll ask around a little?"

Steam builds up in Percy's head. He has come all this way, and she barely knows Isabella? It is all he can do to keep his voice even as he says, "Yes, I would be most grateful for any help."

She indicates the pot. "Will you have tea?"

He shakes his head. "I've not got an appetite for it," he says. No, he has an appetite for something else. Revenge. And the longer it goes unmet, the more it roars.

It is only by chance that he drops in at Hardwick's. He has seen their advertisement in the *Brisbane Courier* in the last issue he read, and has noted that they advertise a large collection of Winterbourne pieces. When he walks past the shop window, it seems the right thing to do to go in.

And from there, only good things happen. While a starstruck Max Hardwick shows him the register of sales, to demonstrate how important Winterbourne stock is to his business, Percy glimpses the name "Mary Harrow."

He jabs his finger at the page. "Mary Harrow," he says. "Who is she?"

"Ah, a young woman who makes her own pieces. Very pretty. We had three or four of them and they sold soon enough, but she hasn't offered me any more."

Percy's ears ring so loud he almost doesn't hear. "I see. And where can I contact her?"

And here is the answer. Lighthouse Bay. Care of the telegraph office, which, Max Hardwick believes, is located at the lighthouse.

Percy strides out the door.

Isabella soaks in a warm tub the night before her departure. She lets the water ease the aches in her bones and back, closes her eyes and lets herself drift for a minute. She and Matthew have been distant, careful not to share the bed, to make love, even to brush against each other in the galley. Every time she feels the ache in her skin to be pressed against him, she dismisses it with her rational mind. They cannot be together, so there is no point in intensifying the pain with long, sad embraces. This time tomorrow, she will be waiting on the wharf for her passage to Sydney, and he will be on his way to a cheap room over the bar at the local hotel for the night, before returning to the lighthouse.

And that will be that.

Isabella opens her eyes. Her towel hangs close by, and she stands, feeling the weight of her body again, to reach for it.

In the lamplight, at this angle, she suddenly sees them: faint blue lines across her breasts. Heat rushes to her heart. She reaches for the lamp instead of the towel and holds it as close as she dares to her bare skin.

Blue lines on her breasts; breasts that have been tender these last two days.

Isabella has seen these lines before. She has felt this tenderness before. She clatters the lamp back into its hanger and grasps her towel, wrapping it around herself as she runs upstairs. She opens the door to the deck and finds Matthew out there, gazing at the ocean.

He turns to her, a puzzled expression on his face. She is, after all, only wearing a towel.

"Isabella?"

A soaring hope has gripped her. The stars seem very close. She lets the towel slide away, so that her breasts are exposed to the evening air, and says, "Matthew, I'm pregnant."

Twenty-nine

*I*sabella wakes from a night of half-dreams and twisted sheets. Today is the day. She and her baby—*her baby*—will be in New York before year's end. All of this will be behind her. But there are dark clouds on this horizon.

She hears Matthew moving around in the next room. The thought of leaving him behind is a bitter taste in the back of her mouth. But even the promise of impending fatherhood cannot convince him to come. He had looked as if he would be sick when she asked him, as shock gave way and the grinding demands of reality pressed on him.

"Go and have a life without me," he had said. The distance they have kept of late seems to have sunk into their souls.

Isabella sits up. She looks down at her bare breasts. They are still heavy and tender this morning, the nipples darker. The regret that she has buried Daniel's bracelet began as a prickle last night, but has now grown acute. She tries to think her way through it, but her thoughts are scattered and she feels pressured by traveling time and ship schedules. Perhaps if she goes to stand in the woods where the bracelet is buried, the answer will become clear. She rises and pulls on stockings and a chemise.

Her dresses, for want of a proper wardrobe, are laid out on top of one another over an armchair. She chooses one to travel in, and folds the others to take in the trunk. She flips open the lid and gasps.

The bottom of the trunk is lined with chunks of gold.

"Matthew?" she calls.

And he is there at the door, with a telegram in his hand and a dark expression on his face.

"Where did this come from?" she asks.

"It's the mace," he replies, as if the fact is self-evident. She has no time to respond as he waves the telegram. "It's for you."

She frowns, takes it from his hand and reads it.

Mary, Percy Winterbourne is looking for you. Have told him nothing, but beware. Berenice.

Isabella's head snaps up. Her heart is cold. "When did she send this?"

"Yesterday morning. Does anybody else know you're here?"

"No," she says, although she knows it isn't true. The jeweler knows where to find her, perhaps one or two of Berenice's friends. "When do you pick up the carriage?"

"In about an hour. Don't delay. Pack the trunk and be ready to fly. Once you're at the wharf, you'll be safe." He looks as though he wants to crush her in his arms to keep her safe, but he keeps the distance they have tacitly agreed on.

"I'm ready now," she says. Her pulse flickers. "I want to go and say good-bye to Daniel in the woods."

His eyebrows draw down. "No, don't leave the lighthouse."

She drops her head. "Yes," she says, but she means no.

And then there is a knock at the lighthouse door. They both jump. It is not unusual for people to come to the telegraph office, but nonetheless he holds a finger to his lips and indicates she stay here in the bedroom. He quietly closes the bedroom door behind him and goes to the main door.

Isabella puts her ear to the bedroom door. Her heart is thundering so hard she can barely hear. Male voices.

"No, I don't know who you are talking about." This is Matthew. Fear rises through her like prickling lights.

More muttered voices. She can't bear it. She cracks open the bedroom door a little and listens hard.

"Then why would a respectable gentleman tell me I could find her here?"

"I have never heard of Isabella Winterbourne."

"She also goes by *Mary Harrow*."

"I can't help you."

It is Percy. The nightmare made flesh. She closes the bedroom door and hides a horrified sob with her hands. Her eyes dart about. The window. She grabs her trunk and hoists it out the window, then pulls up her skirts and climbs out as quickly and quietly as she can. She lands with a thud on the ground and runs for the woods.

Matthew keeps his voice calm and strong, even as Percy Winterbourne—a round-cheeked fellow with a sulky mouth— loses his temper.

"I have already walked up that wretched track in the sun to get here because I have been told that this Mary Harrow, which isn't even her real name, is contactable via this very telegraph office. You should know where she lives."

"You have been given incorrect information. I may have dealt with a Mary Harrow, I may have even kept telegrams for her, but I deal with many, many people, sir. I cannot be expected to remember them all and I certainly don't know where she lives." His heart tightens under his ribs. He needs to protect Isabella, and this gentleman is violently insistent. Matthew is fairly certain he could best Percy in a tussle if there were one, but he continues to hope that Percy will soon be convinced and go away.

"Why don't you go to the village and ask around?" Matthew says, trying to buy any time at all to get Isabella out of here. "If she lives at Lighthouse Bay, then someone will surely know her."

Percy wavers.

"I am terribly busy, sir. I don't mean to be rude, but I really cannot help you."

Percy's eyes narrow, his lips pucker. Finally he says, "I am a rich and powerful man. I hope, for your sake, that you are not lying to me."

Matthew spreads his hands. "What reason do I have to lie?"

Percy looks him up and down, and gives a resigned, "Harrumph."

"Good day, sir," Matthew says, closing the door.

He waits a moment until he hears Percy's footfalls move away. His thoughts spin. Their plans are in disarray. He heads to the bedroom.

Isabella is gone.

He dares not call out to her. He checks the telegraph office, then clatters up the lighthouse stairs, but his blood grows heavy because he already knows where she is—and Percy has to walk right past the woods to get to the village.

He runs, climbs out the back window so he doesn't run into Percy on the path, and enters the woods from the northern edge. A flash of her blue dress. She is bent over, her trunk sitting next to her, digging with her hands. He hurries up to her, and picks her up, wriggling and protesting, and clamps a hand over her mouth. "No, Isabella," he hisses. "There's no time."

She claws his hand away and says in a harsh whisper, "We have an hour."

"You can't be out here."

But she is looking at the ground again, at the bird-shaped rock he moved over the burial site so he could come here and remember her when she was gone. He knows every instinct in her body is to bend to the ground and claw her way through to the bracelet.

Footfalls. His head snaps up. She shrinks against him. In the distance, Percy Winterbourne crackles over the undergrowth through the trees.

Matthew's grip tightens on her, he turns her around and quietly guides her away. But Percy has seen them.

"Isabella, you murdering harlot!" he shrieks, and gives chase.

Matthew grabs Isabella's small trunk, pushes her ahead of him and runs, tree branches whipping his face. They break free of the woods and round the lighthouse. They must now either make their way over the rocks and down to the beach or head inland into the dense woods. The beach is too open, so he hurries Isabella across the grounds of the light station, into the woods and round to the south. Overnight rain has made the ground muddy, and the mud sucks at his shoes. Isabella stumbles, but he rights her, and they go farther into the trees, with no idea whether Percy is still behind them nor how close. He wishes they could run more quietly. Surely Percy can hear Matthew's thundering pulse: it is almost deafening, as are the sounds of fallen branches popping and crunching, their ragged breathing and their footfalls. On they go, making a wide semi-circle around the village, then leaving it behind. Isabella gasps with the effort, and he slows his pace a little so she can catch her breath.

"I can't go on running," she pants.

Ahead there is a creek, a gully. He grabs her hand and drags her at speed towards it. Down they go. He pulls her to the ground, lies flat on his stomach next to her in the tangled, succulent growth that covers the creek banks. They are hidden from sight. He listens as hard as he can.

A pop in the distance sparks in his heart. He strains to hear. No: no more footfalls. Just the sounds of birds and animals moving about, the sea breeze in the treetops making dry leaves fall and land with a soft scratch on the undergrowth.

The sea.

Her breathing.

"Have we lost him?" she whispers.

"It seems so. For now."

$\mathcal{P}$ercy gives chase for a while, then stumbles over a root and falls with a thud. He puts out his hands to break his fall, and a sharp pain shoots into his wrist. He is angry now. So angry that his stomach seems to boil. These woods are nightmarish, full of strange, prehistoric-looking plants and slithering menace in the undergrowth. He remembers the police constable's words, back near the site of the shipwreck: snakes, wild dogs, vicious natives; walking into the mouth of a monster.

Percy sits on the rough ground awhile. He is tired from the horrible overnight voyage up from Brisbane in a private coach. He hadn't wanted to wait two days for the paddle-steamer, but the constant jolting and jiggling, the constant stopping to change horses, had meant a very poor night's sleep. The coach still waited for him, outside the Exchange Hotel. He had hoped to have Isabella in it by now, to take her to Brisbane, to the police. How he would love to see her locked up in a stinking prison in this vile, humid place so far from home. How he would love those long hours of the coach journey with her all to himself, to satisfy himself with a more direct, more personal revenge.

His throat burns at the thought of not getting that revenge, and he has to spit on the ground.

But he is smarter than a woman and a lighthouse keeper. They have to turn up somewhere. And wherever that is, he will find them.

Percy stands and brushes the dirt off his jacket, pushing down an awkward feeling of embarrassment. Nobody needs to know he had fallen. Head high, he makes his way back to the village. The first place he stops is the general store. The woman behind the counter, a thin-faced redhead, smiles at him warmly.

He does not smile in return. "Tell me what you know about Mary Harrow and Matthew Seaward."

The woman stutters, intimidated by his bearing. "Mary Harrow? She was the Fullbrights' nanny for a little while. She's long gone."

"Why, I saw her just this morning. Does everyone in this town lie?"

A well-dressed man who stands, smoking, by the postcard rack on the counter speaks up. "I know Mary Harrow," he says. "She's not lying. Mary Harrow was working for the Fullbrights, but she moved on many months ago. I did, however, see her in the winter."

"Your name?"

"Abel Barrett."

Percy sizes him up. He looks like a gentleman, and is clearly itching to tell what he knows of Mary Harrow. "She has duped you all," Percy says. "Her name is not Mary Harrow, it is Isabella Winterbourne. She is a thief. Possibly a murderer."

The woman behind the counter pipes up, "She stole from Katherine Fullbright."

Barrett holds up his hand to hush the woman. "Who are you?"

"I am Percy Winterbourne, of the Winterbourne jeweling family."

Barrett frowns. "She had jewelry. She sold it in Brisbane."

Percy flinches, thinking about how much of her own jewelry—paid for by his family—she might have sold. And still she has the mace. Why else would she and the lighthouse keeper run away? "It was all stolen," Percy declares in an ominous voice. "Stolen from my family. Stolen from my dead brother. Her dead husband."

The woman gasps. Abel Barrett chews on the end of his cigar thoughtfully, then says, "What has this got to do with Matthew Seaward?"

"They are in league. He's been harboring her."

Barrett shakes his head. "No. That can't be right. Matthew Seaward is as timid as a mouse. Never did a bad thing in his life."

"My husband runs a carriage hire out the back of the store," the woman says dramatically. "Seaward has booked a hire overnight. Says he's going down to Mooloolah Wharf and back. He's meant to be picking it up at ten, if you want to go and wait."

Percy freezes. "Mooloolah Wharf?"

"Ships to Sydney leave from there," she says, clearly enjoying playing her part in the unfolding drama.

And from Sydney . . . anywhere in the world. "Yes, I will wait," he says. They will be back. They have to get away, and they will be back for their carriage—and he will pounce.

In the gully, Isabella rolls onto her back, letting her head fall and her eyes close. Her face is pale and tired and Matthew feels a pang in his heart. He had forgotten, at least while they were running, that she is carrying a child. His child. All of her limbs seem weighed down. He cannot bear the distance anymore. He doesn't care how difficult it makes the good-bye: he folds her into his arms and kisses her face, her ears, her hair.

"I love you, I love you. You're safe," he says, over and over.

She clings to him, crying.

"Sh, sh," he says. "It will be all right."

"How can it be? We can't go back to the village: he might still be there. We can't pick up the carriage, and we can't walk to Mooloolah: it's forty miles."

"But we can walk to Tewantin. The *Plover* leaves tonight for Brisbane. From there you can find another passage to Sydney or Melbourne, and on to New York, where Victoria is waiting for you. I know you are frightened, but once we get you out of Queensland, you will be safe. And one day, not too far in the future, you will be happy. I promise."

She gazes up at him with huge, unblinking eyes. The instinct to protect her is a hard muscle tightening in his gut.

"Come with me," she sobs. "You must come with me all the way to New York. We are a family now. Don't make me do this alone."

We are a family now. It is like a light has turned on inside him. Why did he not realize this before now? A family. His ears ring faintly as he turns this over in his mind. To allow her and his child to travel across the seas alone would make him a dark man indeed. He must travel too. He must protect them. His responsibilities to the light, to the telegraph, to the government office that has paid his wage these last twenty years, are nothing in comparison to his responsibilities to Isabella and her child. *His* child. A feeling stirs inside him. It is fear mixed with wonder. It is awe. All his doubts about petty issues of social correctness are washed away in the great river of morality that a man who will be a father feels.

"Yes, my pretty bird," he says, stroking her hair. "Yes, I will come."

Thirty

Isabella stumbles through the bush behind Matthew. She is reminded, horribly, of her last great trek through the hostile Australian landscape. Much has changed since then, but she is still fearful. They keep the sea on their left, letting the ocean's sound lead them south. In a few hours, they will come to the river, and they will follow it inland to the wharf. She is already tired, but she keeps going. Next time they come to a creek, she will insist that they stop and drink. The humidity weighs her down. The screeching racket of the cicadas pounds in her head. Sweat forms on her brow and under her breasts.

"Are you all right?" Matthew calls over his shoulder. He goes on ahead, breaking twigs and moving branches out of the way for her.

"I'm tired."

"It's only a few hours more."

"It's so hot."

"Let's move a little closer to the sea." He changes direction slightly and she follows him. He still doesn't break the cover of the bushes, but the sea noise becomes louder and the breeze dries the sweat on her skin.

"There's a creek just ahead," he calls back to her. "We'll stop there to rest."

Gratefully, she sinks to the ground at the water's edge and scoops the cool liquid into her mouth. It tastes of dirt and grass, but she drinks anyway.

He sits next to her and drinks his fill. Then he looks at her. "Can you keep going?"

"Not yet."

"I'll feel safer once we get to Tewantin. The paddle-steamer might already be in dock. We can get on and head straight for the berths to rest and hide."

"Let me rest, please," she said. "The baby makes me tired."

He nods his assent, and she sits among the greenery and takes deep breaths. He paces around her, clearly itching to keep going. She closes her eyes and tries to ignore it.

"Will you miss the sea, Matthew?" she asks him.

He is silent for a few moments, then says, "I suppose I will. I hadn't thought of it." She hears that his footsteps have stopped; he is still at last. "I've gone to sleep with the sound of it in my ears every night for twenty years. When we stayed in Brisbane, the world seemed strangely muted. I suppose I will have to get used to that."

She opens her eyes. He stands with the sun behind him, silhouetted. He is turned away from her, looking down the creek towards the ocean.

"I'm sorry that I'm taking you away from here," she says.

He turns, and smiles at her. "You are taking me somewhere I never dreamed I'd go. Into a life with a loving wife, children. A new city. A new world . . ." He trails off, emotion choking his voice.

She rises and goes to him, sliding her arms around his waist. "See now? You've made me keen to keep moving again. Towards that happy new world."

He picks up the trunk and they pick their way across the creek—their shoes are already sodden, so it matters little if they fill up again—and farther south.

The middle of the day approaches and the sun grows warm. Isabella flinches into shade where she can, but she knows her skin is burning. She has a hat to protect her face, but her sleeves are rolled to collect the breeze and she can see that her hands and forearms are growing pink. Her stomach rumbles, and she collects berries and plants to eat. They pick at food as they walk, a little slower for a while, and she tells him about her journey down the beach from the shipwreck. It seems a lifetime ago: a trauma that happened to somebody else. But it didn't happen to somebody else, it happened to her. And if she could survive that, then this short journey will be easy. It gives her the strength and confidence to step up her pace. They make good time down towards the Noosa River.

Next time they stop, it is because Matthew needs to rest. A stone has worked its way into his boot. He sits on the ground and pulls both shoes off to give them a good shake, then sits back a minute to catch his breath. She remains standing, fanning herself with the now-useless ticket from Mooloolah Heads to Sydney. They are not far from their destination now. An hour ago they began to follow the river inland, where the vegetation changed: thick and dark green, ferns to trudge over, the sharp-smelling eucalypts. The opposite bank, cleared for farming, bakes in the hot sun. Soon, no doubt, she will see the wharf. She feels light and happy, almost as if she could run the rest of the way.

Matthew stands and stretches, reaches out to pull her into a hug, then jumps, shouting with pain.

"What is it?" she asks, fear hot under her ribs.

He drops to the ground, grabbing his leg. "Snake," he manages to gasp.

She falls to her knees next to him in time to see a dark shape slither off into the undergrowth. "What do we do? Is it poisonous?"

"I don't know. I . . ." His face is white with fear.

"Let me see."

He moves his hands and she can see two distinct puncture marks in his ankle, just above the bone. "Oh God, Matthew. What do we do? What do we do?"

"Find some vines or long lines of grass. We have to tie it off."

She leaps to her feet and heads down near the riverbank on wobbling knees, yanks down two green vines from a tree and returns. He has fumbled in his pocket for his pen knife, and is scoring two cuts over the bite marks. Blood pours out. At his instruction, she ties one of the vines tightly below his knee, and one above.

"Tighter," he says through gritted teeth.

She pulls tighter. His knee flushes a deep shade of red.

"Isabella," he says, his hand gently but firmly on the back of her head, "you have to suction the poison out."

"Suction the . . . ? How?"

"With your mouth. I can't get my ankle that close to my own mouth. You have to do it. And quickly."

Her heart hammers. She is certain she will somehow do it wrong, fail to save him. She crouches next to him and fastens her mouth over the bite. His skin tastes of salt and mud, but the overwhelming taste is metallic blood. She forms a seal with her lips and sucks as hard as she can. Her mouth fills up with his blood; her stomach lurches.

"Spit it out," he says urgently. "Don't swallow it."

She spits, then returns her mouth to the site and sucks some more, then spits again. She doesn't know what happens next, so she keeps sucking and spitting until he taps her head lightly and says, "Stop now."

"Can you walk?"

"It isn't far. Damn it. I have a snakebite kit back in the light-house. Why didn't I think to bring it?"

"Because you didn't know we'd be rushing off through the woods." She hangs her head, her cheeks flushing. "It's my fault."

He grasps her wrist with cold fingers. "None of this is your fault."

Her eyes fill with tears. "Are you going to die?"

He shakes his head. "I refuse to die." He smiles, but his face is tight. "But I will likely be ill."

"Can you still walk?"

His glance slides sideways. "No. I didn't see what kind of snake it was. There are a number of snakes in these parts, and some are more venomous than others, but I need to stay still. You'll need to go to Tewantin alone and find help. Carbolic acid. I need to poke it into the wound."

The thought of leaving him here, alone and injured, over-whelms her. The next thought, of missing the steamer, or of not having him on it with her, is even worse.

"I'll go," she says. "Carbolic acid."

"Ask at the Royal Mail Hotel. Ask anyone. It doesn't need to be a doctor. Most places in these parts will have a snakebite kit."

She climbs to her feet. "I'll be back soon, my love," she says, and runs.

*   *   *

At least it is shadier along the river. She runs a little, walks a little, alternating. Her heart is back in the gully with Matthew, but her mind remains clear and focused. Around the bend a little, she hears voices. Two men, dressed in their shirtsleeves, sit in a shallow fishing boat.

"Hey there! Hey there!" she shouts, waving to them. She puts on a last desperate burst of speed and runs down to the river's edge. "Hey there!" she calls again, and this time they turn to see her. "I need your help! My friend has been bitten by a snake!"

The man at the oars doesn't hesitate to bring the prow of the boat around and row it towards her.

"Thank you," she says, as they draw closer. She sees that they are both Chinese, probably down from the gold fields. "Can you take me to town? I need to get a snakebite kit. Please!"

"No need," says the first man, who is fumbling away his fishing rod. "We help. You show us the way to your friend." He holds out a hand and she takes it firmly, and steps into the boat.

"This way," she says, indicating down the river. "It's not far."

They talk to each other in their foreign, twanging music and she keeps a steady lookout for the tree she pulled the vines from. Minutes later, she spots it. "There!" she calls, and the men row her to the bank.

While they pull their boat up onto the earth, Isabella trudges as quickly as she can up the bank to Matthew. His eyes are closed, but he opens them when he hears her.

"Isabella? So quick?"

"I found help," she gasps, then the Chinese men come into view. One has a small, cloth bag over his shoulder, the other is carrying a soup pot.

"Carbolic acid?" Matthew says to them, his eyes pleading.

The taller man shakes his head and pats his bag, and says a Chinese word.

Matthew struggles to sit. "No, no. I need carbolic acid. I need—"

The second man puts a hand on Matthew's shoulder. "This is ancient Chinese remedy. We bring it with us to Australia. You trust us now."

Isabella looks from Matthew to the men and doubt creeps into her heart. Has she done the wrong thing? It is too late now. They are here. They are starting a fire and hanging their soup pot over it, boiling water and adding dried herbs while Matthew lies with his head in her lap and his eyes closed.

"Where you going?" the taller man says, indicating the trunk.

"We need to catch the steamer tonight. Will he be well enough to travel?"

"No."

"We have to travel. We have to leave today."

"Then, yes. But keep him still and quiet. He will be sick a few days."

The other man, who is stirring the pot, chimes in. "We take you to Tewantin. No more walking. Still and quiet."

Isabella nods. *Still and quiet.* The smell of the herbs boiling is pungent and musky. Matthew is very pale. She strokes his hair.

Finally, the medicine is poured into a cup, allowed to cool a little, then offered to Matthew to drink. He sits up, and sips it slowly.

"Drink it all," the smaller man says. "Then we take you to the wharf."

Matthew eyes them both dubiously, then takes a deep breath and drinks the whole thing. They fill his cup again, and he drinks that too. His face twists at the taste.

"Come on. Up," the taller man says, hefting her trunk.

Isabella supports Matthew as he climbs to his feet. She feels his size, his weight. Then he balances himself unsteadily and follows the men down to their boat.

The river is quiet and smooth, gliding underneath them as the men row. *What next,* Isabella thinks. *What next?*

*P*ercy waits. He hasn't brought his pocket watch, but he assumes that ten o'clock has come and gone. He sits on a log that has been cut into a stool and harrumphs about the heat and the wait.

The man who has the carriage prepared glances about irritably. "Not like Seaward to be late."

Percy begins to understand that they are not coming. They suspect he is waiting for them, and they are still hiding in the nightmare woodlands. Curse them.

He turns to the man and says, "How far is Mooloolah?"

"About forty miles."

"Any other way he can get there?"

"No, sir. Not unless he walks."

And would they walk forty miles to catch the ship to Sydney? He suspects they would. By his reckoning, Isabella walked fifty to get here after the shipwreck.

"He'll be along shortly, sir, I'm sure."

The longer he waits, the farther away they will be. But if he leaves now, he can be there ahead of them either way. He can put out the word for them.

Percy stands and paces. His eyes sting with tiredness. Finally, he turns to the man. "I'll take my own coach. Meet them there. Don't tell Seaward. Don't tell him anything."

"I won't, sir."

Percy holds up a cautionary finger, then turns and runs back towards his waiting coach.

The driver stops to water his horses some distance south. Percy gets out to stretch his legs, glaring at the dirt road and the flat, yellow-green landscape. He has no food but doesn't want to risk stopping at a hotel on the way, in case Seaward and Isabella got ahead of him on the carriage.

"Do you have any food?" he demands of the driver.

The driver shakes his head.

"Never mind," Percy mutters. "I'll eat when we arrive."

"Seeing someone off at the wharf?" the driver asks. He has accompanied Percy on this journey since Brisbane, and is growing increasingly curious about the continual change of locations.

"I hope to meet somebody there. They're on their way down by foot."

The driver laughs. "From Lighthouse Bay? Unlikely, sir."

"Desperate people," Percy said. "They want to avoid me. Won't I be a surprise?" He smiles, and the driver recoils almost imperceptibly.

"Nearest port to Lighthouse Bay is Tewantin, sir. Nobody in their right mind would walk to Mooloolah. The steamer leaves Tewantin for Brisbane tonight."

Electricity shoots through Percy's veins. What an idiot he has been. This country is like a string of coastal towns, connected by ports and telegraph stations, clinging to the damply hot margins of a great desert. Of course they would go to the nearest port. If only he had thought to ask, before now, where that might be.

"How far is Tewantin, then? Are we nearly there?"

"Passed the turn-off an hour ago."

Percy kicks the wheel of the coach, screaming with frustration and more than a little pain as the blow jolts back up into his foot. "Right, right. No time to lose. Get us back on the road. Tewantin. The port. As quickly as you can."

"Right you are, sir," the driver says.

Percy climbs back into the coach, ants in his belly. For the first time, he starts to fear he might lose her.

The *Plover* isn't yet waiting at the wharf, so Isabella and Matthew sit on a carved wooden bench in the shade of an old whitewashed sawmill, with the trunk at their feet. Matthew is unwell, but he grows no worse and Isabella allows herself to believe that he will recover. If only the steamer would come. She has purchased the last two saloon tickets from the office in town, and she turns them over in her hands, again and again, to make the time go faster. She plays a game with herself: if she looks away for two minutes, when she looks up again she will see the steamer in the distance, plying its way upriver. But the game doesn't work because she cannot stop watching the horizon.

She stands and begins to pace. Across the rough-hewn boards to the water's edge. Back to the seat. Touch the sawmill wall. Across to the water's edge. She counts while she paces. Every hundred paces she stops for a moment to peer downriver. Paces again. A strong wind springs up, rattling the upper branches of the tall gums behind the wharf. Crows and seagulls flap away, startled.

Matthew watches her—stooped and pale—a slight smile on his lips. "Don't worry. If the snake didn't stop us, then nothing can."

"I'll just be happier once we're on the way."

"I know." He moves to get to his feet, but she hurries over to push him back down.

"Still and quiet," she says.

She moves back to the center of the wharf. Three other people have joined them, all men with tickets for the deck. She feels a little safer with more people around. She turns, looks back up the wharf to the road.

And freezes.

In a second, she has her trunk in her hand and she pulls Matthew from his seat and yanks him with her down the wharf.

"What?" he gasps.

"Percy," she replies. They duck in between two wooden buildings. One is the sawmill, abandoned now with its door sagging on its hinges. She cracks open the door and pulls Matthew inside. It is cool and dark, and smells of sawdust and oil. Pigeons roost in the roof beams, up near a series of high, grimy windows.

"Are you sure?" Matthew asks.

"I saw him stepping out of a coach up on the road. He didn't see me. Oh God, how did he find us?" Her heart thuds.

Matthew shakes his head, moving to stand by the door to guard it. "Deduction, I imagine. The nearest port. It was the most likely place for us to go."

"Then why did we come here?" She sinks to her knees, her hands in her hair. "And now, he will wait right there, hoping to see us. And he *will* see us if we try to board the steamer."

Matthew is there a moment later, pulling her to her feet. She remembers that he is ill, and shakes herself out of self-pity.

"Let us wait and see," he says. "The steamer doesn't depart for another two hours."

She searches the space with her eyes. Machinery, dusty and perpetually stopped, fills the building. Wheels with belts on them, pumps and ropes and chains. A large platform catches her eye, and she takes Matthew to it—his arm over hers—and sits him down on the bottom stair. She climbs onto the platform, where she can see a beam of daylight through a chink between boards.

Isabella lowers herself to her knees and presses her left eye against the chink. It affords her a view down to the wharf. She holds her breath. Percy walks past. Then a few moments later he walks back. He is pacing the wharf.

She comes back to sit with Matthew. "He is certainly waiting for us."

"Let me think."

She returns to the chink and watches. There he is, in his yellow waistcoat, reappearing and disappearing in a slow rhythm. More passengers begin to crowd onto the wharf. She knows Percy will search every one of their faces, looking for hers. And then . . .

"What would he do to you?" Matthew asks, as if reading her thoughts. His body flexes forward protectively.

Isabella rises, and comes to sit with him on the step. "He would hand me over to the police."

Matthew nods. "Then why hasn't he called the police? Why does he not have them here with him?"

"Because he wants me alone first." Helpless desperation crosses Matthew's brow. She drops her head, her cheeks flaming as she remembers the liberties Percy took with her in her own home. "Would I hang for stealing the mace?" she asks. It is the first time she has acknowledged it is stealing. Until now, until this moment of reckoning, she saw it as keeping something that was presumed lost, something nobody expected to see again anyway.

He doesn't answer, and she wonders whether he doesn't know or whether he doesn't want to say.

Then, in the distance, they hear the sound of the steamer's whistle.

"She's coming," Isabella breathes.

Matthew puts his elbows on his knees and drops his head to his hands. They wait in the quiet mill, as the sound of the steamer draws closer. Isabella returns to her vantage point to watch the steamer dock, watch the passengers leave, watch supplies be lifted off and on. The crowd disperses a little: many of them were waiting to greet friends. The loading of the steamer takes forever, and still Percy strides about, eyes towards the road, waiting for them.

As the afternoon grows cool and the shadows lengthen, Percy begins to doubt himself. Hours, he has waited. Hours upon hours. He could have been farther along, on the way to Mooloolah. Is that where they are? Or are they still in the bush somewhere? Perhaps they have met their death at the hands of natives or wild dogs. The thought gives him no pleasure. He wants to rip her to pieces with his own hands. A quiet death in the wilderness is not revenge. And he wants the mace back. If it were lost in the bush somewhere, it might be lost forever.

A pain blazes in his head. He has never felt so uncertain and it makes him angry. Why did Arthur have to die? He continues to pace, clenching and unclenching his fists, looking out for any flash of fair hair that might be Isabella.

The passengers begin to board just as dusk comes to the wharf. Saloon class first: mostly gentlemen in their well-cut suits, but an occasional wife or daughter in broad-brimmed hat and fitted coat. Isabella paces now, while Matthew sits—still and quiet and very pale—on his step.

"We are running out of time," she says.

"When is the next steamer to Brisbane?"

"Seven days away."

Matthew climbs to his feet.

"What are you doing?" she asks.

"I am going to end this."

Her stomach turns to water. "Matthew? What do you mean?"

The whistle blows. A bosun walks up and down the wharf ringing a bell. "All aboard who's coming aboard!"

"That's it," she says, panic gripping her. "That's the last call."

He walks to the trunk and picks it up. She rattles down the stairs. "What are you doing? You're not going out there."

He hands her the trunk. "No. You are."

"What?"

"Get on the steamer. I'll try to join you, but don't wait for me. Go inside and go to your berth and keep yourself and our baby safe." He swallows hard. "I will distract Percy long enough."

Her heart feels like it will burst. "Please, Matthew, no. Don't put yourself in danger."

"I still hope to join you," he says.

"But how?"

He grasps her chin gently, his fingers firm and warm on her face. "No matter what you hear, get on the steamer. Do you understand? No matter what you hear."

She is caught in his gaze. Her mouth trembles. She sobs once.

"Do you understand?" he asks again.

"Yes," she says. "Yes, Matthew."

He kisses her softly, then points to the door they came in, and nods once. Then he turns and shuffles to the rear door of the sawmill. He finds it closed and locked, so he picks up a piece of metal from the ground and prizes it open. It gives.

Matthew turns, and points to her door again. She takes a moment to memorize his face, then turns and goes to the door.

She pauses at the corner of the building, in the dark alley between the sawmill and the warehouse next door. The gas lamps along the wharf are now lit. Only one or two people hurry towards the gangplank. Percy, in his yellow waistcoat, stands directly in front of it, with his eyes turned to the road.

Then, she hears her own name called.

"Isabella! Isabella, come on! The steamer is ready to leave!"

At first she is puzzled, because it is Matthew calling her. But he is calling her from the road, his back turned away as though she is up there. Momentarily, the thought flashes across her mind that the snake venom has affected his brain, but then she sees Percy galvanize, start running towards the road, and she knows what to do.

She touches her belly once. "Come, little one." Then she dashes to the gangplank, brandishing her ticket.

"Downstairs to the saloon, ma'am," the bosun says.

"There will be another man. A tall man with a beard. I have his ticket." She shows it to him. "He will be here. I know . . ." She trails off, helplessness stopping up her throat.

"I'll keep an eye out, ma'am. Make yourself comfortable down there."

She cannot stay here and look out for Matthew lest Percy see her. She collects her trunk and makes her way down the stairs, through to the berths. She stores her trunk at one end, then climbs onto the bed and waits, eyes open, hoping for the best, but fearing the very worst.

Time moves slowly, like molasses. Isabella can hear her heart beating. Flick, flick, flick. It is very quiet in the berth. The noises of the steamer, the voices in the saloon, are all muted by the bedding and the curtains.

Flick, flick, flick.

Did he make it? If he'd made it, he would have been here by now.

Flick, flick, flick.

Deep inside her, another heartbeat. Matthew's child. She will raise the child to know all about his father. She will instill all the values Matthew held: constancy, patience, wisdom. Tears brim, but she blinks them back. She has always known she would lose him.

With a clunk, the steamer begins to move. She gasps, closes her eyes. She is on her way. Brisbane to Sydney. Sydney to New York. The long, open miles. Alone.

Then she hears footfalls. Every muscle in her body tenses. Matthew? Percy? She shrinks back into the corner of her berth.

Then, a quiet voice. "Isabella?"

She sits up, hitting her head on the top of the berth. "Matthew?" She flings back the curtain, and there he is: hobbling, but real and present.

She reaches for him, presses him hard in her embrace.

"I must lie down," he gasps.

"Of course, of course. Here is your berth."

He climbs into it while she flutters about him, relief making her joints weak. He lies down and closes his eyes.

"What happened?" she asks.

"I managed to trip him. A pile of logs beside the sawmill. He was flat on his face behind one of the warehouses when I dashed aboard." He groans a little. "I need to rest. The wound is aching."

"I'll get the ship's doctor," she says, pulling away.

But he grasps her wrist gently and tugs her back. "Not now. Soon. Just hold me a moment."

So she leans over him, sinks into him, her face against his neck. She can hear his heartbeat.

His heartbeat. Her heartbeat. And the tiny inaudible heartbeat that will bind them together until death.

The river slides beneath them, carrying them into the future.

*W*hen Percy finally climbs to his feet, his head is sore. So sore. His brain feels as though it is pressing hotly against the tightening cup of his skull. Are they on the boat? Or have they run into town? He tries to track the steamer with his eyes, but his vision blurs, goes almost double. He can't think straight. The pain is ablaze in every coil of his brain. He must lie down so he can regroup and plan his next action. He stumbles from the wharf, clutching his skull, all the pain and judgment of doomsday weighing upon his head.

Thirty-one

2011

*L*ibby still hadn't signed the contract. The solicitor had reassured her that it was all in order, but she still hadn't put pen to paper, and she wasn't sure why. She had already spent the money in her imagination. She was ready, so ready, to leave Lighthouse Bay and get on with her life. But she still hadn't signed the contract.

"They tell me it's been a week since they posted it," Tristan said, as they sat on the small paved area behind her house, soft blue post-sunset air all around them. She smelled the enticing aroma of lamb roasting in the oven and tasted the sweet burn of brandy on her tongue.

"I thought you weren't supposed to have anything to do with the deal?" she shot back, smiling.

"Well, I'm not. But Yann was talking about it and I overheard. Is everything okay?"

"Yes, everything is okay. I'm just waiting for the solicitor to get back to me. He's busy."

"Small-town solicitor. I can give you the number of a good firm in Brisbane."

"It's fine. Don't worry. I'm not worried." She gave him a brief, brittle smile. "Topic change, please."

Tristan tipped back in his chair, stretching out his legs. "Have you decided what you'll do when you move out?"

"I was thinking of heading back to Paris." She glanced at him to judge his reaction.

"For good?"

"I don't know. It depends."

"On what?"

"On a lot of things." This time she looked at him directly, raising her eyebrow.

He smiled slowly in return. "Well, as long as you choose to stay, I'd like to go on seeing you." He reached across and grasped her hand, rubbing her fingers gently. "You know I think you're beautiful."

They sat like that for a while. She sipped her drink, tried to loosen the knots in her neck. The draft brochure was done and sent. She had no more work lined up. This was the interim: the time between before and after. She tried to enjoy it, but the discomfort was still squirming in her belly, and she was just tipsy enough to say something. Tristan had spent all day with her, the night before too, and they still hadn't talked about his "flatmate." So she said, trying to sound more nonchalant than she felt, "So, how's your flatmate?"

His eyes met hers. He looked at her a long time, and she knew he was trying to read her expression, trying to gauge what she suspected, how she would feel.

"It's all right," she said. "I know she's not a flatmate. I never told you about Mark, did I? Twelve years we were together. The whole time he was married to somebody else."

Tristan nodded once. "I didn't lie when I said I wasn't married. I'm not. But she and I have been living together for four years. It's not working out. We sleep in separate beds. She's having trouble letting go. For all intents and purposes, she is a flatmate. I'm helping her see that she needs to find somewhere else to go."

We sleep in separate beds. That was one of Mark's lines. Perhaps it was one of every cheater's lines.

"So, where does she think you are now? Where did she think you were last night?"

"Perth," he confessed.

And Libby remembered how he had told *her* he was in Perth, and he hadn't been. Was *Perth* just shorthand for *with another woman?*

"Do you hate me now?" he asked, and he sounded as vulnerable as a little boy.

"No," she said. "I can hardly judge you without judging myself. If you say it's over—"

"It's definitely over. I think she'll be gone by the end of next month."

Libby considered this. She had no desire to be a mistress for another twelve years, but she could give Tristan till the end of next month. Then, if he was still making excuses, she'd book that ticket to Paris. By then she'd be a rich woman. The thought made her smile.

"You're a good girl, Libby," Tristan said, draining his drink. "Some women . . . They get these ideals in their heads and it makes life very difficult. Relationships are so complicated. So messy and so not ideal. But I have a good time with you."

"Yes, I have a good time too." She shot out of her chair. "I'd best go check on the roast."

She went inside to the kitchen. Through the window she could see his hands, folded behind his head, his broad, well-dressed shoulders. He was good for her in so many ways: intelligent, stable, powerful, good-looking. But he'd lied to her. Indirectly, by denying he was married and not elaborating. And directly, by calling his girlfriend a flatmate. He'd been protecting himself. She understood that. Everybody had an instinct to protect themselves, or to present themselves in the best light, or to take care of their own interests.

But he'd lied. Smoothly. Without blinking.

Libby remembered her first conversation with him. His plans for an eco-resort, his reassurances that nothing would change in Lighthouse Bay. And for the first time, she doubted him. Because if he lied to her about his relationship, what would stop him from lying about everything else?

The phone rang at four in the morning. Libby took a moment to wake up. Tristan slept quietly next to her, on his front so that his smooth, muscular back was exposed to the early-morning air.

He roused, mumbled, "Is that the phone?"

"Uh-huh," she said quietly. "Go back to sleep." She flung back the covers and stumbled to the lounge room. She scooped up her phone. Her voice was croaky. "Hello?"

"Oh, dear," the crisp female voice on the other end of the line said. "I've got my times mixed up, haven't I?"

"Emily?"

"Yes. I'm sorry. I've woken you up."

Libby sat in her office chair and reached across to switch on the lamp. "It's okay," she said gently. "I'd be getting up soon anyway." That wasn't true. She and Tristan hadn't fallen asleep until after one. She cleared her throat, trying to sound businesslike. "I take it you've had a chance to look at the brochure?"

"I love it, Libby," she said. "I can't tell you how much I love it. I had my concerns. I thought perhaps you disagreed with me about the new direction; you'd been doing the catalog so long the traditional way. But now I see that you not only agreed with me, but that you really understood what I said. You really understood how I felt."

Libby smiled. "I sure did," she said.

"Mark would have hated it, you know."

"I know."

Emily adopted a deep voice, mimicking uncannily Mark's cadences. "Winterbourne trades on tradition. Tradition is what our customers want, and it's what they expect to see." Then she laughed, returning to her own voice. "Gosh, he could be such a fuddy-duddy at times."

Libby shared the laugh with her. "I know what you mean," she said, then immediately wondered if she'd gone too far, if Emily would pick up on her fond tone, her casual knowingness.

"By the way," Emily said. "I asked around for you. About the *Aurora*."

"Yes?"

"Yes. It seems Arthur Winterbourne went with the mace because, apparently, he was paranoid about thieves. Wanted to be there with it. There was some question mark over when the company would get paid for the work. When it was lost, nobody was sure if it was property of the Winterbournes, the Queen or the Australian parliament. If it's ever found, it could be quite confusing."

"I see."

"The other thing I found out is that Arthur had his wife, Isabella, on board with him."

"Isabella?" The mysterious "I."

"Yes, the poor lamb. She was half his age. They had a child, but it died very young. There's not much in the family records about her. That's about all I could find. Presumed drowned along with her husband."

Libby's heart lurched. No, not drowned along with her husband. She opened her mouth to tell Emily, but thought better of it. At the moment, all she could do was speculate. "Thanks for that," she said instead. "It adds a dimension to an old local legend."

"I wonder if Mark ever went there to see the wreck," she mused.

"He told me he had."

"Is that so? He didn't mention it to me. But he didn't tell me everything, I suppose. Not about his business trips."

"I expect he told me because I grew up nearby."

"Yes. I expect so. It's good to talk to you about him," Emily said. "You seemed to know him well."

Libby trod cautiously now. "I enjoyed working with him."

"I often wondered . . ." Emily trailed off. The quiet between here and London stretched out. Libby could hear her own pulse. "Libby, don't take this the wrong way, but Mark spoke so fondly of you. His voice, it would go soft when he mentioned your name. I often wondered if you two were . . . seeing each other."

Here was her chance. Come clean. Tell everything. She'd been angry just last night about Tristan's lies. Why not just say it? *Yes. We were in love. I loved Mark. I loved your husband.* Her heart was beating hard. The idea that Mark's voice went soft when he used her name. Oh, it stirred feelings inside her. She wasn't over him. She might never be over him. But he had never been hers to get over.

Damien's advice came back to her. *Forget about what you did in the past. Think about what you can do now, here in the present.* Tristan had lied to protect himself. Libby didn't need to protect herself anymore. She needed to protect Emily.

"I've offended you, haven't I?" Emily asked, in response to the long silence.

"You haven't offended me," Libby said. "I've just been thinking about how to answer you. Mark and I were very good friends. He often visited me in Paris. But you had his whole heart, Emily." As she said it, she knew it was true. He had stayed with Emily. He had protected her. "He loved you very much. Don't trouble yourself with fears that he loved anyone else. He would never have left you." Never.

She could hear Emily crying softly. Then she stopped, and blew her nose. "You are a dear. And I'm so pleased to be working with you. I'll make sure I send more work your way. Thank you, Libby. Thank you so much."

"You're more welcome than I can say."

Libby returned to the bedroom. Tristan was asleep again. She lay down next to him and ran her fingers lightly over his back. He stirred but didn't wake. She would tell him when the sun came up.

She had changed her mind. About everything.

*J*ust as Juliet was stepping out of the shower she heard the doorbell chime.

"Coming!" she called, quickly drying herself and throwing on a red cotton dress. Late-afternoon sunlight slanted through the western windows. Would it be Damien? A week had passed since he'd left, and every day she hoped to hear from him. She could certainly use cheering up after the day she'd had. An unexpected tax bill had arrived right before Cheryl had resigned: she had fallen in love and was off to New Zealand.

But it wasn't Damien's welcome presence waiting when she opened the door to the flat. It was the very unwelcome presence of her sister.

"Can I come in?"

Juliet stood aside wordlessly as Libby walked in, then closed the door behind her.

Libby had a large envelope under her arm. She placed it carefully on the coffee table and sat down. "We need to talk," she said.

"Do we?"

And, curse her, Libby smiled. A big, beautiful, genuine smile. Time telescoped, and she remembered Libby smiling at her when they were children. Playing castles at the B&B, or collecting shells on the beach, or just lying in bed up late in their bedroom talking about boys. Juliet's heart grew tender around the edges.

Juliet sat down. "What's going on?" she said, her voice softer.

Libby tapped the envelope. "Have a look."

Juliet withdrew the papers from the envelope. She saw the words "Agreement between Ashley-Harris Holdings and Elizabeth Leigh Slater" and shoved them back in. "I don't want to know."

Libby took the envelope from her and shook the papers out, flicking to the right page. "Don't worry, Juliet. This story has a happy ending. I'm making sure of it. Look." She held the documents in front of Juliet, pointing to a figure with the bright red nail on her index finger. A figure with a lot of zeroes.

Juliet felt sick.

"I've turned them down," Libby said.

The astonishment winded Juliet. "You've turned down . . ."

"Yeah, I've turned down two and a half million dollars. They said they wanted to build an eco-resort, but . . . I don't know. Sounds a bit suspect. Tristan Catherwood couldn't tell the whole truth if his life depended on it. So, yes, I've turned them down. I'm not selling."

Light and air returned to Juliet's world. "You would have been rich."

"I am rich. I own that place outright. It's right on the beach in one of the most beautiful places in the world. Sure, I don't have a real job just yet, but I'll get by." She leaned forward and put her hand over Juliet's. "I'm so sorry. I'm sorry for everything. I do love you, Juliet. I know you don't believe me, but I do."

The relief had made her vulnerable. Now, these heartfelt words prompted Juliet to cry. First, just silent tears, but then she sobbed once and Libby knelt in front of her and took her in her arms. Juliet pressed her face into her sister's shoulder and sobbed and sobbed. Finally, she sat back, wiping her tears on the hem of her dress. "Sorry," she said. "I'm feeling a little emotional today. I love you too, Libby. I hope we can work all this out."

"Let's start by having a ritual burning of this contract."

They left the B&B behind and walked down the sandy path to the beach. Juliet kicked off her shoes. The sand was cool and soft. They walked along beside the grassy dunes, looking for small dry sticks for kindling, and brought them back to a sheltered spot. The great ocean roared as the sky turned pale and pink. Together, they built a fire and lit it, crouching over it and laughing, their voices snatched by the wind.

"If Scott Lacey sees us, he'll fine us," Juliet said. The wind had whipped her hair into her mouth and she pulled it out strand by strand.

"He'll fine *me*. He hates me."

"No, he doesn't. I think he fancies you, actually."

Libby laughed it off. "Well, I hope I can eventually be accepted here. By Scott Lacey, by everyone. But most of all by you."

"Of course by me. Of course."

"I . . . I'm so sorry about Andy, Juliet. It was my fault."

Juliet found herself momentarily speechless. She wasn't sure how to respond. Yes, it was Libby's fault. But it had been an accident. And twenty years later, Juliet found herself exhausted by the idea of carrying the grudge another twenty years. "I forgive you, Libby." She shrugged. "Andy would have forgiven you ages ago."

Libby tried a smile, offering Juliet the envelope. "You want to do the honors?"

"I think you should."

Libby nodded. Her skin was lit warm by the fire. She held the contract over the fire so the flames caught the corner. They jumped so quickly that Libby let go of the envelope with a little shriek, and they both giggled as they watched the envelope blacken and curl, then turn to ashes. The fire burned down, and they sat on the beach, shoes abandoned and bare feet in the sand, in companionable silence for a while.

Then Libby said, "I have to be really honest with you. At first I said yes. That's why there was a contract to burn."

Juliet's gut twitched, but then she remembered that the contract was now ashes. "What changed your mind?"

"Damien Allbright changed my mind. He's pretty wise for a kid."

A kid. Juliet pressed her lips tightly together, feeling her age, her undesirableness. "Damien's great," she managed.

Then Libby laughed. "You too? Oh, lord."

"What do you mean?" She regarded her sister in the dying firelight as the soft night breeze stirred the ashes.

"Damien wore exactly that expression when he talked about you."

Hope lit up in Juliet's heart. She waited for Libby to explain.

"Look, he told me not to say anything, but I'm forty, not fifteen. Secrets are for teenagers. He's sweet on you, Jules."

"He is?"

"Absolutely."

"You don't think it would be too strange? The age difference?"

"My last partner was eighteen years older than me and it lasted twelve years. There were problems, but it wasn't the age difference that caused them."

Libby had never mentioned a partner. Her voice had grown melancholy.

"What happened to you two?" Juliet asked.

"He died. He left me the cottage."

"Ah. Mark Winterbourne."

"He was married to somebody else. The whole time." Libby smiled bitterly. "I really have to catch you up on my dark past, Jules. Do you think you can still love me?"

Juliet grasped Libby's hand. "I'm sure I can."

The weekend brought a sudden warm spell. Everyone said it would be the last before winter, so Libby took to the ocean for a final swim. The water had an edge of coolness on it, but she soon adjusted and swam a few breakers, then went farther out and floated a little on the waves. The sky was very blue. Beautiful. Home.

She made her way back up the sand, wrapped in her towel, then hosed off her feet by the side of the house. She glanced up at the lighthouse to see Damien letting himself out.

"Damien!" she called, waving with both hands.

He saw her and strode down. "I knocked. You weren't home."

"I was swimming. Hey, you know what? I've decided to stay in Lighthouse Bay." She was amazed at how happy those words made her feel.

"I didn't know you were thinking of leaving."

"Well, I was. And now I'm not."

"That's great news. Are you up for more great news?" He

brandished a folder full of papers. "Photocopies of Matthew Seaward's journal. They were in the boxes at home."

"Including the dates you were missing?"

He nodded. "Libby, you're going to love this."

"And you're going to love this: I think I know who she was. Arthur Winterbourne's wife, Isabella. She was on board the *Aurora* when it went down."

Damien grinned. "Ah, the mysterious past reveals itself. Let's go inside."

She let him into the house and kept him waiting in the lounge room while she scrambled into clothes. By the time she emerged, he had spread the photocopied pages out on the table.

"I take it you've managed to convince Rachel to let you back into your house?"

"And my bank accounts, yes. She's starting to cool off. It won't be easy, but I think we can separate fairly at least." He tapped the documents. "The boxes had all of the journals photocopied. Granddad had made an extra set before he died. Libby, there's buried treasure."

"What?"

He found the page and read to her. *"This morning we buried I's treasure. It is one hundred paces from the front door of the lighthouse, and I will watch over it for her even after she's gone."*

"A hundred paces from . . . That's right on my property."

"I know."

"Graeme Beers . . ."

"Must have the original. That's why the journals were in such a mess at the lighthouse when I first arrived. He'd gone through them."

A light went on in Libby's head. "Of course. He must have read something in Percy Winterbourne's papers that placed the mace at the lighthouse. He came down here, found the part of the diary that mentioned the buried treasure—"

"And he's been coming back ever since, looking for it."

"Buried treasure," Libby murmured, turning the idea over in her head. "Right underneath my feet. What do you think it is?"

He smiled, nodding. "I think it's the mace."

Libby drew her breath in sharply. "When do we start digging?"

He held up his hands. "Slow down. A hundred paces in which direction? This is why Graeme's been poking around but not dug anything up. He's trying to calculate the exact spot. It might even be under the house."

"But we're going to go out and have a look, right?"

"Absolutely."

Within minutes, Libby and Damien were outside, measuring out a hundred paces from the lighthouse in a variety of directions. If they went straight ahead from the lighthouse's doorstep, they wound up exactly where Graeme and his son had been searching.

"What now?" Libby asked.

"Must be what Graeme Beers was thinking."

"Bushes, rocks. No big X marking the spot."

Damien was looking at the ground, an expression of deep concentration on his face. "Or maybe there is."

Libby moved her gaze to where he was looking. "It's a rock. There are plenty of rocks out here."

"Come and stand here, where I am."

She did as he asked.

"Were you ever any good at cloud pictures?" Damien asked.

"No. Juliet was."

"I was a champ. What does this rock look like to you?"

She squinted, then smiled. "A bird."

"'My pretty bird.' Graeme didn't realize because he only had the last few pages of the journal. He hadn't been following the love story like we have."

"You think Matthew Seaward marked the treasure with this rock?"

"Have you got a shovel?"

*A*n hour later, they hit the wooden box. As they cleared the way free with their hands they saw the brass logo on its top: the Winterbourne coat of arms. Libby thought of Mark and swallowed hard.

"I can't believe it," she said. "The mace was here all along. Who does it belong to? The Winterbournes? Or the Australian government?" A thought suddenly grabbed her. "It doesn't belong to me, does it?"

"I have no idea," Damien said. "We're going to need a rope or something to pull it up. He buried it so deep."

Libby went inside and tied a piece of blue rope to a coat hanger, which they dropped in the hole and hooked around the handle. Slowly, they hoisted it up onto the ground. The box was not heavy enough to suggest it held treasure.

Damien grinned at her across the pit. "What will we find?"

"Bugs? Diamonds?"

"Let's see." He flipped the box open. It was empty.

Damien laughed, sitting back on his haunches. "No treasure. Perhaps somebody has been here before us. Graeme Beers?"

"Why would anybody bother re-burying the box?" She reached in and felt around the crevices. Her fingers brushed a small, hard lump and she dug for it and pulled out a tiny bracelet. Not a treasure: the beads were coral and the clasp was silver that had tarnished black. Libby studied it in the afternoon sun. "It's a baby bracelet."

"Why did Seaward call it a treasure?"

Libby remembered what Emily had told her: Isabella Winterbourne had lost a baby. "Things don't have to be worth a lot to be treasured." She fingered the beads gently.

A feeling of the past overlying the present flickered over her skin. Her heart pinched and she found herself overwhelmed. Tears were suddenly in her eyes and she had to look away from Damien, embarrassed.

"Yeah," said Damien softly. "I feel it too."

A moment went by, as the past slipped once again into history, and Libby said, "Look at us. We're filthy. Do you want to come in and have a shower?"

He shook his head. "I'll go back to Juliet's now. I hope she'll be happy to let me stay for a bit longer if I keep working on her kitchen."

"Oh, she'll be happy," Libby said with a broad wink.

Damien looked puzzled and hopeful. "Have you spoken to her about me?"

"Go on," Libby said. "She's waiting for you."

Libby watched him go and then she returned to the house. The photocopied journals still lay on her desk, and she picked them up and fanned herself with the pages a few moments, thinking. Then she slid them carefully into an envelope and sat down to boot up her computer.

Dear Emily, she started to write, *I think I may have solved a Winterbourne family mystery . . .*

* * *

*J*uliet was cleaning down the tables on the deck when she suddenly felt somebody watching her. *Please, no more customers.* She had been working long hours since Cheryl left, not able yet to find a good replacement. Melody was helping all she could, but it was Juliet who had the ultimate responsibility to work harder. She had begun to wonder if she could ask Libby to come and help, but doubted her sister had it in her to be any good at making breakfasts and being nice to customers.

She turned. It was Damien. Her heart fluttered.

"You're filthy," she said.

"I've been digging up treasure." He laughed.

She smiled, puzzled. "How did that go?"

"It was a bit of an anticlimax. Look, Juliet. You're probably busy, but . . ."

Juliet threw down her cleaning cloth and took two steps towards him and encircled him in her arms. He caught his breath, then pressed her hard against him. She could hear his thundering heart. He took her chin gently in his fingers, turned her face up, and moved his lips over hers. Twenty years; she hadn't kissed anyone in twenty years. At first she worried that she had forgotten how, but his lips were warm and soft and molded against hers in such a way that her spine began to sing.

"I'm not busy," she murmured, pulling away. "I'm going to have an afternoon off."

Thirty-two

2012

Libby was glad Juliet had moved back into the front apartment; she deserved a view of the sea from her lounge room.

She let herself in with the spare key. Juliet's usually tidy flat was strewn with unfolded laundry and empty teacups. All was quiet and she didn't want to disturb, but then Juliet's voice rose through the apartment. "Is that you, Damien?"

"No, it's Libby. Just brought your shopping." She dropped the bags on the kitchen bench.

Juliet emerged from the bedroom, still in her pajamas at eleven in the morning, hair a mess, but with an irrepressible smile on her face. "You're a darling. She's sleeping."

"Can I look at her? I'll be very quiet."

Juliet nodded. Libby went to the bedroom, and hung moony-eyed like only a proud aunt can over the crib. "She's so beautiful. She's grown since you came home from hospital."

"I know. It's only been two days."

"Three."

"I lose count."

Libby reached into her handbag. "I have something for you."

"Is it a twenty-four-hour nanny? If it's not, I'm not interested."

Libby laughed. "Have a look for yourself." She pulled out the jewelry box and gave it to Juliet, who looked at it curiously, then flipped it open.

"Oh!" she gasped.

"I had it cleaned and repaired. Doesn't it look beautiful?"

Juliet teared up. But that wasn't unusual at the moment. Since her daughter's birth she seemed to spend all her time blissed out with a smile on her face or sobbing from happiness. She leaned over the crib and picked up the baby's tiny, light arm, and fastened the bracelet around it. The baby stirred but didn't wake.

"It's a bit big," Libby said.

"She'll grow into it," Juliet answered. "Thank you so much. Are you sure you want to give it away?"

"I'm sure. Damien found it, really." She touched Juliet on the shoulder.

"He's going to love it."

"Anyway, I'll leave you to it. Must go prepare for the lunch rush."

"I wonder if Scott Lacey will be in for his usual," Juliet said, a teasing edge in her voice.

"He can ask all he likes. I'm not going out with him."

"You'll change your mind. I've seen you two looking at each other."

Libby hugged her. "Love you, sis."

"Same."

Thirty-three

1902

*I*sabella and Matthew stand in the sunshine on the wharf as Isabella scans the crowd for her sister. The city unfolds around them, noisy and brimming with promise.

"Where is she?" Isabella says.

"Don't be anxious, my pretty bird. If she didn't get the telegram, we will simply make our own way there."

Isabella turns to him and smiles. Her belly is growing round and her cheeks are rosy. He smiles down at her, his new wife. The Captain married them just off the coast of Hawaii, and she has embraced her new name with relish, signing *Isabella Seaward* with a flourish on the exit register of the ship. "You are very reassuring, my dear."

"We have nothing to fear, my pretty bird. Not anymore."

Then Isabella sees Victoria making her way through the crowd in a bell-sleeved jacket and blue skirt. "Isabella!" she calls, her brown hair catching the winter sun. "Isabella!"

Isabella lurches forward, through the crush of people. Her heart hammers inside her throat. Despite the chill air, her face and body flush warm with delight. "Victoria!" she calls, and the crowd parts as though making way for this happy reunion.

And then she is in her sister's arms, crying for joy.

Acknowledgments

Mary-Rose MacColl, whose humor, warmth, and generosity humble me.

Selwa Anthony, who provided all the best ideas in this book.

My "sisters": Bek, Char, Fi, Meg, Nic, and Sal, who went on this journey with me whether they wanted to or not.

Ollie, Mish, and Chad for opening up the Sunshine Coast to my imagination, and opening up their hearts to my arrival.

Angela Hannan for her wonderful job of my website and online community.

Nadene Holm for keeping me sitting at the desk . . . literally; and Shar Edmunds, for keeping my head screwed on.

Special thanks to staff of the John Oxley Library for their knowledge and support, and to Katie Roberts, Laurie Johnson, Ian Wilkins, Michael Berganin, Brian Kennedy and Susan Bush for bits and pieces of research help.

Vanessa and Roberta for their enthusiasm and expert editorial input.

Mum, Luka, and Astrid for the love. And Mirko and Nikki for making it all so easy.

Facebook fanclub: you know who you are.

Lighthouse Bay

In 1901, a ship sinks off the coast of Queensland, Australia. The only survivor is Isabella Winterbourne, now a widow, who carries with her a priceless gift meant for the Australian parliament. In the unfamiliar world of Lighthouse Bay, Isabella must determine who she can trust and where she truly belongs.

Over a century later, Libby Slater returns to her small hometown of Lighthouse Bay after losing her lover. Before she finds the peace she's after, however, she must navigate her dark past and a rocky road to reconciliation with her estranged sister, Juliet. Both Isabella and Libby must learn the hard way that only by leaving the past behind can they discover what lies ahead.

For Discussion

1. The author chooses to unveil the story through several different points of view. What did you think about this decision?

2. Though a century divides them, Lighthouse Bay provides an escape for both Isabella and Libby. In what other ways are the two women alike? How are they different?

3. The sea is an ever-present force in this novel. What significance does it hold for each of the characters?

4. What was Isabella's motivation behind getting rid of the mace? In what ways did her decision surprise you?

5. Discuss Isabella's desire to take Xavier with her to America. What are her reasons for this? How do you think Katarina would have reacted?

6. Describe Matthew's feelings toward his first wife. How does his relationship with Isabella differ? Why is he hesitant to join Isabella on her voyage to America?

7. What role does Berenice play in the story? What effect does she have on Isabella?

8. What is your reaction to Isabella's grief for the loss of her son? Do you believe that she is, as the Captain suggests, one of those who are "in love with their own grief" (p. 38)?

9. "We each mourn in our own way," Isabella says to Berenice (p. 275). Do you think Isabella mourns her husband? Several of the characters in *Lighthouse Bay* have lost loved ones. How do they each deal with their loss?

10. How do you think Emily would react if she knew the truth about Libby and Mark? In what ways was Libby's decision justified?

11. Juliet and Libby carry the burden of their anger and guilt for many years. How does the past shape their adult lives?

12. Why do you think Libby ultimately changes her mind "about everything" (p. 403)? Discuss how her character evolves throughout the story, and what inspires these changes.

13. At the end of the book, Libby discovers that "Things don't have to be worth a lot to be treasured" (p. 411), something Isabella knew all along. What do each of the characters treasure, and what does this say about them?

14. What do you think the future holds for Libby and Isabella?

Enhance Your Book Club

1. Libby is intrigued by the story of a shipwreck in her hometown of Lighthouse Bay. Spend some time researching your own local history. Share a firsthand account or story that you've discovered with your book club.

2. Investigate real Australian shipwrecks online at http://www.environment.gov.au/heritage/shipwrecks/index.html. Write your own first-person diary entry as if you were a passenger aboard one of these ships.

3. If you live near a lighthouse, arrange a meeting with the lighthouse keeper and have him tell you about the harbor's history.

4. Channel Isabella by participating in a jewelry-making class, or try your hand at developing your own line of jewelry made from items you find in nature. The more creative, the better!

A Conversation with Kimberley Freeman

What inspired you to revolve your story around a shipwreck? Was the story of the Aurora *based on an actual event?*

The coastline of Australia is literally crowded with shipwreck history. I grew up in a town where a wrecked ship was used as a breakwater at the bottom of my street. So the wreck of the *Aurora* was imagined after a lot of reading about wrecked ships in Queensland. One particular source was a journal, written by a man who had survived a shipwreck with his wife and dog (everybody else on board was lost). They had eventually been picked up by a passing trade ship and made it back home, where he wrote down everything he could remember. The description of the shipwreck itself was more harrowing than anything I could have imagined. It would be the equivalent of going down in a plane: that kind of horror and feeling of complete helplessness. I really tried to capture that when writing the scene of the *Aurora* going down. In fact, some of the details (for example, the ship breaking into pieces) were taken directly from the journal account. I had no idea that something as large and well-built as a sailing ship could just turn to splinters under the force of rocks and stormy water.

What was your research process like? Did you discover anything in your research that particularly intrigued you?

It's a funny thing, but this is the first time I have written about the area where I live. I've always reached for slightly more exotic places, but I started to realize that where I live doesn't feel exotic just because I'm so used to it. When I started working on the first idea for the novel, I developed a strong friendship (which later grew into a lovely relationship) with a man who lived up at the Sunshine Coast, about two hours' drive away. I spent a lot of time going up there and back, falling in love with the area, mapping out where the story would take place. I also spent a lot of time in the State Library where I live, reading up about local history. It was wonderful to find those deeper layers of history in the place where I live, and to find that my hometown was just as full of romance and intrigue as any of the other places I've written about. In terms of what really intrigued me: when I discovered that paddle-steamers used to take people between the Sunshine Coast and Brisbane. That blew my mind! I think I let out a little whoop of joy in the library and said to myself, "I am SO putting a paddle-steamer in my book!"

Isabella overcomes many physical and emotional hardships in her life. What do you think is the source of her strength?

Isabella was a great character to write in some ways, and in others being trapped inside her head for months on end was unbearable. She was just in so much pain. But I did love the idea that, no matter how bad things got, she was able to stand up and keep going. In some ways, I saw this as an innate stubbornness in her: she gets an idea in her head, and she won't let go of it. Once she sees the lighthouse, she knows she must go there. Of course this gets her in trouble, too—it's the same willfulness that makes her want to take Xavier to America, for example. Isabella is a person who lives a lot in her head, so it's really mental tenacity that gets her through.

Lighthouse Bay *is, in many ways, a story about relationships. It reflects how men and women can build each other up as well as bring each other down. Can you comment on how this idea factored into your writing?*

I had cause to see this fact firsthand during the year around the writing of the story, which was the most difficult time of my life. After twenty years and two children together, my childhood sweetheart and I had parted. The incredible complexity of relationships was very much on my mind, and that's not to say that any of the characters were based on anyone I know. Far from it. I have a lovely relationship with my ex-husband, and he is a wonderful friend and father to the kids. But in the slow breakdown of my marriage and in the horrible, horrible aftermath of the split, I thought a lot about relationships and how impossibly difficult and complicated they can be. And then of course while writing the story, I was trying very hard not to fall in love and eventually capitulating! So I think a lot of that turmoil of the heart has made its way into the story.

Distance and history deeply complicate the relationships between both pairs of sisters. Are you writing from personal experience here?
No, I have no sisters. I have a brother and we have always had a very close relationship. But I remain fascinated by the idea of sisters. I have a handful of incredibly close female friends, I love the company of women, and I imagine having a sister must be the most wonderful thing in the world! Anyone who has one is so lucky (not that I'd trade my gorgeous brother in!).

Isabella's most precious treasure is one that doesn't cost much at all. Is there a particular object in your life that you value in this way?
I have a little box full of bits and pieces I have collected through my children's lives (they are ten and six years old): a paper Darth Vader made out of a toilet roll and black cardboard, a first scribble, a few locks of baby hair, the little wristbands they wore in the hospital. If my house caught fire, they are the things I would grab before I ran for it.

Several of the protagonists in your books are artists. In Lighthouse Bay, *Isabella is a skilled jeweler, and Libby is a painter and graphic designer. What prompted you to make your main characters artists?*
Because I am a writer, I find it easier to write about people who express themselves through art. I would be utterly hopeless writing a book about, say, an Olympic athlete. I wouldn't have a clue of that mindset.

Many of the women in your books struggle with a driving sense of loss. What inspired you to begin writing on this topic?
It was just such a tough time for me, and writing stories is one of the ways I work my feelings out. When I started writing, I knew Isabella was sad, but I didn't know why. When I realized that she had lost a baby, I cried for two days and wouldn't write any more. I kept going through all the other possible scenarios: she'd lost a sister, her mother, anybody but a baby. But it had to be a baby. She had to be all but broken for the story to work. Because what I wanted was for her to have to come back from this horrible loss somehow, so that at the end the reader is left with a sense that hope always returns, even in the worst of circumstances. As

for Libby and Mark, that was much less straightforward. She was grieving a man who had never been hers, so her grief had to be as secret as the affair had been. So while Isabella was openly broken-hearted, to the point that it annoyed her husband, Libby was covertly broken-hearted and couldn't ask for comfort.

You are active on social media, particularly on Facebook. What value do these networks provide for you as a writer?

Oh, dear, they *stop* me writing! I sometimes wonder if there is any value at all because social media are so addictive. But then I get a lovely message from a reader saying, "I stayed up all night to finish your book" (my *favorite* compliment, by the way), and I'm so grateful that the channel exists for them to be able to tell me that. I write in my pajamas first thing in the morning, while the kids are still asleep and the cats and dogs are playing around my feet. Then I get up and get dressed and get on with my day and it's almost as though my writing has taken place in a dream, in another world, which has nothing to do with the real world. So being able to receive contact from other people who've appreciated those morning dream-sessions is just wonderful.

You've provided your readers with glimpses of Isabella and Libby's lives before we meet them in Lighthouse Bay. *Have you considered a prequel for either of them? What's next for you?*

I don't do prequels or sequels. The reader is free to fill in that backstory with her own imagination! I am one quarter of the way into a new book, tentatively called *Ember Island,* about a woman who takes a post as the governess to the prison superintendent's daughter on a prison island in the nineteenth century. Only she is hiding a pretty awful secret, and when she starts to take an interest in one of the female prisoners who manages the superintendent's garden, it all gets very complicated indeed. There's also a present-day frame narrative that sets up some interesting business with an old diary to tease the reader: nothing is as it seems! I'm having a wonderful time writing it.

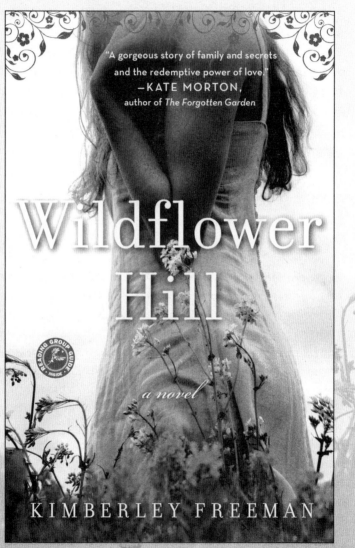